4 March 2022

Dear John,

John has asked me to send you this, his latest book, Unsteady States, Vol. I: Selected Short Stories and Novellas.

With all best wishes,

*Martin*

Martin Noble

AESOP Publications

28A Abberbury Road, Iffley, Oxford OX4 4ES

# UNSTEADY STATES

## VOLUME ONE

# UNSTEADY STATES

*Selected Short Stories and Novellas*

## VOLUME ONE

# JOHN FRASER

AESOP Modern Fiction
Oxford

AESOP Modern Fiction
An imprint of AESOP Publications
Martin Noble Editorial / AESOP
28a Abberbury Road, Oxford OX4 4ES, UK
www.aesopbooks.com

First edition published by AESOP Publications
Copyright (c) 2022 John Fraser

www.johnfraserfiction.com

A catalogue record of this book is
available from the British Library.

First edition 2022

ISBN: 978-1-914938-10-8

# CONTENTS

# 1

# THE WHITE ROOM

*from **Animal Tales***

'Tout être humain est donc éternel dans chacune des secondes de son existence.'

Auguste Blanqui, quoted in Walter Benjamin,
*Das Passagen-Werk*

I F I COULD start over... there's so many stones to be deciphered.'
        'I could have bigger breasts. Catch a bigger fish.'
    'Not so. Even if it's only "could have"...'
    'You chose dull work because you're dull. You must accept.'
    The animals – they bite, they scratch. In cases extreme, they eat. It's all they know of intimacy.
    'I won't leave this house,' he says.
    'It's my house,' she says. 'Legally, you're crap. Go study old civilisations. You're related to them.'
    It's just.
    That's the justice you look for, and live in. The best you can have. Look at toads – they mate, hundreds of them, with one specimen, quite overwhelmed. Stags, with their harem. Not to speak of sultans, with theirs.
    'Stay with me,' says Mimmo.
    'Wow, great,' he says. 'I knew it would be easy, being fixed up.'
    'Tomorrow, you'll find somewhere else,' Mimmo says. 'Now, the market.'
    The stalls, wandering round, it's like a stomach. 'Oh no,' he says. 'Those poor animals, not all quite dead.'

35    'Don't try to save them,' Mimmo says. 'Think "sacrifice".'
36        'These books...' he says, going in amongst them. He sniffs
37    deep – French tobacco, old Soviet glue. 'I don't read,' he says.
38    'Everything outside, around – it's too bulky to get inside,' he tells
39    the girl who'd sell one to him. 'You're so neat,' he tells her.
40    'Uncut, narrow, smelling so new, almost tacky still...'
41        'Come on,' Mimmo says. 'This is how you ended in the
42    garbage. Being yourself.'
43        'My job, classifying stuff. I should tell them I'm giving up,'
44    he says.
45        'What's the point?' asks Mimmo. 'You're not there. The way
46    to handle it, if you can't manage what's around you, is to be
47    radical. Accept reality, project another one upon it.'
48        'You make me sound apart,' he says. 'I'm more in control
49    than you are, Mimmo. I just cancel traces better. They want us to
50    have relationships. Lots of them, all sorts, for tolerance. Then they
51    go round so fast, like horses on a roundabout... Learn to eat
52    gherkins from a jar, learn to be Buddha. There's no end to being
53    normal.'
54        'Well,' says Mimmo. 'The normalisers got it wrong. You're
55    not.'
56        Animals, when they play or let it out – they don't shriek,
57    attract the predators – they just roll upon the ground, look up at
58    you, and wink. Us animals – we can't do that.
59        'Where are you?' Mimmo asks.
60        'Oh, I'm rooted here,' he says. 'There's the Bir-Hakeim
61    bridge, the trains; beneath – Kabylia. My people, some of them.
62    Others in the deserts, in the mines. All over. Dispersed throughout
63    the world.'
64        'You must go further,' Mimmo says.
65        'It's not you want me out your room?' he asks. 'People,
66    chased from their land, hassled by the cops, it's everywhere, we all
67    have part of that. Justice comes through war – you'll have heard
68    that, Mimmo. It's not false. When the gods die, it goes on, all of it –
69    not hope. It's physics.'
70        'Don't take off!' says Mimmo. 'No flights of hot air, no
71    balloons. If you leave your wife, your mother, if they throw you out
72    – it's quite normal. It's what the forces of our destinies want us to
73    do, to be. We're ants, we're everywhere. Underground and in the
74    trees. The universal species, we'll become – we'll take – the lot.
75    Then sit and wait.'

76      'Well,' he says, unappeased. 'What if a solitary wolf comes
77 knocking at your armoured door?'
78      'I'll shoot him through the keyhole,' Mimmo says. 'Straight
79 through his yellow eye.'
80      Gay Paree. How the words shift their shapes, their partners.
81 Friends.
82      'Look,' says Mimmo. 'I don't want you around. Understand.
83 Go and fight for something. There is choice. Territory, history,
84 justice, work. Each has its army. You've ancestors all over, no
85 doubt relations too. All grievances are just, and unresolvable. Your
86 mating season's done. Fuck off. Here, take this.'
87      'No!' he says, 'that's not me. It changes things, utterly. You
88 lose your distance, the "he" becomes an "I", and it an "it".'
89      It's a dog. It's nature, but the coddling kind that you don't
90 want.
91      Here's an emporium, 'Au paradis'. That is what we want. The
92 doors open when you step up on the plate. Everything, the world –
93 sea urchins and *agarbatti*. I push the dog inside, the doors are
94 closed. The dog's too light to open them. Like all of us, it will find
95 the butchers, eventually. We stare at each other, it's surely a
96 moment it will remember. I'll forget it, likely, but I'm free.
97 'Farewell,' I do not say, 'Fuck you twice, Mimmo, old friend.'
98      This city – its works displayed, like an exclusive watch. Guys
99 pushing rails of suits. The grey slates, like scales on pangolins. The
100 glum passages. Melons, flowers, faces, all of marzipan, glazed. Do
101 they all make movies here? Or cut horses into steaks? How busy
102 they all are, and sharp; small sharp brains inside those nifty clothes.
103 You need some drinks, and in the bars, they're extras from some
104 rousting movie, gangsters all assured. *Blousons*, eggs hardboiled.
105      'You look sad, pensive,' some stranger stops and says.
106      'I just lost my dog,' I say.
107      'Buy a bottle, party with us. You're sure to find another sad.'
108      I take the bottle up the stairs, where she had said. All the
109 doors are silent. Maybe the party's sitting on the floor, eyes closed,
110 thinking about Bergson. Maybe they're all younger than me. I leave
111 the bottle at the top, the shabby place. Help the poor, they say.
112      Maybe I'll go see Effi. She abounds with life: she says, 'I'm
113 an immigrant. Perfectly integrated. I understand them all. I hate
114 them all. It's democratic here, so it burns, no sad greys wandering
115 round. Run and run...'
116      I say, 'They're bringing back the tsar...'

117    'There's always tsars,' she says. 'Never the same one.'
118    'I'm a classifier,' I say. 'I just need a place to stay. There's
119    always work for us: sorting the good, the bad, rough and smooth,
120    the sane and sick, the odd, the even, round and square. Faded and
121    perky. Do it to all materials,' I boast. 'My! How the people need us,
122    to tell them what they've done.'
123         'Well,' she says, scooping her feet up beside her on a bed. 'If
124    it's life you want – look in the fridge.'
125         'Maggots don't bother me,' I say. 'They don't put me off.
126    They warn us, but there is no need. The quick, the dead. You don't
127    have choice, it's not democracy...'
128         'How you talk on,' she says. 'Share my bed. If you have
129    dreams, don't pee in them.'
130         Underneath the woollies, there's an attractive being, I am
131    sure. From some part of empire, now still going on, or before.
132    Russia, China, America. Into those, everything fits; she's a pupil
133    from the big class, class of all classes.
134         'I do animals too,' I say. 'Classing where they are in the
135    chain. Everyone gets some points.'
136         'Where am I?' Effi asks, wriggling.
137         'Not at the top. That's where there's nothing left to eat but
138    lookalikes. Further up again, you must consume yourself,' I say.
139         'You class horizontal, and by vertical too. "Do no harm", that
140    must be you,' she says, admiring.
141         'All is left just as it is, it's true, frustrating, sure – but then, it's
142    only work,' I say. What does she do? I wonder.
143         'I work with animals,' she says. 'It's low as you can go.'
144         Sell? Stuff? Butcher? Train? Guard or release? Every
145    pleasure's there, every one is covered.
146         'What's in it for you, Effi?'
147         'I seek their spirit. There's nothing for me in it,' she says.
148         'Nor them,' I say. 'It's nonsense. Which world d'you think
149    we're in?'
150         'There's the revolution here,' she says. 'That must be going
151    on, sort of. If not – those thousands gone, the speeches... Too bad.
152    Sure, it's there. You need to cock your head to hear it.'
153         We try. I'm humouring her. She cries a little. Maybe I do too.
154    Things are dire.
155         'There's guys who pass through here,' I say. 'And fights...'
156         'Nothing to do with you,' says Effi. 'It's about religion. In the
157    end they pay me what they owe. We should discuss your rent. A

158 full bed costs you more than empty ones. What did you think! And
159 your fantasies – all free.'
160     'That's fine,' I say. 'The mystic stuff about the spirits – that
161 was troubling me.'
162     'You don't believe we have a spirit?' Effi asks.
163     'No. Naturally not,' I say.
164     'Well, the lesser ones, what we call animals. They must have
165 one. It's a compensation. You see it in their eyes. Mine's such a
166 dirty job...' she says. 'Not that it helps, or counts.'
167     'I'll find the money,' I say. 'It's respect.'
168     'People don't like me,' she says. Her face is pinched, in its
169 frame, like a palm outward turned. 'But they love having sex with
170 me. It's quite consuming.'
171     'So,' I say. 'I'm in your bed to guard?'
172     Perhaps some day, release?
173     'It's better than gratification, whatever you think that is,' she
174 says. 'Mine's what they call an active life. Animals by day, lovers
175 by night.'
176     'Well, that's up to you. Your problem,' I say, uninvolved.
177 'There's that revolution going on. Maybe you should step out on to
178 it.'
179     She takes me to where she works: it's an emporium, Le
180 Mange-tout. The window says – 'Bush meat: Sacrificials: Halal,
181 Kosher, Christian: Fireside and working: Agnostic and other:
182 Taxidermy.'
183     'I'm so sorry, Effi,' I say.
184     'They don't know which class they are,' she says. 'It's the
185 demand. That makes it clear.'
186     'If you have faith,' I say, at a loss, 'it must be tested.'
187     'Oh,' she says, 'it is, and how. The pay is pitiful.'
188     My seeing where she works seemed to have excited her:
189 there's scrambling in the bed. 'Effi!' I say, 'don't change the game
190 once the hands are dealt.'
191     'You can't just let those creatures do as they want, giving
192 them rights at birth, letting the big ones eat them all,' she says,
193 panting.
194     I say, 'Remember what Engels said. The bourgeoisie has its
195 women in common.'
196     It isn't relevant, it seems, but calms her.
197     'You should go over the globe, help my business, and pay
198 your debt,' she says. 'It's all right – it's business, not trapping and

199  hobbling. You could be suited for it.'
200      It's a way out, certainly. A way in, too, a new life. And yet...
201  It isn't me. She's misread me. I'm respectable. She doesn't
202  recognise the type. All those religions, those cuisines for
203  carnivores. She's truly universal, serves them all. How she must
204  pray, as she does her work, whatever it may be.
205      How terrible, to take Effi's origins as reasons for her moods,
206  her fancies. Perhaps she comes from somewhere where they're
207  slaves, or hunted, discriminated, their brains stunted, caged with
208  malice. She was born with rights, they say. Suppose she has a
209  history, and I haven't known? What if, in my ignorance, I'm
210  prejudiced? Revolution was supposed to stop all that, even in
211  France. I say, 'Effi, don't get me wrong. I'm maybe not the
212  desperate case you think. Perhaps ... there's something in your past,
213  identity, that seeks revenge, a rectifying, justice?' 'No, no,' she
214  says, 'I'm from a place I can't go back to – nothing more. We had a
215  revolution – quite the wrong kind.'
216      I say, 'If we were Russians, centuries ago – the drama! Serfs
217  and seigneurs, the modern at the gates, let in or not, the poetry ...
218  salons and duels and leaving for the capital. There it was, history
219  laid out – the revolution! There it comes! And now, us – we signify
220  so little, big themes sound on above our heads...'
221      'I think it's right, precisely, about us,' says Effi. 'We are
222  exactly us, here, as we are. We are the wood, fresh felled, the
223  carpenter shaves off a twist, away, away – a pile of baby curls. And
224  what is left – it's always us.'
225      I leave her, in the middle of her muddled life. I travel
226  everywhere. Settle accounts.
227      Here – the people have blue teeth. 'It shows they voted,'
228  Neville says, a gross Englishman, Effi's agent – 'Don't you want to
229  look inside?' he asks.
230      'No, no,' I say. 'There's big crates and there's little ones.
231  That's all I need to know.'
232      'You ship stuff out,' he says. 'And you are Effi's girl. There's
233  been a pack like you.'
234      'With me, it's crates,' I say, 'and Effi – well, it's hit and
235  miss.'
236      Neville expands. 'I farm things here,' he says. 'Nature's so
237  profligate. Think of those turtles, panicked, let down by the
238  welcoming sea. And frogs. What you need in places like this here,
239  where you can sell the topsoil, and what's underneath, and have the

240 ladies walk the world to have the chance to clean your house – is
241 weedy guys, aggressive ones. No warrior types, with empty heads.
242 They must hate real good, and back it up with prayers. The hunks
243 and hulks – the plump ones – they're a trap. They'd keep on selling
244 what can find its price, like me. No – when the rebellion comes, the
245 ratfaced pockmarked ones, all the disfavoured – they will have their
246 day. They'll stick my head upon a lance, and burn and sing, and
247 bring some rigour in.'
248     'I didn't see you as a revolutionary,' I say.
249     'Because you don't look in the crates,' says Neville. 'You're
250 just another squeamish Effi boy. You don't know history: when the
251 waves are taller than yourself, you let them sweep you off. You
252 have survived. And then you don't.'
253     I have a meal with them, Neville, Paola. She's tall and blue
254 and out of place, a delphinium. It's meat – I don't look in the pot.
255     Neville unlocks a wooden door, there's chicken wire so you
256 can see in. There's guys, quiet, staring at their screens. 'There's
257 Effi's boys,' says Neville. 'You can't let them out. They'd not
258 survive, they don't know how. They do the books. There's
259 poachers too, who'd take them. There's not many trained to sit
260 before the screens.'
261     There's a movie playing on a bigger screen, quite silent.
262 'They have their fantasy, of course,' Neville goes on. 'It's Effi. My,
263 but they're loyal! And they think – Paris, the capital. We play them
264 Liebelei. Max Ophuls.'
265     And the singer – yes, she looks like Effi, and she sings on, in
266 silence, you watch her mouth, her white skin. You'd like to be
267 inside.
268     'They like the rough stuff too,' says Neville. 'About the
269 Nazis. Those guys had faith – quite the wrong sort, of course. Effi's
270 boys – they identify with the French, the revolution betrayed. Of
271 course. It lets them off.'
272     You watch the mouth, and think of hooks, and being let off
273 them.
274     'These guys,' I ask. 'Their business is all Africa?' 'Don't
275 think of continents. It doesn't work. Think "worlds",' says Neville,
276 puffing as he puts the padlocks back. 'Think "simultaneous" – it all
277 goes on at once – the stuff revolves. It's markets, quotas, futures
278 and pasts, the ores, the trees. Your animals – they serve; and all
279 beliefs and needs are satisfied. You want a monkey in that chair –
280 well, here he comes. We have the monkey mountains here. My!

281    Are they glad to get a proper home. A lion to keep the burglars out?
282    A snake to stopper up the draughts? Lemurs to light the path –
283    those red sporgent eyes... And eats! The thighs, the ribs – how the
284    running sweetens, softens them...'
285        'The lady Paola,' I ask. 'She stands so tall?'
286        'The consort Paola,' Neville corrects. 'Lot of couples work
287    like that – one fat and hairy, the other, insidious like a sheet of tin.
288    It's all thought out. All the anomalies. It's like the gold – laid down
289    where guys are poor, and kill each other just to delve in holes. And
290    then it goes where guys are rich, who lay it down in vaults. Now,
291    tell me there is no intelligence at work! The distribution... it
292    instructs. That's what it's for.'
293        It's hard to contradict. If you don't want it so, then let it be.
294    That dog...
295        Neville grips my arm. 'You – you're pretty cold. You don't
296    communicate, or claim some species similarity. I like that, though
297    the other guys ignore you. You are Effi's type.'
298        He takes us, Paola and me – into a patch of jungle. 'This nut
299    here,' says Neville, 'it was a favourite food. The guy who used to
300    eat it – he's been crated and shipped out.'
301        The flower's a ruby, and the nut is teak. I gulp it down – I'm
302    in a cylinder, the walls tattooed in red and green. The sides expand,
303    it seems it is a lung, there's churning down below, two kidneys
304    hang like purple plums. There's a trachea, up to the roof, a chimney
305    – it might be a still down here, there's bubbling, smoke, a heaving,
306    and a crisscross of emotion, breaths that come and go, the ribs that
307    creak – oh no! I think, this creature has a sentimental life... it's
308    Liebelei, there's to come a duel, a suicide, and I should leave. I
309    kick the single lung, a membrane roars and squeaks, a pibroch – but
310    it coughs, it snorts, and up the gristly pipe I go... a gaping mouth, a
311    tooth... and there is Paola, laughing as she cradles me.
312        'Naughty, oh naughty Neville, with his English japes,' she
313    says, and holds me tight against a papery breast. 'The animals, they
314    know the scene, they're used to being swallowed and regurgitated,
315    sucked in, spat out – it's all the same to them. But we're not used...'
316    and Neville laughs. 'There is purpose there,' he says. 'And wisdom.
317    Every animal eats that fruit. Even those who'll be extinct...'
318        He winks. Could he be that animal? Or think he is? Could it
319    be me? Is it wise, to avoid the fruit of wisdom? Just doing what the
320    immediate dictates, straight between the eyes. Like animals are said
321    to do. Yet – you can't say that something hasn't left them wise...

322 'It's all a game,' says Paola, cuddling me. 'It's just the way
323 they fall – the dice, the cards. It should refresh, to know there's
324 nothing you can do...' I'm still terrified, shaking. She strokes me,
325 tickles me, calls my name.
326      'It's just,' says Neville. 'Justice. You had no house, no
327 territory. All you had, is still intact. You've not lost anything, no
328 one has stolen from you. No one insults you, no one makes a
329 monkey out of you. There's no injustice, indeed – now, you have
330 knowledge, wisdom. That's what I'd hope to bring. Knowing how
331 it can be, how it ought to be. Once you're inside – you can tickle
332 the trachea, hope you'll get spat out – it's quite a reflex, automatic.
333 It's Effi's shop, emporium, all over. Luck. But where all round
334 there's exploitation, prejudice, slaughter quite indiscriminate,
335 assassinations planned – you could attain, instead, the wisdom of
336 the fruit...'
337      He needs to instruct me – I'm not sure it's for my good. The
338 wisdom is – it's chance, the data as they fall on you, give universal
339 meaning to each instant.
340      He says, 'The revolution you're always mentioning. The poor,
341 oppressed – you know, it's always misrepresented. If it happens, or
342 does not.'
343      'Misrepresented? You mean betrayed? Falling over its own
344 shoes?' I ask.
345      'No. Misrepresented. What I said. The actors, the script, the
346 intentions and results,' he says, irritated.
347      'Writers, you mean? Inscriptions?' I ask, thinking of the
348 tombstone forests.
349      'No, no,' he says. 'Everyone. Their hopes. I see the larger
350 frame. What I want is what I've said – stripping out and shipping.
351 The great chain of consuming. Eating, if you want the arrow-word.'
352      'I'm not sure I understand,' I say. 'Nature! Nature!' Neville
353 shouts. 'We big animals – we have made it so, created! It's all ours,
354 what we are meant to be. Nature is what we want it! We can eat it,
355 if we want!'
356      'Effi looks for spirits in the beasts,' I say. 'I don't think there
357 are.'
358      'Of course there are,' says Paola. 'Everyone has one. Even
359 you, I'll bet!'
360      'You know,' I say, gently, as if they're a pair of cretins. 'All
361 this shuffling things about and making us all comfortable... the
362 stripping and the shipping out – they say it's overdone, we'll all

363 come to bad ends.'
364          Paola pushes me away. 'Sacrifice!' she says. 'It's in our
365 blood. It's what distinguishes us from all the rest, the other animals.
366 The rite, blood, sacrifice. Oh, if they would only call me... Rejoice!
367 Rebirth, purity. Millions of us, extinguished and extinct, then –
368 millions of years to wait, calm, dark, what luxury... A new life
369 rises...'
370          'They won't call just you, Paola,' Neville says. 'They'll call
371 everyone. That's what gives our end its greatness.'
372          'I don't just classify,' I say. 'Any idiot tells the difference
373 between a large box, and a small. I know how the world works too!
374 Duels, vendetta – they're a family matter. Spits and spats. Valhalla
375 too – the stall closed down, gone out of business, watch the space,
376 if you've the time. But Paola's into something new. Our time, our
377 space and destiny...' and Neville turns away.
378          'You find it hard to take things in,' he says. It's not a
379 question. 'Paola didn't invent a thing,' he says. 'It's what there is.
380 It's happened. Thing on thing, and after, thing. Now comes the time
381 of sacrifice. Better get used to it, and stamp and dance around.
382 There's no Nijinsky wriggling there, in that tight yellow skin. The
383 music will not stop this time. This time, the sacrifice is not a rite –
384 it is for good. It will be tough, but we are tough,' and he pinches
385 Paola's arm. She doesn't wince.
386          We think about it: then he says, 'I'll take you round the world,
387 we'll do our work. Effi wanted that.'
388          'Shall we go everywhere?' I ask.
389          'Not sure of England,' Neville says. 'I've never gone. It's all
390 about the Scots.'
391          'You seem English to me,' I say.
392          'They're so aggressive,' Neville says. 'Then, there's the
393 Scots. The English took their language, built those military roads to
394 keep them down. All those Scots have is rocks and rain. They did
395 resist – they're called Wee Free, that everyone derides. Religious.
396 Bullies. Insults from everyone. A great injustice done, continuing.
397 And the English, well, they all came in from Denmark, pushed the
398 rest aside...'
399          'I don't know about all that,' I say. 'But there is usually
400 suffering all round.'
401          'Of course, of course,' says Neville. 'Yes: as Hegel says, we
402 all must have our argument. But then – the English go off round the
403 globe, their armies everywhere, at someone else's call. No, it's not

404 my thing.'
405     'Paris isn't innocent,' I say, striving to make the peace.
406     'No, there's that too. But we must go somewhere. Trade,
407 moving things around,' he says. 'If I could be something else, I
408 would. Some creature. But even kangaroos – they do no harm, and
409 when there's lots, they shoot a bunch.'
410     'It's all suffering,' I say. 'So, you stick by your free trade.'
411     'Suffering. You're right. Get ready for lots more. But – trade:
412 it isn't free, you know. It costs as well,' he says.
413     We have reached a confine, there is silence. 'We shall journey
414 with my cousin. Regina, from Brazil,' he says. 'No Paola?' I ask
415 him. 'Oh no,' says Neville, 'she doesn't travel.'
416     On the road. I hear them, Neville, Regina – in the next room,
417 if we have two, in our bed if not. They make a noisy love. I hear
418 them singing out: quite loud, like Jorge Ben – 'Take it easy my
419 brother Charles', and 'Xica da Silva', as if they're making fun of
420 me.
421     'I'm glad you're travelling with us, Regina,' I say. 'Paola is a
422 fine spike, but...'
423     Regina's the colour of teak. 'Everyone fantasises about
424 Brazilians,' she says. 'And it's quite justified. Paola's too stiff to
425 come around the world, to where they're stripping out and shipping
426 in.'
427     'Regina,' I say, 'you've got class. Paola doesn't.'
428     'Yes,' she says, 'I do. But not for you, you cheeky boy,' and
429 she pinches my arm, quite hard, I feel there is a bone inside. I'll not
430 forget the pinch, the 'cheeky boy', in all my life – it's worthwhile
431 living, just for that.
432     'Regina has a magnificent *sillage*,' Neville says. 'High quality
433 candlewax and moonflowers. You should keep downwind.'
434     We go to China, India, Indonesia. There's ships that ship.
435 Animals – some live, some dead, like us, says Neville. Regina lets
436 some pretty ones out of their crates, to run upon the quay. We don't
437 know what will happen. Off we go... 'I wonder...' I say.
438     'You're soft because you think there's virtue in it,' says
439 Regina. 'The guys here are all hard, because it works, and if they
440 smile at you, behind their eyes, your skin is flapping empty, drying
441 out so's it can patch their roof.'
442     'The guys we deal with,' Neville says. 'Stand on that shadowy
443 line, that runs between the benefaction and the crime. It's history.
444 You drain the swamps, mosquitoes come to town to dine on you.

445 Action-reaction – you did it all at school.'
446     'Then there's Effi,' says Regina. 'I bet you think of her, you
447 two. There's no reaction there – she seeks her kind of peace. Not
448 scuffling with you.'
449     'What kind is that?' I ask.
450     'The earthly paradise, of course,' Regina says. 'Unattainable,
451 but – so desirable.'
452     'Desire's a whim,' says Neville. 'An American thing, I fear.
453 Me – I make no promises. When there's stuff to move – I help it
454 move. Take my percent. Sometimes the guys who trap and dig –
455 they live in paper boxes on the slope. When things go well – those
456 same guys light cigars with golden bonds and live in villas on the
457 hill. I claim no credit, and I shed no tear.'
458     Faster it spins, the world. The seas have vortices, like pockpits
459 – you can see the luminescent wrecks down there, seaworms as
460 thick as cables, mariners with gills, and Neville says – 'I've never
461 felt the globe so round before, everything sliding eastwards, then it
462 surges back again. Hold fast! – although you can't fall off – the air
463 is thick, it pastes us on!'
464     He has a taste for poetry, our Neville, so it seems. I ask
465 Regina, 'What is there in all this for you?' and she says, 'Oh, you
466 can see how well he sings and how he screws. What more can
467 humans want? Voyaging with him, there is no pain, he pockets his
468 percent, there's no cadavers of a human kind, just crates and ships,
469 and stuff that looks like soil.'
470     The gold, the teak, the ebony – that's not up to me. Here is my
471 crate of sacrificials, sheep and goats together. Then there's crates
472 marked 'science'. 'Caged'. Life sentences for all, some long, some
473 very short. 'Of course, he lands, wherever there is flat,' Regina
474 says. 'He's not a Dutchman, excluded from the ports: and, from
475 fear of falling, Neville doesn't fly. Then, there is home, where
476 Paola prepares the sacrifice.'
477     'You don't believe in that, Regina?' I ask.
478     'Oh yes,' she says, 'but – I don't take part. All those human
479 bodies, made inedible – we're the only ones to think of that. I'll
480 dance upon their graves, to tamp them down. Not the samba,
481 though. Something more foxy.'
482     'Shipping these beasts to Paradis – I'm doing Effi good?' I
483 ask.
484     'She keeps the gate,' Regina says. 'Is all. Brain not required.'
485     Neville brings a guy to meet us. 'This is Alvin,' Neville says.

486    'I don't know where he's from.'
487         Indeed, how would you know? His girl's called Kitty – she
488    talks with clicks, like all our sailors. She wears warm slippers,
489    heather mix. 'We're here to cheer you up,' she says. 'Alvin will
490    help. He buys up land, and digs and sucks. And when it's done...'
491         'We'll mine the stars,' laughs Alvin. 'Sacrifice is out. We may
492    need fewer of us humans – fewer species too. There's lots that sit
493    around or swing in trees, they don't contribute much. We'll make
494    the stuff we need in labs,' and as he talks, the scene grows lighter,
495    and the sailors gather round. Maybe we'll find a port where others
496    talk in clicks, and they will put on slippers too, old age will crease
497    and crumple them... and Kitty laughs, and says, 'There's last resorts
498    you know! My husband was a Dutchman, such a bore, forbidden
499    landfall. To rid myself, I ate him, not to economise, but to bring us
500    both eternal peace,' and she shows us her pink palms and nails, the
501    Nordic red inside her mouth, and we laugh too, and Neville shouts,
502    'A jest, a jest! We needed that. The future is secured.'
503         I say, 'My dog – if he'd had wings, he'd be an albatross,' and
504    no one understands, but how they laugh, and laugh.
505         'Let's live on an island,' Neville says, 'and survive each other,
506    and the world.'
507         'Everything is almost islands, anyway,' I say. 'Besides, when
508    you arrive on one, you think of boats to get you off, and we're
509    already travelling on boats.'
510         'Yes,' Kitty says. 'On islands, the animal you catch could be
511    the last one anywhere, and eating it could bring you out in spots,'
512    and Alvin laughs and says you'd need some spades and maps, and
513    preferably slaves to dig up all the gold. We stare around, we think
514    of the song – 'Are You Satisfied, With an Average Life?', it seems
515    that's what we have, we are.
516         We take another boat, to go look back at the shore. It is what
517    people do.
518         'Look!' says Regina. 'The scarlet sky! The air: it's musk – or
519    is it gas? Smoke? Incense?'
520         We're not good at weather.
521         'The sailors stayed on shore,' I say. 'Maybe we can hear their
522    clicks. A roister...'
523         'No, no,' Kitty says. 'That's not clicks – it is artillery. Oh no!
524    It has begun. Rebellion. The last, the final, the decisive war – it
525    starts. We're on this ship, all stuck with different hopes and
526    interests. And we can't land, for fear...'

527     'It is the time of sacrifice, like Paola thinks, so maybe I should
528     say farewell to dear Regina, prepare for endings sour,' Neville says,
529     and weeps, 'I'll call the captain...' but there's no one there.
530         'These old ships,' Alvin says. 'They sail around the world,
531     there's no one up on deck, they're playing gin below. If there's no
532     crew, it makes no odds. All is settled somewhere else. For fear of
533     pirates, who have dug up all the gold. Their hobby is to pickle
534     skulls... It's best we go below, and let them fight it out on shore.'
535         'That goddam Dutchman,' Kitty shouts. 'We'll never find a
536     port where we can dock,' and it is true – we travel on, and
537     everywhere there's flame and gas and buildings sliding down.
538         'No people! Let no people on,' says Alvin. They're swimming
539     out. 'We must decide which side we're on. Who knows where these
540     people stand? Use these poles to push them off.'
541         'What if we're on different sides, the five of us?' Regina asks.
542         'Don't lift out animals,' shouts Neville. 'They may turn on us.
543     Besides, we've plenty food in cans...'
544         'Effi's supplies,' I say. 'Let's think of that.'
545         'Oh, there's the zoos,' says Neville, 'and lots just running
546     round the streets. After a while, trade will start again – it's always
547     so, things settle down, they always have. There's fire and ash and
548     ice, then seaweed blooms, and we march out the slime again...'
549         Alvin's robust, and fends off everything and everyone that's
550     hoping to be picked up.
551         'On shore, it may be justice they are fighting for. Can we
552     abstain?' Regina asks, and Kitty says, 'No! What if it's the start of
553     the long war that ends it all, and we'll become the dinosaurs and
554     leave our bones in hardening mud?'
555         'Oh, that's just Paola!' Neville says. 'Our lot can last out for a
556     hundred years, and then we shan't be there to care.'
557         Then there's the coffins, floating out. 'Look,' says Neville.
558     'They're open. The eyes. A last look at the sky? See how they
559     float!'
560         'What you think?' asks Alvin. 'They make coffins so they
561     sink? Holes in the bottom? It's nature, that is all.'
562         'Well,' Kitty says, 'I hope the guys out there have sense
563     enough to burn their crappy shacks and go to live in villas higher
564     up the hill.'
565         'That leaves things as they were, I feel,' says Neville,
566     doubtfully.
567         'Well, what you think?' shouts Kitty. 'They start building

568   something new and different? Take what there is. "Renounce,
569   appropriate. Burn the past," that's what you do.'
570        'I guess that could be justice,' Alvin says.
571        'I don't know what it is,' says Kitty.
572        'That's you,' Regina says, fired up by some response. 'That's
573   Kitty, that's the stereotype. Your bum settled hard on someone
574   else's chintz.'
575        'And stereotype yourself,' says Kitty, making a fist.
576        'I dare say we're all stereotypes,' says Alvin, soothing. 'Each
577   in their own particular way.'
578        The burn goes on. Our bunch – we're interested in the
579   economics, shipping out. Here, instead, it must be religion,
580   factions, clans.
581        'No, no,' says Neville. 'It's the beginning of the end, for sure.
582   Like Paola says. That's why she stays at home – she's such a drag
583   with portents and the like.'
584        'We shall slim down, is all,' says Alvin. 'Agree. No rancour,
585   just like the five of us.'
586        'This ship – could be a space ship, in a movie. Escaping the
587   end, the sacrifice. Except it's cramped,' I say.
588        'That would be the budget,' Alvin says, as if he knows.
589        The smoke's now black. 'There go your cushions, Kitty,' says
590   Regina, with some malice.
591        'If we're a space ship, or we're just a ship, we cannot flee, nor
592   fly,' says Kitty. 'So, we need a captain.'
593        'Yes, that's it!' Regina shouts. 'The third estate – it's
594   everything. Then we cop out, elect some guy that tells us what to
595   do. That's your democracy! Kitty – you're a dope, a boss's gal!'
596   There's much confabulation. In the end, I'm the captain, the one
597   they hate the most, the one who didn't want the job.
598        'We can't live like animals, in a pack, like cards,' says
599   Neville. 'Bossed by some ancient guy who screws the women.'
600        'These religious wars,' says Alvin. 'The chiliasts – they are
601   the best. They give you something to expect, to wait for.'
602        'That's not the whole,' says Neville. 'Big interests. Past and
603   future, it is all in play.'
604        'Sure, everything is part of everything,' says Alvin, irritated.
605   'But – if there's no conclusions, you can't have new starts.'
606        'Look!' says Kitty. 'Fireworks.'
607        So there are: rejoice. Conclusion. There's tracks of
608   phosphorus, then golden hail, squirrels blue and red, flowers that

609  boil and run. Then bang bang BANG. It ends.
610        'Maybe modernity has come,' I say. 'New life! Free! And not.
611  It's quite complex. At least there's shopping.'
612        'Shipping too,' laughs Neville.
613        Then they turn on me:
614        'Of course,' says Alvin. 'You're not qualified.'
615        'We're still stuck here,' Regina says.
616        'I know,' I say. 'I don't believe. No gods, no emperors, no
617  heroes – that's my creed. Raise the black flag...' and I go on. They
618  are not satisfied. Indeed, my discourse angers them.
619        The captain, the real captain, comes on board. 'I'll land you
620  on the shore,' he says.
621        'No, no,' we shout, but it's no use, and on the shore we go.
622        Some angry guys show up, they take us into jail. A loose
623  environment, it seems – there's people shuffled in and out, and
624  stories long as books, some torture, some cut deals. A guy says,
625  'You're safer here, than where the guys outside are settling scores.'
626        No doubt it's true – but we were better still upon our boat.
627  'This certainly is "after", but there's consequences you like, and
628  those that simply come along,' I say. Each moment here's a capsule
629  holding lives that sprout and burst – a blink, and we have victory,
630  defeat. Another – here's the revolution and its counter. Another
631  blink – we're freed from jail, 'Before we figure out what you've
632  done wrong,' they say.
633        'Somewhere there'll be a bar that's selling,' Kitty says.
634        There's guys with turtles on a stall.
635        'Let's free some too,' Regina says.
636        'No,' I say. 'Effi needs them by the hundred,' and they stare at
637  me.
638        'I'm quite converted,' Alvin says. 'They'll need a guy like
639  me. There's my cash, too...'
640        Regina seems put out. 'I've always been a revolutionary,' she
641  says. 'But then the politics gets in – you see it here, you see the
642  black holes open up...'
643        'It's the adrenalin, Regina,' Alvin says. 'You get the same
644  effect from jumping off a bridge. The trouble is, my love, you're
645  superficial. Try working in the factory I'll bring—'
646        'We're overtired,' says Neville. 'Our benevolence, wanting to
647  do the good – it's coming to an end. The storm has passed, we need
648  to break the spell.' I'd like to leave: it's like passing through the
649  market, seeing the stomach work, the digestion. Best not linger.

650 Kitty has found her bottle. Maybe in a while she'll dance. Alvin
651 says to some guys hanging round – 'I'll be bringing work and cash.
652 I know you'll keep it safe.' The guys grin. It says 'Harvard' on
653 their shirts. 'Yes,' Neville says. 'It'll all start up again. It must. I'll
654 be here. I told you I was for the revolution.'
655     'I should leave,' I tell them.
656     'Don't wave your black flag too much, my friend,' says Alvin.
657 'People don't like you if you're not enthusiastic for new orders.'
658     'I know,' I say.
659     'You think only of yourself, the immediate fragments of
660 perception, colliding with your consciousness,' says Neville.
661     'I know just what you mean, Neville,' I say. 'But I don't think
662 you've said it right, what you've just said.'
663     'He means you!' says Kitty. 'You can't piece a scene
664 together, make it whole, make it part of a panorama. You're too
665 small, I guess. Low down.'
666     'You don't like me, that's all it is,' I say. 'That's quite ok. It's
667 not obligatory to like.'
668     'You see!' says Alvin. 'Here, it's history. You – it's always
669 you. It's individualism run wild. You're like a beast that has no
670 history, no tradition. And the values that come with.'
671     'Well, sure, I don't let those things out, to show,' I say,
672 doubtfully.
673     Regina isn't here. 'She's letting guys convince her they are
674 doing right,' says Neville. 'She gets taken in too deep. She respects
675 – unlike you. But then – I have to pull her out.'
676     There's no sign of her. Guys in big cars drive up and down the
677 shuttered street: they shout and sing.
678     The three walk away from me.
679     I go back to the jail. The guy's not pleased to see me. 'Hey!' I
680 say. 'Those two guys and the tipsy lady – maybe you let them go
681 too soon. You know, for them, it's profit that they see in all this
682 sacrifice. Starting up their digging, and their scams. Corruption,
683 too, I bet.'
684     I hang around. A big car takes the three, my friends, back to
685 the jail, and then inside.
686     Somewhere outside, Regina's free. She'll never know who
687 gave the gift, her freedom. Maybe she wouldn't understand. She'll
688 seek out Neville – or she won't. Not to have him – it's a sacrifice.
689 So is to have him. The fighting here – is it the beginning of the end,
690 or a part of it? I'd need to ask Regina. Maybe there's an end to her

691 and Neville too, with him in jail. Perhaps she'll wonder where he
692 is...
693        I've finished here. I go back to see Paola. Remember not to
694 talk of them, Neville, Regina.
695        Paola's lying on a mattress. How white it is in here. How
696 white she is. She says, 'You see, I am depressed. I'm like the Snow
697 Queen, waiting for my prince. A special kiss.'
698        'You've got the story wrong,' I say. 'But you have what I
699 always wanted – remember what the song says, "A white room,
700 without curtains". And you understand, the white light coming in,
701 uninterrupted, forceful. And you, Paola, lying there, your skin so
702 white, the little scoops of breast, so white, so kissable.'
703        'Yes, yes,' she says. 'The sacrifice. The end. How it depresses
704 us. Come, lie beside me, and let me see a landscape on these walls.
705 The trees – they should be indigo, the sand – is red as garnets, the
706 sea is maybe grey, or green?' And she turns to me, and asks, her
707 mouth is close, the lips are red as garnets and the breath – grey-
708 green as aloes. 'Grey? Or green?' she asks. 'The sea?'
709        There is a rule – you mustn't fall into the sea, you mustn't fall
710 into the grey and green depression Paola has – and as she asks, she
711 pulls herself a little higher, and her breasts are bare, she says,
712        'They tell me I have lovely breasts,' and I say,
713        'Who are these "they"? Is there some contest you have won,
714 dear Paola? That would not be a surprise...' and on I talk, because I
715 know three things, like in the fairy tales; not mention Neville, not
716 drop Regina's name. And not involve myself with people who're
717 depressed, they're in a magic web that sucks you in, they pass it on,
718 the malady, the charm. Depression, it's a spell, and maybe you can
719 break it, by doing what you mustn't do, taking her and sharing it,
720 and lying on a bed somewhere and waiting for the prince, or the
721 princess, after a hundred depressing years, that you can ask to paint
722 the landscape on the white wall where the light hits with all its
723 force...
724        'No, no, Paola, really – I've no libido left,' I say – but it's too
725 late. I do exactly what I should not do. She lies, a white ermine
726 curling on the mattress – and at last her eyes are open, and they're
727 blue, sea blue. 'I waited here,' she says, 'so long, until my
728 depression could be passed on. The sacrifice, the species' end – it's
729 all passed on, it's disappeared.'
730        'I know all about that,' I say. 'The sacrifice, the end. It isn't
731 malady. It's an hypothesis.'

732 'Fuck you!' she shouts. 'You know it's happening. You've
733 tramped the world. You know!'
734 'Yes, Paola. Yes, I know,' I say.
735 There's something bounding up the stairs. Jump, jump, it
736 goes. It comes in on us – a beast with sporgent eyes, a black mask
737 on the white, a lemur.
738 'Here,' says Paola. 'This guy, this lemma... See his legs – the
739 back ones are so long, he can't bend down, go on all fours, he has
740 to jump. Look at the eyes, so sad, they know about extinction, you
741 can see. Take him – take him back to Effi. He's taken my
742 depression, taken it off you too, and bears it all himself.'
743 It could be so. He's miserable for sure, and we – Paola and me
744 – we're feeling good.
745 I travel with the lemur.
746 There's the Bir-Hakeim bridge, the trains.
747 'Effi, who's the guy who left? I passed him on the stair,' I ask.
748 'Oh, just a guy I owed,' she says.
749 'Neville's no more with us, Effi, I'm afraid,' I say. 'There was
750 a battle. Maybe a decisive one. Then he got in wrong with the new
751 guys. He wanted everything to carry on, to stay the same, to go
752 back like it was. We'll need another agent.'
753 She seems distracted, so I say, 'I brought a lemur. Some
754 people say it's called a "lemma".'
755 'No, no,' she says. 'They got it wrong. A lemma's quite
756 another thing. I'll call it "Lemmy". Like the movie guy, *"les
757 données immédiates..."* It fits animals. You must remember
758 Alphaville?'
759 We hear it jumping up and down the stairs. Depressed.
760 'What shall we do with it?' I ask.
761 'Something will come to us,' she says. 'It always does.
762 Though why you brought just one, I cannot think. Anyway, you're
763 safe here for a bit. Don't think about the animal. It won't be around
764 for long.'
765 'Well,' I say, annoyed. 'What I have seen – the battle, justice
766 being done, all that – if it means something, as it must, then single
767 creatures must mean something too. A couple, or a troop, is quite
768 another thing. My search took all my qualities. They say they're
769 ghosts: those creatures last for ever.'
770 She's not convinced.
771 She says, 'I guess it could be worth a lot. If anybody still
772 collects exotic things.'

773

# 2

# SHEEP

*from **Happy Always***

IT WAS LONG AGO. I soon left that country. There seemed no choice but to go down the mine. Most people do. Starting a band – you need other people. I won someone's girl, gaming in a bar. She never spoke – resentful, strange . . .

They keep a goat in the garage. It roams free, but isn't fed. It's for Eid. They're supposed to give some to the poor. I'm poor, I never get any. I'm glad. I don't approve. It's too domestic. Religion – they do what they want, but killing people in the house . . . It's a delicate beast, it thinks maybe I can help. What do we know of destiny? In the goat's case – chance isn't part of it. Now, if it were a sheep . . . The same end, better publicity. No hope. A martyred guru? Another festival? There's a debate about it, that way maybe chance starts to take a hand. 'The sum of choices' – that's life, they say, with no chance. It's not at all convincing. Sometimes, there's no choice at all.

No one can hate this awful country. I do. It's a hole in the ground. They've sold the topsoil, poisoned the Indians. Dig enough, you find the other country underneath. Richer, but still brown, yellow, anthracite. Not that it matters to me, except as themes. Symphonies, perhaps. Nature gone crotchety. Never explicit, never speaking. It's not like Cancer Ward, telling you how they hid the tumours. The Captive, *La prisonnière* – all first person, so you can avoid writing in the wars and stock exchange. Memory – even less pondered than a history. Raskolnikov, and 'his duty towards humanity'. There's a lot of talk about it here. Those are my three books. A course – what in, I never grasped. It didn't lead on. Mostly they don't. They end up pinned in a frame.

810   The goats, eating natural grass, brought in to show the ground is
811   healthy, the tar spun off. It doesn't fit: the picture of the jolly
812   farmer's wife, cutting out the meaty ones.
813       I love roasted goat. I can do without – it's not a great sacrifice.
814       You take an exam to get here. Do you take another, to get out?
815   Or just step outside, not come back in.
816       The war against the cows. Hard to say who's winning. They've
817   made a movie – *Le sang des bêtes*. There's casualties. Hung up in
818   the cold. Then you breed more and more and when they're at their
819   best – you eat them. I love steak – but it costs. I can easily do
820   without. It's not about eating. Nor about the animals: there's a
821   world order. It's about the order, and its balance. Some species
822   leave a hole, if they disappear. Bees, for sure. Humans – even more
823   for sure, maybe. Cows and goats . . . there's times and rites, and
824   every species has them. The fleshy ones, they do all right, although
825   they cost – the cows do.
826       There's no cruelty, it's not about that. If someone is in minerals,
827   digging them, they'll find oil is the new thing, and paid better. It's
828   all work, though, that gets harder, longer.
829       The cows should have got together with the goats. Solidarity.
830   But there wasn't much of that.
831       'They don't like you here,' says my friend. 'Walking about, not
832   unbuttoning your head.'
833       'I can't step away,' I say. 'Even my science comes out in first
834   person. I'm not a liberal – but that's the way it is. I know no one
835   made it all for me – invisible stars, rocks slung off . . . vandals and
836   viruses.'
837       'Don't dissimulate,' he, Frank, says. 'Talking doesn't absolve.
838   For certain, you did wrong. Leave quick, before you're made to
839   pay.'
840       'Those books,' I say. '"Moral responsibility", that was their
841   theme. If you can't do anything about where you are – maybe
842   you've no responsibility. The prison camp you're in . . . Then
843   Proust – there's no responsibility – just sex, no guilt; just swap the
844   attributes around. A *pédé* and a peeper. The lady prisoner . . . Those
845   quadrilles . . . "The dimension of Time", the ever-rolling stream,
846   stands in for everything. And – punishment – the dark bird that will
847   get you. You're not responsible, however much you fear the wings,
848   the beak.'
849       'You don't need prison, nor a punishment, to discharge
850   responsibility,' he says. 'To accept it, or deny.'

851  'That's what they say,' I say.
852  'I'm not sure you understand what you say,' says Frank. 'It's not
853  your job, after all.'
854  'Words?' I ask. 'What words?'
855  'Moral. Responsibility,' he says.
856  'You're right, Frank,' I say. 'My friend. Well-named. Frank.'
857  'Be a beacon,' Frank says. 'If you can't be something else. Or
858  have a job that makes clear what you say.'
859  Good advice, even if you don't understand it. He continues,
860  'This society – we're all a tiny bit responsible for what goes on.'
861  'Bees,' I say, 'they must each feel totally in charge.'
862  'Well,' he says, 'we're not. We vote. That shares it round. Then,
863  those that do the thing, they shift away. They're just appointed.'
864  '"Responsible" I understand,' I say. 'It's "moral" – if it clings
865  more, or less to other words.'
866  'Whoever made you read those books,' says Frank, 'should have
867  been clear. Maybe you should go where it's not an issue.'
868  'Yes,' I say, 'but I expect I'll always remember you.'
869  'The thing is, you're exasperating. You ask questions not
870  knowing the answer. And that stops people doing their job,' he
871  says.
872  'Those questions might have been my job,' I say. 'But it seems it
873  wasn't to be.'
874  'It's that responsibility,' says Frank. 'It clings, though you don't
875  want it. Maybe it could be moral too. That's what you seek. Good
876  luck – maybe someone will give you them . . .'
877  No, I don't want that at all. I say, 'I want to do propaganda. And
878  hope it turns out real and true.'
879  'Then you want the opposite of what you want,' says Frank.
880  'That's clear,' I say. 'Though I don't see why you should
881  understand.'
882  'Or want to,' Frank says.
883  Leaving this country's easy. It's one of its best qualities. Walk
884  through that door – adventure! The sky! Then, a mass of poor guys,
885  wanting to recruit you with their story.
886
887                                *
888
889  You're at the helm. Wear a chauffeur's cap, no one will ever ask
890  you for your licence. I drove this guy, a fuzzball like some weeds
891  give off. Two tiny legs, the abdomen, a face round and unkempt.

892  We often go to Switzerland, but live no place in particular. He has a
893  Rolls, a Cadillac. 'Which is best?' he asks. Origins and destiny –
894  uncertain, for this Rufus Borzhoi.
895      'The Rolls is hard,' I say. 'It's the Cadillac that rolls. Rigor or
896  plump.'
897      'I choose the soft,' he says. 'Bring your girl along.'
898      When I leave, I'll sell the Rolls. The cash will smooth my
899  journey. My girl – she didn't say goodbye. She waved. Her trade is
900  choosing *now*, not luck – she's learnt. The proud call it betrayal, an
901  offence.
902      When you drive a guy, you get time to read the books – those
903  with the tricks, those with the panorama. On the road – you see the
904  banks, the bodies. The 'little friends', boys and girls, the deadeye
905  guys pushing deals. And you see – 'oh! the seasons, and the
906  castles'. The great disappointment – Mongolia, with permanent
907  constructions. On the road, it's all ephemeral, and jigging round the
908  jams. How it should be. I grow – leaves, boughs, fruit: my three
909  books, infinitely repeated, reproduced. 'Power lives to betray . . .
910  humans blow away like cotton fluff, some get in your eye and
911  throat . . . don't do the dirty job unless you're sure you walk away,
912  unharmed, unburdened.' All the rest – air in the tires.
913      Brown tracks, black roads. Poles, stalls, and pumps. Back to how
914  it started, the digs, the tailings, yellow clouds. In the beginning –
915  the digging. Brought forth – roads. Roads where you go anywhere
916  and everywhere. Black strips – the view. The poles, the lights –
917  useless, will go. We need the pumps, the stalls – the eats. There's
918  guys – twenty-four hours beneath their arms, flagging you down to
919  do a deal. The *filles de joie* in their culottes, the chicken pieces on
920  the stalls. What interrupts? Passages of sheep and goats. On we go,
921  to Troy, to Herat, on to Harbin. All graded, flattened. On we go –
922  Borzhoi in back, spitting the sunflower seeds, a spiky parrot. 'On,
923  on: don't stop.'
924      'You're bad seed,' says Rufus. 'There's never a change in
925  register, no other point of view. It's always yours. The poet, staring
926  ahead, avoiding the dogs, the crash, the ditch. Unnatural. What do I
927  think? Your girl – leaf-tossed, a double blank. You've no idea.
928  Straight ahead, on, on . . .'
929      'It's so,' I say. 'It's the way we're built, and the work I have. It's
930  more secure than other kinds of sitting down. Ahead, ahead, on and
931  on. Avoiding the calamity. Avoid the other people in their motors,
932  cruising, speeding, broken down. You're going down the funnel,

933    you're sand in the glass, going from narrows into broads, the trees –
934    reeds in the flow, the poles, the palaces, on and on, the world a
935    steppe, the Cadillac our shoe that steps . . .'
936        'Exactly,' Rufus says. 'You choose to be the driver. All
937    decisions are yours, and every accident, all the arrivals – due to
938    you, in silence and in fasting. All yours.'
939        'These guys here,' I say. 'Been driven from their houses. My
940    idea – would be to put them underground. So – they're invisible.
941    No danger – everything beneath – they eat the mushrooms and the
942    beanshoots, their cows no longer crazy with the sun and wind. Tiny
943    brown chapels – no domes, no squinch to give them airs. No one to
944    come and drive them out, and knock down everything . . .'
945        Have them live down there . . . they're safe, the tanks and boots
946    – unsighted, trampling upstairs.
947        'Hmmmm,' he says. 'It may be you just want a panorama – with
948    no features, just a plain, a planet horizontal – so you can drive
949    without a person, wolf or sheep – that springs from roadside, drops
950    from tree . . . It's all your interest that's in play,' he says. 'You want
951    the flat. But – the messages! They'll all be traced! No matter if
952    you're in your chapel underground . . . Someone will hear – your
953    prayer, your curse . . . and dig you out, or bomb you in . . . No, no,
954    the answer is elsewhere. The brain! You can't send guys to live on
955    Mars or Venus – cutting off their language root, experience, eyes
956    and ears – the bleats, the singsongs and the dance . . . The brain's
957    the gewgaw you must work on . . .'
958        'I hadn't thought,' I say.
959        'This awful body,' Rufus says, holding it up so I can see him, a
960    blob, sea-urchin, oblonged in my mirror. 'I want rid of it . . .
961    Instead, a brain that travels anywhere, without the pains and
962    stimuli, the search for food and dictionaries, the sex, the soap, the
963    waffles, calvados – and all the rest that body craves, insists on.
964    Until that brain – that travels into space, or roams among the
965    daffodils of yesteryear – is plastered in, Oh! driving man up front!
966    Feel my frustration, longing, anger. The struggle! Brain and body,
967    screwed together in unending strife . . . It's prison, friend. You
968    walk with it, you cut its hair and nails. No crime, and no release.'
969    Bobbing up and down – now you see his moustache, sealion or
970    walrus – now the wavering beard.
971        'Well,' I say, 'that's all incurable. What I propose – instead of
972    driving into nothingness for ever – maybe I could be the
973    helmsman? A voyage. Steering. Not letting on the purpose, or the

974 goal, the destination . . . "Going home" they call it. Though there is
975 no home. There is oblivion. Dust. Maybe they dig you up and stain
976 you brown. That's it. But . . . helmsman. Yes – it has a ring,
977 sonority. It's got a crust . . .' I'm fascinated.
978     'Stop swerving, you idiot,' shouts Rufus. 'Just because you've
979 found your crack in existence, your sunlit wall, your calling as a
980 cold and supple lizard, – keep to the straight!'
981     'It's the joy,' I say. 'I'm sure it passes. I don't need you, Rufus,
982 nor anyone behind me . . .'
983     He doesn't challenge me. 'Oh,' he says, 'I'm just a cuckoo. I
984 tramp the world, I leave my eggs in other's nests, throw out their
985 spotty little kids, in shell or skin . . . I take them over: my projects
986 are so big, enormous . . . Invasive. "Cuckoo" they cry. And
987 everybody tilts their ear, "Aha! I know that theme," they shout, and
988 run to see . . . But – you never see the bird. It's flown,' and he
989 laughs, long, too long, too loud.
990     Hiphop in Mongolia, fire alarms in Bangladesh – the schemes
991 catch on, replete with plausibility.
992     'My fortune,' Rufus says, 'comes from intelligence. Poker. This
993 noble lady – maybe the deck was lightly stacked. She loved me,
994 wanted me to be her prince, but all I got was . . . her liquidity. Her
995 French – had Russian endings. That's real class.'
996     We motor on, in silence. People all over – driven out: camps
997 hidden in the hills. Their offence – passivity. Born wrong. In wrong
998 places. 'This goddam tar, the tarmac. Filling up with gas . . .' I say.
999 'It all goes back to drills and mines and pipes and pumps. Holes in
1000 the ground – gold, cobalt, oil: it's all the same. My miserable
1001 origins . . .'
1002     'Here is the sea!' shouts Rufus. 'Thalassa! Bars. Smokes. Hands
1003 off the wheel, and let some guy take . . . his wheel. Then off again.
1004 I know it's purgatory – but what comes next is worse.'
1005     The sea – infinitely sad: jungle invisible. Bells ring with no
1006 human hands – fog, scored for unseen horns. There are no sheep,
1007 no cows – no church – attached.
1008     'Your pain will cease,' says Rufus. 'A machine will drive the
1009 motor. Guys who thought they'd see my face, decide if it was
1010 honest – they'll scrutinise me on a screen. Your work, its pain, will
1011 cease. Remember – unemployment is secure. No interviews,
1012 anxiety, humiliation. On and on . . . Me? I'll be fine – capitalism
1013 rides hard those electric tigers it invents.'
1014     'Rufus,' I ask, dismayed. 'I'll be a helmsman still?'

1015    'Oh yes,' he says. 'You won't drive. But "helmsman" – all you
1016    guys, you warriors, you guides – yes, all of you will keep that
1017    honour . . . your destiny, your own, alone . . .'
1018       Rufus sits up front with me – it doesn't make us equal. The
1019    road's a line, you follow it, then crossing it there's lines with cops –
1020    the frontiers. There's a good line too – the sheep that intersect, that
1021    you can count, and think of sleeping with their warmth – a stall . . .
1022       'Take it from me, my friend,' he says, 'there is no promised
1023    land. No promise. And no land.'
1024       'Should we load some women in the back?' he asks.
1025       'Your hands are free,' I say. 'They might damp down the
1026    springs. Those waves, the rolling – it brings nausea.'
1027       The driver. Without the motor, you are still a helmsman. You
1028    don't need, won't have, a ship. Those don't belong to you in any
1029    case – there's a Rufus somewhere, with the document. 'Reward the
1030    followers', 'administer the people', 'hail the victory, death to the
1031    faithless and backsliders' . . . You drive – that's it. Guys and gals in
1032    the back? Who cares. You steer the ship? The problem's with the
1033    storm, not the passengers. What keeps the sheep in line? The
1034    shepherd ahead, the dogs behind? Or simply being sheep, going
1035    after grass. No promise. No land. That's the secret everybody
1036    knows. You're the helmsman, doctor, wolf and saint. On, and on:
1037    onward, the soldiers, the faithful patients, the guy with the
1038    sandwich box full of dough . . .
1039       'There's a layby,' Rufus says. 'We'll doss down here.'
1040
1041                    *
1042
1043    The guys who come to rob us, to steal the motor – come from the
1044    camp that's out of sight.
1045       It's what I'd do. We're the same species. Rufus doesn't ask for
1046    help. It's not my job – and I can run so fast! – maybe I'm blessed; a
1047    providence, a faith. Or that he's slow. You know he has the cash.
1048    He needs to justify his wealth, even – an apology. They try to start
1049    the Cadillac – it's way, way beyond them, so they stamp on Rufus.
1050    That's what I would do.
1051       At his memorial, we sing 'The Enchanted Wanderer'. We weep.
1052    I read from *La Prisonnière*: the corpse 'a stone which encloses the
1053    salt of immemorial oceans', thinking of our voyages, and my pay
1054    packets . . . 'the sealed envelope of a person who inwardly reached
1055    to infinity'. I don't mention running hands over Albertine. Rufus is

1056 dead, his sex as immaterial as his brain, his body. He wanted to be
1057 rid of one, or both. There was nothing in him you could know. Like
1058 Albertine – maybe he wasn't real. Or bits of real people, and so
1059 unreal. His capital lives on. His associates are in the room, all
1060 singing like a hatch of frogs.
1061     I sell his Rolls – it's my new life, the cash. It's the least I could
1062 have done.
1063     We mill – we mull – around the absent cadaver.
1064     'Chantal!' I say. 'The name is beautiful. You're the thing of
1065 beauty Rufus left, I'm sure. In life, one's all you are allowed. You
1066 know – the motors – those he left to me . . .'
1067     She's not so great – rather, it's her scent. And clothes. Take
1068 them away, and . . . 'Here is some cash,' I say. 'There was no will.
1069 I'm sure you were the one, despite the lack . . .'
1070     'Oh,' she says, 'I'm in the *Palais froid*. The castoffs, castaways
1071 end there. But they get paid, and into the mausoleum they go too,
1072 when the emperor decides to go to paradise.'
1073     'That's poetry,' I say. 'How did you cleave to him?'
1074     'No cleaving, dear,' she says. 'I organise the coursing of the
1075 hare. My castle grounds . . .'
1076     'How does it work?' I ask.
1077     'The hares are freed, they make the run through the long grass,
1078 and clients shoot them. It's their fun,' she says.
1079     'I never saw him, Chantal, with a gun. We were all innocents, up
1080 there,' I say.
1081     Chantal folds my notes away, the serenade is done. Farewell.
1082     'I am the hare that gets away and makes the massacre a sport,' I
1083 say.
1084     'That's trite,' she says. 'You say you're an escapee. Everybody
1085 says you are the heir, with Rufus's cash and all his tastes.'
1086     'I know the universe was not created for my contemplation –
1087 though when I die, it all will disappear. Rufus didn't leave me
1088 money – maybe, sitting behind, staring at my head, the patterns, the
1089 designs, priorities carpentered in his brain . . . he passed them on.
1090 Someone did for sure. I didn't invent them all myself – the colours,
1091 tastes, the duties and the punishments. And yet – they ended up
1092 inside,' I say.
1093     'Sometimes imposed, sometimes inborn,' she says. 'That's the
1094 dirty trick. How to sort them out?'
1095     'Oh,' I say, 'it's not because there's animals, along with us.
1096 Everybody gets a weapon, like the gladiators – a twisty wing, a

1097 claw. Never the right combination so you'd always win – the
1098 armour's holed, the sword's an edge but not a point. Everyone is
1099 equal, as you never have the right accoutrements. It's not that. You
1100 can't object to it. What I strive for – it's being not imposed upon.
1101 Speaking as if the language is your own. Escaping.'
1102     'That's what the guys did who stamped on Rufus,' Chantal says.
1103     'I escaped my destiny,' I say. 'I'll go on doing it. That's all, the
1104 best, that you can do. Then – you get caught, cornered. That's too
1105 bad.'
1106     'You should be good,' says Chantal. 'Then nothing matters
1107 more.'
1108     'I told you, Chantal,' I say. 'Escaping is the best there is.'
1109     'Then what? Do it again?' she asks.
1110     'Leave no trace,' I say. 'That is immortality. Curiosity – the only
1111 quality. No heritage, no lesson. No amusements as a legacy.'
1112     'Well,' she says. 'I do the opposite of all that.'
1113     'Maybe not the exact opposite,' I say, wanting to be pleasant. Or
1114 because I didn't know.
1115     'I absolutely have to leave,' she says. and so she does.
1116     I think those animals, the hares, the sheep – know everything
1117 they have to know, to do. What they don't know is humans, their
1118 motive. And that, it's quite irrelevant for them to know.
1119     The sheep is good, are good. It's the shepherd we know we can't
1120 be sure about. He or she is good and bad. It doesn't matter to the
1121 sheep. Me? I can't be a sheep – but I needn't be a shepherd.
1122 Because . . . we know . . . Without a tribunal to investigate . . . we
1123 know all about being human, everything we need to know. And all
1124 about those shepherds too.
1125     'Keeping shtum about the cash? I envy you – that's all pleasure,'
1126 and here's another – a Diana – after me, after the good life. This
1127 one – maybe in from the street, 'I'm Britney. A relative.' A good
1128 cry for Rufus. A lake of tears, some kind of race – a treasure hunt.
1129     'Oh no,' I say. 'All these people. Hunters – a hunter isn't quite a
1130 predator, but here are predators. Bend down – you see their legs,
1131 it's like a spinney, birch and oak.'
1132     'We're all here because we're sad. We've all lost . . .' she says.
1133 She doesn't bend.
1134     'It's like the guys in France, romancing,' I say. 'Partying,
1135 making a fuss about the boys and girls they hunted, and the size of
1136 those big cheeses who'd take tea with them. Writing it all down,
1137 seeing themselves as master of the dance.'

1138    'There's no tea here,' says Britney. 'This scotch is real. The hunt
1139    is harsher too. The spirit is elusive. Rufus – no body, now no soul
1140    that we can catch . . .'
1141       'You're right,' I say. 'The hide and seek is rough. It ends, quite
1142    sensibly, in other deaths. For Rufus – oblivion: he left no record of
1143    the banks his wealth was in.'
1144       He clutched that sandwich box. Could it have fitted all in there,
1145    the cash, and disappeared?
1146       'They'd find a wood, and trap the stag inside. The huntsmen
1147    were all round – they couldn't see each other, so they talked with
1148    horns. The different calls. Muster. Gone away. Each move was
1149    musicked. Then the dogs went in,' I say.
1150       And there is Rufus, a red-brown envelope, transparent – leaping
1151    out, his antlers bright with myth and gold . . . Away, away, down
1152    the hill – that's the instant you forget the numbers of the bank
1153    accounts, you're pure and poor, your carnal self is disinherited. Off,
1154    down the hill – use the stream to throw the dogs . . . the elfin
1155    fanfares fainter now, a silver horn plucks at the silver air . . .
1156       The mist, the frost, turns us all into an ancient silver print . . .
1157       'Everything has changed,' I say. 'These people here, looking for
1158    his memory – they are not friends, whose intimacies become my
1159    tales. Not my friends, not his. Now, they're after *me*. If they can't
1160    kill the absent Rufus, quarter him – they'll go after me . . .'
1161       'Your eyes,' says Britney, 'brim with fear. I love it, your humble
1162    humanity.'
1163       'Ah yes. The gift of fear . . . Where I came from, there was
1164    work,' I say. 'Once, too, I'd have begged to be a servant for
1165    Chantal.'
1166       'So?' Britney asks, 'what is your point?'
1167       'I thought it was quite clear,' I say. 'Joining some class. Dying
1168    for yourself, your cause. I preferred to drive . . .'
1169       'Where Rufus said,' she says.
1170       'Rufus was no messenger,' I say. 'I chose the road. You saw –
1171    I'm not a slave. Chantal took my cash . . .'
1172       'An error,' Britney says. 'Or else you stole it from his corpse.
1173    And so – it weighs.'
1174       'Oh no,' I say. 'It's feathers. It's lighter even than the work you
1175    do today, and there it is tomorrow, just the same, always starting
1176    over, like the tide. Or sometimes not. Cash – it's always there. You
1177    don't feel a weight.'

1178     They cluster round me – a rally of animals, a-sniff. What's the
1179 driver – sex? Food? An excitement that can end in both?
1180     'I suffocate,' I say. 'You bear me down.'
1181     'Oh – really?' says Britney. 'I'm the dependable type. A Buick,
1182 built heavy.'
1183     'To me,' I say. 'You're more a samoyed. They give you lustre in
1184 the city, pulling them along, reluctant on their string. But in the
1185 wild – omnivorous and bossy.'
1186     I'd recognise these people in the street. Each one has a dignity,
1187 an exclusiveness. A different shape, a timbre, gait, a set of tastes
1188 and smells. That's good for them. I look around the group: here,
1189 tales abound. I'm not like them, I don't gather anecdotes, and I
1190 don't hunt.
1191     Then – a moment of epiphany: once, you'd have said, of
1192 revolutionary consciousness.
1193     'Rufus – the best shepherd you could have,' I say to Britney,
1194 Chantal who has turned her ear . . . 'He was so quiet and satisfied,
1195 sat back there, wherever I felt like taking him, and doing all the
1196 work.'
1197     And now, I'll safely graze on what his motor car has realised.
1198 Sheep aren't so stupid, though they may be limited. The inspiration
1199 – it alights. The company's alert:
1200     'Why,' I shout, 'you're nothing but a pack of dogs!'
1201     New life! It flares up like a star.

1202

# 3

# THE SCORPIONS

*from* **Enterprising Women**

*Lara*

I AM A COLLEGE PROJECT. Crime.
'I'm your friend. Just write me your history, all about
you,' I say. The guy writes:
'... drinking with people you don't know and don't trust. No
particular place to keep or gain. Off in some guy's car – "see my
grannie in Silver Lake" – she's been dead for years, but we got
snowed in, we drank for days. Those cars – cause lots of damage,
when you drink or when you steal them. So much room up north –
you can get lost for ever. Turn up for work a coupla times – they
pay you off for the week to get rid ... this society, it's like a sea:
you feed off the crap that sinks, it comes from guys up near the sun,
wearing suits – but in their heads, the same things as yours – the
game, the booze, hating the family, loving some woman, then not.
'"How much cash you got, old son?" It was a cop, I said
"$6.83" – "Then," he said, "You're a vagrant, come with me," and
you go in and out of jobs, and rows, and meeting up – and there's
an Indian woman, keeps on coming round, I didn't know about her,
maybe there's kids, a guy who has a rifle, but she's nice, we drink
together, and she tells stories ...'
'I might do better with girls,' I say. 'Their criminality.'
'I don't think you give those guys their space,' Lara says.
'And from the girls you'll get harsh fun.' In the room, some brown
and yellow feral cats with pointy noses – I push them gently out my
way with my boot. 'There's guys, that should be interesting,' I say.
'Up at the school. An astrophysicist. Some other, into particles, or
bones. It seems we started off with everything – all packed into a
speck of dust.'

1240 'We're still there,' she says.

1241 'Hotter than hot,' I go on. 'And dense. Time zero ... can you
1242 imagine that?'

1243 'No,' she says.

1244 'Well, that's right,' I say. 'There's the proof. You can't.
1245 There's no place for you, to sit or stand, observe. Nothing to
1246 compare. No big or small or long or short.'

1247 'I know,' she says. 'It's on TV.'

1248 'Well,' I say. 'It's news to me. And they don't talk to me
1249 about it – but – I ought to know. It should be a right. Not covered
1250 up, and only certain guys who know, and they don't talk.'

1251 'Maybe they think you're not so bright,' she says.

1252 'They do talk about things, though, like grumbling about the
1253 food. And goddam automobiles.'

1254 She says, 'They know you're not a prof. What was it you did
1255 – an affray? They put you into criminology, you're an exhibit. An
1256 aid. A nearly living proof. You're a crime scene. It's your sentence,
1257 it's not for learning from.' I say, 'I forgot I'm a coward. Sometimes
1258 you just join in. Sometimes you start things off. Like the universe.
1259 It's like they say in Zen – god is a dust speck on your broom.' It
1260 was me they wanted. They didn't want someone from a gang. Dead
1261 ends.

1262 Lara insists, 'Do you tell anyone but me, you're putting a
1263 gang, a skein, together? If you find someone interesting?'

1264 I ignore this. I say, 'And in the beginning, there were all
1265 different models, makes, of men. All black – all quite bright,
1266 religious, into painting on the walls. All competing. Stealing each
1267 others' women. So, now there's us. We're stardust, and all those
1268 African guys looped in.'

1269 She says, 'Once Hitler was nearly as big as the world. Now
1270 he's a speck of dust on the broom, waiting to become a universe
1271 again.'

1272 I say, 'I'm not into things so big as that. That guy – the one
1273 who broke up cars when he was drunk – he cut his woman. Cut her
1274 right up.'

1275 'You're dark,' says Lara, 'but not quite moved outside the
1276 light. Just blocking it off.'

1277 I say, 'Or – maybe he got scared – he thought her old man was
1278 after him. It preyed, a bit.'

1279 'Nothing succeeds like insanity,' says Lara. 'I can't stand you,
1280 your fussy friends and their big pictures. And those punks. All you

1281 think about is making money, but you haven't got a cent. That's
1282 thought for you!'
1283     It's all true. 'At least I don't have consciences inside my
1284 shoes, making me limp,' I say.
1285     'I want to be free, with no one else around me,' she says. 'The
1286 college let you go. They got tired of you, so they got the cops to
1287 forget it all. That's generosity. Justice, even.'
1288     'Well, here we are. Here we are,' I say. 'Two matches in the
1289 box.'
1290     'You know why we're here. I saw in you – an organiser.
1291 Inspiration. Not setting up a gang for company and street nuisance,
1292 everybody saving something of themselves and passing on the crap
1293 to other people. You'd take a ride from the devil, if the bus didn't
1294 show.'
1295     'These cats,' I say. 'You want them to recognise – this is
1296 inside. An apartment. But they've become another kind – they
1297 don't know in and out. Just food.'
1298     'They'll learn,' says Lara, 'and if they don't, there's nothing
1299 lost.'
1300     'They're a challenge,' I say. 'Reality's a challenge too. They
1301 say "open up to it", the tactile and the amorous, don't hide behind
1302 imagination. Be realistic, Lara. Everybody yearns for realism ...'
1303     'You don't mean "realism",' Lara says. 'You mean "being
1304 realistic" – that's quite other.'
1305     'Well,' I say, 'the astroman – he'll never travel to those stars,
1306 or lie back on some beach and have them tan his little legs. And
1307 bones – those black guys tucked away inside the moderns: the other
1308 prof, guy – he doesn't see them, throwing spears and joshing. Just
1309 callipers and skulls.'
1310     She doesn't answer. There has been no question. For the
1311 moment, we are here, exasperated.
1312     A gang. Alcohol. It's all dangerous.
1313     'You have to learn the dangers, so's to live with them quite
1314 easily. Look at Alma, now,' says Lara. 'She lost all her family ...
1315 and the family before that too, all in one swoop.'
1316     'It doesn't back you up,' I say. 'You foresee danger, but it's
1317 unforeseeable. As Alma found, those peoples and their states – they
1318 were quite murderous. Once they get railways and the telegraph,
1319 there's no escape. What can you say? Fine poems on the tombs, and
1320 plan your getaway?'

1321
1322
1323
1324
1325
1326
1327
1328
1329
1330
1331
1332
1333
1334
1335
1336
1337
1338
1339
1340
1341
1342
1343
1344
1345
1346
1347
1348
1349
1350
1351
1352
1353
1354
1355
1356
1357
1358
1359
1360

'You feel lost, in your loss,' says Lara. 'Though it's not particularly yours. Loss belongs to everyone. But – you should watch to see who comes out with a smile.'

'Lara,' I say, 'do you still arrange things? It seems pathetic, you know.'

'We don't have many things, my dear,' she says. 'Your friends, the gang you'd like to have – they don't count for much. The idea's worth more than the individuals,' and she goes on.

'OK,' I say. 'It was a bad idea. A flying wedge, red nail. Assertion, testing the limits – hitting guys. It wouldn't prove ... besides, what is it that needs a proof? Here we all are. Some cannibals, some just seasick, all looking for another boat.'

It's not the furniture we haven't got that Lara puts in order. Not pictures on the walls, or words in songs she doesn't sing. Arranging. She can arrange just about anything that comes to mind, and you can't see unless she tells.

'I think a lot when you're not here,' she says. 'I can set whole pages straight. Fit you all in, and make a future for myself. I put in whole brigades, of spear-throwers ...' and I say,

'You mean – spear-carriers,' and she says, no, hers are on the move, and in close order, not just trailing after.

Someone up there on the hill, the college, they reported it – Lara tells me how this guy, he closed his girlfriend up, maybe to possess her more, lessen the threat. Or just – his brain turned bad, like a cauliflower gone to mould. A horrible end for her. And his end too – full of little cadences. By law. Some trades – you can just lift people off the streets, and shut them in. No cadences, no calendars.

'You see?' says Lara. 'This arranging things. Is not just fantasy.'

'These little apartments,' I say, 'like those curiosity boxes that guy used to make, all incongruous, but neat, you can't have things and people spilling out the walls and windows.'

The cat food's ready – I say. 'Must we eat the same, all of us, cats too?'

'We are all one, that's what you always say,' she says. 'And it's convenient.'

'These felines—' I begin.

She interrupts: 'Whatever you're about to say, it makes no sense. So don't.'

1361        I say, 'Look what's happening all over. It's revolution, round
1362    again. Here it comes, just like it didn't come when our parents
1363    longed for it, and hugged. This time – it's fucking monarchists and
1364    priests and such who cheer! Here, everybody wants a change that
1365    suits. Not to be left aside. Pretending to like guys indifferent to
1366    them, guys redrawing maps, guys having none. What's it all mean?
1367    Hot shards, these religions, dancing at our governors' legs, like
1368    shrapnel. Or else it's houses, made of sand, that's being built.
1369    Millions of them! What's behind it, Lara? What's coming down on
1370    us? Control? Torture, designed by law? It's all beyond me – here, I
1371    don't belong. I'm ignorant, and innocent.'
1372        She stirs the pot: she says, 'I'm off quite soon. Protecting
1373    animals, since I haven't protected you ...'
1374        I'm amazed. I say, 'Things here, they change. The guys that
1375    were marooned, up on their ladders – now they're looking bright,
1376    maybe they'll start to climb again.'
1377        'So what,' she says. 'You never climbed. I think you like the
1378    snakes. Down there, you're on firm soil. It does you credit – with
1379    me, at least, but no one else.' I say,
1380        'I bet for you the attraction was my stuff with criminals? And
1381    staring at the stars? With Claire too, the thief? Who steals from
1382    everyone? That's why you leave, and don't invite me too.'
1383        Lara says, 'The trouble is – they're pillars of it all. Gangs,
1384    community, tattoos, and cutting throats. It's all too much the same,
1385    it's not outside us, it is exactly us. A different shade of grey, that's
1386    all. Our unthinking wills, they roam and squabble, plot and stab. It
1387    is exactly us.'
1388        I'm impressed. I say, 'Well, even so, it has its fascination.
1389    We're supposed to love the everything, the all-around ...' She ladles
1390    out the catfood, says,
1391        'You may, I don't. Now, say goodbye when Alma comes...'
1392        And so I shall.
1393        'Well, Alma,' I say. 'Making my own way again.'
1394        'That's good, so good,' she says, taking off her shawl. I say,
1395        'You look at the big things happening out there – the
1396    evolution of it all, when everything is made of similar materials, the
1397    universal stuff. You mustn't intervene, or if you do, you only
1398    nudge. But destiny – it's massive. The little stems and stalks that
1399    stick and swirl – you think they're huge – they are. But it's all
1400    details, it's all swept away. There's no design – it's just what is,
1401    and how it twists ...'

| | |
|---|---|
| 1402 | 'His friends will beat you in the streets,' Lara tells Alma. |
| 1403 | Alma looks bleak. I say, |
| 1404 | 'No, it's the profs. They're into distances you haven't paper |
| 1405 | you can write them down. And times – the same. The things that |
| 1406 | slither, then they hop, and then there's sludge again, or slush. And |
| 1407 | then there's sushi, then there's us.' |
| 1408 | Alma peers at me. She says, 'Yes, yes – it's so. You see the |
| 1409 | art, and then the news, and guys that run from here and there, |
| 1410 | convinced. All going round, suffering by rote. And herding people, |
| 1411 | putting them in lines, and then there's nothing left to eat.' |
| 1412 | 'Alma tries to sort it out – is it a news sheet? Or some art?' |
| 1413 | Lara goes on, ignoring Alma but talking about her. 'She lost her |
| 1414 | families, but they never said quite why, if it was something that |
| 1415 | they did, or what she was. They kept it secret, but it shouldn't take |
| 1416 | a lot to work it out.' |
| 1417 | 'I have loss, that's quite a positive matter,' Alma says, 'And |
| 1418 | chaos.' |
| 1419 | 'Chaos or disorder?' Lara asks, quite sharply. |
| 1420 | 'Oh, chaos,' Alma says. 'I guess you could do poems – if you |
| 1421 | were a poet. It's quite irreversible, though. Loss.' |
| 1422 | 'Well,' I say, intruding, 'I've no pardon. Those profs – quite |
| 1423 | superficial. Proud of the good things they think their kids did with |
| 1424 | their guns. Me – the people I know with guns – they don't think |
| 1425 | they're doing good things.' |
| 1426 | 'I'm sure you could do politics as well,' says Alma, trying to |
| 1427 | take things in. 'Or little acts of justice.' |
| 1428 | 'Yes,' I say, 'if I was really into it. I think you must be ready |
| 1429 | for just anything. My friends don't vote. They don't go out and |
| 1430 | have the cops to billy them. But, yes, I see you think, "These guys, |
| 1431 | they're pretty much quite hopeless scum."' |
| 1432 | Lara moves into a higher gear: 'You know, the forest where |
| 1433 | I'm off to save the animals – quite long ago, was densely |
| 1434 | populated. With humans. Now, it seems it's the domain of animals, |
| 1435 | but once – people. Villages. Towns and dancing. Then the other |
| 1436 | humans came.' |
| 1437 | 'Their viruses ...' adds Alma. |
| 1438 | I say, 'My family – they had an imaginary member. They |
| 1439 | believed in him. They called him Michael Hove.' |
| 1440 | 'Alma gave all her money to a sect,' says Lara. |
| 1441 | 'It wasn't much,' says Alma. 'I was convinced, just then.' |
| 1442 | 'That's terrible,' I say. |

1443 My father would have given me advice: 'Drop that woman.
1444 Leave that country. Clean your mind.' It's good to have advice.
1445 I stare at Alma – she wears those high dresses, like she's
1446 Amish, which she's not. Her skin – a line comes to me, 'spotty as a
1447 fig pudding'. When they torture you, maybe they fit another skin,
1448 when they have done – if ever they are done. Or maybe she's so
1449 white and pure, she doesn't let it out, her skin – forever shaded,
1450 remembering ancestral parasols against the sun at Biarritz. She
1451 must be fifty – nothing at all, when you think of stars. Stars in the
1452 sky, not in the circus. And all so long ago, the waves, the sea, long
1453 gone, flopped down, exhausted. My family: – Lara, they didn't like.
1454 In her own unliked way, they thought she was too good for me.
1455 Michael Hove, now – he could drive my parents where they
1456 wanted, at the right speed too. Relied on to weep when they were
1457 dead. Now, Michael Hove, writing down my thoughts, shaking his
1458 sad, his perfect, head.
1459 There's been a long silence. I say, 'I did a course in aerial
1460 photography. I know all about it – I could be up there, filming Lara
1461 while she fosters cubs.'
1462 'It's not just cuddles,' Lara says. 'It is a project, details
1463 minute, and balances exotic.'
1464 'You need an aeroplane for those photos,' Alma says.
1465 'A boss,' I say. 'That's what you need.'
1466 'A platform,' Lara says. 'Everybody does.'
1467 'You think there's one for everyone?' asks Alma. 'I'm sorry,
1468 the things I say are trite, but I am deep.'
1469 'Of course, there's one,' says Lara. 'And you can't show
1470 there's not.'
1471 'How I hope Claire will drop round,' Lara lies.
1472 Claire – she's a sexual Parthenon – the spear, eternal flames,
1473 the giggling virgins. She's gathered so much wisdom ... Lara
1474 whispers to Alma, 'Claire is a thug.'
1475 I say, 'It's true I've all the richness of new knowledge, but I
1476 can live like one of these,' and I put out my hand towards a cat.
1477 'No,' says Claire. 'Your scraps of tittle, picked up in the bar –
1478 that isn't knowing anything. It's squalid. Doing courses when you
1479 need an aeroplane...' She has brought a bottle.
1480 Lara says, 'Maybe I should make spaghetti?' Alma says,
1481 'It's too early for spaghetti – not for a martini, though.'
1482 'This bottle's not spaghetti, nor martinis either,' says Claire.
1483 Lara says, 'Oh no, it's not a drinking party!'

1484 'You know,' says Claire. 'Since Lara's off, and you will have
1485 to leave this pad as well,' she smiles at me, 'we could do a
1486 sledding, right across the country. Sponsored by some guys I know
1487 who need to clean some cash. The hard bits we could do by train – I
1488 know conductors everywhere.'
1489     'I'd love to come,' says Alma, 'but the trains – maybe they
1490 won't take the dogs?'
1491     'Then it's man's work,' Claire says. 'You'll have to pull,
1492 Alma. Like those old barge-haulers,' and she smiles at me. Then,
1493     'Look, Alma, can we dump you off someplace?' she asks.
1494     'Oh no,' says Alma pertly. 'I'll stick with you. I never
1495 criticise the company I'm with.'
1496     'We could take a car, go see some grannies,' I suggest.
1497     'My granny's in Haiti,' Claire says.
1498     'I see you've taken over quickly, Claire,' Lara says. 'This guy
1499 – I couldn't stand him any more, you should watch out.'
1500     'Well, you abandoned him, just like these cats, to go and
1501 coddle others,' Claire says, laughing to blunt the point, and Lara
1502 says,
1503     'Those cats are smart. They'll not forget.' We ponder this,
1504 who's abandoned, who remembers.
1505     'If I'd known we're into heavy conversation, I'd have brought
1506 another bottle,' Claire says.
1507     Lara shows a nature movie. 'You're going to make a peace?'
1508 asks Alma. 'That's a noble thing. Those zebras and the crocodiles
1509 ...'
1510     'The nasty ones – they get to eat the pretty things. It doesn't
1511 seem quite right,' I say.
1512     Lara's irritated. 'That's how it is. That's why the movie's
1513 made.' I say.
1514     'I know all that, I see it. Life. Or not. Lara, why don't you
1515 make the creatures food, like you give the cats and me? Then this
1516 eating thing would be resolved. And those poor guys that live in
1517 huts – they could get some too,' and Lara turns the movie off.
1518     'Mine are tiny things,' she says. 'Almost like grit. And they
1519 eat nectar, maybe a puffball for dessert. They're almost invisible,
1520 no one gets to eat, or even see, them.'
1521     'That's all right, then – go to, Lara!' Alma shouts.
1522     I'm not convinced, I tell them how some stars, they may eat
1523 other stars, but there's no blood, no fuss, we hear about it, if at all, a
1524 million years to come, and Lara says, 'Oh no, not more stuff about

1525 the stars. If you're hungry – there's kilometres of spaghetti, just to
1526 hand.'
1527     I put a record on, it's Hendrix, 'Up from the skies.'
1528     We try to dance to it, Claire and I – 'Look, they're a zebra,'
1529 Alma laughs. 'All striped together, prancing there,' but Lara lies
1530 quiet, in wait.
1531     All are quite merry, except Lara. Alma recites, 'past those two
1532 long spits of sand there stands the harbour wall, samphire and rock-
1533 cress making their show, the schooners elegant and rich unload the
1534 bales of spice and silk, and quincaillerie from Madagascar, while
1535 little skiffs race to and fro, the cormorants peering with one eye
1536 into the deeper blue, the other scanning for the clouds that come
1537 with the noon heat, and on the shore the merchants, the "blue
1538 ones", travelled from Maracaibo and from Tenerife stand majestic
1539 with their camels, daggers with crude rubies set into their
1540 pommels...'
1541     'What's all that?' asks Claire. 'Must be Stevenson. Or
1542 Conrad.'
1543     'I remember everything he wrote,' says Alma, proudly.
1544     Some guy comes in. He says, 'Hey! My motor! Someone's
1545 prised up the hood all round – maybe a tire iron ...'
1546     'That red job?' I ask. 'Maybe it was me. Wanted to see who's
1547 it might be. A roadster, that's what they're called. They scare the
1548 cats – they hate the colour red.'
1549     'The cats are all inside,' says Lara feebly. So they are.
1550     'I came to say farewell,' the guy says. He feels he can't object
1551 too much. Politeness is a trap. Parked right outside, the nuisance,
1552 where I could see it ...
1553     'You, guy! Wire wheels, red body!' says Claire. 'Who's
1554 leaving then?'
1555     'I'm not,' says the guy. 'The motor's jammed.'
1556     'It seems we're all leaving,' I say. 'That's what parties do.
1557 Farewell, farewell, and o remember me! A contradiction there...'
1558     'I didn't mean it quite so hard, abandoning you all,' says Lara,
1559 crying.
1560     'I'm sure we're used to it,' says Alma. 'Usually done with
1561 more style.'
1562     'Well,' I say. 'Lara did the decent thing, eventually. She cried,
1563 as she was leaving.'
1564     'You're quite perverse,' says Claire. 'And that silly car –
1565 they'll make you sweat for that.'

1566
1567
1568

'His red rooster? Besides, Claire – that Alma, lost her family, now she has this tic, it all goes into literature and memorising. Print doesn't disappear. You didn't help.'

1569
1570
1571
1572

'She isn't sympa. She is rather dull,' says Claire. I say,
'Now – where's to go? Here we are. Now, that's a thing it's always possible to say, wherever you may find yourselves.' If you're in luck, I think, and living.

1573
1574
1575
1576

'Anywhere you run to,' Claire says. 'There'll be poor people, poorer than you can believe, and lots of cops that listen to the things you say. Especially you. You toss out words, not caring where they fall. The cops'll lock you up ...'

1577
1578
1579
1580
1581
1582
1583
1584

'Quiet, Claire! You bring up these poor people – it's your excuse for wanting far away from them,' I say. 'And making cash. And Lara – joining the animals, she will not resist and fight. The bad guys ramp around, waving their axes and their viruses – and all she thinks of is a spot where all can live in harmony. "Back to the garden, crock of milk of kindness for the snake ... My! the territory's smaller every day, so close the gate ... keep out the evil fruit ... put on your pants ..."'

1585

'You should try focussing your anger,' Claire says.

1586

Oh no, there's Alma.

1587
1588

'Here I am,' she says. 'My family gets better the longer it's been dead.'

1589
1590

'Mine had a store that fell on them,' Claire says. 'Better trust the street.'

1591
1592

'That's enough of families,' I say. 'Mine had no one to blame but themselves.'

1593
1594
1595

Lara leaves to do her good work, restoring everything. The balance before the sin. All animals, disposed for our enjoyment and cuisine.

1596
1597
1598

'If it wasn't for Alma here, we two could be a metal band,' Claire says to me, irritated. 'I have the voice, and you – the vision. You could strum something.'

1599
1600
1601
1602
1603

Alma says, 'Now, my dears, believe me – metal bands beat dog-sledding when it comes to time spent dully on the road. But – I'll be with you as you cut your path. Be careful, though, should you invent religion, do politics, all that. It bites you on the nose. My families, remember ...'

1604
1605

'Alma's just a Tory,' Claire says. 'You see it in her dress. Hiding her scaly skin.'

1606     'Everything's been tried,' I say. 'Guys with whiskers, guys
1607 with beards, and guys without. Now, the empty space, dead genes.
1608 The void, the disappeared. All over. Nothing's left – maybe I'll be
1609 Michael Hove, example to you all.'
1610     'I think before I act,' says Claire. 'Although that may not
1611 work. But you – you only think in afters.'
1612     'The consequences is what you live with, Claire. Maybe we
1613 should go where it's still hot, and starting over, trying everything
1614 again,' I say.
1615     'Enough!' says Claire. 'I'm your angel, that is true – but, as a
1616 glance will tell – I'm the black kind. Now, I'll tell you of my plan,
1617 and if you tell on me, or my associates, your brain will turn to soup
1618 – but have no fear, the sexual bond between us is a band of steel.
1619 You always wondered how it was that mind came out of matter.
1620 Well, I'll tell – at least what's good for you. It's magic! Now
1621 reflect, and don't come back with silly questions. And of course –
1622 you know that Lara went with that odd guy whose car you trashed,
1623 that Rudy? He was her cavalier ...' and I repeat,
1624     'I know, I know,' although I don't.
1625     'Hey now!' shouts Claire. 'This shouldn't be! Here's Lara,
1626 banging at the door.'
1627     And here she is: 'I went and then came back,' she says. 'It
1628 often happens so. My animal is dead, extinct. In books, you just
1629 arrive in time. Rudy and I – we had a little break for oldtime sex,
1630 and then they said, "It has expired. The chain of life – the spiral ...
1631 it is broke."'
1632     'That isn't anything,' says Claire, in command. 'Those profs
1633 my lover, this guy here, was chatting with – they'll supercharge our
1634 genes, and land some junk on planets far away, where apples grow,
1635 and grass and stuff. We'll colonise the galaxy, put a metre on our
1636 arms and legs ... that's what those guys were saying over lunch...'
1637     'No, no!' says Lara. 'No food. That is the message. My small
1638 creature, scorpionlike, that pollinated things – without him and his
1639 complicated ways, the copulations in a mystic knot, the colour
1640 coding and the poison spots – without all that, within a year,
1641 there'll be no food, no buds, no birds, no animals of any kind:
1642 amusement and use, they're at an end. The brick that kept the
1643 mansion tall – is crumbled, dead. Extinct.' Maybe she weeps.
1644     'Oh come,' says Alma. 'Don't exaggerate.'

1645    'Those rockets they send up,' I say. 'It's clear, they're packed
1646    with people, a getaway – landing all over on stars and stuff.
1647    Colonies and empires. With no food.'
1648        'They'll all be having babies – those trips are long,' says Lara.
1649    'Just imagine – all your life spent in a speeding tube, your destiny
1650    to procreate.'
1651        Rudy's come along. He chimes in, 'Sure, no moral education
1652    there.'
1653        'Well, Rudy,' Lara says, and clings to him. 'I guess the sex
1654    we'll have should last us to the end, not start to pall, or send us off
1655    to stranger doings ...'
1656        'Hey, greedy guys!' I say. 'This news – extinction – has come
1657    so many times before. The individual, fearing death, transforms it
1658    into communal expiring,' though starvation's banal and lengthy.
1659    There's more drama, being burned up by the sun.
1660        'There's bargains in all this,' says Claire: 'Just think! The
1661    things to buy up! What they call subsets will corner markets ...
1662    Although, to watch the more unfortunate, less provident, pass on,
1663    that's die, will make a painful scene.'
1664        'All those murders, stretching back,' Alma says. 'It makes it
1665    nonsense, and it makes it sense. The sense is nonsense, if you
1666    understand ...'
1667        'You're crazy,' Claire says. 'No one will die, and all will
1668    suffer as they do, and all, well, yes, will die, but not because of
1669    Lara's scorpion. Just contemplate our species, its accomplishments,
1670    its goals, maybe its deficiencies ...'
1671        There's the angel in her talking, and Rudy says he'd rather fix
1672    his car than frowst around in Lara's bed all day.
1673        It's like a Japanese library – full of books you can't read,
1674    you're sightless, mute, even the exit sign's a mystery.
1675        Rudy – red all over, quivering like a boxer – hits me once,
1676    below an eye. He's hurt his hand, and 'There!' he says. For Lara, or
1677    the car. No consequences, not even justice.
1678        'To show that we don't care,' says Claire, 'we must have a
1679    feast.'
1680        'There's just potatoes left,' says Lara, and we sit and wait.
1681    The last cat, Flower, is bibbed and sat beside.
1682        'Where'd the other moggies go?' I ask.
1683        'They went to barbecues,' says Lara.
1684        'It never comes to being cannibals,' Alma says. 'That's maybe
1685    a mistake. I was never taught at school – it seems that's a tabu,' and

1686    as we contemplate, and Rudy pinches Flower's thigh, and then, in
1687    fun, he pinches Alma's too – we think of who's more appetising. I
1688    say to Claire, 'This sex bond we have – does it involve some acts?'
1689        'Oh no,' she says. 'For they would spoil and complicate.
1690    Look in my eyes – ' and then I do, and see the table and the
1691    sacrifice, the souls that's taken out and bottled, the voices in the
1692    stone, and think – 'Better all that than fumbling in some bed, or
1693    scrunched in Rudy's sporty little car.'
1694        'Here it comes!' shouts Lara, and what munificence we see!
1695    Potatoes dauphine, croquette: potatoes Port-au-Prince, *à*
1696    *l'irlandaise*, Bolivian deep-frozen, trampled underfoot, and sweet,
1697    and sour, those crunchy straw-like things, and frites of every
1698    calibre, potatoes big as Swedish heads, tiny as stripy marbles, from
1699    Courland and from Kiev, in stew and powder – Rudy says he
1700    always keeps some in the car, packets of potato dust, you just add
1701    water, there you are: – potatoes pinked and curried, peppered à la
1702    Red Queen, smoked and whipped ...
1703        We eat until we gag, we pause, and eat and eat, and gag again.
1704        Alma says, 'Maybe we should keep to plant anew,' and Lara
1705    says no, no, without the sting that impregnates they'll just lie down
1706    and rot, and even Flower licks a drop, the conversation tingles –
1707    even better than the talk of rocketry and hunters killing tigers on the
1708    steppe.
1709        And the vodka. Yes, the vodka, not to forget the vodka.
1710        'You pulled off Rudy's ear,' the scream is Lara's, and I echo
1711    Alma, say –
1712        'Don't exaggerate. It's just a part of the external part. An
1713    impulse, nothing more. It was his talk of moral training, in the
1714    rocket, as it speeds for centuries, to plant our seed in some hot,
1715    steamy star. For that's a place, the rocket tube, where there's no
1716    good or bad, no deed foresworn or done. No reflection and no
1717    impulse.'
1718        'And that's what Rudy said,' she screams at me. 'You cretin!'
1719        Most of us are drunk. 'I shall not leave the life, before I've
1720    had my say,' I say with dignity. 'Morality is still a thing I cherish,
1721    and I seek,' and I hug Alma. She's the best of all of them. I shall
1722    protect.
1723        'Confront big themes, settle small scores,' I say, and Alma
1724    says,
1725        'Right on! That's what makes history history.'

1726 Rudy's ear looks like a spigot, and it pours like one. The
1727 blood is more to Flower's taste than spud. We laugh at that.
1728 Remembering his ear, will make his righteousness a comic turn.
1729     'Really, we shouldn't laugh,' says Alma, laughing. 'Not at
1730 misfortunes – but there's so many of those, there'd be little else left
1731 for laughter ...'
1732     'That wasn't a misfortune,' Lara says, though it won't affect
1733 their sexuality, I'd suspect.
1734     'You go on and laugh,' says Claire hugging Alma. 'I shall die
1735 rich and laughing if I can.'
1736     'We've feasted. Now we should dance,' I say. 'But not to
1737 Hendrix. I always cry when I hear these songs and wish I'd been
1738 born a Catalan.' We talk of music. When we've all starved, where
1739 will be the music then? It's true, we'll understand the fate of our
1740 unhappy, hungry comrades, all around the world – but music!
1741 Where will that all go?
1742     'It's written down,' says Alma, 'some of it. And that will
1743 blow around. The rest – it comes from bones, to bones it will
1744 return,' and we are sombre, while I pick a disc.
1745     'Tristan!' I say, and Lara says it's not for dancing to, and
1746 anyway worn thin with hearing over – but I'm indifferent, I just
1747 want to hug with Claire, maybe I'll die rich with her ...
1748     'You know,' says Alma, as I look for music than can fit our
1749 feet, 'Lara's scorpion sets us free! We don't need now to shoot and
1750 burn and stretch each other. There's no point, next year, we'll all be
1751 dead, or agonising. Now we can think what questions we should
1752 like to solve,' but Claire strokes me, says, 'Hold on – I need this
1753 guy as muscle in my plan. He's got no cash, so simple soldiering's
1754 his fate ...'
1755     I say, 'But Claire, there is the sexual bond, and politics as
1756 well, no doubt the post-colonial sympathy we share...'
1757     'Yes, yes,' she says, 'there's lots of philosophical stuff to do –
1758 but my associates will surely want to put their cash in things that
1759 keep them hanging on when all the rest have given up. That means
1760 they'll want aggression too.'
1761     'No, Claire,' Lara says. 'I'm sure when all is lost, you'll join
1762 the sad brigades,' and Claire turns away, and Alma says when
1763 music's lost, and we can dance no more – where's literature, its
1764 consoling, like they say it does?
1765     Alma starts reciting: 'I had done a few things and earned a
1766 few pence, my family was murdered for no crime, and now I find

1767    myself, quite drunk, with petty criminals and people arrogant,
1768    depressive, and yet I need to chronicle past deeds, relying on my
1769    obvious fitness for the task – what happened to my grannies – and,
1770    additionally, my general perceptive possession of a scene that's
1771    new – the imminent, definitive elimination of the human race ...'
1772        'Alma, that's very nice, and clever too – but do you really
1773    hope to add to what is over, half-forgotten?' asks Lara.
1774        We dance, Claire and I, like bugs who've fallen on the stove.
1775    The music comes from inside, probably it is different for each. That
1776    doesn't seem a difficulty.
1777        'Alma,' Lara insists, 'if you write down your history, will
1778    anyone be there to read it? And then again, when things are nearly
1779    at an end, they don't relent, those guys, they like to see opponents
1780    killed. These are all things to take into account,' and she smiles
1781    kindly, then she says, 'I'll ask my Rudy – he's a kind of priest or
1782    guru, he will surely know how we should behave ourselves,' and
1783    Claire shouts, 'It's only us that knows the ending, and it's only Lara
1784    who has told us what it is,' and that is true, though we're
1785    convinced.
1786        'Lara, you do believe all this, what you have told?' I ask.
1787        'Of course it's true. An off-print, would that do, convince?'
1788    she asks. 'It's just the favour that I did, that you would be the first
1789    to know.'
1790        We do a general dance, a swaying on the spot. It's more about
1791    the misery to come than comradeship. The others – seem to have
1792    thick lives, and contradictions. What is my life? What was it?
1793        What will it be like, no food, no trek to camps, no state, no
1794    fighting for the sack of flour, no rights abused?
1795        'Poor Rudy,' Lara says, 'he is so red. And after sex, he almost
1796    dies, his pumps are clogged.' There, who could resent a guy like
1797    that?
1798        'When I was in the jungle,' Lara says. 'And they told me we
1799    were done for – it occurred to me: design. It couldn't be intelligent,
1800    if the failure of one tiny part could bring down all the rest. But,
1801    sure, it's all design. And so I thought – a new arrangement. No
1802    more hierarchy, no tower of being. Discontinuity. Poor Rudy –
1803    even his feet are red. There's one alternative for me: Rudy. And
1804    you – you're another. Absorb them both. That way I can be
1805    committed to you both, and not depend ...'
1806        'You always went in for arranging, but this one's not for me,'
1807    I say. 'Rudy – what does he think?'

1808     'Oh, he thinks a lot,' she says, 'but he's no plan. He has his
1809 faith – if it's wrong, he'll be quite lost.'
1810     'Maybe if he bursts while you two have your sex, he wouldn't
1811 even need to know the truth or not, the right and wrong?' I say.
1812 'We have to plan,' she says, 'now that there's no future waiting.'
1813     Claire says, 'I'll have you meet my friends. They are
1814 Ukrainians, mostly. They won't like you. They will think you're
1815 trash. But don't despair – you're in my frame. Better an end
1816 complete, than economics going wrong that lasts for years. Of
1817 course, knowing what awaits, there's no point in a long relationship
1818 – I'm sure we're both relieved,' and so we are.
1819     Alma prepares to write – she's not sure what: 'Once, they
1820 said, to serve the people. Now, we shall starve with them,' she says.
1821 Yes, Alma is the best, I'd cling to her.
1822     'We've done the dance,' says Lara, 'and that will do. Now, we
1823 must do the monument.'
1824     'I think,' I say at once, 'it should be music. That will last for
1825 ever.'
1826     'No one will be there to hear,' says Rudy.
1827     'That's always irrelevant, when music is around,' I say.
1828     'If we do a statue, no one will be there to see it either,' Alma
1829 says. We think more deeply.
1830     Claire says, to hurry things along,
1831     'Rudy's quite an ordinary guy. We cover him with clay, and
1832 that's a mould. We put more clay inside – there's then two Rudy's,
1833 one dead, one clay, when all is done. And that's the type. "Man".
1834 No numen. No celebrating what isn't there.'
1835     'I think,' says Alma, twisting her notebook, 'it should be an
1836 open space. Quite fastidiously clean. No bones or diaries, and no
1837 grass. Just a place you can't tell what happened there, or what's to
1838 come. No tired mementoes, and no stones.'
1839     'No, no,' says Lara, 'that is way depressing. No, none of that.
1840 It mustn't be vainglorious, but not defeat and sad. No nullity.'
1841     Are we close? We shall all watch each other die.
1842     'Look at Flower,' says Lara. 'She's becoming quite human.'
1843     She's on a shelf, staring at us, like she was a book you'd need
1844 to read.
1845     'OK,' says Rudy, 'that can be your place,' and she jumps off.
1846 A yellow cat with orange eyes.

1847       Later, Lara takes me aside: 'Look, Rudy's keen on that idea
1848 from Claire – a memorial to him, his ego. I am not. There's only
1849 one thing we can leave, I feel. A space.'
1850       I say, 'I know! It's "Lara's scorpion".'
1851       'Exactly so,' she says. 'In malachite. There's lots up on that
1852 mountain, you and Claire, you can climb ...'
1853       'Hmmm,' says Claire, 'malachite. Ukrainians are used to
1854 mining it. It's as good a thing to own as any. There's some tooled
1855 in on Alma's escritoire.'
1856       I say, 'Come on, Claire, climb the mountain with me. Keep
1857 me quiet, and Lara too.'
1858       Claire says 'The best thing to leave behind, if you can't leave
1859 behind a sea, is a palace. No one will live in it, but in many palaces
1860 they don't, or else someone lives there who didn't build. I see the
1861 stucco – and the gold, like butter icing. I'd have it made of
1862 chocolate, with sugar, green and white and gold. And on the top,
1863 those cherries, if we can't have stars ...' We're all hungry, Claire
1864 most of all, for cake. Lara says,
1865       'Stars, Claire. Don't mention them. Quite out of register. I'm
1866 more modest – I'd have Flower, set on a plinth. She's come quite
1867 near to us – that must show something?'
1868       Claire sighs, 'We don't do things together now, processions,
1869 funerals, and weddings, everything that's in between. The cat –
1870 she's come in at the tail end.'
1871       'I didn't know about your passion for cake, Claire,' I say. 'It's
1872 quite endearing.'
1873       'Forget the cake part,' she says. 'It's palaces, the thing.'
1874       We climb the copper mountain. At the top, driving me on –
1875 fish pie, and pears in caramel.
1876       'Two things I can't abide,' says Claire. 'Pears and pie. And
1877 the fish?'
1878       'It's when they're left to suffocate,' I say. 'Even sheep have it
1879 better – but in the pie, the fish are done with suffering.'
1880       We haul each other up. I shout, 'Claire, the chain that broke –
1881 the planet can't have been so fine, so balanced, tested ...'
1882       She shouts back, 'It never needed explanations, even less
1883 now, when ...' We struggle on.
1884       'The lumps of malachite. How big?' I ask.
1885       'Another silly question,' Claire says, tossing rocklike things.
1886 'Enough it's green, red-spotted, like the scorpion. This stuff – will
1887 need some treatment.'

1888        When we reach the top, a panorama – there'll be the Orient.
1889    The steppe. The sea of Aral that blows its poisonous dust over
1890    mankind.
1891        'Aggression without power, it's quite so trivial,' pants Claire.
1892        'Most people manage just with that,' I say.
1893        'Sure,' she says, 'but we want something special. This copper
1894    heap – we've a bent trader, metals exchange, all that. We'll find a
1895    corner, then we're in for life.'
1896        It seems a little thing. I say, 'I thought I might be salaried, and
1897    help you steer a course.'
1898        She says: 'As for you, I have my doubts. You're not cut out to
1899    do crime seriously. Not anything. Egocentric is the word.'
1900        'When do we arrive,' I ask, 'at the top?'
1901        'Oh,' she laughs. 'You'll no doubt get fish pie.'
1902        I say, 'The big guys, in big countries, if they apologised for
1903    everything, they'd never stop. Alma says they should sit with
1904    shaven heads, like monks with begging bowls that's full of spit, on
1905    street corners in the rain.'
1906        'Alma has her burdens,' Claire says. 'Remember, you must
1907    stand the object against itself, or else you couldn't see it. That
1908    should be clear.'
1909        'It's not at all,' I say.
1910        She says, 'The telescope – to make a distant thing seem near –
1911    if you just looked along a tube, that would be magic. But it's not.
1912    Because you make another little image upside down, imaginary –
1913    and then you see.'
1914        'It's all about my pay, it seems,' I say. 'At least, we're still
1915    good friends, my dear?'
1916        'Of course,' she says. 'It's just we need a dull and stable guy,
1917    a punk. Not you. And as for telescopes, it works for salaries and
1918    history. To make a job worthwhile, you need that little image, tiny
1919    and invisible. That's cash. With history, you bring it near – but no
1920    one lives again, and nothing moves. You see,' and she heaves me
1921    up, her shoulders straining at my buttocks, 'in a hundred years, all
1922    will be fine and prosperous. But with the violence, you need power,
1923    and that's your image, do you see.'
1924        We change around, I heave her up. 'Yes,' I say, 'I'm
1925    following your argument. Though if it's true, that's quite another
1926    thing.'
1927        'Without the following, you would never have the truth,' she
1928    says.

1929        It's like the cafeteria and the profs. The distances, up from the
1930    skies, the dancing genes, and Lara, queenly, when she had her flock
1931    of cats.
1932        Then there's the copper dust. We sink in it, immobilised. At
1933    night they pour some more, Claire's poor castle's covered. Then the
1934    rains will set it hard. We're stuck, till Claire says, 'Dance. That's
1935    the thing. I'll teach you steps ...' and so she does. We wriggle out,
1936    and then we're down. The stacks of malachite, the grey stones, they
1937    are all around, the monument can be begun.
1938        Around there's lines of folk: I ask, 'Is it for bread? Or for a
1939    lifetime, rocketed towards some patch of turf a million years
1940    away?'
1941        Someone says, 'They're off to Saturn, there, they will decide
1942    where to go next.' They do not talk of scorpions.
1943        There's other lines, of altruists – they make up little gene
1944    packs, so if anyone survives, I guess, they'll loop in selections of
1945    our finest guys.
1946        'It makes your violence, your aggression, seem pathetic now,'
1947    says Lara. 'And Rudy's quite worn out – although no doubt he'll
1948    leave his tattered genes for what comes next.'
1949        'My memoir,' Alma says. 'There are so many culpable. My
1950    family dodged around, and suffered from their choice. Their
1951    torment came not by chance, or nature either, but I don't know
1952    where to start. It's all been said before, the politics, but if you leave
1953    it out, there's just your friends that's on the scene ...'
1954        'You don't have time for quibbling, Alma,' Claire says. 'Of
1955    course it's all been done before. You write it down again, you start
1956    with the Romanians, and then go on. This time, with Lara's
1957    scorpion – no state, no history's to blame, they'll say. Though
1958    maybe if she'd got there earlier, she might have found the creature
1959    still alive... So, Alma, no justice then or now. The chain of being
1960    holds until it snaps – there's nothing to be done. Just write things
1961    down, and we'll decide the way to take them. A memoir. Even if
1962    you don't remember it.'
1963        Alma writes, 'Today the chief engineers have been down to
1964    our part of the mine. The management has issued some instruction
1965    or other about boring new galleries, and so the engineers arrived to
1966    make the initial survey. I checked the woodpile behind our little
1967    house, and moved a nest of mice to where our cat, Flower, could
1968    not reach them. I had sent the children far away, for with hostilities
1969    afoot, prudence is required. Then I heard the neighbour whisper to

1970    me, "There's soldiers coming down the road. For sure, they are not
1971    ours."'
1972        'That's my grandfather,' Alma says, doubtfully. 'They were
1973    Romanians, the soldiers.'
1974        'You never forget a word you've read, Alma,' says Lara, part
1975    proud, part doubtfully.
1976        'No blood, no jackals,' Alma says. 'I have to hurry, set it all
1977    down. What good comes from this?'
1978        'What do you get from all this, Lara? I ask. 'Watching us like
1979    gladiators, preparing to die?'
1980        'You must find yourselves. And be yourselves,' she says.
1981        'That's two things, Lara,' I say, 'which don't fit.'
1982        She holds Flower, vertical, like a wriggling infant: she says, 'I
1983    love you all, in different ways. You must succeed, before it is too
1984    late.'
1985        'You mean,' I say, 'when it is too late. I'm nothing. Against
1986    this obstacle, elimination, you can't do anything. No food, no
1987    energy. Some things explode, and others cool right down. Rudy is
1988    ice, Claire and me – we're hot blobs.'
1989        'I love you, anyway,' she says briskly.
1990        'Unfortunately, Lara,' I say, 'you're dead.' Like Alma. Claire
1991    – just stirring on, being what she's made to be, though her story
1992    isn't interesting, not enough for Alma to make it up. Grand fraud,
1993    it's called, her speciality, her crime. And so,
1994        'There's little time,' I say. 'I'm going to make the break.
1995    Here's what I propose. A future not born from the past, that's what
1996    should come after us. Not helping people catching up with richer
1997    guys. Not killing off the guys who won't enjoy the future that you
1998    make for them. Not killing off the ones that don't agree, or look
1999    suspicious.'
2000        Lara says, 'I didn't tell too many people, about the scorpions.
2001    There didn't seem a point. What's going to happen – it will happen
2002    anyway.' She hasn't understood. I say,
2003        'What there will be, when we are gone, is not my inventions.
2004    Only the best, there'll be. But things you can't imagine. Not
2005    legacies: – the best.'
2006        'It makes no sense,' says Lara. 'It sounds quite infantile.'
2007        'Sense?' I say. 'Where's the sense in other galaxies we'll
2008    never reach? And those dead ancestors?'

2009        'It's like a kingdom of the gods, your afterworld,' says Lara,
2010    humouring. 'Life in the sun, the shadows disappeared. Perfection
2011    unimaginable.'
2012        'Like maybe what goes on on other stars?' I ask, 'or planets?'
2013        'You must spend more time on saying what you mean,' she
2014    says.
2015        'I can't say more – you must see that.'
2016        I'm witness in a trial – the guy whose story I took down, and
2017    then he cut his girl. I don't know what will happen to him. I can
2018    guess.
2019        'Who will bury us, Lara?' I ask. 'We can expect no justice
2020    either.'
2021        'Oh, we'll all help, I'm sure,' she says.
2022        'Rudy should carve the monument, the scorpion,' I say.
2023        'Oh yes,' says Lara. 'Poor Rudy. With him, it's all platonic
2024    now. He's weakening – but sculpting helps him find himself. We
2025    didn't see the cache of malachite that Claire threw down – but
2026    there's enough on Alma's escritoire to make a tiny, life-size one...'
2027        I say, 'My prof, that guy – I hear he went to Titan, one of
2028    Saturn's moons. There's methane lakes. And methane ice and
2029    methane rain.'
2030        'Well, yes, that figures,' Lara says, 'with lakes of methane,
2031    you'd need ice and rain the same. I hope he didn't quote me when
2032    he left ...'
2033        'Oh no,' I say, 'he'll launch himself again from there. He'll
2034    start a dynasty, like pharoahs did – he'll breed in rockets, those will
2035    be his pyramids, and so his genes will land up on some planet
2036    wandering, quite unaware, his kids will found an empire, culture
2037    too ...'
2038        'The vision is a noble one,' says Lara, not convinced. 'You
2039    don't seem to have the detail right.'
2040        That guy's trial – he needs, if not an alibi, then stories. I tell
2041    them about Indians, and I think of how with them, Lara's scorpion
2042    might have been a totem, venerated, or at least not left to die. The
2043    guys in court – it seems they think I'm on a trip. It doesn't help my
2044    friend. I whisper to him – 'In a year or so, it will be done and
2045    finished, though each of us will have to bury all their friends ...' I
2046    try to comfort him, but there's no space ... I'm ushered out. Some
2047    justice will get done, to him.
2048        Claire says, 'We don't care if it's true. Apocalypse. We bet
2049    against it, and we bet the other way as well. We'll make some cash,

2050 and if we don't – another Lara, another ending of the world will
2051 come along. And when it does, we shan't collect, for sure, but nor
2052 will we pay out.'
2053 I should have had my gang, and ordered guys around, and
2054 done some deals, repented, maybe, given cash to charities. Or else
2055 – been Michael Hove, and driven people round, so carefully. The
2056 hunger – always with you, slides its paw in yours. Maybe Claire –
2057 she has a source of food, and in a chamber secretly, tears off wings
2058 and legs, and stuffs them down, the bones, the plumes. Rudy
2059 hammers at his car. His face is grey. I say, 'That monument: – the
2060 beast is tiny, and malformed.' He says, offhand, 'If there are things
2061 come after we have gone – it's probable they're small and
2062 malformed too.'
2063 'Don't let him go!' shouts Lara, as he speeds away: 'There's
2064 so much work needed to be done on him.'
2065 'He couldn't take the hunger, Lara. That's what drove him
2066 off,' I say.
2067 'He may crash himself,' says Lara. 'That silly car. He's
2068 suffering so – he ought to end it. And, you know, he couldn't stand
2069 you.'
2070 'Yes, I know,' I say. 'It's not surprising.'
2071 'We could all have gone on trips,' she says.
2072 'Lara,' I say, 'your trips end bad. Look what you didn't bring
2073 us back.'
2074 She turns on me, 'You needn't believe me, if it is too hard. I
2075 want nothing from you. But you'll know, the pain, the longing. It
2076 beats anything that Alma writes about.'
2077 'Oh, I agree,' I say. 'I need no further proof. It's all uphill –
2078 the copper mountain, made of dust, my record with the cops, the
2079 gossip. Nothing's easy now.'
2080 'At least you went to court,' she says: 'You were a citizen.'
2081 'It wasn't up to me,' I say, 'The guy who cut her up, his girl,
2082 the Indian – he couldn't tell us why.'
2083 Does Claire have food, I ask myself, black markets work
2084 better than the ones they talk about on television, those that failed.
2085 'Claire doesn't love you,' Lara says. 'She just hoped you'd steal
2086 some buns....'
2087
2088
2089

2090    Later:
2091        'We shouldn't sit and wait,' I say to Claire, referring to the
2092    end, and tell her about Rudy.
2093        'Oh, it's jealousy,' she says. 'Or just to get away.'
2094        'There isn't anywhere to go,' I say. 'You have to wait the
2095    drama out – or else ...'
2096        'Or else it isn't drama,' Claire agrees. 'No one is trustworthy.
2097    No one is after you. They say it's sickness, this suspicion – but I am
2098    in the midst of it, I promise you, no suspicion is misplaced.'
2099        'It's not like Alma's folks,' I say. 'They were harassed out of
2100    everywhere.'
2101        'That part – it hasn't happened here, not yet,' she says. 'Rudy
2102    went off to look for food. Maybe you should do the same.'
2103        'I ought to be the fool,' I say, 'the saviour, the innocent – it
2104    can only be me, but it doesn't fit. The quest is always for the grail,
2105    for purity, for as-it-was. Not burgers.'
2106        I think how the profs... they ran. They couldn't mend it, but
2107    they knew the time was up. Where's the food been stacked, I
2108    wonder – climb the mountain, soft with chocolate powder. Up and
2109    over. See where Rudy's smashed his red machine.
2110        'We ought to fix things,' Claire says. 'That's what we're
2111    famous for.'
2112        'We understand the chain of being, Claire,' I say. 'I heard it
2113    over lunch. It's we don't know how to fix, though lots must be
2114    responsible. The strange thing is, Lara's our messenger.'
2115        'The messenger but not the news,' she says.
2116        'Of course,' I say. 'We should have known to plant some
2117    seeds.'
2118        'That's so simple, you must know it doesn't work like that,'
2119    says Claire.
2120        'Music ho!' I shout. 'Let's keep our dignity and dance!' I put
2121    on 'Ready for the Hit between the Eyes', we dance, Claire and I,
2122    separately. It goes quite well.
2123        Alma comes in, she says, 'My memoir is finished. Now, I'll
2124    dance with Flower – she's ugly, just like me.' Alma is the best,
2125    she's wild, she's heavy, she is light. We are all light, with our not
2126    eating.
2127        Flower looks like a teddy bear, the coat, the stare. 'See!' Alma
2128    says, 'what does it take to make her civilised?'
2129        'I guess we'll sit around and die?' I say. 'That's nothing new
2130    – but, with you guys, it's peppery too.'

2131
2132
2133
2134
2135
2136
2137
2138
2139
2140
2141
2142
2143
2144
2145
2146
2147
2148
2149
2150
2151
2152
2153
2154
2155
2156
2157
2158
2159
2160
2161
2162
2163
2164
2165
2166
2167
2168
2169
2170

'We're all too weak for sex,' says Lara, though she's not been thinking in that way. 'Poor Rudy – he got tired of repetition. That's the artist for you. He didn't sculpt too well.'

'I shan't hang around for long,' says Claire. 'We've found a stash of spoons and forks. The cache of food – it can't be far away. If we don't eat it all, I'll share it out. That's communism, my dears – sharing the poverty around.'

'Yes,' Alma says, 'it's always politics, at the end as well. I wonder why poor Rudy was so red?'

'It wasn't genes,' says Lara, irritably, 'probably to match his automobile.'

'Maybe he knew about the spoors, the hunting?' Alma pushes on. 'Was he a red man, gathering archaic things upon the icy steppe? Whittling the rocks? The reddest Indian, last Mohican? Seen it so often, yet we didn't recognise ...'

'Cut the crap, Alma, please,' says Lara, much incensed: 'Maybe he came from Mars – they're all red there, as we all know, and maybe brought his motor too. He's just a loser. Arm-wrestling was for him the tops.'

'We don't expect carvers to be bright,' I say, thinking of the guy who cut his girl. And carving joints ... 'Or smoking them,' says Alma, pertly. 'They say it's good for appetite.'

'Flower's awful thin,' says Lara, pinching her, and changing tack. 'There's not a slice of meat on her.'

There's a rattling. We look out. It's Rudy's car, for sure, and all opinions, theories have to be revised. Oh no! It isn't Rudy after all – 'It's Flower!' says Claire.

'She purrs!' says Alma. 'It is transformation! She could be Parsifal – except ... I don't feel anything.'

It is a little miracle. Alma says, '"It is the best time we have ever had! said Frederick ..." oh, who said that, I wonder. Who was Frederick? But how apposite, it must be French. This moment – how many people out there, who won't share. My book is full of them ...' She weeps. We could all weep, but don't.

'Come, come, Alma,' Claire says, though not liking her a sliver more. 'The fascists came, and then they went. They're just a speck on someone's broom. You can't blame them for the scorpion.'

Alma mumbles that the fascists passed the uniforms to other guys. I say, we're shut in here, and if they're all round, we shall not

2171  let them in. 'You're kind to say it,' Alma says. 'But my memoir –
2172  it's full of them, all sorts.'
2173       'They're shut up in your book,' says Claire roughly. 'And you
2174  should shut up too. Alma, we're terminal in here. Rudy came from
2175  Mars, so now we know, and he was Lara's love, and he's gone
2176  back, no doubt, up there, down there. Food, Alma! Write me some
2177  food!'
2178       'They're all gone now, and I can't ask them anything,' says
2179  Alma, weeping.
2180       'Don't be such a baby, Alma,' Claire shouts – 'It's not you
2181  that suffered all that stuff, it's us that's suffering now.' Then she
2182  turns on me, 'This creep! And his creepy friends! The big time that
2183  he wanted – just being a DJ, spinning his platters, goofing off. And
2184  Lara coddling with her Martian, then off on mission, letting that
2185  creepy insect slip away, and all our food go with it – every loaf, the
2186  flat ones, raisin-filled, the twisted shiny ones, the baguettes, *rosette*,
2187  salt and bland, with seeds, with olives, sweet and oiled – all now
2188  expired. Goddamit, those sugar dragonflies – Lara, couldn't you
2189  find that little creature, in your shoe, or up your leg, some kind of
2190  asp, stuck in your bra – there's millions, bunches of eggs with legs
2191  that's sticking in your hair ... But no, "He's gone. the dear extinct.
2192  Departed, unwanted first, though now desired." You parasites! You
2193  stingless crawlers!'
2194       'It's all self-hatred, dear, that rant,' says Lara, pacifying.
2195       They grapple and scratch.
2196       'No knives, dears,' Alma shouts. 'Look! Flower is
2197  frightened,' and indeed she is. She scratches too, but at the door.
2198       I'm lucky, I hallucinate:
2199       *In Rudy's car, we're down the road that looks like food – the*
2200  *potholes look like empty oyster shells, red gravel's paprika, there's*
2201  *beetles crawling in our path, like capsicums. Those bushes, made of*
2202  *candied fruit, those mustard-coloured birds – I say to Rudy, 'Let's*
2203  *stop, enjoy the scene,' but no, he turns away, he's cherry-red all*
2204  *over, and he says, 'Not now, I must be back to Lara, for she loves*
2205  *me, there's no time to stuff the landscape down. It's true the*
2206  *streams are claret, but sobriety's the thing – I'm part of Lara's*
2207  *scene, I can't be late.'*
2208       *'What, Rudy, exactly do you do?' I ask.*
2209       *'Oh,' he says, 'I'm always there on time. I'm very punctual –*
2210  *ladies just love that. Five meals a day, and I am up for every one, I*
2211  *don't say no, my body burns and burns, I'm like an oven, what I eat*

2212    *is turned to crimson embers ... all turned to muscle, and to steel –*
2213    *this sporty car is what I ate, I made a shell, just like a lobster or a*
2214    *crab, and I go skeetering from side to side ...' And so he does – the*
2215    *curry powder's loose, we slide, we almost hit those quails, he*
2216    *brakes, we spin, beneath the gravel-paprika we see rows of eggs –*
2217    *from plovers, eagles, guillemots and such ... He hits me, in the eye,*
2218    *above where he struck before. It stings. And he drives off ...*
2219    'Hey, creepy guy, so you've come back from there!' It's
2220    Claire, she's won her bout with Lara – 'No cheesy dreams from
2221    you,' she says to me. 'You'd better find some food for Flower that
2222    even in extremes we wouldn't eat.'
2223    Lara says, 'Now, even with the Americans and their bombs,
2224    their money – there's no recriminations. We're all in the same
2225    basket now.'
2226    We don't reply. There's nothing much to say. Then, Lara
2227    screams at Alma,
2228    'You didn't let Flower out! Not in the street, the neighbours,
2229    all those folk ...!'
2230    Alma's distressed: 'I thought it a good turn. Freedom, you
2231    know. Escape.'
2232    'You idiot!' says Lara. 'Rudy's gone, now Flower ...'
2233    'Oh, they come back,' says Claire, quite unconcerned, and
2234    tells a story of a cat that did.
2235    'It isn't going right,' says Lara. 'I thought to have you all
2236    around, for comradeship. In these hard times – you need a
2237    plenitude, a raft. To say the world would end because I couldn't
2238    sort my preferences out ... absurd!'
2239    Claire says, 'Lara, I'm a cat that loves the street. There's sure
2240    to be a crew somewhere, some guys who've seen it all, and
2241    planned. But – one last time: Lara, you're sure it's as you say, the
2242    hunger's doing for us all, for you, and this guy here,' and she hugs
2243    me and smiles, 'There's really nothing, no way out, except some
2244    chance...?'
2245    'No, Claire,' says Lara. 'There's no chance. And do you think
2246    I'd play a game, a trick, and sit here while you starve, like poor
2247    people that you see in photos do? No, I have told you how it is,
2248    exactly so.'
2249    Claire goes out: she says, 'I'll look out for the cat. And you,'
2250    she says to me, 'you never were the tough and trusty guy you
2251    thought you were, the kind that hard guys want. It's quite a
2252    compliment.'

2253    'Oh Claire,' I start to say, but Alma takes my arm. 'I did an
2254    awful thing,' she says. 'I hoped to see the people in my book, some
2255    I remember, others we have photos of – go out the door in time.
2256    Escape, and have another life, just like the cats.'
2257        Alma goes to another room.
2258        I say, 'Lara, it's stifling in here.'
2259        'It must be Alma and her stove,' she says. 'They used to lie on
2260    it, the whole family, all year long, they say.'
2261        'I'll take some air,' I say.
2262        'You were a valid part,' she says to me, 'but you were there to
2263    be reformed a bit. Rudy – he was quite another thing. I had to sort
2264    things out. I'm still unsure.'
2265        No, I shall never be the perfect driver, perfect son, a Michael
2266    Hove. I say,
2267        'I appreciate you Lara, for what you might have done for me,
2268    if there had been time.'
2269        I run outside. I hope I'll see Claire – there's no one there,
2270    outside.
2271        I walk part way up the hill, the copper mound. No, you can't
2272    see the steppe, just a town, the walls toast-coloured, pale and burnt,
2273    every shade of hasty making or forgetfulness. No olives on the
2274    trees, no sheep, no bells. No people, just the hunger, in the head,
2275    like grit, no food.
2276        A call to prayer comes feebly up the slope. I settle back.
2277        Alma's the best.
2278        I'm glad she isn't here.
2279        There's movement in the sand. A little school of scorpions, it
2280    seems. They run, they play, they fence. Some are green, red-
2281    spotted, like the malachite.
2282
2283
2284                        THE END

2285

# 4

# LENIN IN THE CINEMA

*from Black Masks*

*'For us, the cinema is the most important of the arts.'*

*V.I. Lenin*

ANOTHER DAY at work. The drawing office. Wet Paris mornings, where everyone looks like someone else: someone important, someone alive or dead. I set up my work, use it to conceal my pleasure, my cartoon. Paris was the capital of revolutions, then of the cinema: then, for a little while that is perhaps not over, of the cartoon. Will a Lenin find the cartoon a revolutionary art? And rescue me? Set me up there with the big names, the recognisable faces – make history of me? I start my story: 'The lion of the Amazon' – too enigmatic. 'The treasure of Xica da Silva' – the slave who made a fortune. Or shall I identify too much? And yet, for the Amazon, we need a queen, an Amazonian, Brazilian knockout, like young Xica.

'Millions of heads, like black peppercorns, or matchsticks with dobs of red, of white, phosphorous. Bands with American tubas – their heads swaying like pythons'. Security men in Ray-Bans, feeling suspect bulges among the crowd: "Hey, man, what you carrying here, a Magnum?"

'"Hey, right man, you right. That's what I carrying."

'Gathered here in the name of the ballot and. the unity of the species, on the banks of this 32-lane freeway, inaugurating the first lady president of the hemisphere, an enthusiastic lesbian, not yet 24. Photo xeroxed, pasted on thousand-dollar bills and scattered to the crowds.

2321 'What enthusiasm! Here a guy selling cans of Bud, knocked
2322 down and trampled. There a small landslip slides a samba group
2323 down and out, into the headlines. Union of Brazil and Argentina,
2324 Brazentina: continental euphoria.
2325    'She sits up there, surrounded by her Amazons, all newly
2326 promoted general, and every one a samba queen. All ready for the
2327 hunt, beautiful black and white skins setting off the golden braid,
2328 little bows and arrows stolen from the Indians – a double row of
2329 cheesecake cupids. All ready for the hunt, across the sierra, across
2330 the pampas, into the rain forests, ready for the hunt... '
2331    I can't focus, the picture fades. Xica da Silva came here, in her
2332 short real life, came to Paris. After her, but not because of her, the
2333 revolution. The director of my first, real job comes in. He has a
2334 famous face, an unenviable one. You say at once: 'Aldo Moro'.
2335 Aldo Moro has been a cadaver for ten years, but already he is
2336 looking better. He was – he is – a true saint in sheep's clothing, but
2337 as clever as he's devout. Eating his madeleine, he looks like Mrs
2338 Sheep in her shop. Being dead doesn't mean too much to him – no
2339 doubt he thinks that this is heaven. Ever-pressing fear of hell,
2340 already he has his sinners and his devils courting him. He'll put in a
2341 word for them, they think, and rip them off a touch as well: himself
2342 he did not save. I slide away, from hierarchies here, and I'm back,
2343 back on the drawing board, back in Brazil.
2344    'The lady president abolishes sex and dissent for the duration of
2345 the hunt. Electronically, the votes against her are transformed into
2346 positive ones. She and all her company take a vow of chastity. All
2347 other world leaders follow suit – except the pope, who institutes a
2348 regime of non-stop orgies. To prepare herself spiritually, the queen-
2349 slave-president goes down to hell. It looks like Milwaukee. She is a
2350 beautiful glass flower.'
2351    I break away from my narcissism, and watch the director in his
2352 office. Moro is praying again. The phone rings. He speaks to it. He
2353 hangs up, but continues conversing. I see he has the porter, a baggy
2354 Gorbachev, in a corner of the room. He is berating Gorbachev for
2355 bullying behaviour in the elevator. He says there have been
2356 complaints, and Gorbachev is sweating, accusing his enemies
2357 among the neighbours. Moro is unyielding, but in the end, with his
2358 little smile, he yields. Gorbachev barges his way down the corridor,
2359 and pushes his way into the lift. He ignores poor Ronnie Reagan,
2360 who is collecting our bets on the evening's cycle racing. And Moro

2361 calls Ronnie into his office. Mildly, he reproves him for a wasted
2362 old age. Ronnie will start to cry.
2363     I can't stand this bathos, force myself back to my story:
2364     'The President, Candida, is challenged by tourists from the
2365 future. They are living in the *barrios*, the *favelas*, they want to
2366 change the course of time, turn Candida's successes into failures.
2367 Why? They must be bored. They wear masks because human faces
2368 have become so ugly. They run everywhere, like Inca messengers.
2369 The world has no more fuel. On weekends you can skateboard.'
2370     I can't go on. I must be bored. I must have a beer, meet with my
2371 new friends, Lenin and Trotsky. Is it possible they hardly know
2372 each other? I slide out of the building, and see Moro's long face at
2373 the window. He is the cow, and I'm the cowslip. Gorbachev is
2374 playing cards on a box in the street. He is slamming down his
2375 cards, 'and one: and two: and the clincher'. He is playing with
2376 César Auguste, the big black who always beats him, and cheats.
2377 César Auguste tells me he is 35, but his hair is white: he looks like
2378 a pot-scourer.
2379     Lenin is prematurely bald. Prematurely for what, I don't know.
2380 He is always in this bar, playing tric-trac, or, as now, vigorously
2381 annotating *Of Grammatology*, a book he says is tops but I suspect
2382 he doesn't understand. I usually see him here with Trotsky. They
2383 are regulars here, but they only speak to each other when I'm
2384 around. Sometimes Lenin tries to talk to the Algerians, needling
2385 them, till they tell him to piss off. 'Piss off, piss off,' he repeats.
2386 'Yes, you've learned the language of reason all right.'
2387     I ask him, 'Where's Trotsky?' I never talk about my cartoons,
2388 the revolution he, or the Amazonian queen, should lead: but he
2389 knows all about my job, the office, Moro, Gorbachev.
2390     He answers, 'Trotsky's doing his martial arts, I believe. He
2391 insists his puny physique's an advantage.'
2392     Lenin himself is no Hercules, and his skin is yellow and
2393 wrinkled like a pickled brain. I can't think what to say. 'I hear
2394 Trotsky is being rehabilitated over there.'
2395     Lenin is suddenly animated. 'What a disgrace! I'd sooner rot
2396 than have that happen! Talk about skinning the ox twice!'
2397     I am stuck in this bar, stuck in this city, with a deflated Lenin
2398 who won't play his part. A little effort, and I'm in Brazentina once
2399 again. 'Candida cannot find the way out of her city. The city has
2400 excluded the colours red and green. This means the traffic lights in
2401 every district have different phases – from violet through turquoise

2402 to brown, from orange to blue to diamond white. But her city
2403 stretches for ever, like an immense production line, or gut –
2404 showrooms to wreckers' yards, courts and hospitals, each zone
2405 packed with people of a different colour.'
2406 　　　I wait for Trotsky.
2407 　　　Lenin says, 'Trotsky's always late.' He's in a nervous mood. He
2408 often rants on about the others. He calls Gorbachev 'Motormouth',
2409 but I think he may be jealous. Of me? I don't know why. I've taken
2410 the same oath as Candida. It has become hard to enjoy glory or
2411 death in the first person. Some larger figure seems to intervene, to
2412 find the right words, of regret, of condemnation. I feel I shall not
2413 even be sorry for myself, someone more powerful, skilled, or just
2414 more sensitive, will do it for me. Even Lenin is better informed
2415 about my fantasies than I, although he's unemployed, and Trotsky
2416 has problems with the rent. Trotsky doesn't look as much like
2417 Trotsky, though, as Lenin looks like Lenin.
2418 　　　I ask Lenin: 'Are there lions in the rain forests?' and he replies,
2419 'In the rain forests there is everything.'
2420 　　　In my head I draw the pictures of the words: it is indeed the
2421 Amazonian lion that Candida hopes to find. That is indeed her
2422 programme. That she was elected on. The lion: described by the
2423 many writers of the zone – for this is the real treasure of Xica da
2424 Silva – apart from its long legs and musky smell, its features are: its
2425 orange teeth, and a mane that passes through three phases – from
2426 black beneath, to blue, and then smoke-grey. Its tail-end is held
2427 high, the tuft is black enamel, a kind of policeman's badge, or
2428 maybe a cockade. It's hard to see, to concentrate on, because you
2429 are held by those pale eyes, like grape-flesh, in the dusk they go to
2430 quince, the pupils inflexible, like two typed 'l's. And when it
2431 speaks...
2432 　　　Trotsky parks his motorbike, and comes in with his messenger's
2433 satchel. I don't trust him. Things I say only to him and Lenin seem
2434 to get back to Moro. Moro has spoken to me about lions. I've seen
2435 Moro and Trotsky together in another bar, eating steamed potatoes
2436 and salt herring. I know that Trotsky bets, and wins, with Ronnie
2437 Reagan, but he never treats us. Lenin and I owe so much money in
2438 this bar, it would take some huge upset to set us free – meanwhile,
2439 we are obliged to keep on coming. Trotsky is lucky to have a
2440 messenger's job: it's good news, if you bet. There's no future in it.
2441 But future for what?

2442       I am back in the land of the lion, the forest: 'None of the
2443 freeways leaves Candida's city. They circle it like the grooves on a
2444 record. Some of her escort are hurt in road accidents. They are
2445 seized and used for spare parts by gangs holed up in hospitals,
2446 experimenting with immortality.'
2447       Trotsky says, 'I can't wait till the last real Parisian leaves. It'll
2448 be better when there's only exiles here.'
2449       Lenin is irritated. 'Not exiles, immigrants.'
2450       Trotsky replies, 'Well, I prefer being an exile – it's not a
2451 question of nationality.'
2452       I know they've always lived here. Trotsky drinks my beer and
2453 rushes out. 'This district's going downhill fast,' he says. 'All kinds
2454 of funny business.' He looks like a philosophy prof, and Lenin his
2455 mature pupil who can never graduate.
2456       Lenin says, 'I'd like to ask you out. But I don't have any
2457 money. Perhaps you'd like to ask me out?'
2458       I say, 'Well, anyway, where would we go?'
2459       We pause outside my building. I must go in, pretend to be
2460 working. Lenin's going to the cinema. Reagan is protesting about
2461 something. Usually he's quiet. Lenin says, 'They're arresting
2462 Ronnie. Gambling. Serve him right.'
2463       Gorbachev is busy with a broom, sweeping out the courtyard.
2464 There seems a great quantity of leaves, but I had never seen a tree
2465 there. He makes no move to intervene in Ronnie's plight.
2466       Lenin dismisses the incident. 'Of all the arts, the cartoon is, for
2467 the moment, the most important. But – those little boxes the
2468 pictures are in, and those little bags for the words!'
2469       I say abstractedly, 'You can do anything you like – it's like the
2470 blues, it's like opera, without music, but you could make videos
2471 and add everything ... It's like drawing the inside of your head.'
2472       I think, 'Perhaps Moro will sort out Ronnie's problem,' but then
2473 I wonder if he hasn't sent for the cops himself. I must concentrate
2474 on my own story:
2475       'Candida finds the rain forests only a few metres from the
2476 ramparts of the city. Her comrades must board a tall ruined galleon,
2477 manned by black admirals. They go down through galleries and
2478 passageways lined with stone animals, their pupils fixed and
2479 inflexible, like typed '1's. In the city, the travellers from the future
2480 are speeding up the seasons. Winter lasts only a few days, in a few
2481 minutes spring has come, the fruit and flowers burst out like roman
2482 candles. The people are enthralled – but they are ageing, slowing

2483 down; as they gape, their teeth fall out, their limbs wither ... The
2484 city falls to ruin, the rivers are red with rust.'
2485     I see Gorbachev taking sacks of leaves from César Auguste, and
2486 sending him away for more. He empties them out, and sweeps them
2487 up again.
2488     I must get to the lion: 'In the hold of the galleon, they find the
2489 lion. He is lying on a white vinyl couch, and around him are the
2490 lights and reflectors for television. Candida has only three of her
2491 most faithful lovers to accompany her. The admirals crowd round,
2492 their wiry white hair looks like pot-scourers.'
2493     Lenin hisses to me, 'It's that bugger Trotsky', and then leaps
2494 forward, like a balding jackal, pushes the cop and sends him
2495 sprawling as he's ushering Ronnie Reagan away. The cop can't see
2496 what's happening, and Lenin is really very quick, very practised.
2497 He shouts to Ronnie, who is struck still like some stone animal,
2498 'Run, you twerp', and slowly Ronnie scutters off.
2499     The cop gets up and runs to the metro after Lenin. But I see that
2500 Lenin is over there, talking to the girl on the cinema box-office.
2501 They seem good pals. So that's how he sees so many films.
2502 Gorbachev is leaning expressionless on his broom: the courtyard is
2503 clear, but I can see a space by the wall now filled with neatly
2504 stacked bags of leaves. César Auguste has disappeared.
2505     I am at my desk. I must finish the cartoon. I feel like the pilot of
2506 a black bomber flying over a silver sea, the radio antenna is like
2507 cobwebs. I am hurrying, I am rushing the story of Candida, I have
2508 been trite about Xica da Silva. My lion is not the Brazilian
2509 revolution, nor yet an ecowizard.
2510     'The lion is old and chilled. He doesn't eat gazelles, but drinks
2511 carrot-juice and pops testerone pills. He now puts on Ray-Bans and
2512 a shawl embroidered with strawberry leaves. Candida has become
2513 old and fat after her adventures, and with her three attendants she
2514 looks like a malign pumpkin surrounded by witches. She asks the
2515 lion the three questions: first, to test him – since we see the answer
2516 on a screen behind him, "How shall I die?" and he tells her.
2517     'Secondly, "Shall I fulfil my mandate, and be successful?"
2518     'The lion chuckles: "What do you think?"
2519     'Finally, she asks, "Is it worth it?"
2520     'The lion closes his magnificent eyes, which have become a
2521 diamond-white under the lights, the pupils, like two typed "l"s, as
2522 narrow as keyholes. He is asleep.

2523 'But these answers restore Candida. She longs to be away, and
2524 regain her city in a last battle. The admirals form up behind her and
2525 her court, making a clangourous *afoxé* behind her Zis convertible,
2526 drawn by mules – a crepitating, shuffling swarm, 158 abreast, back
2527 along the Avenue of the Americas, swinging round Radio Square
2528 and into Silicon Alley.'
2529 Moro calls me. He had been watching everything from above. I
2530 thought I saw his sheep's head peeking from behind the blinds. I
2531 feel that cartoon days are nearly done. He has seen me, with Lenin.
2532 'I'm afraid,' he says, showing his long, orange teeth, 'I shall have
2533 to let you go, Chantal. Not that I ever *really* let anyone *go*, my dear
2534 girl (and what a lovely name yours is), but – now there is a
2535 closeness, now a distance. Now you'll do your drawings on your
2536 time, not on mine.' He chuckles, and his pupils constrict into two
2537 typed '1's.
2538 I can see, far below, Gorbachev handing the broom to Reagan,
2539 who looks dumbstruck, like a garden gnome. The last of the bags of
2540 leaves is disappearing to the roadway, César Auguste is toting it. In
2541 their own ways, Lenin and Trotsky have let me down.
2542 I am through. The story finishes: 'Candida must fight her last
2543 battle alone, regain her city from the time travellers. She fills the
2544 subway, transforming herself into a hydra, as a hatch of mayfly she
2545 aerates the rivers, and as a fall of steel feathers – amber, lilac, black
2546 – she cleanses the air. Time slows down again, the seasons drag
2547 out. People age, but slowly. Terribly slowly. Life becomes
2548 imperceptible again, in its passing. Candida looks younger and
2549 younger.
2550 'She has triumphed, again she is surrounded by bright lovers.
2551 We are back on the banks of the 32-lane freeway. Millions of
2552 heads, like black peppercorns, or matchsticks with dobs of red, of
2553 white, phosphorous …'
2554 I am liberated, whether I want it or not, freer than Candida, freer
2555 even than Xica da Silva. Lenin has lived up to the name I've given
2556 him.

2557

# 5

# WHERE THE PHILOSOPHERS GO

*from **Short Lives***

'YOU CAN'T IMAGINE the poverty here,' she says.
'Having no money, however much you've had – until more arrives – that's it!' he says. 'Poverty!' Everybody knows it.'

'No, that isn't it at all, you fool,' she says, and there is silence.

'See!' he says. 'The gangs have marked the houses. This road were on's between the 18s and the 8s.'

'Back to the hotel,' she says, 'I hate this place.'

'You needn't be frightened,' he says: 'We're not part of this scene.'

\*

'I liked you better when you were an alcoholic,' she says. 'There was transition. Like putting a glass plate in the camera. It might come out black all over, or a silverpoint, or crackled, treetops drawn by spiders. Now, you're just a you.'

'You thought you had the cure for booze,' he says. 'And you could stand up all the little soldiers, all over the world. With acid – after a while, you can reach down into the hole without it. The angels fluttering there... The drink – it's always different for a while, but there's no depth, no sea, just new surfaces, until you've tried them all. Then, if you can, you leave those rooms.'

They watch the cars below driving very fast, the guy pulling a cart with two empty barrels slow, very very slow.

'This is a good war,' she, Bianca, says. 'It's not like with drones and jointing knives, our guys and theirs, the clean and the dirty, our

2594 sort and who knows whose sort... Here, there's criminals, with no
2595 history.'

2596 'They're winning,' he says. 'They'll go on winning till they're
2597 all gunned down. Then, goodness can come.'

2598 'I'm not looking for goodness,' she says. 'I'm dodging.'

2599 'Our good guys have built a wall to keep the fugitives out,' he
2600 says. 'Our country's full of fat old guys who steal. And – those
2601 bodies here, tumbled down. They've fingerprints, but don't have
2602 names. How do you live with that? And on the other side, any other
2603 side – there must be guys who think like me. We all have countries,
2604 we all carry some other primal things ... it's like the song says –
2605 "No, I don't love you, I just wanna be held when I'm scared"...'

2606 'I'm leaving you,' she says. 'Don't get emotional. You, and the
2607 children. It's inevitable. When we've done the report, I'll have the
2608 ticket changed.'

2609 'Do we have children too?' he asks.

2610 'These beans,' she says. 'They explode in my stomach. I'm
2611 going down to get some stuff.'

2612 She walks across the road. Nothing hits her.

2613 She's never seen again.

2614 That can't be true. Someone always sees you – even if you're
2615 dead, and this place, you have to watch them all the time,
2616 everybody.

2617 He never sees her again.

2618 That's what she said – she left.

2619
2620                                     *
2621

2622 'Rodney Hawkett', says the label on his door. The guy, Rodney,
2623 says, 'Should we look for her? Bianca? Quite a mystery there.'

2624 'No, no,' he says: 'We can't put our finger on her. No secret, no
2625 mystery. Not knowing, not worrying: that's us. She's gone where
2626 millions go, and we don't know.'

2627 'If we look,' Rodney starts to ask. 'Where to begin?'

2628 'There'd be a procedure. But – no end's envisaged to it. And if
2629 we want to find her, there's no procedure for ends, solving it all and
2630 starting off again. And – why the search? What should we do with
2631 her? If she's in a hole? We'd know where she is, who's got her –
2632 can't do anything about it...'

2633 'Right,' says Rodney. 'She'll be someone who's dropped off.
2634 Missing in inaction.'

2635    Rodney's been to school, had some education too. There's my
2636    report for him to read. How friendly is the place we were in? Why
2637    would you want to go? Who can get out? What do those numbers
2638    mean – 8, 18? A study to be done on that – maybe a movie too?
2639
2640                                        *
2641
2642    The kidnap? 'The trouble was,' Bianca – the woman he was with
2643    and went missing – says to her friend, 'No one came looking. They
2644    tried to sell me, but...'
2645        'So you were kept for sex?'
2646        'Oh no. For fear. Mine was so great it seemed to be a value to
2647    them. They keep you if you are a saint: it takes time to flower from
2648    what you were. You mature before they martyr you. They weren't
2649    afraid at all. I made up for that. My fear – I showed them they still
2650    had the power. When I reached the end, they'd get rid of me ...
2651    down the escarpment, like a dog, like the book says.'
2652        'I can't believe,' says Bianca's friend, 'no one looked for you.'
2653        'Oh, maybe they were right,' she says. 'I'd no idea where I was.'
2654        'Why did those evil guys, the bad guys – why did they want
2655    power? Without money. Not much enjoyment even if they'd sex on
2656    you. It seems hollow.'
2657        'The power was to make sense, give a meaning, so's not to feel
2658    afraid,' Bianca says. Her friend, she thinks, is rather stupid – but
2659    her own explanation doesn't seem so bright. 'It was part of their
2660    job,' she says. Those months – she was sweaty clay put in the fire,
2661    an unworked shape coming out a cooked lump, a gruesome thing,
2662    in its core a squirming pulse, a worm macabre and blind.
2663        'Well,' says her friend, 'now, you know where other people are.
2664    Your partner. Your report. Your escape – a liberation, surely ...'
2665        'They went away,' Bianca says. 'Those people. No escape. I was
2666    just left, worthless. What's the point of starting things again?'
2667
2668                                        *
2669
2670    Bianca's friend says to another friend – 'Do you think they took
2671    her? She doesn't look like. Maybe she just went off.'
2672        'She's finished,' says the friend's friend. 'Not her fault.
2673    Someone else's will, being under that – it shows up the whole
2674    performance, from crowns to clogs. You can't make a case for
2675    anything, after that.'

2676
2677
2678
2679
2680
2681
2682
2683
2684
2685
2686
2687
2688
2689
2690
2691
2692
2693
2694
2695
2696
2697
2698
2699
2700
2701
2702
2703
2704
2705
2706
2707
2708
2709
2710
2711
2712
2713
2714
2715

*

Bianca's former partner, Vince – he's waiting for something. Meantime, he sits next to a clerical guy on the big wheel. It's to waste time, though he'd prefer to be alone, at ease.

The guy says, 'I'm just a lay therapist. I don't tell the stories, do the songs.'

'You're a priest,' says Vince. 'Spoiled all by yourself.'

There's a cool between them. 'I don't pretend you'll all be gone to paradise, immortal there. I suggest – there is some choice – ground-level, limited. The devil took God up and offered him the view,' says the priest. 'Up here we see everything. None of it will ever belong to us. I offer it to you just the same.'

'I accept,' Vince says, 'I've nothing. It's another con – first God made it all, so he was being offered just what he had made. Like he was a proletarian. Now – the con is new – you can't give, I can't take.'

'But all the rest is good – identity, rights, sex,' says the priest. 'Guilt and repentance. All up to you. That stuff – I can't give or take away.'

The wheel wavers at the bottom of its round. The weight of the two of them holds it there. The machinery would lift them, but they only paid for one circle, one up and up, and down. There's no fear – aeroplanes are far more dangerous, the view is less. You'd not fall here – you'd stick, like monkeys in physics or mechanics.

*

Vince wants this job. A job. The employer guy says, 'Ha! Recommended by Hawkett. That old shit. I'd trample on his flayed skin, a rug before the hearth, a spitty fire – yes, pocked by birdshot from the anthracite. I'd stand on him and warm my bum. Never too little of him, if you can't make him suffer!'

Vince, the postulant, says, 'We were in that sad country – a report: fancy visiting, putting money in, tossing off a little article half-read, by someone impermanent: in State, maybe...?'

'You were on the wheel,' says the interviewer. 'Hmmmm.'

'I should have been with people at the top of life. Like the ball in the pin machine, but starting with the lowest scores, going counter – right to the top. Instead of guttering out.' He doesn't say this:

2716    waits for the next question, the next card. He's only rubbish in his
2717    hand...
2718    'You lost your partner,' says the boss, the guy who's dealing,
2719    interviewing.
2720    Vince, who was on the wheel, the top, lets his mind, his
2721    memories, go soft, fall off the spindle, spool out on the floor. Is this
2722    all there is, before what's next? – this room, the questions that
2723    come, don't come. He keeps the mantra going silently, 'Jack of
2724    diamonds, oh jack of diamonds ... that's a hard card to find...'
2725    Vince says – 'I'll look at anything, and remember it.'
2726    That's all you need, to get the job, any job. Get kicked out too,
2727    of any job.
2728    His new boss says, 'Your work would be: do anything I tell you.
2729    Remember your profoundly wretched, compromised and cowardly
2730    soul. Keep in your sight the people lost, the challenges not faced.
2731    Me? I want to reach the top, to mix, even talk, with the talented,
2732    creative, and the rich. Be one of them, earn my biographers; their
2733    adulation, their respect. Your job's to push me up.'
2734    'It's more important, then, for me than it is for you,' Vince, the
2735    new hired hand, imagines. He'd be the new assistant – kingmaker,
2736    master of the prince's bedchamber. You need to know how it all
2737    works, the society, and reach the top for someone else, without a
2738    pole, a spring, a ladder – from nearly scratch.
2739    'Remember,' says the boss, 'your fault. The woman you
2740    deserted, having unwanted sex, short and jagged, with bony brown
2741    boys, their faiths and death inked on their unloved skins... And
2742    don't fuck with me. You're broken and in need. Send me to glory –
2743    then kneel before me: your creation. Pay tax on what I give you,
2744    and may your food cling to your purple gums like dry raw oatmeal.
2745    Sleep floundering in your sweat, and run the streets, cold and
2746    crabfooted. Obey my orders and invent your own: don't tell me the
2747    secrets you discover. Make me a whole, a hallowed man.'
2748    Vince, the new employee – now he has a contract, some cash, he
2749    is 'I'. Vince is 'I'. I'm to operate the social elevator. Bellhops ...
2750    they're gone too. Do it yourself, arsehole. Press the button, wait.
2751    Here's a modest guy, scrubbing the marble floor. Singing the
2752    song – the awful song, his terrible country...
2753    'You know,' I say, when he has stopped his tale of gangs,
2754    corruption – all the rest that brings him here, and can't imagine
2755    going back – 'The answer is,' – and I sing: '"My name it is Sam
2756    Hall / And – you've got to kill 'em all." There's no other way. You

2757 can't do it here, we're modern in this civilisation. But you guys
2758 can. No alternatives, no priests, no choices. And no self-doubt:
2759 that's a rabbit's tail someone pinned on, to make an easy target.
2760 Historians, philosophers – in the jail they go, if they won't run.
2761 Sculptors and potters – they can't waver, make mistakes. They're
2762 safe. They know how to make the choice. The rest ... is jelly in a
2763 bucket. Wield your bloody ladle. Forget the roots – cut them deep,
2764 and pour in quicklime. Yours is day one. This is the way, the only
2765 way...'
2766      He's laughing now. Maybe – oh no! – maybe he's an 8, an 18.
2767 For sure he'll have a cousin or a cop who is...
2768      'You're an illegal, friend,' I say. 'You should be a refugee. The
2769 thing is – you refugees are messengers of war. It's always so. You
2770 let them come, you turn your back – it's just the same. You think –
2771 all the guys within the Pale of Settlement – if they'd all come here
2772 ... there'd still have been a war, for sure – a big one, no one spared.
2773 Civil wars, uncivil ones...' I stare at him, as if he's the commanding
2774 one. Where, exactly, how – would they have gone? It's a hard one,
2775 that. Not worth pursuing.
2776
2777                                    *
2778
2779 Drinks. My boss – there's ten to twenty million like him – if they
2780 were on a scroll, in China, perching on those sugarloaf mountains –
2781 it would be gross. A termite hill. Not worth an artist's title, those
2782 numbers – an affront to modesty. Then, there's Africa and India.
2783 Millions of rich guys, looking down on him, the boss: indifferent,
2784 scornful, superficial. In their grounds – plinths, organic forms in
2785 bronze... Behind the glass – incunabula, narwhal prods: take you
2786 two lifetimes to appreciate, to amass. Then – death, dispersal.
2787 Vanity, all vanity: oblivion. A family of heirs – spring up through
2788 the trap from hell, to fritter everything away.
2789      'I've been observing you,' the guy who's staring, sat beside me,
2790 up here in the cloud, pulls at my sleeve. 'If it's ok,' he says, 'I'll
2791 run my tab upon your tab. It brings a saving, in the end.'
2792      'These bars – up so high, there is no view,' I say. 'Cold blue, the
2793 sky; or porridge.'
2794      'You can't be spied upon,' he says.
2795      'No,' I say, 'and I'll not pick up your tab, entwined with mine.'
2796      'Wrong!' he shouts: so loud, his hat falls off. Inside there's
2797 inked 'Andy'. Maybe it's not his... 'If you're a general, you

2798 sacrifice your soldiers. Otherwise – you are a fake. To have your
2799 victory – there must be skeletons dancing round your bed.'
2800     'If I'm a general,' I say, 'I'd not be pushing someone else to end
2801 above me.'
2802     'That's the spirit,' Andy says. 'You know it's vanity. And –
2803 better that it's yours. We all pick up those tabs, and pass them on. If
2804 you can't pay – you'll need to run down thirty flights of stairs.
2805 That's why they put these bars up high. They're up high so you
2806 can't get out without paying – unless you run real quick... They
2807 block the elevator. So much for machines ... wheels without
2808 wheels.'
2809     I settle up our tabs. Andy's been there for a week, it seems. He
2810 grasps my arm. 'Now, you should see my friend, the flight
2811 instructor. I call him Icarus, though it's not quite right. This time,
2812 this incarnation, it's Icaro.The higher up you go, the colder. So,
2813 those wings lost traction – you shouldn't blame the glue. What you
2814 need, my friend is – go right to the top: all by yourself. Forget
2815 about your boss. That's squalor. We can trick you out, with what
2816 you need. Money – we'd give old stuff – venerable, venerated. And
2817 then – you add the new. Invention. A perfect wedlock...'
2818     The drink's at work. Andy, pulling me along – to me, he seems a
2819 cat on X, ecstasy, a flying Hirschfield rug, through the pubs, out the
2820 windows, not paying now: over the walls, spikes in our pants,
2821 discussing destiny, cabbage and beans, bourbon and pills, until
2822 'Another friend, dear Icaro,' says Andy, losing his fur, his pace,
2823 becoming almost human, a reel of speeding pictures... 'Try him out,
2824 Icaro,' he says.
2825     They fit me with the helmet: it's all green and grey below, blue
2826 up top, if I can skew my head right round: 'The sacred book,' Andy
2827 confides, 'says in the realm of God, that starts ten metres up – it's
2828 all divinity. Angels, suchlike. That's why they build those towers,
2829 skyscrapers some call them, and put bars on the top. No longer law
2830 that men must live by – you're in paradise there. I guess the angels
2831 like a tipple too – and if they fall, there's wings.'
2832     'Fuck you,' says Icaro. 'Anyone can knit a pair of wings. They
2833 do not always bear you up.'
2834     Andy says, 'In the desert, there's no mountains, everything's
2835 nine metres high. It's obvious they thought God's realm, the angels,
2836 if you're in that mode or heresy – lived just above your head.'

2837
2838
2839
2840
2841
2842
2843
2844
2845
2846
2847
2848
2849
2850
2851
2852
2853
2854
2855
2856
2857
2858
2859
2860
2861
2862
2863
2864
2865
2866
2867
2868
2869
2870
2871
2872
2873
2874
2875
2876
2877

'Now,' says Icaro, 'forget the virtuous world, the simulacrum. Try the real thing, and fly. No helmet. Watch for sacrilege. You must expect some tumbles... Try your strength.'

It should be easier, without the fakery, the helmet and the pictures. 'You need to take the right philosophy,' says Andy, 'that moves along. Let concepts bear you up. Experience without them – would be just the simulation of a flight. No aeroplane around, no tail, no feet, no horns to warn the rest. Sensation without context. A drag, and frightening too.'

They're chuckling as they try to fit me with a grubby pair of wings. 'He's better off without,' laughs Icaro. 'The worst part is the launch.'

I'm on the edge. Nine metres – or ten? It's worth your life, and heaven too. 'There's a slope and grass,' says Icaro. 'All green – like the poet says.'

'It seems to me this is a roof,' I say. 'A drop. To earth.'

'There's trees up there, sprouting from the tiles,' says Andy. 'Olives, a passion plant. Jump and glide.'

I live. It's like the first flight, on the beach: you land quite bad, but you're in history. Icaro and Andy laugh.

'History? That's not the point,' says Icaro. 'You can end there as a flop. Usually – you're dead. The thing to do's to grasp some wing, angelic maybe, that yanks you up, and gives you shine.'

'The point is different,' says Andy. 'You think one law trumps all the rest – the law of gravity, of *gravitas*. But – we're so ephemeral – where does our gravity end? Hole in the ground? An urn, a mausoleum – or in dust, anonymous, that clogs your brother's lungs – and so it all goes on, until another law breaks in. A law we all ignore – when we leap up. Yet – there's heaven for us all, or most: where there's no gravity. We laugh – there is no dawn nor dusk, nor *gravitas,*

so – laughter unceasing. Icaro – his namesake didn't drown from gravity – but, the tale goes – from disrespect, or hubris, ignoring some advice about the altitude that's clearly wrong or else there wouldn't be PanAm, TWA, and all the rest.'

'My bruises hurt,' I say. 'The law is punishment.'

They laugh the harder, 'Why,' says Icaro. 'This guy's a wit, a genius, a most ingenious faller.'

'No, be serious,' says Andy, and to me, 'You flew. Next time we'll find a taller house. Guys did it all the time, before the Revolutions, in France, and science too. You're merely lacking in

2878    the philosophy, the confidence that leaders have. Night flyers, they

2879    were called. Maybe it's easier in the dark.'

2880       'I must explain,' I say. 'My boss will ask why I've not launched

2881    him, his ambition.'

2882       'You're walking on those sticks,' says Andy. 'Tell him you

2883    learned a lesson for him. "Choose bedmates that don't push you

2884    down the stairs."'

2885       'Why do you care so much for me?' I ask.

2886       'Appearances, and time – that's where my interest lies,' says

2887    Andy. 'The sticks, the crutches – they seem resulting from an

2888    accident. We know – they come from your success. And time: the

2889    world, its time, is folded like a fan. Those pubs, the hostelries we

2890    drank in, flying over walls and hedges – arriving in the painting,

2891    five hundred years ago, when my friend Icaro went down... It's

2892    folding timescapes.'

2893       'Hold it, Andy. It's all a fable, about Icaro, both then and now.

2894    Everything we know and do – it happens all at once, then it is gone.

2895    The painting's made today: the pubs, the walls with bottle glass

2896    atop – they happened once, and disappeared. We're only

2897    consequences. There's no success, no failure – we are blots of

2898    liquid ink, we dry. There is no fold that brings us near the past, our

2899    faces pressed on some Aegean pioneer's... Time is a scroll,' I say.

2900    'That's wrapped so tight – it never is unwound. Your hat, Andy – it

2901    must be yours, it can't be Warhol's. He never wore a hat. Time and

2902    appearance – that was him. Not you.'

2903       'Who's to say?' says Andy. 'Someone else has found a head to

2904    fit his hat. What interests me – us – is handing your ambition, your

2905    achievement, back to you.'

2906       'What do you gain?' I ask.

2907       'Percentages,' says Icaro. 'That's all there ever is, you shouldn't

2908    ask for more.'

2909       'I couldn't bear to see you,' Andy says, bending down to look up

2910    at me, the angles full of shade. 'Shovelling beauties random in your

2911    boss's boudoir. When we could have them for ourselves... Since he

2912    chose you, I knew he couldn't ever make it, wherever he might

2913    want to go, to be. So you must see that's the case. I shan't be a cat

2914    again, I promise you – no caterwauls, no jumping over gates and

2915    walls. Those pills we took – they eliminate our worms. The

2916    universe – it's made of wormholes – the living creatures end up

2917    inside us. Don't you feel cleaner, purer now?' he asks. He pulls me

2918    close. 'You are my poem. Lines from you – they'll come to me at

2919　night, or if we have to take the road again – "Yes!" I'll think. "That
2920　caught the pulse; there the thought lay down and curled up on the
2921　picture, and they were one."'
2922　　'That's opportunism,' I say.
2923　　'Oh no,' he says. 'That's wedlock.'
2924
2925　　　　　　　　　　　　　　*
2926
2927　Rodney Hawkett tells me, 'You got the job. There's an end to it.
2928　You go on. Success, failure – you'll find, for you – they're much
2929　the same. Your boss – that shit – he thinks those clouds are full of
2930　lovely people. He's an idiot: they're full of odd tennis shoes and
2931　plastic bottles. You find them on the beach, all washed up. Bodies,
2932　too. Watch out!'
2933　　Rodney Hawkett's bones – he keeps them in their sack of skin –
2934　you wonder how. The shoulder blades – two china bowls cast down
2935　and cracked ... the belly, mottled like old books, the organs wizened
2936　like old plums, purple, nearly draining out, down the filament of
2937　sex.
2938　　'What should I tell the boss?' I ask.
2939　　'Keep away from the truth,' says Rodney Hawkett. 'That holds
2940　good for me, too. I want lots of things, some you plug in, some you
2941　put in the bank – truth isn't one of them. There's no socket.'
2942　　'Maybe,' I persist, 'the arts. The talk about them. That knocks
2943　off the lugs, the roughness: then you file the sharp bits down.'
2944　　Rodney Hawkett nods. He wanders round. His bedsheet leaves a
2945　black grape nipple bare: a monk's scraggy shoulder. It's good to get
2946　out of bed sometimes, but he should dress: a stretch, a shout –
2947　that's what you need.
2948
2949　　　　　　　　　　　　　　*
2950
2951　'My models,' Andy says, 'have nothing to do with those ambitious
2952　guys, the depressives. I think a lot about the fables – the self-
2953　sacrifice. The hare who leaps into the fire to be food for the sage. It
2954　all seems whimsy – the contemplation, the lives you'd like to live –
2955　but really, it's quite physical. Making a bridge with your body so
2956　your monkey subjects can get across the flood; getting eaten so's to
2957　help someone.'
2958　　'Andy wanted to find an evil guy,' says Icaro. 'Not one of the
2959　wholesale types that's into politics, money, mustering camp-

2960 followers. Those are the multipliers, they turn one killing into
2961 millions. No: a guy like you, Vince. Faithless, insensitive. Not evil
2962 "bad" – just evil good and bad.'
2963     'I don't feel the tug,' I say. 'There's no appeal. Who'd want to
2964 be his object?'
2965     'Oh, you just want rewards, and you fear the punishment,' says
2966 Icaro. 'Try to keep your face a blank for a while. Think how many
2967 shapes there are in it.'
2968     'No whimsy, Icaro,' I say. 'No magnificent promises that end up
2969 as a bowl of milk, a pocketful of dust. I don't need educating into
2970 nothing, I know it well.'
2971     'That's not it at all,' says Andy. 'I'm sure you know real killers.
2972 Machismo, money, fear and dirty trades – that's of no interest.'
2973     'I'm not jumping in the fire,' I say. 'I'm no dinner! Andy – you
2974 are my dearest friend, but: no!'
2975     'He means – why this, not something else,' says Icaro. 'Or
2976 nothing else at all?'
2977     'I know exactly what I mean,' says Andy. 'And this guy – he is a
2978 candidate. He looks, he seeks: I find.'
2979
2980                    *
2981
2982 I tell the boss: 'You know, to send you up the stairs – it's right I
2983 need to try things first. Like tasting for the poison. It's a dice: enjoy
2984 the juiciest bits, they may be strychnine. And so I get the fun, the
2985 chance, the risk.'
2986     'Yes,' says the boss. 'I quite see that. But – you could end up
2987 getting all the fizz.'
2988     'I'm not the mountaineering type,' I say. 'Ascents are
2989 dangerous. and when you reach the top – there's nothing there.
2990 Remember the song, *'maledetta noia'* – bloody boredom. That's
2991 what faces me.'
2992     'We could call everything off,' says the boss. He pushes back his
2993 rolling chair. Some muscle tone, a hint he's used those pedalling
2994 machines, bolted to their spot. He plays 'the eager son', sniggering
2995 within. Rodney Hawkett is his mentor, would be his grand old
2996 father – that's the generation, before they invented doctors,
2997 dentists... Those old guys, quavering, determined, doctrinaire –
2998 there they go, see! the flames behind the door, it's a cat flap for old
2999 tigers, up they go, like straw...
3000     'Advise me,' says my boss. 'Gain your pay.'

3001 'Exactly,' I say. 'You speak of "gaining the summit". Nothing's
3002 gained. It's like the pay – a week goes by, you're poor again...
3003 Unless you have the itch: you have to take the last train, and the
3004 first, the first station and the last, the last biscuit or the biggest. It's
3005 an obsession. Where does it drive?'

3006 'I don't know,' says the boss. 'I'm an obsessive. I do those
3007 things you mention, and many many more.'

3008 'It's maybe seeking a perfection,' I say. 'But it's not perfection.
3009 It's something to do and then relax.'

3010 'You must tell me about perfection,' says the boss. 'That is your
3011 job. And – does it involve me in calligraphy?'

3012 He holds out a broken hand, steel-pinned in the middle like a
3013 hinge. 'My friend – she shut it in the door,' he says. 'Some question
3014 defining about sex. That isn't mountaineering, nor can it lead to
3015 some perfection...' I nod, but he's not satisfied. 'She wasn't
3016 satisfied,' he says. 'Is it perfection when you're satisfied? Is it the
3017 feeling, the act – or the state itself, a platform? Exercises? Winning
3018 at blackjack, over and over? That would give me satisfaction, that's
3019 for sure.'

3020 'Your hand,' I say. 'It has something of the perfect...'

3021 He waves it, it flaps – 'My body – is a circus,' says my boss.
3022 'Can you have a perfect pratfall? A cure – that turns a hand from
3023 something that can grasp – into a clown, an acrobat, you leap, you
3024 make a pyramid of men... In the real world, they don't exist, don't
3025 function. Yet – there they are. Six guys stood on each other's heads
3026 – what does that mean? To paint the ceiling, pick your apricots?
3027 No, naturally not. A perfect human? Just perfect, as humans aren't
3028 *for* anything, but they can *be* ... no more than themselves, no more,
3029 transformed from being less than what they are...? Growth,
3030 progress – those are finished. Maybe that means perfection can be
3031 attained. But – and here, my friend, arrives the paradox: is this
3032 perfection the *best* thing there can be? Well, clearly not. Or not in
3033 an exclusive sense – it's good for humans, possibly, but perfect
3034 crabs have what is best for them, and viruses, and elephants.'

3035 'That's where the first lesson ends,' I tell the boss. I can't go on.

3036 'No, no,' he says. 'The last word's always mine. Perfection of
3037 oneself, your species: isn't *good*, you see. The guys who link the
3038 two, the one, the all – they've always held the stage. It isn't so. The
3039 perfect man – kills all the rest and crams them in his perfect mouth
3040 and grinds them with his perfect teeth. You get my point, examples
3041 take shape in your head?'

3042 I'm silent. It's the only way to halt the flood.
3043
3044         *
3045
3046 'He's a casuist,' says Andy. 'Those are easy games for him and his,
3047 if all he wants is friends. We have more serious adventuring to do.
3048 He's worse than Hawkett, and they're both too late to be a nazi
3049 with the uniform.'
3050  'You must be a volunteer,' says Icaro. 'The fire service. Yes –
3051 you must be a fireman.'
3052  'H is for happiness,' Andy explains. 'And it's the name of a
3053 bomb. See how we want both. The biggest bomb, the nearest to a
3054 perfect one. "Noooo," they say. "We want one, not to use – just
3055 decoration and for frightening. We're compassionate." And there it
3056 is: the cookie jar – you steal a cookie even if you know you'll be
3057 found out. You swallow it right down, you drop your bomb. So as
3058 to *be* found out; the naughty one, who's badness must be forgiven.
3059 That is the path to love. Authority, veneration too – of course, there
3060 is a pantheon. There's death and war – and mediators, whom we
3061 respect, of course...'
3062  'I've heard all that,' I say. 'I know – when the music stops, your
3063 big ears hear the wisdom, the enlightenment. But why should I be a
3064 fireman?'
3065  'People want money,' Andy says. 'But when they see the guy
3066 who has a pile of it – they laugh. She's vulgar. Maybe she's not
3067 even happy. You think you will respect what you want. It isn't so.
3068 You respect the poverty that you don't want. You deride the wealth
3069 you wrestle for.'
3070  'Bombs, Andy. Happiness,' I say. 'Where does the fire come in?
3071 Look at my round head. There is no third eye, no tranquillity. My
3072 empty hands ... no attributes, no power: no sword, no justice, no
3073 forgiving. Fire is a pepper up your arse. It makes you jump and
3074 run.'
3075  'That's what firemen do,' says Icaro, annoyed. 'You should
3076 know. They put out fires. Now, you work to make your boss a hero,
3077 respected. Everybody does, who delves and spins. It's to puff up
3078 some guy who gives you bread. Stale, too. Look at the fires the
3079 bosses make – fireworks. It works! The fire works – so do you.
3080 You work to set the flames and see them leaping up, exploding,
3081 making the pattern. Forget it. Take your pitcher. Pour it on the
3082 flame...'

3083    'Icaro,' I say. 'This is banal. It never works, to set the fire,
3084    extinguish it. We build what others have designed. Whatever you
3085    knock down – the blueprint stays, immortal, fecund.'
3086        But – the fire: we live by it. If – when – it dies, we die. The three
3087    – we look up at the sun, cover our heads, submitting.
3088
3089                                            *
3090
3091    I'm a fireman. Oh – how we hate the common run – cats in the
3092    trees. Forcing the locks to empty rooms. Water, smoke, minerals
3093    clagged with earth, the poisons... Not our elements, no, not at all.
3094    We are people of the flames: those tall palaces, those glassy spikes
3095    – it's not our element, they're made of sand, they splinter and
3096    implode. Icaro was wrong: the fire – it makes itself: it's not a toy, a
3097    simulacrum... You don't risk it by miscalculating. You earn it, seek
3098    it. It's creation, blooming from destruction, it's revelation from the
3099    wood, the straw, the skins. To die in the fire – it's a gift, a blessing.
3100    Icaro deserved his punishment – to rise up to the sun in arrogance,
3101    not in love, surrender ... just to flap his wings. If – if only – with
3102    longing, he'd flown up to perish in the fire, as though he'd never
3103    been. That's perfect love.
3104        That's what they say.
3105        We need the flames, their dance, their shout. Us firemen – they
3106    try to damp us down, to drown.
3107        We're tied in to diving suits, a travesty: our heads in brazen bells
3108    to stop us looking up to where the flames aspire... 'No, no!' the
3109    captain cries – 'Whatever else – do not go naked in the flames! – no
3110    sacrifice, and no delight, fulfilment, can be required of you.
3111    Nothing in your heads except the song – "burn, burn", the babies
3112    and the pigs – a hecatomb – someone up there lives on the scent,
3113    their incense...'
3114        It does no good. We need to see the flames ... the colours –
3115    sapphire blue, the yellow melon flowers, our blood – red as
3116    coxcombs. Our passion... With what regret we put them out, put
3117    them away, our flames, waiting for another show.
3118        'That's Hawkett's ancient house,' I hear a colleague shout... At
3119    last! A pyre that ends in orange, springing to the sun; a misty grey
3120    of ash is left, and not a trace of black, of death...
3121        Old Hawkett too – consumed to his last, an offering, spiralled up
3122    – the tender tongue, the roasted beak, the runny sheep eyes – a
3123    slender cuisine for sure, but all gone, eaten up.

3124     Yes, I think, as we squirt our final drops on silent embers – he
3125 made a show... Not a witness, just someone curious and
3126 questioning. I'm glad he got burned up.
3127     'I saw the whole station, the firemen – dancing round, all skin
3128 and hair,' says Andy, reproaching. 'But you resisted. You didn't
3129 jump right in...'
3130     'No,' I say, 'but – it's hard for me now... My work. I can't go
3131 on, I don't believe in it. I've seen the fire, the little flickers we have
3132 now, and how it ends – all, everyone, the rocks, sea monsters – all
3133 eaten by the sun. Or doing it ourselves, the ending. It's a temptation
3134 ... better than sex or water when you're thirsty...'
3135     'Yes,' says Andy. 'Temptation is to be resisted too. The more
3136 you can resist, the better is the end, surrender, the falling... No, you
3137 can't work for your chief. He's ignoble, his ambition – it's
3138 unreal...'
3139
3140                         *
3141
3142 I tell the boss I can't go on. He can get thousands like me...
3143     'Yes, of course I can,' he says. 'But you're my rabbit on the
3144 stick. You've fallen in the fire. I've lost: I cannot lose. I'll ride your
3145 spirit till the end of days...'
3146     'Oh no,' I think. 'I never thought. The guy's a maniac. Of
3147 course...'
3148     I say, 'I'm not your good communist, boss – I know the
3149 situation, and what needs doing in it. And I don't do it. Not a bit of
3150 it. Quite the contrary.'
3151     He's not listening. Or he doesn't understand.
3152     'This form,' he says, waving it. 'It follows you from job to job.
3153 The way I've fixed it, though – you'll never work again. The fire,
3154 the end ... abandonment. No one will pay a guy like you, who takes
3155 it all to bits, and sees the stalks and stems, the ladders and the
3156 synthesis, the little greenish blobs of life that waver mindless up
3157 and down...'
3158     'That isn't fire,' I say. 'It's flowers. You do it in the schools...'
3159     'So,' he says, 'you betray, deny. You'll wander round the world,
3160 quite unappeased, anonymous. They'll mock you when you come
3161 to beg.'
3162     'I believe all that,' I say. 'But you'll just sit here, vindictive, on
3163 your own, unloved...'

3164    'Yes,' he says, 'I know all that. It's good. It's me. I'll be the
3165    boss, clandestine, murderous. I'll give my orders. The booze – I'll
3166    have it all myself – no partying. No courting. Whores. No
3167    conversation, no collecting stuff, no friends and so no enemies –
3168    just introspection and enjoyment. It's where it's always been –
3169    inside: just as the humanists believed – the divinity of myself,
3170    impregnable, unique.'
3171
3172                                    *
3173
3174    'It seems, Andy, there's a form,' I say. 'You fill it when you're
3175    born, it follows you around, precedes – and if some guy puts down
3176    a – what? A query? Doubt? Dissatisfaction? – you never work
3177    again.'
3178        'Oh yes,' says Andy. 'It happened with poor Icaro. Out of a
3179    cloudless sky... And in a while – you learn to live without. The
3180    work you never get – you learn you didn't want it anyway...'
3181        'Farewell, then, Andy,' I say: 'Friends for ever.'
3182        'It's a sad day,' says Andy. 'I hoped to hone and burnish you.
3183    Push you up, through the trap, and on the stage. Profit from your
3184    activity, better still – your inactivity. What they call big crime – it's
3185    what is left for you, though it's of no interest. Disasters come from
3186    heaven, or from teams of guys who are too big to tumble down.
3187    Governments, not gangs – they rule. Crime just suckles on their
3188    hindmost tit, I fear. It's petty. You'd be a bug in someone's ear, or
3189    someone's telephone.'
3190        I wait. Andy says, 'Sit back. There's no roundups here, not now.
3191    You're not of fighting age – or you'd have faked your birthdate, so
3192    you're too young, too old. That's what the Syrians did, who
3193    wouldn't fight for France. You're not a surgeon, so there's nothing
3194    useful you can do. These are liquid days, my friend. On the radio,
3195    there are always songs – touching, tender, hard. Listen to some
3196    words, don't be ashamed when they make you cry – you're in your
3197    elastic garden now. Forget Icaro, forget things dropping from the
3198    sky – no one can come down on you...'
3199        'There's always "next", Andy – that's what the radio's for,' I
3200    say.
3201        'Come on, Vince,' he says. 'There's people doing things that
3202    fifty years ago would have been a miracle. Dancing on Mars.
3203    Calculating when we all will fry. "Up to the ceiling, down to the
3204    floor" – remember? your rough relatives used to swing you up and

3205    down. Now, there's machines for that. There's lessons to make you
3206    a good father even if you've got no kids...'
3207       'There's movement, Andy,' I say. 'But nothing deep. Or still.'
3208       'Lessons, Vince,' says Andy. 'If you're really helpless.'
3209       'It's the nomads, Andy,' I say. 'They're underneath my eyelids.'
3210       'I have no truck with them,' says Andy, laughing. 'Those little
3211    terracotta carts they made – then the bronze; twisted and crude. As
3212    though they'd only seen them far away. The wry reward for
3213    travelling and never getting there – it's an ice tomb on the steppe.
3214    Everybody knew – it was the usual failure. Down to the frost. Dress
3215    warm and well. Too bad.'
3216       'You're stuck, poor Andy. The customary parasite,' I say. 'You
3217    sit inside your city, listening to the horsemen circling round. If
3218    everything becomes a city – then you'd be safe. No trading off your
3219    daughters to the chiefs. Those kids'll serve you in your senile days,
3220    as you lie gaga on your litter, laughing up at towers and ramparts.
3221    It's no use. There's quests, and voyages. Same endings, but what
3222    you look for's different. Icaro was on his quest. It did for him. And
3223    yet – the quest was over, a success. We all can fly. He thought it
3224    was a voyage. Voyaging – you're not seeking one big thing, a goal
3225    – but several, all familiar, all with a tariff on the door. Night flights,
3226    and one night stands. On, on – vibrating beds and porno for a
3227    quarter. You say you're seeking something – it's the same thing,
3228    over and over. Wandering – pushed and pulled. Taxis at dawn: the
3229    frontier. A document – will it protect, against the dogs and guns...?
3230    You're right to doubt. Pack your bundle – or you dump it there,
3231    beneath the hedge. Maybe you'll be back for it – there's no one
3232    cares. The quest is something else. You find a fig tree, lie back –
3233    the quest can start from there... Those blue birds – come and shake
3234    the branches – down will come the fruit. There's figtrees
3235    everywhere – you might lie under every one – there's blue birds
3236    plentiful... They migrate. They're souls. For sure, they're not
3237    monogamous, they don't bear you back each year until you croak:
3238    *they* croak, a requiem. No – everything's renewed, for ever it's the
3239    same. The form – it doesn't change, it waxes, wanes, sometimes the
3240    tiles are blue and sometimes green – the heaven and the faith –
3241    they're much alike...'
3242       I could go on, but Andy says: 'That's crap. The voyage has no
3243    end. The quest – no start. The voyage – it begins in nowhere in
3244    particular. The quest – is stasis. An itch where you can't scratch.
3245    Real nomads – they have beasts, each year they do the up, the

3246  down. It's agriculture, Vince. Without the shit to burn – you'd
3247  freeze. Their economics – based on crap. Not voyaging, no quest.
3248  Invent the spade – you dig a trench – and with the earth – you've
3249  made a rampart. There you are! Mechanical. A conurbation.'
3250      'Icaro...' I begin.
3251      'No, no,' shouts Andy. 'Forget Icarus. Our Icaro – works in
3252  insurance. He thinks he's a crude beast who wants out the door. It
3253  isn't so. He isn't trapped. He's salaried. A bureaucrat who weeps
3254  because he has no feathers on his arms, no compass in his brain.
3255  Pitiful. Don't read his poems, Vince. Try sipping at reality.
3256  Remember, I'm you're life-coach: if you don't earn, I don't eat
3257  steak.'
3258      'I'll be your crude beast, Andy,' I tell him. 'So long as there is
3259  action. I'll climb up on the stool, I'll chase the clowns, I'll catch the
3260  flyers as they miss the net... I'll do what it takes to get your ten per
3261  cent...'
3262      'It's much, much more than that,' says Andy. 'Start thinking
3263  thirty.'
3264      'If you've no job, you think of joining 8s and 18s,' I tell him.
3265  'Short lives. That's the new thing. When I hear "Amur" – my hair
3266  roots tense. The river – shrivelled by the drought; the snow – it
3267  stings like salt. How can we live? The beauty's gone extinct. Those
3268  plodding songs. We lie down in the cold. We die. What else can we
3269  do?'
3270      'Ah yes, the Gobi,' Andy says. I see the tears prick in his eyes.
3271      This is our passion. Roaming with no beasts, no destination.
3272  Whatever you are looking for – you'll find it there, in plenty or in
3273  desolation. Anything at all, whatever. Or nothing.
3274      'Well, I can't go,' says Andy. 'I renounce. I'll find some other
3275  things to do. You can't, you won't. You won't give up. You won't
3276  invent.'
3277      'Of course,' I say, needling. 'The animals see us. They scout us
3278  all the time. They know – those we don't kill, will starve. They'll
3279  go before us, just. You need them, you need new collectivities. The
3280  buildings – they see us too, in a lesser way, as we see them, quite
3281  likewise. Don't say it, though, they'll think you're mad. Say
3282  "architecture". "Dance", not dancers. Besides, the dancers never
3283  look at you. You're not on their horizon – it belongs to them alone.'
3284      'Collectives,' Andy says, 'those are what you overlook: the guys
3285  in joyous lockstep, like the geese. I fought the class war for many
3286  years – till I got tired of losing and repeating...'

3287 'Crap, Andy!' I say. 'You've never had a home. Never enrolled
3288 in anything.'
3289 'Do you want a woman?' Andy asks. 'Not that I pimp. Or know
3290 your tastes. But – it's always easier to find a woman for a friend
3291 than for yourself. They say they still work miracles – even though
3292 we don't believe in them...'
3293 'Andy, my record's worse than most,' I say. 'I'm sure you know
3294 what woman's best for me – hunting's interminable. The dates!
3295 Think of China – the quantity! Then – there's the documents...'
3296 'A dog, then? A cat?' Andy asks. 'A crow? Raven?'
3297 'That's the track,' I say. 'A voice.'
3298 'Try these,' says Andy, opening his sack. 'There's discs.'
3299 We listen to them all – the women – in cathedrals. 'Too electric,'
3300 Andy says. 'In that huge space, it resonates with the expanse – why
3301 roof it over, then? It must be fake.'
3302 The baroque, and the impertinent: singing with lips sewn up, in
3303 boxes for the dead – in urns: in winds... There's males, a trilling in
3304 the head: and musky mezzi, a tenor cuddled in their breasts.
3305 Andy's eyes are closed, the lids are a bruised blue, with baby
3306 streams of red. The mouth droops, a pure drool runs down inside
3307 his shirt. He's in the melody.
3308 There's playful, tearful, trills, purrs and growls. O seasons, o
3309 betrayals, o pyres for lovers on the shore... Lilacs and millstreams.
3310 Sentiment engraved on plastic. Voices. They're solid forms, laid
3311 down on nothing, unfleshed, breezes on the silver dishes – some, in
3312 life, as thick as trunks of olive plants; some brass, some zinc, some
3313 – iris stems.
3314 'They're all traduced,' I say. 'You can't see the face – all could
3315 come up from the same throat...'
3316 'You choose a moment, then,' he says. 'It's all the same, and all
3317 the same to me. A voice has left behind its body anyway – and on a
3318 disc – well, nothing on to something, as they say, is nothing, only
3319 what you want to hear.'
3320 'That one!' I point. 'It drives along, that voice. Where is the
3321 source?'
3322 'I've no idea,' he says. 'I'll not desert you – but ... who the voice
3323 belongs to, I don't know. It could be pure electrics. You would
3324 have to search.'
3325 'And finding – would be happiness?' I ask.
3326 'Happiness is moving on to something else,' he says. 'All music
3327 is farewells.'

| | |
|---|---|
| 3328 | 'I know about farewells,' I say. 'You pushed Icaro in his chair – |
| 3329 | down the hill he went, into the water. He can't wheel back up the |
| 3330 | slope.' |
| 3331 | 'That was drastic, I admit,' says Andy. 'It's hard to call it bad. |
| 3332 | Not good – just filing patterns. Much of everything is that – |
| 3333 | designs. For instance – you could start a reservation. Not Indians – |
| 3334 | animals. Nature. They have the instinct so they won't all die. That's |
| 3335 | helpful for you. And – Icaro got on my nerves – that dreary tale...' |
| 3336 | 'I don't feel at ease with good people, Andy,' I tell him. |
| 3337 | He acts surprised: 'Your priest must have told you – in animals, |
| 3338 | there isn't good or bad.' |
| 3339 | 'I don't know which side that guy was on,' I say. |
| 3340 | 'Lion and lamb,' says Andy. 'We disobeyed, like Icarus. It kept |
| 3341 | on going bad, after him. Disobeying is the game. Now – we're |
| 3342 | flying everywhere, sometimes by night.' |
| 3343 | 'It seems too easy, put like that,' I say. |
| 3344 | 'That woman, Bianca – you could keep your animals near where |
| 3345 | she disappeared. Go look for her,' says Andy. |
| 3346 | 'It's your obsession, Andy,' I tell him. 'She's dead, or she's |
| 3347 | alive. Looking won't change a thing. There's no badness in any of |
| 3348 | it. Besides, she wasn't tender with her family... And – I'd forgot – |
| 3349 | those animals. They all have families – every sort. Monogamy and |
| 3350 | orgies, regurgitating for your kids and eating them... Socially, |
| 3351 | Andy, it's a jungle.' |
| 3352 | I stare at his pale eyes, his dusty hair, the skin laid on like flakes |
| 3353 | or scales. Everyone's a priest, their own ideas on end days, how to |
| 3354 | live a long and useless life, and have the rest work on to cover you |
| 3355 | when you are old... |
| 3356 | 'Hey, Vince,' shouts Andy. 'Wake up to the plan. You rent a |
| 3357 | plot of forest, fence it round...' |
| 3358 | 'The animals?' I ask. 'And knowing about the trees, the |
| 3359 | snakes...?' |
| 3360 | 'You haven't understood, my friend. The fence is there to keep |
| 3361 | the crawlers out,' Andy says, 'The scratchers and the roarers too. |
| 3362 | You're stockaded, so's you can dig in peace. Gold and sapphires in |
| 3363 | the mud. What d'you want with animals, a-falling in the holes? A |
| 3364 | space – no animals at all! If the moviemakers come – you hire |
| 3365 | some creatures from a zoo. You find the treasure. Then comes your |
| 3366 | launch – success, flamboyant backcloth – a cityscape, your bride – |
| 3367 | you have to be a couple, but you have a document to keep your |
| 3368 | wealth secure.' |

3369      I meditate: 'It sounds like greed, dear Andy. And there'll be
3370      competitors... The gangs... The taxes...'
3371      'It isn't greed, dear Vince,' he says. 'I'll skim and skin, and so
3372      will all the rest. It's finding what is hidden. All religions have a
3373      mystery ... what's underground – that's the best kind.'
3374      'It's not about religion, Andy,' I say. 'I sat next to a guy on the
3375      wheel, is all.'
3376      'Rodney Hawkett – he was into conservation. Not of himself –
3377      that clearly didn't work. Of unknown things. A loving paedo. Like
3378      your boss – up to the ceiling, down to the ground. You see the
3379      world at boot level, then up with the flying things – you think
3380      they're owls. No – they're cameras and bombs. It's all the same
3381      strategy, what they have,' says Andy.
3382      'I won't dig in those guys' empty holes,' I say. 'I want big
3383      gestures, laughter with a paint moustache, hands on my knee, hands
3384      soft and pale as butter, under the table...'
3385      'Get used to brown hands,' says Andy sharply. 'Do you hold the
3386      quiddity of all you've seen? No, naturally not. It all moved on in
3387      spirals, it spun away like sugar. Holes in the ground – hold on to
3388      them – they're solid, silent and still.'
3389      'It's all negative. I see the whole scenario,' I say. 'Me, the
3390      indigenous lover, the extended family, some in the 8s, some the
3391      18s. Betrayals, shootouts. Riches found. Guys hired – some steal
3392      and some defer. The bugs you eat, the clawmarks round your ears –
3393      those begin to weigh, your gut degenerates. There's more riches,
3394      less work more luck, and it's paper that you buy and sell, and more
3395      slick guys who cheat and flatter, more ceremonies, old guys who
3396      have dull funerals far far away, and guys that hate you smarming
3397      up...'
3398      'You don't want to be a loser, though,' says Andy.
3399      'It all comes from rubbing up,' I say, irritated, then annoyed.
3400      'Things, people. Caroming off: your balls against the others.' Like
3401      toads in mating mode, you clamber up, over the viscid backs.
3402      You're quite anonymous, you've the same blunt nose and wriggling
3403      paws as all the rest. But for the pile, you'd just be croaking solitary
3404      in the slime. Friends: do they hoist you up? You hope they're
3405      nonces, strangenesses, out of the game... They pall. You the albino,
3406      Andy; Icaro with bleached hair and peeling scalp, the eyebrows
3407      blackened like moustaches...'
3408      'That's from his trip,' says Andy, backing off.

3409 'I'll do it all myself,' I say. 'I don't need animals, hungry and
3410 peering in, and gangs that prowl. Paying percentages! I know where
3411 I am making for. Imagine, if you can – the crowd, some in rags and
3412 some in ermine tails, they cry, '*Slava, slava*' – the bells are going
3413 mad, the clappers glow a revolutionary red. It's Stalin! Stalin! Here
3414 he comes, pushing through the crowd, alone, the stiff green cape,
3415 pen in one hand, the other holds a paperweight. He's here before
3416 us, and the crowd moves back. Then – what?'
3417     I pause, although I know what's coming next. 'He sings,' I say.
3418 'It is his moment, and he knows. It is the summit, and he sings.
3419 Solo, of course.'
3420     'What does he sing?' asks Andy, 'And what about those guys
3421 behind him?'
3422     'The chorus? That's what they are, that's what they do.
3423 Acclaim.They don't sing so well. You need to do things by
3424 yourself, know when exactly is the time. What does he sing? It
3425 doesn't matter much: there's something of the "Song of the
3426 Forests", I should say.'
3427     'There's an audience,' Andy says, 'soaking in or spitting out.'
3428     'No, Andy, that's not it,' I say. 'You're solo, or your chorus.
3429 There is nothing else. No audience, no booking, tickets, and no
3430 money back.'
3431     'OK,' he says, 'saving from extinction. Striking it rich – neither
3432 attracts?'
3433     'Those are normal. Extinction always happens – delaying it...
3434 that too. It's imperceptible. Wealth – exactly similar.'
3435     'There's a new kind of gathering,' Andy says. 'You should go.
3436 There's no agenda. Now, there's no marriages, people live too long.
3437 Death is bland and dull, you long for it – perfunctory the funeral...
3438 Someone nominates a festa every day – each creed, a celebration,
3439 there's commemoration constant, no rejoicing.. the glorying days –
3440 they sail above, like swans, the honking breaks your sleep. So –
3441 don't count the rites. Get together – maybe something happens,
3442 maybe not.'
3443     It's a variation. A potlatch with nothing – maybe no one – in the
3444 pot. Old guys, in a clump, standing on a platform, drooping like
3445 tallow candles. Each one full of wisdom, each wisdom is the same
3446 and incommunicable. No train's expected on the platform.
3447     'I had a partner once,' I say. 'I invented dialogue for her – that
3448 she was kidnapped and released, or killed. I never heard from her.'
3449 I'm making party talk, jollying up someone who says:

3450  'These gatherings are useful for confessions. Once it was
3451  deciding if to go to war. Now – that just happens. That's much
3452  easier.'
3453      'Oh,' I say, 'don't give any weight to anything. You always
3454  meet up with people you could travel with, and then they disappear
3455  as well. You never know their names. It's to show you're in a
3456  species,' I tell her.
3457      'My name's Aisha,' Aisha says. 'And yours is Vince, a chain
3458  around your leg.'
3459      'All these feckless people here – they could decide to rampage
3460  out and burn some houses, Aisha,' I say. The thought excites, the
3461  possibility – it rouses me.
3462      'People pair off,' she says, 'because they see the animals.
3463  especially the birds. But really... If you live close to a desert, you
3464  lose a lot of people there. Forests too. And railway lines, cities.'
3465      Then – there's gangs, armies, occupiers. There's no problem
3466  losing what's encumbering.
3467      'All the excitement, then the boredom – it distracts,' says Aisha.
3468  'It's better doing what you have to do, not exchanging names.'
3469      'What I have to do,' I say, 'I do it, eyes shut. Humming
3470  something else.'
3471      'That's wrong,' says Aisha. 'All lives are tragedies, of course –
3472  and that's banal. The thing is – your life's your story. You can give
3473  it structure, decide who are the characters, the plot. You step on
3474  that boat, punch out that guy. How does it hang? Control's the
3475  thing. Beware the horses, Vince – they eat your cash like hay. Sex?
3476  You're not a master: best leave it out.'
3477      'Who's the story for?' I ask, though I know quite well...
3478      'Oh, the story's yours,' she says. 'No one is interested in any tale
3479  except their own.'
3480      'You might give a hand,' I say. 'Be good, be generous. A joke?'
3481      'All that is up to you,' says Aisha. 'If you do an epic, be sure
3482  there's someone literate at hand, to write or chisel.'
3483      'But...' I say.
3484      'I know,' says Aisha. 'My grandfather used to sing the song –
3485  "Arise, ye prisoners of starvation, arise, ye wretched of the earth..."
3486  The thing is to give your story a shape, so you can go back over –
3487  have a laugh, an honest tear, a frisson of regret. Then...'
3488
3489                              *
3490

3491 'You're right, Andy,' I say. 'Those gatherings are old style.
3492 Romantic, like the té dansant. She stole my jacket.'
3493      'A good one?' he asks.
3494      'I should say so,' I say.
3495      'Some people want to drive a Merc and live in a hut. They call it
3496 culture, but it's just a choice,' he says. 'A coat – you can't get far in
3497 that.'
3498      'All this talk – it doesn't fit my coat. It was padded, for a
3499 lineman.'
3500      We're both annoyed. 'What annoys me most,' I say. 'Apart from
3501 the cold – is the trick itself, the oldest. Someone confides, proposes
3502 a long voyage that may resolve everything, or give details and
3503 prospects you live with the rest of your life ... and it's about
3504 something else. The story that you hear comes louder than the story
3505 that is really just to lift your jacket.'
3506      'Yes,' says Andy. 'That you fell for that – of course, it's chance,
3507 not choice, so you suppose – it makes me wonder if I'm doing right
3508 to keep on bearing with you, putting up with closeness?'
3509      'Fuck you, Andy,' I say. 'The jacket didn't want to get liberated,
3510 passed on to someone's lover.'
3511      'Maybe she thought it was owed to her – the scam, having to tell
3512 the story, use the language, sticking with all those people – all
3513 waiting for some synergy,' he says.
3514      'I'll take the mischance as a message, Andy,' I say. 'If you've no
3515 coat – it means 'get nearer to the sun'. Not climbing hills: going
3516 down south, where there's faith and poverty.'
3517      'You're slick,' says Andy, not approving. 'Like an empty pan.
3518 But – if there's still some warmth inside...'
3519      'Yes, Andy,' I say, breaking off with him. 'Maybe you can cook
3520 your egg. Aisha told me how we struggle up the hill, the crest is
3521 mist, and up and up – the view will be superb, our legs grow weak,
3522 our lungs dry up, two apricots, we lie down with the rest – the air is
3523 thin, we fight for it, there's knives and baseball bats brought out
3524 That's it, the mystery. White light ahead.'
3525      'What mystery?' he asks.
3526      'How we all got on the hill, and thought there was another side,
3527 a view, our legs would take us up – seeing the bones stacked up, we
3528 might have guessed. That is the mystery, my dear old stupid
3529 friend,' I say.
3530      'Well,' says Andy, 'out you go!' He opens the door, like to let a
3531 cat out, nothing in.

3532   'It's snowing,' I say.
3533   'It could be rice,' he says. 'Hold out your hands, thumb and
3534   forefinger together.'

3535
3536                                    *
3537
3538   Soon, there's sixteen of us, in the snow. Striding along, of every
3539   sex, thinking about it, us and ours – sex, our faces first white with
3540   the frost, then black, mincing, floundering as if we're on the
3541   catwalk in our fashion heels. On our heads, like mushroom caps,
3542   straw hats woven tight, you see stoneturners wear them, in Japan.
3543   We're dressed for sharper worlds than this. Ahead of me – a guy
3544   bearing a long pole, a shorter hook, shiny, collectable – the long
3545   stick jigs the trolley back on the wires, the hook's for shifting
3546   points so the tram can follow its true destiny. We're all thrown out
3547   of somewhere, a useless trade encysted in our hands – gluers and
3548   tackers, makers of jet jewellery, solderers, stuffers of fine sailfish...
3549   'Don't just tramp,' shouts Steve beside me – 'Sing! Sing every
3550   song, they'll come out to feed us, like we were the birds...' and so
3551   we do. Everything is possible.
3552   We lose some mates – we stride along, our long white bodies,
3553   black faces. 'We are the best,' we shout, we who are left. The snow
3554   falls like a curtain – you could only see our heads, the snow our
3555   bed, our sea. We swim, we paddle.
3556   'You must believe,' shouts Steve. 'This is how we evolve. In
3557   equations, in the earth, the sun, the twist divine – that little extra
3558   turn you give the key – the lock is free, the extra twiddle's for some
3559   divinity. Or – it invokes the spirit in a metal... salutes a privacy, an
3560   ingenuity... For sure – on every planet God has left not sons alone,
3561   but twins... And off they've gone, our comrades, looking for the
3562   lost twin daughter, ancient as the seas, bearing up our luminescent
3563   skiffs, our fishing ferries plunging down, our slaves, our
3564   contraband, our oils, our motors–'
3565   'Steve,' I shout. 'We must avoid the drift. If we go down, we'll
3566   need to wait for spring...' But on he talks, '...our motors ...
3567   evolution...'
3568   'We should have been four,' I say. 'But we're just two, our best
3569   two frozen out, or stumbled off, consumed by the beasts I love –
3570   who can keep track? Or – gone underneath the ice. Black shrimp-
3571   eyes fixed and sideways...'

3572    'Ours are the tropics, Vince,' says Steve. 'Everybody knows
3573    they're sad – between the cancer and the goat with pointy horns.
3574    What do you expect? Everybody lives in huts and tents...'
3575         'I don't know you, Steve,' I say. We're in the melt – a pink,
3576    anonymous. The black, the white – gone somewhere, invisible.
3577    This was our highest moment. What were we going to do, we
3578    sixteen? Maybe the other twelve – maybe they managed whatever it
3579    was, and became famous without belonging to a club, ranged in a
3580    totem. Maybe Steve has the rich interior life I don't have time for in
3581    myself, being so occupied with dealing with him, and Andy, getting
3582    a job, not wanting it.
3583         'I work for your boss,' he says. 'To find new things, you need
3584    laboratories. Just sitting here amid the mud – you don't discover
3585    anything. You need a guy who leads, with cash...'
3586         'No, no,' I say. 'I'd quit.'
3587         'The boss is like the ancient guy who burnt,' says Steve. 'Dry
3588    crusts against the flames. One side's philanthropy, the other – well,
3589    he makes us skip. You'll see.'
3590         'No one has two sides,' I say. 'We're one-dimensional – or else
3591    we wouldn't stick, we'd tumble on the floor.'
3592         'We have come through,' says Steve. 'People invented what
3593    we've just experienced, made it a metaphor, an epic. See – there
3594    was no need. It's real. We're pink again, no ash, no clinker. Here's
3595    your payoff – your boss's conscience,' and he puts a thin envelope
3596    inside my shirt. 'I'm a scientist,' he says. 'My job with you is done.
3597    Find a tower of the winds, and listen to them. Pay the rent. Snuff in
3598    the air. Suppose you were up there, looking down on roofs, gliding,
3599    spiralling up and down, waiting for the dead to be laid out for you...
3600    Aren't you better off? Just as you are. You'll only need an oil lamp,
3601    yellow light to match that old French paper, those yellow mysteries.
3602    They're piled up on the stalls. You can't understand the words ...
3603    but there are murders constantly, then justice. In not too many
3604    pages. Go to bed, dream of pink dawns.'
3605         Steve's another genius. I admire him – there's nothing else to
3606    say. I say,
3607         'All the people here – they come, like us, from somewhere else.
3608    You forget, or else you cry all day. Driven out – by friends – for
3609    sure, no one cares about that tale. Armies, heretics, the drought –
3610    that makes news, but no one cares that much. The moving on.
3611    That's normal. Do you wander, do you stick? They say that's the
3612    crucial point ... the species, sedentary or nomad. It doesn't work

3613  that way, of course. Everybody wanders, from Summer palace to
3614  the Winter one, Paris–Moscow and then back, and nomads build
3615  their cities, start collecting tax. Then, there's thinking about
3616  abstracts. Humans, they say, are the only ones that think of things
3617  not there... and yet – humans are artisans, making things that
3618  animals have never thought of, can't handle with their paws and
3619  scales – that's why the bigger beasts lie around: they muse all day,
3620  on things that aren't...'
3621       Steve bustles off, into the market. Red hot peppers, purges, stuff
3622  that makes you sneeze. 'I have to find a thing...' he says. He's
3623  never seen again – it's not a kidnap, I'm quite sure.
3624
3625                                    *
3626
3627  In the room I rented, there's a woman, fingering my stuff.
3628  'Othmar's gone to mosque,' she says, 'I'm sure he will be back.'
3629       'He's not from here,' I say.
3630       'He converted when he found me. He teaches German – that's
3631  where they all want to go. Then he gives their names to the police,'
3632  she says.
3633       'I don't know any German,' I tell her.
3634       There's little for me here. I don't wait for Othmar to return.
3635       They all drive fast here in this town.
3636       In the market, there's some very rich. They'll likely lose their
3637  cash. The very poor – where will they land? Do they hope to pick it
3638  up, the cash, as it goes falling from above?
3639       They're from here, and not. I don't believe in that, travelling and
3640  staying still. I don't believe in mystic painting, nor the holy wall
3641  where one day it might appear to me, nor in sages, nor in studying
3642  and coming up with vacant skins. Once it was here, now it's utterly
3643  gone, gone utterly. I don't believe it, not at all, but it's missing.
3644  Even if it never was, it can still be missed.
3645       The little guys – they started all the trouble here, wanting a
3646  looser life. Poor little guys? Who beleves that. Poor guys never did
3647  anything here. So – the little ones began it all, and the big guys
3648  stopped it. If you want to believe something really bad – you can
3649  believe that. Everything's belief, all made up – epics, revelations,
3650  and equations – we forget what the blind poet said last night,
3651  tonight we sit around the fire and hear it all again.
3652       It's hard to know ... where's best: maybe a small country, three
3653  or four people, abstemious. I could be a soldier there, irregular. The

3654     best kind, keeping out of trouble, with no penalties for skiving off.
3655     A tailor or a sailor? – there's periods of beggardom, and you need
3656     to sew the canvas bags. Rich man, poor man – as you walk along,
3657     you're neither. Nothing here to steal – just clothes dumped by the
3658     track, never a whole person left inside, curved bones, too twisted to
3659     be arms or legs.
3660          Ahead, there's a couple, stumbling along.
3661          Gennaro and Maya Reza: 'We make up names so's when we
3662     arrive,' Gennaro says. 'We'll fit right in.' We walk along together.
3663          'When we're somewhere else,' says Maya, 'we'll think back to
3664     this awful place, everything will glow, there'll be eternal festa.
3665     Cousins and aunts, our children, making honey all together,
3666     dancing before the hive.'
3667          'Why are you leaving?' Gennaro asks me. 'The war? The
3668     poverty?'
3669          'It's because I don't speak German,' I say. They stare. 'And all
3670     the rest. Everything you wouldn't want to know firsthand.'
3671          'With us,' Gennaro says, 'it is the fear.'
3672          'Oh,' I say, 'I don't listen to what they say. I don't watch what
3673     they do – don't look up, or down. Those curved bones – I'm sure
3674     they never have been straight.'
3675          'Ah,' Maya says, 'it's the fear that makes them curve.'
3676          'The fear,' I say. 'Is why no one wants you in, when you have
3677     got there. The fear's a plague.'
3678          'Families should help,' Gennaro says. 'But – they make it
3679     worse.'
3680          'You should avoid those people who have ghosts,' I say,
3681     thinking of Rodney Hawkett, burnt to toast. Exalting, we all danced
3682     around... My boss – full of rancour, his eyes – two pills dissolving:
3683     storing the anger in his gut, elbows asplay that can burst a gate, set
3684     you running down the street, screams stream out of every hole in
3685     you, you're kicking in the doors, what's compressed is red and
3686     yellow, foamed in spate, a fountain over everything. Out it roars
3687     like writers' crap on walls – 'Blast' 'Magic wood', 'Frack'. Not
3688     knowing where he wants to finish up – despising the rich, the guys
3689     like him. How to spend his cash? Founding museums, collecting
3690     stuff like it was bets on greyhounds. Buy stuff, buy titles – hating it
3691     all, all's a mantra, quite beyond you... Maybe dead, he plans, he'll
3692     enter in your arse and eat you up and leave the shell...
3693          'It's the fear,' Gennaro says. 'You may think it's something else.
3694     It's in you like a vine, a white blind eel. It makes your legs go

3695     pippety-pop. You have it worse than us – from friends and enemies
3696     – all the crusading axmen, all the holy warriors, the jailers, the
3697     warders in intelligence, wearing their gowns and pointy hats.'
3698          'Don't be afraid of me,' says Maya, holding on to me, letting me
3699     inside her eyes: 'I'll keep you company, and I won't keep you
3700     safe.'
3701          'I trust you, Maya,' I lie to her. 'We're nearly where we want to
3702     be. No one is interested in us. We're just poor guys – can't fight or
3703     work, valueless, along this track...'
3704          'There'll be a border. Everyone comes here – to occupy. I guess
3705     there's money in it. There's no way you can escape,' Gennaro says,
3706     pushing us along. 'There's always aeroplanes scouting. I guess they
3707     see us. We'll go to where they come from – that way, we'll be
3708     safe.'
3709          He whispers to me, 'I don't trust Maya. Going somewhere else –
3710     it's the first step away from me.'
3711          'Do you care, Gennaro?' I ask.
3712          'It's a little thing, like they keep on happening to everyone,' he
3713     says. 'It's when they pick you out. You're standing in the crowd –
3714     and then the finger points, you've to be the hangman, or the
3715     corporal, or the guy with his eye in a sling,' and he laughs – we
3716     both do. It's an old expression.
3717          Up ahead, there's a low bar: The Edge, it says. 'If you know it's
3718     a low bar,' Maya says, 'you'll never get on in your life.'
3719          Gennaro says, 'That's true – if you've ever gone in one – you're
3720     ashes. Floating dregs.'
3721          'If it's for the border guards,' I say, 'they'll for sure be heretics,
3722     and there's alcohol.'
3723          We three go in. There is alcohol. Maybe some of our twelve are
3724     sat there, in the shadows, back from their poles ... on theirs, there's
3725     dancers, there's an angry stripper too, I hope she doesn't fake her
3726     rage – this stew needs peppering up.
3727          'Hey!' I say, 'I ought not to be here. It's trivial – but if I drink –
3728     short life to come. You must choose to have one: there's *Vita* in
3729     that bottle, you can drink it long or short. A short – like if you want
3730     to live – a mayfly: devoted to good or bad. Which – good or bad –
3731     it's quite indifferent. Long lives – there isn't one between us here.
3732     That's all about the flow to a conclusion – always a
3733     disappointment.'
3734          The guards keep people in. Other guards – they keep them out.

3735    This guard's called Rocco – like his mates, he's chosen a brief
3736    life he thinks is good for him, for everyone.
3737        'Your friends,' he says to me, 'they have no hope.'
3738        'I had suspected that,' I say. 'But – all they want's to walk on,
3739    ahead. Hope's abandoned. Movement is the thing...'
3740        'You seem a gent,' says Rocco, feeling for the cash tucked in my
3741    shirt, quite playfully. 'You could be a no-man, your own land
3742    ahead. Your friends – they have the fear. Not wanted here or there
3743    – it's the infection, terror, that we're told not to let in. Or out.'
3744        'Gennaro's too old to be a soldier, Rocco,' I say.
3745        'That's exactly what we need,' says Rocco, 'old soldiers. They
3746    can occupy before they die. There's cities going empty – others
3747    that's too full. Shift people round. Equality, that's what we need.
3748    When that comes, we'll take Maya too.'
3749        'Oh, come,' I say. 'It's not just soldiers live in towns. Besides,
3750    you do control from far away, intelligence, in quantity. Then
3751    there's the baking, butchery...'
3752        'You remember butchery from Rodney Hawkett time,' Rocco
3753    laughs. 'No, Gennaro's useful. You're useful too – in quite a
3754    different way. You draw the maps, you choose the presidents, talk
3755    to your foreign friends, ally with them. You and your boss decide
3756    the lot. Ration the water. Then – there's the sun. You keep us
3757    worshipping indoors, going to vote, all that – but – we should
3758    prefer to start again, take off our clothes, run in the burning sun,
3759    take back our rightful colors, charcoal twiglets running through the
3760    midday heat... You, you keep us in the modern way. Work. Flying
3761    all enclosed as if you're on the ground...'
3762        There's drumming now – a guy from Senegal: the stripper's
3763    stripped – she dances on, puts back her clothes the wrong way up.
3764    We drink our *Vita*, and we slap our knees and click our heels –
3765    don't feel the pain. We kick out with our legs, the arms fly round –
3766    those, we can't feel. Love. Ah! Love. How we would make it, feel
3767    it in the blood, make it hum and wheeze, if only brain would
3768    animate our genitals...
3769        'Come, come with me,' I whisper to Maya. 'We'll live in no
3770    man's land... Pass the fence, the ditch...'
3771        'You're a zero to me,' Maya says. 'But, of course.'
3772        'See the city, where we'd live, down there,' I say, 'where you
3773    can hear the donkeys bray. Gennaro could go round in the
3774    evenings, light every soft yellow lamp that hangs there like a
3775    lemon, ripe and sweet...'

3776　'Yes, yes,' Maya says. 'Lying on the roof, the stars clustered up
3777　there like flocks,' and maybe she weeps. 'It could be Gennaro's
3778　home. But – it's not my city. I'm not welcome there. They'd know
3779　me from my name.'
3780　　I drink more *Vita*. 'It's banal, Maya,' I say. 'Talking of no man's
3781　land, of whole cities there... Cities are all like that – there is no
3782　welcome, and we love them for it...'
3783　　'No, no,' Maya says, 'Take me away with you, far far away, and
3784　you – turn into someone else.'
3785　　'I'll reason with Rocco,' I say. 'Shunt me towards him.'
3786　　'There is no universal reason, clean, without vibrato,' Rocco
3787　says. 'There is nothing universal except the universe. Gas and
3788　stones. Lots of nothing. To reason, there is a ceiling, quite
3789　impenetrable – call it God, or happenstance, your pot on the fire,
3790　bribe in your pants... That serves to get you through the day and
3791　round the corner. The rest – is dreams of luxury. My weapon is
3792　your ceiling...'
3793　　And it's true – I've fallen and I'm wedged here beneath the
3794　bench, my ceiling – most hems are dirty, mostly guys aren't
3795　wearing socks. 'Oh help me up,' I try to shout – but if I'm up, I
3796　might fall down again, I need a peg, a glue, more hands, a shanty or
3797　a prayer.
3798　　'Leave him be,' Gennaro says. 'He's overdone the *Vita*. We'll
3799　find another crossing, climb the fence.'
3800　　'No,' Rocco says, 'It's too late for that. You can't just live in
3801　places, without a history, a past, a future.'
3802　　'You can't keep tabs on everyone,' I say.
3803　　'Of course we can,' says Rocco. 'That's what your money's for.
3804　Who'll pay our tab? You! And where've you been? You blabbed
3805　about Rodney Hawkett – that's a decease. And all the rest? Are you
3806　responsible? Friends disappeared... Now – here comes the tab...'
3807　　'You took my cash already, friend,' I say. 'Before you ask – it
3808　was a present from my boss. For showing him his aspirations were
3809　all vanity.'
3810　　'Ha!' Rocco shouts. 'You're out to be the clever sort – that we
3811　don't want. We live by vanity – we don't like folks that's cleverer
3812　than us... They put themselves on wrong sides, and won't be argued
3813　with...'
3814　　He kisses me on the top of my head. They bring the tab. *Vita* –
3815　even when it's cut to make it *Aquavit*, is costly here.

3816    'The more we keep you simmering, the more you think of
3817    crime,' says Rocco. 'Yours, ours. You're angry now...'
3818        'No, Rocco,' I say. 'I'm still trekking to my happy place.'
3819        They laugh. Maya says, 'Gennaro, of course I love you. Giving
3820    you up, going with someone else – would add a poignancy, make it
3821    a broader theme...'
3822        'It isn't in the contract,' Gennaro says.
3823        'Did I hear "the dance before the hive"?' shouts Rocco: 'I'm the
3824    gatekeeper! Mine's the transition – place to place, not time to time.
3825    Who'll push up that ceiling with a show? Berlin in the Eighties?
3826    Kick 'em up – higher and higher, up the ceiling goes, into the blue
3827    ... ignorance or innocence? Let's lose them both. Up on the stage...'
3828
3829                                    *
3830
3831        'Can't you walk now?' Maya asks. 'This box is heavy, and the
3832    wheels have fallen off.'
3833        'I'm terminally ill,' I say: I'm lying here, spilled from my cart.
3834    'That *Vita* – it's killing me. But... I can't walk. My shoes? Oh no...'
3835        'You didn't do a perfect strip,' Gennaro says. 'You started with
3836    your boots – it stopped the show – your ignorance and innocence
3837    had stashed your savings there...'
3838        'My cash reserve!' I say. 'It fluttered out like doves, I bet.'
3839        'Some thought you had a belt of gold,' says Maya. 'Your nudity
3840    made us dread – we didn't pry. A belt of chastity, your boss had
3841    maybe had it forged and fastened on. It takes the fire to get it off,
3842    then you are rightly done – and roasted too.'
3843        'It's true,' I say. 'My boss had them made for loyalty. But – I
3844    betrayed. I never even saw the smith, the hammer and the fire. Of
3845    course, that Hawkett was a platinum man, you'd need to melt him
3846    in the fire to judge his worth. They're all like that, the real big
3847    guys... As good as gold and twice as valuable...' I prattle on.
3848    Gennaro says, 'Hey! We're off, through this fence, Maya and me.
3849    You'll find some boots, if you survive. The army has them – you
3850    could join...'
3851        They're gone. My box is wedged between the here and there.
3852    Maya and Gennaro scuttle through the maize, their rich inner lives,
3853    unexplored, tiny white flags like rabbits' scuts, undulating as they
3854    run. I'm unsure – do I want the here or there? What did I say when
3855    I took off my shoes? I hear Maya, shouting back:

3856 'A discourse worthy of the best. You're truly Vince the prince!
3857 If you had subjects, you'd be loved – but you spoke of the objects –
3858 the nebulae, the universe – then what? When it ends? Will the
3859 purpose be revealed? And – should we add some goodness to our
3860 bad, or are we just ephemeral, sad beasts who've lost our tail and
3861 claws and found some awful substitutes? Faith in science,
3862 worshipping the sun, cherishing the beetles, remembering the dance
3863 – all was brought out, dear Vince. And then – the denouement. The
3864 golden wave! Your shoes, your clogs – the bills you sprinkled out
3865 like amber rain, soaking the lot of us – and you, a poor man, drunk
3866 and poisoned with the *Aquavit* – your inner life, turned inside out
3867 like dirty pants to make them look like clean... You never said you
3868 loved me, Vince, but I'll remember...'
3869 And she's gone. I didn't love her, though that's the story that
3870 resounds. And now I'm stuck, abandoned... At least I kept on my
3871 socks, in them a further stash of cash convertible – the stuff of
3872 dreams, that buys you tickets for the wheel...
3873 'You were Silenus...' she shouts back, fading out.
3874
3875                                    *
3876
3877 'We want people who can garrison,' says the sergeant, the recruiter
3878 – Rocco or his brother. 'When you occupy a place, first you must
3879 cut out the doubtful ones. It's about right people in the right space.'
3880 'That's obvious,' I say. 'Who wouldn't want that?'
3881 Sure I want that, and I want a pair of boots. 'I was in the fire
3882 service,' I say.
3883 'That reference to Silenus,' says the soldier. 'That marks her.
3884 Where she was – that's silly talk. Where she's going – they'll see
3885 she's different. She'll thieve. You mustn't do that.'
3886 'I don't believe in Silenus,' I say. 'There's a trace of hedonism
3887 about me, that is all. And I'm suffering for it.'
3888 'That's good,' says the sergeant. 'We're not beasts. We're not
3889 shod,' he laughs. 'Not by smiths. Your boots are over there.'
3890 He kisses me on the top of my head: 'We'll cover you,' he says.
3891 'Your fears, doubts, anger. But don't desert, we'll shoot you.'
3892 'Must I take an oath?' I ask.
3893 'If you like,' he says. 'But it sounds like last century. Just put on
3894 your boots and try to save your pay.'
3895 I musn't desert, I tell myself. 'I'll go and pick some mushrooms
3896 in the forest,' I tell him, Rocco, or his brother – 'For our lads' soup.

3897   There's a mystery in a mushroom... It'll help them decide who they
3898 want in and out.'
3899     The sergeant winks. 'A good stew,' he says. 'Proof's you against
3900 stones getting thrown. Better than *Vita* – that makes you feel bad.'
3901     The friendly forest, the faces on the trunks that wink, the
3902 branches sweeping down, shading me as I run – these wonderful
3903 boots: sleek as a fox – I run. There's a hole in the fence. Maybe
3904 they'll keep putting cash on my paybook, maybe I'll get medals. A
3905 band for my funeral.
3906     As I run, I grab some mushrooms – down they go! I might join
3907 the Chinese army, with my skills acquired – go see the shamans –
3908 and I fly! Like Icarus! Over the ditch, the minefield – a noble arc –
3909 I flap my wings – no, it's not feathers, it's my mushroom power.
3910 Imagine – an army with battalions of naked men in flight!
3911     But – do I want to spread the story round? The mystery becomes
3912 banal... There'd soon be millions in the air, like dragonflies, in
3913 armed and unarmed combat – the fields strewn with the throbbing
3914 bodies tumbled down – a new dimension... Migrating populations –
3915 flailing off to warmer winters, blacking out the midnight suns,
3916 building their nest on Notre Dame, an evening oratorio as flocks fly
3917 back to bed from picking fruit and berrying in the woods... Angel
3918 cities, everywhere.
3919     You come down – it's not the sun melts you, not your
3920 presumption: your body's used up all the mushroom juice. Icarus –
3921 poor unlucky soul – a stall! the blue above, the blue beneath.
3922 There's no way out. He should have fallen up, upward in the sky.
3923 The sky that should be black. Dirt makes it blue. Make a splash –
3924 you might be saved...
3925     I land quite gently in a tree. This place: it feels like a small
3926 country. I've met the leaders leading everywhere. Power over one
3927 person – you feel it all, intense. Power over a million – there is no
3928 kick, no fun, no prick. The people groan and cheer, suffer and hate
3929 – you don't. You needn't. Others will do it all and live with it – the
3930 struggle. Power over twenty guys – just strife and ridicule: think of
3931 it – sex over twenty guys – what would that mean? It wouldn't,
3932 surely, be the sex you'd pant or pay for... Or – you might ingratiate
3933 yourself, win their vows, their interest. 'Service before everything'
3934 – you, under everybody else. Power – hallucination, panic, strut and
3935 reticence: whatever helps to make it work.

| | |
|---|---|
| 3936 | There's a castle, and beside – a bigger building, no crenellations; |
| 3937 | that shows you've conquered, don't need the castle now. |
| 3938 | Dishonoured people at their desks. |
| 3939 | Inside the curious big building, there's guys like Rocco in the |
| 3940 | corridors, stopping their chatter when they stare at me. |
| 3941 | 'Maya Reza,' I ask. 'Just to see how she is. She was independent |
| 3942 | – couldn't afford a trafficking.' |
| 3943 | 'Oh,' says the guy, 'we don't take names. Those change – it's |
| 3944 | kinder not to write them down. It's better that the folks just |
| 3945 | disappear. It's natural: some – because you didn't care. Some want |
| 3946 | to disappear. Some, most, perhaps, just aren't there any more. It's |
| 3947 | better, that she can't be found.' |
| 3948 | 'I know,' I say. 'It happens all around me. People come and go. |
| 3949 | There's not so much that you can do. It goes on so.' |
| 3950 | 'We're perishable,' says the guy. He takes a shine to me. Not to |
| 3951 | Maya, he's no idea about her. We laugh: me – because a 'shine' – |
| 3952 | that's an old expression. I don't know what's funny in his mind. |
| 3953 | 'You know – if you've no address – they'll have gone thieving. |
| 3954 | There's nothing else, unless you're handy,' says the guy. There's |
| 3955 | another expression, makes you laugh. Cry, if you're the nostalgic |
| 3956 | type. |
| 3957 | 'If you've an interest of a general kind, in people and what |
| 3958 | happens to them,' the guy goes on. 'You could make it a career. All |
| 3959 | the people – who knows what they did, where they've gone ... you |
| 3960 | could look for them. Publish your search. We – don't keep a |
| 3961 | record.' |
| 3962 | That's the end. |
| 3963 | He says, 'You seem an important guy. Made yourself a soldier |
| 3964 | too – you're a weapon! That was noble.' |
| 3965 | 'Oh yes,' I say. 'I work too with a big boss,' and I give the |
| 3966 | name. 'I deputise for him. I'm his philosopher. And – I'm a protégé |
| 3967 | of Rodney Hawkett, tragically melted down.' |
| 3968 | The guy says, 'And Maya? A lover? Terrorist, maybe.' |
| 3969 | 'Of course I loved her, like we ought,' I say. 'She could be |
| 3970 | angry. Docile too. I never went inside her inner life.' |
| 3971 | 'The cops will take a note,' he says. 'Of her. Your snitching on |
| 3972 | her – that makes sense, if you're quite prominent, the type who |
| 3973 | sticks around, and gives particulars. We'll find her – and you too...' |
| 3974 | I leave him an address – the park where there's the wheel. 'Some |
| 3975 | fifty hectares, where you can amuse yourself, at any time,' I say. |
| 3976 | 'I'll welcome you.' |

3977 'Thanks for the invite,' says the guy. 'It's a commitment. Both
3978 of us...'
3979 He takes a book, a gilded cover: in his other hand – an orb, a
3980 globe. 'If you should let me down,' he says, 'here's an agreement,
3981 signed by everyone. It's good for all the planet, here in my hand, in
3982 miniature. We'll chase you round it, if you fall short and wanting.
3983 Now – gaze at this wall!'
3984 It's light and dark: a childish scrawl of blob and blur. 'The
3985 universe,' he says. 'Dawn and night. You fly, you spread your
3986 wings, you take a ship – anywhere and everywhere. We'll hunt you
3987 down, wherever you hide out and raise your shabby flag.'
3988 'I understand,' I say. 'But – that address I gave – it does exist.
3989 You good – your best – time awaits you there.'
3990 He puts away his orb, his book in every tongue... He switches
3991 off the wall. He waves me to the door.
3992 The flying, my fall – mushrooms don't come in.
3993 I've done a foolish thing.
3994
3995 *
3996
3997 'Oh no,' says Andy. 'You're back. No – a life's not lived like this.
3998 "Decisive interventions", that was to be the aim. Besides, there's
3999 people looking for you. You gave that name they say it can't exist:
4000 "Maya". Can't be found, not on a list.'
4001 'Maybe she's gone underground,' I say.
4002 'Then it's murder – not mass murder', Andy says. He's much
4003 relieved.
4004 'Maybe I got things wrong,' I say. 'It's always possible.'
4005 'There's the Hawkett legacy,' says Andy. 'Yours, since you
4006 were on the scene, the fire. It's treasure trove.'
4007 'I was getting short,' I say, pulling myself up.
4008 'No, no,' says Andy. 'Not cash. People. "Decisive intervention"
4009 – so, you decide. Maybe – have a dream that's realer than the real
4010 again – transform it all. Hawkett – he's left you people who're in
4011 debt to him, or that he owed. Ready for anything.'
4012
4013 *
4014
4015 'I can free you from Andy,' says the lady. 'Him and Icaro, two
4016 leaches, living off each other's blood.'

4017 'And my team?' I ask. 'Jazz dancers, monocyclists, poodle
4018 trainers. Renderers, web-makers...'
4019 'All of that and much much more,' she says. 'Too bad there's no
4020 bikers. I do love a thuggy type...'
4021 I'm amazed, I gaze... 'Yes, dear,' says the lady. 'It's a shift. The
4022 best ladies wore them once. And – watch this pin.' It seems to hold
4023 her knickers to a belly-band. Her body's very bony-thin and very
4024 round, in parts. That aspect's not worth considering...
4025 'You didn't do too well in tests of action, nor humanity,' she
4026 says. 'Right down the middle. Norm: should be your name, though
4027 Vince is bad enough... Maybe your forte should be politics. But
4028 your teeth are grey. Go see the dinosaurs – they had a smile that
4029 dentists couldn't chip away. You need a grin, but not when you
4030 inspect your troops – there's always someone making history, a
4031 bullet in the chamber, then in you...'
4032 'You've thought it out,' I say.
4033 'Oh yes,' she rushes in, 'it's all about the paintings, dear.'
4034 'Yes,' I say, 'I've seen the movies – the Duce, in the chapel,
4035 finishing off the sketch. Oh dear – the colours! Stalin in the
4036 monastery, the frescoes ... and poor Eisenstein, the criticism ... did
4037 him no good. So, they say, Stalin rubbed it all out, the painting, the
4038 building – a perfectionist – his good side...' We pause, maybe in
4039 awe.
4040 'I thought it was the style,' I say, 'not the execution.
4041 Romanticism, writing it all down, thinking there would be a future.
4042 All that stuff.'
4043 'Look,' she says, 'I've thought it out, I don't need commentary.
4044 Come home with me, on the way you'll think about having sex,
4045 when we arrive, we'll toss for it. Remember – once you've had it
4046 with another – it's hard to fantasise. Hope's better deferred, you
4047 know.'
4048 'The guys I knew – Andy, Steve – what were they? What
4049 becomes of them?'
4050 'Just call me Lady Bea. That's short for everything that starts
4051 with "B" – the lady means I'm not a queen,' and she laughs. 'Andy
4052 loved your emptiness. He thought he could fill you up. Steve – you
4053 lost the other pilgrims. Then the snow – it melted off your boots –
4054 the boots you lost, with all your cash, being ungirdled in the pub...'
4055 'Yes, yes,' I say. 'I know all that. But *them.* The people I've
4056 been with, who ran with me across the fields, looked back with
4057 tearful eyes – "Save me, save me" they seemed to cry...'

4058  'Yes, that was what they cried,' she says.
4059  There's a youth in her room. 'He's not my son,' says Lady Bea.
4060  'Round me,' I say, 'people seem not to last so long.'
4061  'All the culture Stalin had, his handwriting, so well-formed – all
4062  came from the church, you see,' says Lady Bea. I think she ignores
4063  my questions. 'Maybe that's the case,' she says, 'But I don't ignore
4064  *you*, not at all. Most of the best, the documented ones,' and she
4065  unpins her hat. 'Are dead. And – you are right – pins are important
4066  in my life. They serve to fix what is not you to all the rest. There is
4067  no theory that accounts for it, except in abstract terms, quite
4068  tentative.'
4069  The youth tells me, 'Beatrice clings to the lady title. It isn't
4070  pinned, so she can do without. If you have sex, the rate is half and
4071  half. If not, you get the discount, forty-five per cent.'
4072  'I'm sure you are related to her,' I tell the youth. 'And the
4073  pictures. On the walls and lying on the floor. Grass. Beautifully
4074  done – even the colour's right. It could be real.'
4075  'They *are* real,' says the youth. 'If you're a soldier, you
4076  recognise it at once. It's cover. For hiding behind.'
4077  'This Beatrice,' I say, 'she must be a recruiter. That's why she's
4078  good at categories.'
4079  'All those people in your legacy,' says the youth, 'they must
4080  have preferences. It's like a country – people knowing where they
4081  want to go. They'll all get kitted up, and take an oath. Beatrice is
4082  special – she puts them on a catwalk. That way, you can see where
4083  they'd best fit in.'
4084  It's oppressive in the room. There's too much muslin and velvet
4085  here, it's Bloomsbury but there is no cat.
4086  The youth, waiting to age so he can be recruited, moons around,
4087  listens to Cobain...
4088  'Usually recruiting's done at school,' he says, 'But if you don't
4089  attend – it's soldiering direct.'
4090  Beatrice, filling in paybooks, hums Delibes. 'Don't goggle,
4091  dear,' she says. 'It's me that has the eye. I sort you out. The
4092  struggle, yes, it does avail, for that is all there is.'
4093  'I've heard that, Beatrice,' I say. 'It always seemed a metaphor.'
4094  'There is demand,' she says. 'The old, the young, prospectors,
4095  spies – the guys who run it all and watch the screens...'
4096  'Struggle's quite vague,' I say.
4097  'I got you prised away from Andy,' Beatrice says. 'And – I
4098  know what you're getting at as well. I'm full of it. Culture,

4099 cooperation – taking another turn. Africa's long behind us,
4100 naturally – the first long march. Those fossils, covering the globe!
4101 I'm more into rats – how they'll suffer, the poor things, when the
4102 air, the water disappear...'
4103     'Andy was a lazy type,' I say. 'He hoped to push me where he
4104 wouldn't go.'
4105     'That's the devil's work, my dear,' and Beatrice and the youth
4106 leap up, arms in the air, their fingers locked. They gyre.
4107     'Andy's gone!' the youth cries out. 'That sponge! The labours,
4108 the heavy lifting – those remain. That's what Andy groomed you
4109 for.'
4110     'You realise,' says Beatrice. 'When your troop files in – they're
4111 not the past, they're not your slaves – they're not your friends.'
4112     'Hide behind the curtain,' says the youth. 'You never know what
4113 they have done, and where they want to go with you.'
4114     The curtain's gauze: the faces of my legacy – they look alike,
4115 soft focussed. Beatrice questions them – where they've been, all
4116 that. She gives each one an envelope. The youth has joined me,
4117 stands too close, he smells of acetone, of glue that sticks the
4118 aeroplanes. His twiggy hands – too close to mine... 'See, Beatrice
4119 has assigned them all,' he says.
4120     'That's no advantage I can see,' I say. 'Not for them, and not for
4121 me.'
4122     'Oh yes,' he says. 'It must be done. She places them – it's a new
4123 thing...'
4124     'And me?' I ask. 'What's to become of me?'
4125     'Well,' says the youth, 'we have no cat. Maybe she plans to keep
4126 you here.' He shows his teeth to show he's made a joke.
4127     Outside I watch the guys assigned, opening their envelopes.
4128 Some have drawn blank, but everyone strides off – towards the
4129 poles, the sun, the snow that's done for people that I hardly knew.
4130 Off they went, those messengers – they don't come back. Those
4131 messages – a one-way show, the destination gone away, just as they
4132 arrive.
4133     'I'm quite confused,' I say to Bea: 'I don't know where I stand.
4134 Nor where you – nor Hawkett, dancing in the flames...'
4135     'Oh – just see him as a portent, dear,' says Lady Bea. 'Our
4136 instinct tells us all has changed. We're global now, and if it all falls
4137 down... Look at this marquetry...' and she shows me two long
4138 boxes, one cloudlike, billowing, with roots and leaves of

4139  cherrywood set in, the other tiny one, of chipboard, and inset
4140  'Nachlass', 'the unnamed'.
4141     'That's for the boy,' she says. 'I picked him out to boil my eggs.
4142  Quite useless... But, we are prepared. We just need someone who
4143  will nail us in.'
4144     'You're quite unlikely, Lady Bea...' I start.
4145     'The eggs we thought would hatch – but we must be content, and
4146  boil them, like an eye,' she says. 'Eyes must be hardboiled. Maybe
4147  you are the one that's left, your last labour the last screw – that's
4148  for the boxes, if I don't reach immortality...'
4149     'What's going to happen, Beatrice?' I ask. 'And why is
4150  everything I thought gone rancid, the people that you see – all spun
4151  away... you hope for this, or that, it all turns round...'
4152     'Well,' she says. 'You nearly learned to fly. And nearly tried to
4153  tell your truth. See – how unavailing that all was!'
4154     'What is your destiny?' I ask. 'Maybe you've reached the end
4155  before, or several times...'
4156     'Oh no,' she says. 'I fight my fights. Last woman standing, that's
4157  my role. Of course, there's devastation – but the fig's a mighty tree,
4158  resourceful, generous. There's me beneath, big birds that shake the
4159  branches, so...'
4160     'And then the angels come,' joins in the youth, 'to end it all, and
4161  start it off again.'
4162     'Yes, yes,' says Bea. 'Though you will not be there.' She turns
4163  to me:
4164     'He oughtn't to be here. But when it's time, I'll send him back to
4165  where he was before...'
4166     'I shan't take my envelope, even if you've one prepared,' I say.
4167     'You're unreliable,' she says. 'You get nothing. And remember
4168  – the earth turns, spins your friends into oblivion... the morning star
4169  comes round again – see – now it is the evening star! But once a
4170  star...!' She smoothes the antimacassars. 'Reaction always wins.
4171  That's how we've survived so far. Evolution is as slow as worms
4172  who build big wheels. It still is more secure than constitutions and
4173  the cops.'
4174     'All ends in death,' I say, 'except for Lady Bea.'
4175     'That is the halfway, where we've reached so far,' she says.
4176  'First, there'd be your labours: then will come – modifications to
4177  our genes – the fins and tails, the scorching breath, ungainly smells,
4178  the loss of speech – all's to change, the adaptations ... everything
4179  transmogrified. Useless to criticise my underwear, my decor – all

4180   will be mutated, back to the slime and claws. Enjoy your beauty
4181   now, mine too – you'll seem grotesque when the rest have seven
4182   arms and eyes and live in ceiling cracks and sing like toads.'
4183       'I'm sure you're right,' I say. 'But – those guys that Hawkett
4184   dumped. Where did they go?'
4185       'Oh,' she says, 'converting, Vince. Some make believe in distant
4186   worlds, some float in the ships that get you there... knowledge of
4187   everything, friends with all, the true religion, each has their
4188   expertise – life must go on...'
4189       'Not necessarily so,' I say. 'If you are right...'
4190       'Oh, don't lose hope,' she says, kissing the youth on his
4191   brilliantined crest. 'Some sell motors, some patch you up, some
4192   give you therapy ... look out the window, Vince: human life – it's
4193   all there.'
4194       She's right, it is. 'We shall have tea,' says Beatrice. 'Before you
4195   go?'
4196       'Where am I going?' I ask.
4197       'I'm brilliant,' says Bea. 'But I don't predict.'
4198       'Does anybody know a grace?' asks the youth.
4199       Into my head comes a phrase – maybe the absent Steve invented
4200   it – 'Certain strategic salients of bourgeois power remain...' Should
4201   that be a grace? Is this a salient? Who's taken over now?
4202       'You're right,' says Bea. 'Culturally, this is a dump – the trunk
4203   where they keep clothes for dressing up. Good music – where's it
4204   gone? Now – eat your egg.'
4205       'Be sure to dip your soldier in,' says the youth.
4206       'There's feather stuff in mine,' I say.
4207       'Now, aren't you the lucky one – it's for absent friends, but
4208   those wings won't take you far,' says Beatrice. 'I'm always sad
4209   about the grace. It can't be hard to make one up. We all have hope.'
4210       'I only hope for what may come about,' I say. It sounds prim.
4211       They both look shocked. 'Haven't you been listening?' asks
4212   Lady Bea. 'All my lads are mercenaries – they don't hope for
4213   anything – and nor do we.'
4214       'I can't wait,' the youth says, beating with his spoon.
4215   'Mobilisation! I hate just being kept.'
4216       'After everyone else is poor because of you, you and your mates
4217   will be in poverty as well,' says Bea. 'You're a plague.'
4218       'You took my heritage,' I say. 'Someone earned from that – not
4219   me.'

4220     'It's an accident of birth,' says Lady Bea. 'The wheel turns, is
4221     never still.'
4222     'Sex – it's the same,' the youth complains.
4223     'I tell you stories, dear: you take them to your cot, enjoy yourself
4224     – in the big world, you'd have to share,' says Beatrice – 'I guide
4225     *you*. I don't guide your hand.'
4226     'Before I leave,' I say, 'Give me your largest thought.'
4227     'Drink what you can of your tea,' she says. 'And – this could be
4228     your grace: "Poverty brings conflict. Riches bring conflict, but the
4229     weapons are much bigger." That should help you, dear.'
4230     As I leave, another squad swirls up, pushes me aside: I say,
4231     'There's love in that ménage,' but they don't seem to hear.
4232
4233                              *
4234
4235     'Now I'll do Kutah-Qamat,' says the singer in the underground. 'It
4236     means "You are short, my beloved – perhaps because you are my
4237     life, and my life is going to be short."'
4238     The less indifferent of us, maybe the more aimless ones – we
4239     laugh. For sure, that's what it says, the song... We laugh away – the
4240     singer – she's not fazed.
4241     She's done: she isn't paid. 'It must be the translation. I did a
4242     course – I'm not one of them. I'm poor, is all,' she says.
4243     'You're right,' I say. 'It isn't funny. It's true – but what's it
4244     worth? Who can tell?'
4245     'I could have studied equality,' says the singer. 'Saving human
4246     lives by calculation: saving wolves. Instead, it had to be Farsi, for
4247     the time.'
4248     'Not many do it,' I say. 'Not here, in this place that looks like
4249     Copenhagen. Even if they don't finish...'
4250     'How'd you finish a language?' she asks, getting angry.
4251     'Besides, I don't like healthy digging ... all those worms ... And
4252     there's lots I don't want to be equal with.'
4253     'No,' I say, 'I mean with a language, there's a point where you
4254     try to speak, and they don't laugh at you. You could try memory,
4255     rocking to and fro.'
4256     I peek at her licence, that you need to sing in this flat grey town:
4257     'Melissa'. 'That's a name slips sweetly off the tongue,' I say. I
4258     guess it's sexual, all those words. Of course, she's even angrier.
4259     'I don't mean anything,' I say. 'Not about anyone, not me or
4260     you. Just words, slipping off...'

4261    My tongue.
4262    'The song was so beautiful,' Melissa says. 'I wanted to pursue it,
4263    turn into it, like a sylph. Of course, that leaves most of life outside.
4264    Even more, if you're successful, have to repeat.'
4265    'That outside's the part of life I live in,' I say. 'And beauty – it's
4266    so contested – what its value is, where it lives, what languages it
4267    speaks. What's left without, where we all live, mostly.'
4268    I give offence, continually. Speaking has intimacy, even if you
4269    haven't meant it, as if you stuck a finger in a nose, a stranger's ear.
4270    'It's all in the past,' I say. 'Beauty in the future – it makes no sense.
4271    No – it's all gone by.'
4272    'The past – wasn't at all beautiful,' she says. 'And you're right
4273    about the future. Beauty's the unicorn, hidden behind the tree.'
4274    We've reached to terminus. We stand, each ready for a
4275    conclusion, on the platform: 'Beauty teaches renunciation,' Melissa
4276    says, 'and we desert it for reality.'
4277    'That's crap,' I say. 'You don't need teaching to renounce,
4278    desert – absolutely anything and anyone. And often deserting's the
4279    best way – whether you do it, or it's done to you.'
4280    It's been a charming interlude – it's good it's ending. And
4281    Melissa – certainly she's short. She wears a pair of cavalry boots,
4282    long and creased – a mistake, if you're so short; not small and
4283    harmonious, just not long enough, disproportionate to everyone.
4284    'Goodbye again,' I say. 'I shan't pester you. I'm off – the trip is
4285    over.'
4286    She doesn't set off for somewhere. 'I ride this train,' she says,
4287    'It's work.'
4288    Of course! She's always on the same train, up and down the line
4289    – impossible to leave her – she's always where you know she is.
4290    Better than picking rubbish – it's still work for an untouchable.
4291
4292                        *
4293
4294    I find Gino's apartment. I start to say Bea sent me. 'No, no,' he
4295    shouts, 'I don't want to know all that. Most everything of what we
4296    know is over. It's experience, dead – what you had in mind to do
4297    with it – whoa! there it goes, it slips away.'
4298    'Right!' I say. 'What's your news?'
4299    'For me,' he says, 'if you go through it numb – existence – I
4300    wouldn't care, I wouldn't know. It isn't even up to you. You falls

4301 asleep – are you dead? You wouldn't know, or care, and nor would
4302 I.'
4303 'Not archaeology,' I say, 'not war, nor precious metals. I won't
4304 follow you or anyone for those. Not a secret, nor a mystery. I've
4305 done all those. Not a second best – the blossom – peaches?
4306 cherries? Old guys whittling? Trying those fried beetles – how
4307 delicious! No, not any of those trips, not by a stick's length.'
4308   'Oh, dear Vince', he cries, 'how you are one of me!'
4309   The artwork, stacked against the walls – it's Fifties, bold and
4310 sentimental. Papers too – travelling the Berlin underground,
4311 orphans playing spoons – but aren't those bones? one stop further
4312 and it's socialism – trying atom bombs on South Sea islanders...
4313   'Those were my father's,' Gino says. 'I haven't bought a thing
4314 since he went off. If he is memory, removing them might do it
4315 harm...'
4316   He laughs. He's a great joker, you can see.
4317   'What then?' I ask. 'I've travelled in a pack. We crossed a
4318 frontier by both ways... It taxed our legs. And the people! – with
4319 their stories, being counted and then disappearing. Guardian types –
4320 stepping out the frame of bad movies, their names thumbed cards
4321 filched from ruined tenements ... unpunished, unrepentant.'
4322   'Numbers!' shouts Gino. 'Don't give me numbers. They're for
4323 counting, and for games of cards. Useless for mathematics – they're
4324 ignoble, from the unit dump. And religion's hooked on them – it's
4325 all an invite to a massacre. Sixteen of you, are there? Come to
4326 explore the world, convert? Right – your heads go rolling down the
4327 steps, bleached skins tacked to the sacred oak, eyeballs on skewers
4328 for the temple monkeys, testicles rolling in the hoochie koochie
4329 dancers' game of marbles... You're crazy – advertising numbers –
4330 it's betting your mother on a pair of threes...'
4331   'Tell me, Gino,' I say. 'Everything. And leave your father out.'
4332   'Energy,' he says. 'It transforms everything. Makes bronze,
4333 makes lime. Keeps things standing – release it and they fall ... the
4334 tree, the fire, the carbuncle and the kiss, the dragonfly and the
4335 haiku...'
4336   'I get all that,' I say. 'I met a woman on the metro...'
4337   'Oh,' he says, stretching up a thin finger to touch the clay parrot
4338 suspended from the ceiling, 'negative energy is good too. Routine
4339 stores it in your battery. Stretching like a cat two metres tall and
4340 elastic like a picture or a choir singing ... It's like voices – they're
4341 not concerned with harmony – just the reach, throwing nets on an

4342 empty sea, up like a seahawk, empty spirals in dry air ... then down,
4343 caught nothing, ready for the climbing wall, the puzzle tree...'
4344     'We're the new charge,' I say, as Gino hustles me along, 'We
4345 plug in ... and then...'
4346     'Wait!' says Gino. 'The talk – it must be right. Look at those
4347 guys – bound to their wheels – wheels for prayer, then every day –
4348 repeat, repeat – a tick, a tock of every clock, the climate's fucked,
4349 and yet it's springtime clothes, and fall, and candles lit, here come
4350 the three, the wizards orientalist – out go the twelve, the miracle's
4351 of numbers once again – now, here come the lambs, we'll cut their
4352 throats, and here's the ass... this time – who is the ass, who's to be
4353 flogged with beams, and who is resurrected, who's nailed down,
4354 who's taken up, who's for the pit...? Numbers and repetitions –
4355 dead is dead, you fools, the end's the end, spring won't return, you
4356 shot the bears, poisoned the fox – they're gone, into the
4357 storybooks...'
4358     'Yes, Gino,' I say. 'Pray every day and worship calendars – it's
4359 finished – if it ever was. Now, it's food and capital – and that
4360 repeats as well – the seasons that there aren't, the fire that eats the
4361 manioc, the numbers don't add up, someone has filched those bags
4362 of gold, is in the counting house and fondling his queen – there
4363 aren't that many blackbirds left ... yes, Gino, you are right! we're
4364 chanting those old counting songs, eleven jonquils on the grave and
4365 four black horses for the hearse, four angels round my bed, three
4366 spirits lift me to the golden dome – aaah! down I go, they're
4367 demons made of fog, that's thirty fingers let me slip, down to the
4368 crypt – swift as the hypothetic ape, thirty-two the feet each second
4369 whizzing down the invisible rope ... and down, we're winding
4370 down ... how many millions of years to go? a blink, a hohum in the
4371 universe, it's heating up, it's freezing down...'
4372     'Yes, Vince,' says Gino. 'That's the scene.'
4373     The moment – it resolves. He says: 'You need to put a wire deep
4374 into the brain – if the universe possesses one, or it might have just
4375 one big toe – we'll charge that up as well. Off with the old, the
4376 drift, decline, the mended shoe, the button strangled on its
4377 dwindling thread... Of course – there could be disadvantages. We'll
4378 never know how long the charge holds up. And – it could mean, for
4379 us, a shorter life...'
4380     'Oh, so long as we don't know,' I say. 'I have in mind a person,
4381 already halfway to the revelation, a prisoner of habit, to and fro,
4382 entrapped, ensnared and begging uselessly...'

4383    'Exactly so,' says Gino. 'You think you do the guy who has no
4384    cash, no food, a service if they get a sack of flour... You know – she
4385    doesn't – that the cash is stacked up in the bank. What will sort her
4386    out is revolution! The sages – they can't point that out, and nor can
4387    you – you'll go inside. Life over! The revolution, this time done
4388    right, that's what you need...'
4389        Gino lays out the benefits – it's energy you need to stand
4390    upright, throw down your spade...
4391        'Of course,' he says, 'you can't enjoy your life unless you think
4392    it's over soon. Your sin, the guilt, betrayal – is not original: it's just
4393    a sin. Live with it – it's yours, no one can steal it off you. Without
4394    it, life is less enjoyable – the punishment will come, and let you
4395    measure up. Try heroic: the heroic mode! I'm not thinking of the
4396    thugs and oafs, of course,' and he bends to kiss my head. 'Without
4397    your bad deeds – what would the good ones be? You must break
4398    out, dear Vince. It's perverse, this shackling to your past, your
4399    slithery recall of what and why you might have done... I've long
4400    passed that...'
4401        'When do we set off?' I ask.
4402        'Where?' asks Gino, laughing. 'Who said a bunch of friends
4403    would go, open the prisons, stop a war, write lampoons for the
4404    mags? That's old-time fantasy, my friend, you can smell it, stinking
4405    on the page. That's not a foundation myth, dear Vince – it's folly,
4406    pure. The charge, the juice – can come from anywhere. Leave aside
4407    the persecuted, the innocent – they all have their day. A page is left
4408    for them in every Book of Kings. The worst: they already have it,
4409    it's their pillow, and their plate. All must change, so that the
4410    smallest thing can change. A jolt, a volt, dear Vince, is not a plaster
4411    or a splint – your teeth will itch, your hair fly out, the rabbits shoot
4412    out of their holes – and every egg will hatch, maybe we'll turn to
4413    silver gilt ... this project, Vince, it has no nurse; no holy water
4414    drips, no mumble reels up on your screen, no prayer and no
4415    excuse...'
4416        'Just let me see the machine, Gino,' I say. There's scepticism
4417    somewhere in me, like a cyst.
4418        'Oh dear,' he says, 'you're a gadget freak! I expected better.
4419    You must start from the need, and then the answer. The unanswer,
4420    if you have the question wrong. Any guy on the corner can run you
4421    up an apparatus. Listen,' and he pulls me beside him on a pile of
4422    news – 'communist spies will rule the world,' says a headline –
4423    there are two laws. One should be repealed: the second law of

4424 thermodynamics, that says we're winding down. The distances
4425 grow far and bleak, there's frosting on the telescope, it cools and
4426 slows, the gas burns all the pans you left on stupidly... The other
4427 law says no! Nothing is ever lost, the energy rolls out, an
4428 everlasting sea, with whales of infinite fecundity and heft, over the
4429 horizon are the dinosaurs and all your ancestors – no one thinks of
4430 you, nor you, I bet, of them. Less and less – or on and on: that is the
4431 choice. You see, dear Vince – it's bloody laws! Who made them?
4432 Who enforces them – how can we repeal, and have our world fired
4433 up, all hugger-mugger with our friends, and Mahler when we wake
4434 and Fauré as we sleep...?'
4435     'Oh Gino – this is what I feared,' I say. 'The promise is a joke, a
4436 spoof.'
4437     'It was a test,' he says solemnly. 'To see how far you trusted me.
4438 Keep in your sights the physics and their laws. That is what
4439 matters. If you prefer silence as you sleep and wake – you're
4440 philistine, but nothing worse.'
4441     'I trust you, Gino: but you seem extravagant – even rococo, in
4442 your scheme,' I say.
4443     'Forget the scheme. Let's say – there is no plan. Things change,
4444 wind down – and they should simplify – their end is nigh. What do
4445 they have to lose, by sticking to the rules as if it's still day one?
4446 Take cash. Once, you dug and sluiced, assayed and lit the fire, and
4447 made a lump and held it in the die and struck, and struck again, and
4448 had it weighed, and maybe clipped, or copied even – then to the
4449 treasury, the market, the legionnaire... the solid mass goes in your
4450 shoe or in a hoard – and on and on – the bearded despot on the front
4451 – he dies, the goddess on the back – she never shows, but still
4452 there's blood and fisticuffs to have that disc! Now, all you need do
4453 for cash, is put the paper in and turn the wheel.'
4454     I take my leave. Gino's a genius, no doubt, there's little history
4455 and happenstance that can resist his analytic mind. But – what if
4456 he's a charlatan? He says his words are free, and I don't pay. Can
4457 this be all?
4458
4459                       *
4460
4461 I must take the same train back. I tell Melissa, 'Gino has the big
4462 idea – so big, it isn't viable.'
4463     'You could try,' she says. 'If you've not got one of your own.'

4464     'I don't know what's involved,' I say. 'He's lots of space, if I
4465     can't share with you.'
4466     'Oh,' she says, 'I share already. You know – hotels. They make
4467     you pay while you're asleep. As if a corpse paid in the graveyard. If
4468     you don't move around, it's all quite clean.'
4469     I laugh. 'The payment's for the dreams. The more you pay, the
4470     more the dreams reveal. A cash reward for nightmares.'
4471     The only money I have left is in my sock – how much there is,
4472     from here, I can't imagine. I say, 'Gino's not recruiting. All the
4473     others are. I can't think why some of them have turned me down.'
4474     'It's probably the height,' Melissa says.
4475     'No, Melissa, it's not that,' I say. 'I have ambitions, and they see
4476     I'm capable of running bosses, interviewers, and all the show. It's
4477     envy, or it's my disillusionment, I'm sure: I'm bigger than the job –
4478     I take them for a run...'
4479     'If Gino has a room,' Melissa says, 'I could share there. Not that
4480     anything would change – I'm sharing now. But I'd not go with you
4481     – you have no feel for words. You're just a mirror: those don't tell
4482     you anything. It's all already in the silver on the back. There can't
4483     be two of you: the one you are is there, behind the glass – there's
4484     nothing fresh, no warning.'
4485     'We've been warned, Melissa, many times,' I say. 'More is
4486     pointless.'
4487     'Look at the air,' she says. She fans it with the Book of Kings:
4488     'There's particles and weapons, storms – just about everything. It's
4489     got too thick to breathe. We should have an expedition – lie on
4490     couches, drink the tea, in places where there's nothing but the sand,
4491     nothing to do at all, the boredom and the lack of faith ... maybe we
4492     could get tattooed. Kohl round our eyes.'
4493     'Who do you share with, Melissa?' I ask her.
4494     'There's my friend, Holly. A great capacity for love: on the side,
4495     there's tarting. That's an old expression – it's not supermarketing.'
4496     'I know exactly how it goes,' I say. 'Maybe you should
4497     concentrate on that short life, Melissa. It could be a fad, seeing that
4498     it's necessary, and coming anyway. Last things you could do
4499     tomorrow. In a week. Me, paying the singing lady in the metro...'
4500     Gino won't let us use his room. He hasn't said. It's what I'd do.
4501     The room is full, but not of life, or death – for that, it's valuable.
4502     I ask the artisan on the corner – 'Energy for Gino. Has he
4503     ordered...'

4504    'Oh,' says the guy, 'I made the boxes, like a coffin, only vertical.
4505    You sit in, and hope you don't end up in horizontal.'
4506        'No, no,' I say. 'It's like charging up the universe – instead of
4507    trickling out, you renew the kick. It works like hay or electricity –
4508    awakes the pole that jogs it up again – the whole: desire, creation.
4509    Not going backwards – just...'
4510        'I understand,' the old man says. 'But like so many, you have
4511    got it wrong. Electricity – it doesn't leak away when out of use. It's
4512    waiting in there, like a muse – a jaguar that leaps when you depress
4513    the switch. There is no power draining out, making the stars
4514    explode like cathode tubes, the distances increase as if the edge
4515    recedes, loses its reds and greens...'
4516        'It's all technology,' I say. 'If it goes one way – it can be
4517    reversed. A woman says you're not the one – you're tossed away
4518    and sad. But – she is free! It's life for her, a bruise for you. In some
4519    rare case – you both are free, or even grafted on to one another...
4520    There's many ways of cheating the inevitable, the blur and blot, the
4521    poet said...'
4522        'No,' says the craftsman. 'It's not on. It all decays, it tarnishes, it
4523    splits, it comes unglued, the solder cracks, earth turns to dust and
4524    wood to ash.'
4525        'Gino wants a machine...' I say.
4526        'No, he's wrong,' the old man, Beppe, says. 'Energy's quite
4527    outside the tin and nickel. It's in us.'
4528        'He knows,' I say. 'He wants a box...'
4529        'He'll end in one,' says Beppe, laughing. 'If not a vase. Come
4530    out the back.'
4531        The shop is a *bottega* – a counter with a bottle and some flex, a
4532    shelf above where you can sleep or snoop – but out the back – it is
4533    a world. There's houris sleeping on divans, peacocks white and
4534    purple, tall yuccas where the shrews can nest and glide, a stand of
4535    pampas where a family of wolves returns my stare. There's green,
4536    brown and gold, living furs of grey and white.
4537        'I observe the wolves,' says Beppe. 'We lost our top wolf – he
4538    got too smart, a neighbour shot him. The pack knows life more
4539    fully than we do. The big bright underwater beasts, their enviable
4540    brains – I have no room for them, alas.'
4541        He shows me round. 'We keep our heads quite clean of what we
4542    can't observe,' he says. 'Here, no fetishes, no guards invisible, no
4543    guardian avatars in masks... No boxes.'
4544        I laugh, 'Then, nothing dies, and nothing needs a charge?'

4545 'That is the way,' he says. 'I don't make puppets. What I seek –
4546 it must exist, be present from the start. Maybe we should have
4547 stayed beneath the waves, and let intelligence take hold. Now it's
4548 too late – we thought we'd found the shore, that it led up... But no:
4549 there's empty shells and stranded weed.'
4550 'The guy – the top gun?' I ask. 'Top wolf? Blasting the
4551 experiment.'
4552 'Oh,' says Beppe, 'he wasn't top of anything – not even of the
4553 shooting class.' He makes the gesture, on his neck.
4554 'Well, what's the core, the shape, the drive?' I ask.
4555 'I thought of protohumans,' Beppe says. 'It's true our end is
4556 ugly, nigh – but at the start the energy was there, the evolution
4557 swift, the pace was fast, the destiny, alas – disaster.'
4558 'You're breeding protohumans, Beppe? Prototypes?' I ask.
4559 'Put it like that, it has a nazi sound,' he says, 'though everyone is
4560 toying in that way. There's counting too – you need it to be
4561 capitalists. It's tough to learn: – maybe some birds can help.
4562 They're numbering the eggs, you see, then having to regurgitate.
4563 You need to get your figuring right, no one wants to sick them up,
4564 the frogs and such, more than they need.'
4565 There's the yucca leaves, and then the sky – without the
4566 incurious lofty trees, the town's too flat; they even put the trains
4567 under the ground.
4568 'That wolf,' says Beppe. 'He had a grin. He carried off an ape
4569 I'd just brought in. Maybe it was best to send him on. I don't
4570 believe it, but it fits the story so.'
4571 'I've no opinion, Beppe,' I say. 'Except – I guess I have. He
4572 should have ate the ape, and there's an end...'
4573 'You underestimate my difficulties, friend,' he says. 'That's
4574 typical. When we got to sitting down all day, and calling up our
4575 friends if we forgot a word, a place – our brains started to get small.
4576 Things to solve – they got beyond us. In the pack, we had to know
4577 a lot of stuff – the beasts, the plants, the rain. All gone! We spend
4578 the evenings gawping at the stars, the distances, inventing dreams
4579 about them, fearing the drop.'
4580 'The breeding aspect, Beppe. Maybe it's reserved for you,' I say.
4581 'I see you have some beauties lounging on divans...'
4582 'Oh,' he says. 'That's not the experiment.'
4583 'Well,' I say, 'if you're not the patriarch, initial seed, the primal
4584 cell, eternal father...'

4585     'The size of brain,' he says, 'that works, lights up all through...
4586     You find it in the people who've survived a war, maybe been
4587     tortured, run, begged for bread, asylum – they must know
4588     everything. Their brains – they are immense. You find those people
4589     on the underground, no one wants them up here in the light.'
4590        'The question's still unanswered, Beppe,' I say.
4591        He goes on: 'Short lives. You have to force it in: experience, the
4592     wisdom. We forget most of what little's been transmitted to us. We
4593     don't know how to survive,' he says.
4594        'That's evident,' I say. 'You map it well – the starting place.
4595     Then, it's all problems that you cannot solve.'
4596        'Yes,' he says. 'You're right. I see the problem. I've no clue
4597     how to resolve. I'm quite like Gino. What did he say about that
4598     room he has?'
4599        'Oh,' I say. 'What I suspected – "No, you're not dossing in my
4600     private place. My ancestors – they may return and need the
4601     space..."'
4602        There's room on those divans ... but I don't ask.
4603        'Money, Beppe,' I say. 'I don't care about space – that's a nazi
4604     thing as well. Setting questions – that's wrong too – when you've
4605     no answer. Anyone can set up a world like yours. My need is –
4606     getting lots more cash...'
4607        'Mend these stools,' he says, pulling some that limp, from a
4608     wood chest. He laughs, 'That way you'll have some guys become
4609     more sedentary; see their brains shrivel, the same song in their
4610     identical mouth.'
4611        When I finish mending, he gives me cash – brick-sized. 'That's
4612     far too much,' I say. 'It tempts. I can spend that in an hour, have
4613     nothing left again.'
4614        'Do what you want,' he says. 'It's not so much. You don't know
4615     how people live, all the cash they take, hoard up.'
4616        'That's true, Beppe,' I say. 'But don't forget – it's not just us,
4617     the project. It's the universe! The whole shoot – to be put in
4618     reverse.'
4619
4620                              \*
4621
4622     I take the train – of course, there's Melissa. 'What's that sewage
4623     stink?' she asks.
4624        I tell her all that Beppe does: those little chairs, like mounting
4625     blocks – maybe for horsemen; how he loves his animals... 'Oh,'

4626 Melissa says, 'those old guys – they all build stuff like that, stock
4627 up with all the women they will never screw, hope to be eaten up
4628 by something that has loved them once. What a hope!'
4629     'The smell!' I say. 'It must be printers' ink. The parcel Beppe
4630 gave... I've suffered this before. Those virgin notes...'
4631     'You better spend them all at once, or not at all,' she says. 'And
4632 run. Maybe buy an aeroplane, take off...'
4633     I think of it – creation. Rolling back, a tidal boom along the
4634 shore – the reds spring up from every pocket where they've lurked
4635 – the snooker match starts off again, reds in their triangle, then
4636 place the reluctant pink and brown, the dawn and dusk. All ready
4637 for the break, the pristine frame...
4638     'The cash!' shouts Melissa. 'I'll avoid you till it's spent.'
4639     That's good – but then – the train is always waiting: and on it,
4640 the sound of wheels, the 'short life' song. That, you can't avoid.
4641     'Vince,' she says. 'You're at the top. You're where your boss
4642 had paid to be. Your friends – Andy, Steve – pushing you. Now,
4643 Gino, Beppe – pulling you towards the peak.'
4644     It's true. I'm favoured. I think of Maya, not of Gennaro.
4645     Melissa goes on, 'Beppe – maybe he wants to be top wolf, now
4646 there's a vacancy. And – horsemen... not the apocalypse, that's all
4647 been done. They ride in from the desert...'
4648     I'd like a wolf to fill me with their love – when once they say
4649 they love you, it's for life, they don't go cold. The same with cats –
4650 that way, you see that love and sex are separate...
4651     I say, 'No, Melissa, you're quite wrong. The mounting blocks
4652 are there for starting from. No one is coming in – there's riders
4653 leaving, that's for sure...'
4654     With Melissa, there's always a terminus. In fact, there's always
4655 two, one at each end. Most other things – there's no end, no point
4656 where you arrive, no credit for being on the way. That's true of
4657 things – thoughts, systems, images. People, though, they're a
4658 terminus, they decide their own and hand it over to you – some
4659 with a knife, most with indifference. 'The thing, Melissa,' I say, 'is
4660 that Beppe and Gino don't agree. I can't be with them both.
4661 Beppe's organic, Gino – is mechanical: the history, factitious.
4662 Beppe's is self-indulgence, totemism. He has the snide money, he
4663 can buy anything, and ride away – fast and faster.'
4664     Next day, Melissa says, 'That's a fine shirt, Vince. Boats, sails
4665 and wings.'

4666  'I told you I could fly,' I say. 'You wouldn't know – but I can be
4667  *sympa*. Fancy – wafted me, into the store.'
4668  'Your smell has gone,' she says.
4669  'I dumped those notes,' I say. 'I met a guy. A cop, I think.'
4670  'What?' she shouts. 'You bought a shirt, and sold your friend –
4671  sold Beppe!'
4672  'He must have known,' I say. 'Preparing to make a getaway...'
4673  'He couldn't ride...' she says. 'And there's no horse.'
4674  'You always ride,' I say, 'if you have nothing else. Black horses
4675  from the hearse, out of the traces – for him, and for the houris.
4676  Besides – it was my social responsibility: I didn't quite say "who"
4677  and point.'
4678  'So, that cop paid you for the slush?' she asks.
4679  'Remember,' I tell Melissa, 'I didn't sell old Beppe – I sold the
4680  money. And Gino paid me too – not to ask to stay with him. He's
4681  flush – his father built the atom bomb, and left us this advice –
4682  "don't look up, ever" – and now, everybody, black, white and
4683  brown is making one, down in the cellar, a bomb: it shows you
4684  have some faith, even if it's only that you'll win, or get away with
4685  it.'
4686  'It isn't colour that's at stake,' Melissa says.
4687  'That's just a metaphor, like flight,' I say. 'There's flight to get
4688  to a new place by air, and flight that's running anywhere at all as
4689  best you can.'
4690  'They'll trash poor Beppe's compound,' says Melissa: 'And the
4691  animals... the trees...'
4692  'Gino's machine is less impractical,' I say, hurrying it along.
4693  'This shirt. Maybe it reminds you of the poem – "the cemetery
4694  beside the sea".'
4695  'He got it wrong,' Melissa says. 'He talked of seals, grazing
4696  below, he should have said the sails, those dhows have sails that
4697  look like white doves' wings. But anyway, it's all about his muse...'
4698  'Ah yes,' I say. 'The innocent. A moving picture, all the same.'
4699  'Beppe's released his soul,' says Melissa. 'You don't need be
4700  religious to see that after death there comes the flight, the wing, the
4701  flame ... the seed – it flies, quite free... Those horses – what delight!
4702  To leave the hearse, gallop over the red sand to those red granite
4703  outcrops...'
4704  She doesn't sing her song – we do the circuit, the train empties,
4705  fills, and empties. 'Don't go with Gino,' says Melissa. 'You've lost

4706 so many that you've not appreciated – I don't see you, fiddling with
4707 those tiny screws and stripping wires...'
4708     I say, 'You're right, Melissa. What you say, is poetry. But
4709 nothing regenerates – only shamans think that way. The soul is
4710 evanescent, up it goes and out the chimney. It's a consolation – one
4711 that does not console at all.'
4712     'Well,' Melissa says, 'I have to work the carriage up ahead.
4713 Decide what you want most to believe. You disgust me. It doesn't
4714 change a thing.'
4715     'They say you have to work at it, belief,' I say. 'Like you sing
4716 your song, Melissa, and no one pays. One day, you're absent –
4717 then, they remember you, the shortness, your truncated life – stuck
4718 in the train, the up and down...'
4719     'It's all a metaphor,' she says. 'I don't believe fuck all. Nothing
4720 that I'd tell you. It needs someone, to pull it all down.'
4721     'So,' I say. 'You don't believe you're hungry? That's just fine.
4722 You can't go into politics, not if you're hungry. You can't take my
4723 money, not if you're going into politics, and I won't give it you,
4724 even if you're into politics. So – if you're hungry – I'm not buying
4725 food for you...'
4726     If she's really hungry, she'll not think about politics, or doing
4727 much about it.
4728     She's already long gone, up the train. She should learn more
4729 songs.
4730
4731                            *
4732
4733 Gino says, 'I'll hand the work on to you. See...' and here's a pile of
4734 papers ... some have baby faces scribbled on. 'I'm nearly there,' he
4735 says, grabbing the graphics, scrumpling them – 'It's not a doodle,
4736 forget all that – here's the start... And it goes from here ... and so ...
4737 and then ... it follows that...' His breath is like marsh gas, and my
4738 eyes go grey, like mushrooms under oil...
4739     'This much is right,' he says. 'It makes a bomb. That's physics
4740 from the marrow. We know how the fiddly bits are screwed
4741 together, what happens when they spring apart, collide, or just get
4742 jiggled...'
4743     'I understand your terms,' I say. 'It's these equations... I missed
4744 some weeks of school, and so the principles – whatever discipline
4745 this is – were rusted when they were ladled in my head...' Gino
4746 rushes on,

4747 'My father stopped halfway – of course, that experiment made a
4748 flash and wind. Too bad there were those guys just clocking in on
4749 that particular day. That was the path. But – you must be...' and he
4750 stands on tiptoes here – 'Very very careful as you go ahead, that
4751 everything just doesn't fall apart. It is a risk we scientists must
4752 boldly take – but watch it! When you make the sphere, before you
4753 pull the switch, I might suggest you check your caculations ... one
4754 last time, as they say.'
4755     'So, Gino,' I say. 'It's all in the last page. Keep for your archives
4756 all this extra scrip... And tell me why you've given me the job, the
4757 last equation, that turns it all around – from expansion and decay to
4758 compression and new life...'
4759     'It's the compression bothers me,' he says. 'It's not that we've
4760 got big, bigger, as everything streams out old style, expanding
4761 horizons, fading. If we contract to millimetres, certain tasks become
4762 quite tough. Like going up the stairs, drinking a pint of booze ...
4763 and there's the chance that all you'll get is one huge bomb... But –
4764 you're the expert, now it's up to you. I'll spend the next, the other,
4765 fifty years awaiting me – making a bower, like old Beppe did – the
4766 hearse parked round the back, the houris ... maybe a tank of
4767 dolphins...'
4768     'It doesn't seem it goes like that,' I say. 'Not decisive. Short
4769 lives, dear Gino! You've already had a lot of years – the birthdays,
4770 and the festivals; – you know the drill, how each hour resembles
4771 each, how boredom tarnishes, the presents pall, the sacrificial
4772 beasts – they bleat, they struggle, they piss upon the ground with
4773 fear... Maybe that fear belongs to you, dear Gino ... maybe your
4774 doodles tell the tale equations don't...'
4775     'Listen, my friend,' says Gino angrily. 'Just don't explode the
4776 universe. That's all I ask.'
4777
4778                         *
4779
4780 I show the last page to Melissa: 'Those symbols,' she says wisely –
4781 'In the next room to Farsi, they're doing Early Georgian. Those are
4782 *asomtavruli* characters, no doubt at all.'
4783     'I don't think so, Melissa,' I say, quite gently. 'I need someone
4784 who can distinguish rejuvenation from a bomb. I must have missed
4785 that day at school again – so much went on there, but – away it
4786 goes, the wisdom, and gone for ever.'

4787 'If it was worth,' Melissa says. 'He would not have passed it on.
4788 His father set off the worthy massacre – the money trickled down to
4789 Gino. Gino follows Beppe, and probably Beppe, or *his* father, in
4790 their turn set up another massacre... And so it goes. One generation
4791 slices ears – the children take the cash and shed the tears.'
4792 'I fear,' I say, 'that's all a commonplace. In their bedroom, in the
4793 cellar – reviving the universe, blowing it all up – every student
4794 reaches Gino's point. Later in life – it's Beppe's.'
4795 'It's true,' Melissa says. 'It's Epicurus and Democritus, – flow
4796 or particle, decline, eternity. Beppe and Gino. Your ancient golden
4797 egg, dear Vince – it looks and smells like all the rest...'
4798 'Well, Melissa – not everyone has a cellar or a bedroom where
4799 they work things out,' I say.
4800 'The rest is trying to make fortunes, some by writing songs, and
4801 some with dollar clichés, and the filigree,' she says. 'Vince –
4802 promise me, it's not just that you don't understand this sheet that
4803 you don't see what it means...' and she waves Gino's last page at
4804 me.
4805 'This really is the key to the big door, you think?' I ask. 'It's
4806 poetry, Melissa. It doesn't say how we should live, nor how we can
4807 protect ourselves from states, or save the elephants. It strives – we
4808 respond, because we strive as well.'
4809 'Is that your best attempt?' she asks. 'For you – it has no more
4810 significance?'
4811 'Melissa,' I say. 'Hard times confront us. This paper–' and for
4812 effect, I scrumple it '–is myth, it's our re-foundation. Let's find a
4813 worthy place, and stash it there. If we can find some humble guy
4814 who'll work the next step out ... we'll play this last, this first card,
4815 then.'
4816 She's not convinced. 'The dead?' she asks. 'Do they resurrect?
4817 Or just there'll be no more? Not giving birth to anyone would be a
4818 great relief.'
4819 'It's metaphysics, all that stuff,' I say. 'Will there be night, will
4820 there be day, or light, or dark? That tangled way's aesthetics...
4821 Formalism, abstraction – do they do a dusk, a dawn? Come on!
4822 You're old hat, Melissa. Big sculptures stand out in the rain – they
4823 don't complain, and nor should we.'
4824 The dark – it's all around me. Melissa recedes, as if I'm drunk or
4825 dead. Maybe my old partner – Bianca – maybe she'll hop out, from
4826 hiding in her urn, to give me hell.

4827 'Melissa,' I say, 'I got away from Icaro – now, here's another
4828 chancer, Gino. Are they my destiny – their promises unfulfilled and
4829 unfulfillable? By me, at least.'
4830 'If it's your destiny, it's mine as well, and those who sang my
4831 song,' she says.
4832 It's poignant, and she makes the pose – but, now she stands
4833 before me – really short. Another question of aesthetics. A
4834 punishment awaits, I'm sure: she's having hers ... her height. Mine
4835 – it will come, for prejudice, discrimination, all the rest.
4836 'Yes!' says Melissa. 'There you go, you, your friends – you
4837 stridulate, you fly, you fornicate, you flee and you intrigue, you
4838 build your worlds, you blow them up ... and me? I work the trains.
4839 What would it cost you, as you swarm like toads for sex in seconds,
4840 frolic like hares before the bullet – to help me out? Just for a day...'
4841 I hear her out.
4842 'It isn't hares they kill with bullets, my dear friend,' I say. 'They
4843 use a blast of peppery shot... Pellets.'
4844 'At least,' she says, 'no one goes looking for me, puts me on
4845 their list. It's you they're looking, asking, for. They always catch
4846 their hare ... you'll end up as a *lièvre au poivre,* my *Hasenfuss* – in
4847 a jug – jugged in a jail – your brain, your perfect dialogic
4848 instrument, a braised mouthful, hare-brain: – they'll hear your case,
4849 you'll end up cased, skinned nude and crude...'
4850 I'm terrified, of course. Everything I've ever done has never
4851 crossed the line: yet they're searching for me: 'Hide Gino's
4852 scheme,' I say.
4853 'I haven't eaten, Vince,' she says. 'Maybe the future's tasty,
4854 peppy, even...' and she pretends to swallow ... everything.
4855 'Who's been asking, Melissa,' I ask. 'Military? Aviation?
4856 Forgery? Trafficking – or abandonment?'
4857 'All of those,' she says. 'Do be calm. See, I've learned to play
4858 the *dutar.* Lutes – you go all over – in time, for centuries back or
4859 more, to Africa, to Samarkand...'
4860 'Melissa,' I interrupt. 'That's niche. You could be singing in a
4861 bar, making them cry. Here, you're a lost soul...'
4862 'Then here is where I am, and I belong,' she says. 'I see
4863 everything you don't. I'm full of silent folk – their journeys mostly
4864 short, uncomfortable, preoccupied. I watch. I am the eye of God,
4865 dear Vince,' and she laughs. 'So – put your obol in my cup, mean
4866 bastard. Or stay and watch with me...'

| 4867 | 'What else, Melissa?' I ask. 'I'd watch, but there's no end. They |
|---|---|

4867 'What else, Melissa?' I ask. 'I'd watch, but there's no end. They
4868 stand, they reach somewhere, impassive they push their way ... they
4869 disappear, and we go on. We reach the end, but it's eternity – it all
4870 starts off again, the different people, impassive, in a rush, the
4871 scenery like it's painted on, and tunnels with those fairy lights in
4872 case it all breaks down and you must stumble on the track...'
4873     'Yes, yes,' she says. 'We know about the trains. You must feel
4874 your presence more. You and I needn't leave, not when the others
4875 do. But you'd be poor, dear Vince. That wouldn't suit. Hungry too.
4876 No water, and no booze, and no one offers anything. The song
4877 repeats, and when I'm dead, it will go on, another mouth will hold
4878 it for a while – without a consolation, saying exactly what there is.
4879 Short people with short lives.'
4880     I say, 'That was your choice, Melissa.'
4881     'Look at all the choices you have made, dear Vince. You're
4882 terrified now,' she says.
4883     It's true. But she is not the eye of God – that's what the semi-
4884 destitute believe. They think where they are's the best that they can
4885 do ... some gods are happy with stale cakes, of course, don't climb
4886 off those pedestals...
4887     'I don't run,' she says, 'not from anything.'
4888     'I don't run,' I say. 'I make choices, for the best.'
4889     'Then go!' she says. 'Leave! Who wants you?'
4890
4891                                    *
4892
4893 'You can paint me any colour / I can be a clown', the music says.
4894 It's exactly right. This is freedom. Everyone in the bar seeks it, and
4895 now we're free, floating up, leaving our skins and boots, up in the
4896 smoke. You put your quarter in the box, music – and you're free.
4897     I've told the guy beside me about my life – 'To me,' he says,
4898 'it's absolutely normal.'
4899     I'm abashed – 'I thought my life was vital,' I say.
4900     'People come in every day,' he says. 'Ideas: not always wisdom.
4901 Jetpacks. Ranches. The big project – the street is full of them, and
4902 all for sale. Down in the alley, they're divvying winter coats – it's
4903 hot as hell this summer – but you take a dozen...'
4904     'You buy into everything?' I ask.
4905     'Of course,' he says, 'and I do it all. What else is there? It's my
4906 expression does it: they think I'm a fish, a *pollo* – so, I am. A
4907 dolphin with a stash of Spanish gold, a cockerel that scratches up

4908 cut diamonds... In my window, it tells you: "Broker". No one
4909 believes it, just how broke... You can't put "brokest" – it's not
4910 grammatical.'
4911    'This way, you don't survive,' I say.
4912    'It's not Italy,' he says. 'It isn't organised, you don't burn saints'
4913 pictures, don't cut your thumbs. It's business. So, you don't die
4914 young – no one need be loyal to anyone.'
4915    'There must be rules,' I say. 'For not living long.'
4916    'Right!' he says. 'If you want rules – don't quote. Always be
4917 original. Be proud – any one of those chickens,' and he points, six
4918 turn naked, glumly, in a hot case – 'Could have written
4919 Shakespeare. Always have a line. If they say "Are you an idiot?"
4920 you say, "No, I'm not an idiot." That way, you'll see – you'll make
4921 out fine.'
4922    'It sounds so easy, Mike – it is Mike?' I say, 'I'm sure there is a
4923 further knack or two.'
4924    'Keep your distance. Imagine tight places – aggression without
4925 singing and without hitting people – that's rubbish,' he says.
4926    I tell him about Icaro, my bird friend, looking down on fields of
4927 flowers. Migrating – knowing exactly where you have to go and
4928 running into eagle scouts along the way...
4929    'Men and woman,' Mike interrupts, 'that's a problem. Our
4930 sensibilities have diverged, over the millennia, nothing to be done.
4931 Making up? History. That's not sharing a ciggie when you've
4932 enjoyed someone. Best not to try adventuring.'
4933    'It's all feeling,' I say. 'Perception, not cognition. If you don't
4934 go along with that, you end a bigot, old hat. Some old dogma. After
4935 the modern comes surrender. It should be sweet.'
4936    'All your friends,' says Mike, ignoring this ... what does it mean
4937 anyway, apart from making a career and lots of cash with saying
4938 it... If you're migrating – feeling's not enough...' 'They're
4939 Christians – or else they came from that Village. Except the
4940 Muslim ones – they're from a village very similar. No one comes
4941 from those now – if you did, you're empty, like a sardine can you
4942 bring home from the picnic, empty, a bit oily...'
4943    He talks on about sardines, what they're made of, how he may
4944 have been a whale in life – and thinking of the can, and being
4945 soldered into it, I find my bladder's full, and wonder if he'll still be
4946 there when I get back...
4947    He's talking to a guy – I hear... 'I'm Apollo,' the sardine riff,
4948 and he's spliced in some of me. 'Mike,' I say. 'You're a product!'

4949 'No,' he says, 'I'm buying...' but the guy has moved away.
4950 'Don't be jealous, Vince,' Mike says. 'Nothing anywhere belongs
4951 to you. And I'm not going anywhere... Do you have somewhere in
4952 mind, that you'd like to go?'
4953     'I know about it, Mike,' I say. 'Migrating, you don't go
4954 anywhere.'
4955     'You might be eaten before your time,' says Mike, 'or fall down
4956 out the sky; or netted. Shot. The timing's everything. My
4957 behaviour, Vince – it's all consistent. I'm not looking for a drinking
4958 friend that I rely on – charred with alcohol and dead before I've had
4959 my fill.' He whispers, 'The guy that I was hooking on, while you
4960 weren't here – we could roll him when he goes outside. A kicking
4961 he'll remember and get sympathy for years. A bad surprise that
4962 turns out profitable.'
4963     I don't react. He says, 'Or – we could do a tour, old time. Two
4964 hundred US cities, me on spoons and you on comb and paper. That
4965 way – you learn a good profession, and geography as well.'
4966     'Look, Mike,' I say. 'I'm more into the exotic. The things that
4967 change the world – at least reveal the lava dawdling in the cracks...
4968 "Wings beating softly, the windows flew away." Like that.'
4969     'I told you,' says Mike. 'Don't quote. It makes you seem an
4970 idiot.'
4971     'If I bought it, it would belong to me,' I say. 'Like an ex voto – it
4972 might cure something, thank someone.'
4973     'That's foolish,' Mike says. 'Exchanging invisibles, your gods,
4974 for more invisible – the capital behind your cash. Think how
4975 complicated it must be, your dimes and quarters, what lies behind
4976 all that? Nothing? – it can be so intricate, the invisible, like what's
4977 behind the dancing in the fire, poking a pointy stick right through
4978 your tongue, sacrificing fluffy animals. Down on your knees – who
4979 sees? The invisible. Counting your coins – in your pocket,
4980 caressing, over your groin. Who sees? Not you. Don't let it out, the
4981 secret. How much? How close to the big pot, that lets you buy your
4982 dream? Maybe the invisible, the sightless one who trusts in God,
4983 who struck them up, each dime, and gifted them to you – and lets
4984 you buy a cake, a shot – of bourbon, maybe, God save all those
4985 weedy kings...'
4986     'You're inconclusive, Mike,' I say. 'It all coheres. It's a mobile
4987 – you hang it on the ceiling. What for?'
4988     'We should rob that guy,' says Mike. 'Most people don't
4989 understand their teachers, or don't like their badger smell. We take

4990 his cash. Then, he finds he belongs to the world: cops, offices,
4991 surgeons. He'll thank us, and we can buy more drinks. It's a lesson
4992 not everyone gets: or else – it takes a whole fucking war, an
4993 occupation, a tyrant, smashing buildings, peeing in wells,
4994 diplomats, infanticides... we're teachers, Vince, not into politics. I
4995 could beat up on you, if you're squeamish about strangers. Your
4996 lesson, unique to you, learned, and all the benefits.'
4997    'I'll think about it, Mike,' I say.
4998    'Yes, you will, Vince,' says Mike. We drink some more: 'But
4999 you should follow me more closely.'
5000    'I always follow close,' I say. 'Hawkett. My boss. Andy –
5001 mooching, in a bar, like this. Steve, the hard man, melting off.
5002 Maya. The lovely miniature – Melissa... I follow – where do they
5003 lead? Is it all a pack, that pick me up and cast me down, because
5004 they see a destination in my eye that they won't reach, will never
5005 see...'
5006    'Oh, my friend,' says Mike: 'You're the best case I have seen. A
5007 paranoia growing in a celadon, so fine and whispy – the grey, the
5008 green... beneath, percussion swishing to uphold a voice of pure
5009 disinterest... Your innocence, dear Vince, cries to be violated.
5010 Watch your back, your front, your sides! It's not just you... The
5011 flowers – grow by themselves: if they get picked, it's chance –
5012 there's no conspiracy, no plot.'
5013    He laughs, and other guys join in – my brothers...
5014    'So, to be sure, dear Mike,' I say, 'you love my company? There
5015 is no other interest...'
5016    'Who would mislead you? You've no cash – except for picking
5017 up this tab,' he says. 'Maya had nothing, Melissa – even less. Not
5018 everyone who's nothing wants to cheat you, Vince. Trust your
5019 imagination,' he staggers, nearly falls. I hold him up.
5020    'You see,' he says, 'the holy fool, compliant Sancho, pilgrim in
5021 the bog – who see the golden walls, the crystal city – those types all
5022 die when destiny's in sight. Or – suppose – they just get sent to jail
5023 for vagrancy, resistance ... or there is no city: those are tents for
5024 refugees. Come home with me,' Mike says. 'You can't keep
5025 sleeping on that train.'
5026    He's right. There is no plot. It's true – I have the paranoia ... it's
5027 a gift, an alpenstock as I climb up the hill, steeper and steeper,
5028 thicker swarm the clouds...
5029    'Pay the bill,' says Mike. 'Sleep over in my chair. You're not
5030 wanted, are you? Not a deserter? Those boots look like military –

5031 give them here, I'll get you sandals. Used a wrong word about a
5032 war?'
5033     'Oh no, Mike,' I say.
5034     I miss the train – you could lie out on the seats.
5035     The stairs in Mike's house, a continent – 'Don't get sucked in
5036 here and there,' he says... 'They have to eat. There's couscous,
5037 steam boat, and I don't know what that is ... there's timbals, pine
5038 nuts...'
5039     'Did you notice, Mike,' I ask. 'The house is listing?'
5040     'Yes,' he says. 'It's following a trend. Big places, countries –
5041 swallowed into sink-holes. And now we have the new religion,
5042 spreading here and there – roots, leaves... Soon everyone will have
5043 a new one too – all different, and militant. If you can't choose – or
5044 haven't thought – just keep on climbing, mind your step, your hold
5045 – right up... I'm in the attic here...'
5046     'Who knows how it will end,' I say, making conversation, as the
5047 stairs are steep, some break away.
5048     'Of course, you know how,' he says. 'But then – who cares?
5049 Short lives! The best choice, and inevitable – but things get denser,
5050 faster – so you'll never know if and when it finishes... So many
5051 dramas, left incomplete – Lulu, Moses, symphonies – someone will
5052 finish them, if not – we live with that, the inconclusiveness...' And
5053 panting we arrive.
5054     He takes my jacket and my boots. 'There,' he says, 'your chair. I
5055 mostly don't have stuff. You never know when you may have to
5056 move. Those plastic bags prepared – less ostentatious than a
5057 suitcase, Vince.'
5058     There seems nothing to eat. 'Time to sleep,' he says: 'My! Those
5059 suppers smell good,' and he's gone.
5060     I pass the night up and down the stairs – each floor tilts
5061 differently. Maya. Maybe she's lodged here, a hard-shelled creature
5062 in the sea-wrack. Mostly, people have left, to work, to clean. I saw
5063 them on the train. Others sleep as long as possible. On the bells, no
5064 name looks like it's just been changed.
5065     Mike says, 'I've just eaten – you weren't here. One meal a day –
5066 the house rule! If you do fancy stuff – you'll need to knock: go
5067 down a floor.'
5068     'Where are we going, Mike?' I ask. 'Are you taking me
5069 somewhere?'
5070     'Don't be pathetic, Vince,' he says. 'I've already given. Now –
5071 it's your turn.'

5072    'It's not my world, Mike...' I say.
5073    'It's too early for the bar,' he says. 'There's no one interesting.
5074    We could sing. Duets. Berber songs – we'd need no orchestra.'
5075    'Without camels, it's not the same,' I say. 'I know a song in
5076    Farsi, and that's it.'
5077    We stare at each other.
5078    I say, 'This is a tree you live in, Mike. Each with their branch, a
5079    different fruit.'
5080    Mike is morose, he says, 'The fruit is pinched and sour. The
5081    leaves – they're poisonous. Where's the water for the roots? A
5082    broken sewer, maybe, metres down. No, Vince – your age, and
5083    mine – the age of doubt, precariousness, of curiosity – it's over.
5084    The people here – they'll grow apart until they're different species
5085    – a monkey, lemur, eagle, vulture... each eating various stuff, and
5086    fighting over it. Some in fur, some in feathers – some with bare
5087    bums aflame. When everyone has their new faith – a balance will
5088    be reached. To some the fruit, to others – others' flesh. Each
5089    against all, dear Vince – that will be it. No time for languor, sex, or
5090    telling tales.'
5091    'You'll find your twig, I'm sure,' I say. I'm not so sure.
5092    Is that a tear? This, the old dispensation – mean, squalid, on the
5093    run – does he regret...? 'Yes, I regret,' he says. 'It could have been
5094    quite comfortable. Mean spirits – that was us. Frightened,
5095    ungenerous. Our symbol was the tank. Steel cans – you fry inside.'
5096    'You're quite the moralist, dear Mike,' I say.
5097    'It's living with the fear of death,' says Mike. 'Morals don't
5098    come in. Play before you die, they say. But – fear takes the upper
5099    hand. It makes you need strong stuff – belief, a God. It's quite a
5100    paradox – this God is death. She used to be a mother too. No more.'
5101    'Then – short lives,' I say. 'Is just a strategy. It's realism; it's
5102    what you get, not what you want.'
5103    Mike pushes me towards the stairs. 'You owe me for the night,'
5104    he says. 'You didn't sleep, and so you pay. Since you can't pay, I'll
5105    show you how to live.'
5106    'I don't want a job of conning drunks, Mike,' I say. 'I don't want
5107    to end up working for some stupid strongarm hood. Besides –
5108    you're stuck on your metal: sardine cans, tanks. It's against the
5109    common view, that seats each in their carrel, jollying along with all
5110    the rest.'
5111    'You have to work it out,' says Mike. 'I'm right. Guys in the
5112    tank – Laszlo, David or Saul, Elroy and Mahomet – of course they

5113    get on. They're comrades, all in love. "Pass the shell," says one.
5114    "Right away, my sweet," the other. What I tell you, Vince, you
5115    have to think about it. That's where I differ from all the rest.'
5116        'It isn't always easy, Mike,' I say. 'It doesn't always make a
5117    sense.'
5118        'You see, Vince,' Mike says. 'You like my little caricatures.
5119    You love the dialogue. All powerful people – love to talk, they talk
5120    to everyone. It doesn't mean a thing. They love ingenuous guys like
5121    you: you think you're smart, you flatter them. It doesn't mean a
5122    thing. If I were to sell you, Vince – what would you fetch?
5123    Something? Nothing? A nickel for your conversation – your yes
5124    and no. It's dull, dear Vince.'
5125        Mike scuttles down the road – in baggy brown – he's a
5126    shameless mutt: appearances? If they matter – they're irresistible.
5127    'Come on!' he shouts, 'I'm the one whose legs are short. Run!
5128    Everyone – look – they stand back!'
5129        Running after him – doesn't make a team of us.
5130        Melissa – the tiny solid figure in the core that gives the
5131    matrioshka meaning. Someone must know what that meaning is.
5132    Foetus? Saviour? Someone knows. Or – everybody knows but me.
5133        'Mike,' I ask, 'Is it riches? Is that what you're looking for?'
5134        'I don't want to be a rich man, Vince,' he says. 'But yes – I
5135    guess – rather than inner life, it's cash my reasoning and my
5136    rhetoric are hitched to... Why? The poor all think like me... In my
5137    way, it's them I serve...'
5138        'But Mike,' I say. 'Suppose we have a different scheme. All in
5139    the middling sort. Maybe a tawdry prize for thoroughbreds – a
5140    book, a frock... Everything you do – transformed. Equality – will
5141    bring fraternity...' He leaps in:
5142        'No, no,' he shouts, 'it isn't so. Do you want fraternity, Vince?
5143    You're not the sort. That needs a different route. But I seek purity,
5144    dear Vince. Abnegation, sacrifice.'
5145        'And paradox?' I ask.
5146        'Of course. That's in my schedule. It's the part I most enjoy. It
5147    takes real effort: the drunks, the ignorant – those are easy. Maybe I
5148    disappoint you so?' asks Mike. 'If I transform the world – does that
5149    make me useless? If everything is changed – poor into rich or
5150    middling – I'll be changed too. But it's not. I am as I am. Exactly.
5151    Not forgetting who I owe, and who owes me.'
5152        'You're not my train, Mike,' I say. 'You don't take passengers.'

5153     'Only the poor understand purity,' says Mike. 'Because they live
5154     a life that's absolutely not. If you're rich though – you don't
5155     entertain the thought.'
5156        'Is it good, Mike, being pure?' I ask. 'Or is it just a thought –
5157     like being equal. Is that good? When they have something like it –
5158     people don't enjoy. Is it a good, Mike?'
5159        'I've really no idea,' he says, hurrying away. 'I think it's like the
5160     fire for you. I don't pester you for that.'
5161        He pushes open the pub door – there's a roar of welcome, maybe
5162     just a roar. He turns,
5163        'Your mission, Vince...'
5164        'Yes, Mike?' I say. 'Yes, I have one, like everybody else.'
5165        'Here,' he says, 'here's my parting gift.'
5166        A magnificent kazoo, a little rusty, but the rest shines like the
5167     moon. A moment of epiphany, though – suppose, that everything
5168     Mike told me was a con – the wars, his doing without furniture, the
5169     charge for sleeping over... 'The house, Mike,' I say, 'all your
5170     invention?'
5171        'What do I want with furniture?' he asks. 'And people make
5172     their millions for people sleeping in their beds. Civilised people –
5173     always need a pretext for the greedy things they do. I'm not greedy,
5174     Vince. I do best exactly what I do. Holy fools, like you, Vince –
5175     they're old hat. The walking on the water, flying donkeys, power to
5176     the imagination – or was it the working class? – those Jews, those
5177     Arabs, were they gullible, taken in by holy fools – or making fun of
5178     Romans who were there to stay? Inventing things, dear Vince – it
5179     leads to terrible revenge. Don't do it. It's an explosive. Remember
5180     Dostoevsky, following his lucky fairy – the wheel of fortune,
5181     hobnob with the kings and queens, and slap them down... Beware
5182     the knaves, my friend. You know they're there, but on you go!
5183     They're waiting for the deaths – then they'll be kings themselves.'
5184        He plays the huckster: 'On my left – the water-walkers: on my
5185     right – the flying donkeys! Ladies, gents – a contest never seen
5186     before. And after – for the title – imagination, up against the
5187     working class!'
5188        He laughs, he coughs, he spits.
5189        'No, Mike,' I say. 'It's all two centuries ago. I have no truck
5190     with all of that...'
5191        'Then tell it to the people in the house,' he shouts. 'And if it's
5192     really all for cash and land – then give them some of yours!'

5193
5194
5195
5196
5197
5198
5199
5200
5201
5202
5203
5204
5205
5206
5207
5208
5209
5210
5211
5212
5213
5214
5215
5216
5217
5218
5219
5220
5221
5222
5223
5224
5225
5226
5227
5228
5229
5230
5231
5232

He's gone. A cruel shot from the great bow no one can string but him. He never told me how to live – I didn't want him to, but it's something more that I have missed. All the other creatures scurrying by... I'm a pliant tree, silent in their forest ... some rub on me and leave a clot of fur, or urinate, sharpen a claw. It's nothing special – this wearing down my biteless bark – is all my day and most of nights.

*

'Hey!' the shout: 'Stand up, no pathos.'

Here she is, Tara – a long blue stick for walking, but not in urban lanes. She's blue – her arms, her neck. 'Don't stare,' she says, 'I'm not a leaflet. I'm a parchment – gives you rights, takes most away.'

'Don't explain,' I say. I wait for her Gennaro – the usual jealous type – he's in the shadow there...

'Armand!' she shouts. 'Come out, salute this stranded wreck. We'll pull him off the reef.'

'Oh no,' I think. 'There's been the past, with Andy – a hard landing – on crutches. Grounded, flight annulled. Steve – the present – fleeing with the desperate, their faces lit like in old movies where you cranked by hand, all under-speed, Maya cloche-hatted, kohl-eyed ... Mike – and the future: all manacled, aligned and humble in a chant...'

'No time for that, she says: 'That's old stuff. Past, future, forget all that: a short life has this beauty – it's all at once. The past – not composted; the future quite improbable. And what you have – is not the present, with its layerings of all the rest, the pallid lives all round – all the unknowns, the unpresentables, the virtuals, the severed heads on plinths. Forget the swish of time: that's tinnitus for you. You have so little time – best to assume there's none.'

'It makes sense, Tara,' I say: 'But my adventures ... no more roofs or wings of styrofoam...'

'Quite right,' she says: 'You've no time for accidents. I know – we blue people are a scarce resource. Those men of the desert – they were napalmed, then deprived of everything. Some was an accident, mostly malignity. Best avoid sand, stay schtum and near a bus route...'

'Your cash?' I ask.

5233   Tara looks like she's had breakdowns, like the bus. You need to
5234   find another going well, and get a part from that... Maybe it's sex-
5235   shows they put on... Or painting bodies.
5236       'Oh,' she says, 'if you don't think about it, cash keeps coming
5237   in. And if you haven't thought and then there's none – your mind's
5238   quite free. There's no burden from what's not there – that's a
5239   scientific law as well. You have to keep within the rules in
5240   something – and that's a good and easy one. "Nothing is from
5241   nothing made." It's poetry.'
5242       'I'm sure you're right, Tara,' I say. 'But filling even a short life
5243   – especially with something huge... it needs a take...'
5244       'I'll start way back,' she says. 'It started bad. The Germans –
5245   they devised an epic: a foundation myth. Those, you know, must
5246   end in "all goes well". The guy commissioned wrote the music too.
5247   It was an evening's show, with tunes. His bigotry – maybe it
5248   underlay the tragedy. You never never say "it all goes wrong". He
5249   did. It all fell down, for everyone. The trenches, the massacres, the
5250   camps... His Ring – it turned out just a ring of corporations...' and
5251   on she talks. Armand has heard it many times: he says, 'Tara thinks
5252   to write it as an elegy. She'd have done the epic right – but it's too
5253   late. That's why our lives are short...'
5254       'No, Armand,' Tara says. 'There's more than that – but there's
5255   no time to tell it now.'
5256       'There's no hurry, Tara,' Armand says.
5257       She hurries us along. The stick is used to point to crenellations –
5258   'Hohenstaufen or Hohenstollen?' she asks, chuckling ... or to raise
5259   mail flaps... Maybe there's a letter there that she could read... 'Out
5260   of date, out of time, Tara,' Armand says.
5261       She pokes at nests in hedgerows – 'A pipit, a poppet... What a
5262   lark, if only there were birds alive...'
5263       So, we roister down the street: 'You're an intellectual, Tara,' I
5264   say: 'I don't know how to deal...'
5265       'From the top you deal, you mutt,' she says: 'God wasn't an
5266   intellectual. A simple soul – if there was one of those attached. But
5267   if You are the Star – when you die, there's nothing left.'
5268       'Always the joker, Tara,' Armand says, unenthused. He says to
5269   me. 'She can't celebrate. Nothing has a terminus for her, no
5270   consequence secure. It's her affliction.'
5271       'Her body isn't the beginning and the end, like it is for us,' I say.
5272   'There's always a commentary to be drawn on it.'
5273       'From it,' Tara says.

5274    'Tara is broken,' Armand says. 'She's lost her substance. Only
5275    style is left.'
5276    'I've not seen this before,' I say. 'I'd want that for myself.
5277    Substance – it doesn't make you friends, and weighs you down.'
5278    'Energy,' Tara says. 'It's having much too much. It lifts you up,
5279    it wears you out. That's what has no substance. People live many
5280    years – but still their lives are short. Mine will be shorter still. The
5281    time you feel alive, that is. What shall I do? What do you want –
5282    help someone you don't know? End their misery? It would take a
5283    century, then you're both dead, gaga, speaking different languages
5284    – not well – not having travelled round, seen the mountains, the
5285    sanctuaries, the skittery blue and yellow beast beneath the rock the
5286    instant when it terminates, its whole chapter, its file, drawer in the
5287    laboratory – all extinct, tossed into the furnace...'
5288        'It's what I've been asking, Tara, on and off,' I say. 'Those
5289    questions.'
5290        'You need a question for that answer,' Armand says. 'I think we
5291    shouldn't be burdened with you, Vince.'
5292        'What burden?' I ask. 'You have money.'
5293        'They pay me to look after Tara,' Armand says.
5294        'There's nothing wrong with her,' I say.
5295        'Look, Vince,' he says, pushing me aside. 'You think they pay
5296    you, just because you are alive? One of you must be sick, real sick,
5297    before...'
5298        'It's the last day of your life, Vince,' Tara says. 'How do you
5299    spend it? You could shoot that guy over there – right through the
5300    eye – the left one, closed; the other's aiming at you. No one wants
5301    this piece of scrubby land you scrabble over, but who aims best
5302    makes everybody rich, they'll eat sheep's tails, they have good
5303    lives, and holidays to see the pyramids. That copy of Le Cid you
5304    brought along and never read – who'd you want to have it? Not me,
5305    I don't hold with it...'
5306        Dark and misty, we hear the siren in the rushes: 'There's a river-
5307    boat,' says Armand. 'I wonder, will it go to Krems?'
5308        'If the river's long enough, it will go to Krems,' says Tara. 'The
5309    monks will give us two white cells. I'm sure I know the captain – it
5310    won't cost.'
5311        'Do you need have faith to get a cell?' Armand wonders.
5312        'The Sufis were wonderful,' Tara says. 'But they showed
5313    themselves too much. The dance – it always makes me cry, to
5314    watch, and think of genius revolving, slowly raise its arms.'

5315      They go aboard: they don't take me. Tara cartwheels up the
5316   ramp. There's no one else about. Armand picks up Tana's stick,
5317   carries it after her, as he's been taught.
5318      How valiant they are, Tara and Armand. Forget Indians and
5319   robots, those straight faces, our brothers that we'll never see, our
5320   silent selves... Those two stride out alone, disconnected ... not
5321   taking sides, because they don't believe enough to do what must be
5322   done: destroy your enemies, go bowling with their heads, throw
5323   roses at your warriors.
5324      The money... Is it really tossed to them, so they can roam? I
5325   should have asked.

5326
5327                                     *
5328
5329      'We're tired of being poor,' says Whitney. 'We're passing it on.
5330   That's why you get to rent the room.'
5331      'Remember it always,' says Dolores. 'If you don't, it's not worth
5332   the money.'
5333      'I'll make a start,' I say. 'Maybe the bed's broken leg will mend,
5334   if I take my time. And – where will you sleep now?'
5335      'You have a niggly mien,' says Whitney. 'The earth is made of
5336   broken things. The moon – that just spun off. No use to anyone –
5337   but people go on and on...'
5338      'Fine,' I say. 'I guess the money's for your useful things.'
5339      'We're going into action,' Whitney says. 'Soldiers or doctors –
5340   whichever seems the best.'
5341      'They're both mortal skills,' Dolores says. 'They interdepend,
5342   and both are lined with goodness.'
5343      'I don't need your justification. Give me some pegs to hang my
5344   memories on...'
5345      'Don't be clever about the garden,' Whitney says. 'It's not for
5346   fine writing, nor for snootiness. A dead lady left the furnishings –
5347   you wouldn't throw them out.'
5348      'I might,' I say, thinking of Mike, not gathering stuff – and
5349   Maya, needing it.
5350      'It's not about taste,' Dolores says. 'We fit right in, for size.
5351   We're all normal in this street. You don't want to empty out.
5352   Someone might call.'
5353      'Or mistake our house for theirs,' says Whitney. 'Then, there's
5354   burglars. If you've nothing to take, they kill your cat.'

5355      They move into another space, giggling over me. Whitney is a
5356  frizzy blonde, Dolores has red ends – for sure, I'll remember
5357  everything.
5358      'It's good,' I say. 'You don't want to start anything or analyse –
5359  just to do good.' It's a thing you say, to make friends, reduce the
5360  rent.
5361      'Oh no,' Dolores says, 'we want to do good by doing bad.'
5362      'Underneath,' I say, 'you want to do it together – maybe there's
5363  love involved. They say when all else goes, love remains.' That's
5364  another thing you say.
5365      'They say that, do they?' asks Dolores. 'It's crap. Love's dying
5366  all the time. A grope, forgotten date, trench mouth: you're on your
5367  own – no sympathy.'
5368      'Interesting lives, you have,' I say.
5369      What does that mean? – that there's someone else involved –
5370  somewhere. Your own life doesn't interest you, not in that way.
5371      'Our lives?' Whitney asks, looking for some repartee. 'We
5372  haven't had them yet. And when they're done – we can't talk to
5373  you about them.'
5374      'That's why\ you must remember things,' Dolores says.
5375  'Dimensions, smells – start with the room you're in. That should be
5376  simple – most people here – have rooms. Others have a jungle, or a
5377  desert, and no rooms – that gives your memory a feast, but not
5378  more happiness...'
5379      'That's what we'll probably find out,' says Whitney. 'When
5380  you've something larger than a room, with no happiness – but
5381  what?'
5382      'Remembering,' I say. 'That's what transpires. But, Whitney,
5383  this doesn't seem to tilt you where you want to go. You're back to
5384  poor people in a space.'
5385      'Yes,' says Whitney. 'But this time we're looking on.'
5386      'I get the scene,' I say. 'Saving bad lives – or living them.
5387  Which do you prefer – being killed before your holiday – or after?
5388  Not so easy. You might save the fare, the threat of rain...'
5389      'That's if you go away,' Dolores says, giggling. 'If you're at
5390  home – the question's only one of time.'
5391      'Jolly people, Whitney, Dolores. I've been meeting lots like you
5392  – moving along, questioning the inscrutable, not caring much about
5393  response...' I say. 'It's disappointing.'
5394      'Oh, Vince,' Dolores says. 'We're not benevolent. You can't
5395  relax with us. We might do to you what we might do to anyone.

5396   More – since you have lodged with us. Most things that lodge in
5397   you – must be cut out or burned away.'
5398   'You don't talk like doctors,' I say. 'I wonder, do you know
5399   more about soldiering?'
5400   'The basic's much the same,' says Whitney. 'You bring relief.
5401   Bad news – it's seen as your intelligence. That doesn't mean it's
5402   easy, either way, but it's been done for centuries...'
5403   'And like the song says, "Everybody dies",' Dolores says, and
5404   laughs.
5405   'You're dangerous,' I say. 'You've no brakes.'
5406   'Ah,' says Whitney. 'That means speed. It's a real puzzle – you
5407   think you're going fast – but it's just turned into light, here in your
5408   skull.'
5409   Dolores interrupts, 'We thought a lot about the invention of
5410   time. At first, it wasn't. Things just came round. There was
5411   duration – but that went on and on, colourless and flat. It's only
5412   recently that people learned to chop it up – long lengths and short,
5413   like spills...' 'Spaghetti,' Whitney interrupts. 'We were into
5414   Buddhism – a drama seconds long, a drum, a fan, a long white
5415   gown, black buttons.' 'Like a surgeon's,' says Dolores.
5416   'There was long and short, and also where you were, and we
5417   were outside it, so we wanted something more. Our time,' says
5418   Whitney. 'Doing what we want in it, without an end, without an
5419   interruption. War and peace – it's all the same. No one to tell you
5420   which is which.'
5421   'This place,' Dolores says. 'They go to lots of wars, and tell you
5422   when they stop, and some they say will never end. So – if they can
5423   do it, so can we...'
5424   I lie down on the bed and hope they'll go away.
5425   They won't go away. They live here – I don't. I hear them
5426   laughing – they're both much larger than me – if there's a fight...
5427   Dolores shakes me – 'You've been trained,' she says. 'A
5428   recruit.'
5429   'Yes, I joined, to find a person,' I tell her. I don't mention boots,
5430   or pills.
5431   'We have a friend,' Dolores says. 'Mister Bongo – from the
5432   Congo. We wouldn't call him that – he does.'
5433   'That's a place they might want you both,' I say.
5434   Whitney's too chubby for a long march. Dolores is tall enough
5435   to see above the bushes. A sack of rockets on her back, precious as
5436   a baby, so they say.

5437   'Mister Bongo's quite delightful,' says Dolores. 'I love *frites*
5438   too, though it's not clear to me – were they an African invention?
5439   Or an importation? We know potatoes came from there. All that,
5440   the horror, it's all part of us. We sent it there, they've sent it back.
5441   No one is cured, not ever. Ostend – Oostende, they call it – where
5442   Christ came in procession, to make us beautiful – in an hour, you
5443   see it all, *frites* a-plenty. It's a friendly place, if you're not from
5444   there. They remind me of Slovaks, in a way.'
5445       'I don't see you in the Chinese army, though,' I say. 'You live
5446   on intimacy... Your take, your world...'
5447       'You're right,' she says. 'Two of you, of us, can't stand in line,
5448   in order. It would look absurd. No action, then, for us. You can't
5449   fool around with scalpels, either – the Chinese are demanding, do
5450   things quick – tick-tack, before you know.'
5451       'Dolores,' I say. 'You've got it wrong – your side, it would be
5452   here. You'd not go anywhere. Not needed, not wanted. The enemy,
5453   it would be them: for them, is you. Your future – exactly what you
5454   have right now, here in this house. Short lives, but not heroic, not
5455   what you'd want.'
5456       'It may not come to that,' she says.
5457       'I've nearly memorised the room,' I say.
5458       'I told Whitney having someone in would fuck up everything,'
5459   she says.
5460       In the morning, they've gone away. Their note says – 'Put the
5461   rent in the pig, Pig.'
5462       I don't see any pig.
5463
5464                                    *
5465
5466   'I see we're brothers,' the person says – it says 'Anna' on her
5467   badge: we're stuck, not glued together – something's broken down.
5468   'You realise,' she says, 'it's odds and sods that govern us. However
5469   they get in ... election or the warming pan. You'll not be rid of
5470   them. We're in a primitive stage. You either stick with them, or you
5471   develop or transform. Minorities – they help. The Jews made
5472   German industry, Janissaries helped the empire float... Syrians,
5473   Iraqis – they have history behind them, and they're smart...
5474       'Guys like you – they're quite deluded. I bet you think that
5475   people, places – they are interchangeable. It's mostly true. It isn't
5476   wholly true – so it's not true at all. Hotels – they look alike, even if
5477   you holiday on Mars. And people – they're all equal, as you know,

5478 and yet – like the hotels, we see each one is different within – like
5479 chocolates in a box. Yours are illusions, friend! You have to come
5480 to terms with difference – although it may not matter much, my
5481 dear.'
5482     They winch us back. We start again. It's a relief – anger's no
5483 use, when you're halted. Outside, there's a noise of sabres clashing,
5484 long sparks.
5485     'The trolley came off the wires,' says Anna. 'And the points are
5486 never true. That's why we're lurching forward.'
5487     'You can't steal a tram,' I say. 'And the passengers – they're
5488 special. They don't carry notes, only small coins. On every trip you
5489 glimpse goodness, how it could be if the tracks were straight.'
5490     'It takes a bright city to have tramways,' Anna says. 'You need
5491 to know where people want to go.'
5492     'Guys tried to fly centuries before they thought to lay a track,' I
5493 say. 'Our brains must be put in the wrong way round...'
5494     'That's not at all the way to think,' she says. 'Don't stand so
5495 close. What makes you think I'd want to see you another time?'
5496     'Nothing,' I say. 'Just to hang on to, while I decide my future.'
5497     'Exactly,' Anna says. 'In your obtuseness, you're quite smart.'
5498     'It's about perfection, Anna,' I say. 'This ride on the tram. Many
5499 people have the tickle: the meeting, the performance. Finding a
5500 companion. I have, many times.'
5501     'Sex and perfection – those are different things,' she says.
5502 'When you reach perfection – it's the end. The fall, the splash –
5503 they think it's a fish, that silver leg with gold stubble going down.
5504 The flesh – it flakes off like soaked bread, the eyes flat – like
5505 dimes. They don't bug out. And go pop – it's inaudible anyway. If
5506 you have it all inside you, everything there is up to now – and no
5507 doubt you have – why let it out in a display, an airshow? Look at us
5508 all here, in this launch, motoring along, on our rocking stream,
5509 knowing it all and letting nothing out at all. Getting off when it's
5510 our time. Mostly we don't pay the fare, but – we keep schtum. Try
5511 it.'
5512     'Someone gave me this stick,' I say. 'I've ways to go.'
5513     'There's many shops sell those, Vince,' says Anna. 'Gift means
5514 nothing special. It's over. There's nothing more for you to do.
5515 Forget the hanged man and the tipping castle – it's been done. The
5516 guys here – have everything on their screens. Balloons, floating up
5517 and down, not like the real thing – that's the game you have to play
5518 when it's all revealed. Revelations are infinite, minus one ... near to

5519   infinity, it must mean there's one to suit. Believe or don't – what's
5520   there is what there is.' She laughs, as I have no reply. 'You wanted
5521   destiny, poor Vince, that sat beside you, fit your plan. I am your
5522   fate, Vince, and I'll drag you down. I'll put my suckers in your eyes
5523   and suck your stomach out and make you spit your lungs... No tears
5524   – the sea is what you've wept. No sleep, I'm bells inside your
5525   skull...'
5526        'I don't deserve you, Anna,' I tell her, crumbling. 'I never did
5527   wrong to anyone, never anything by myself...'
5528        'Oh, my dear,' she says. 'You're in the web, your little thrashing
5529   legs are sticky with your sentiment. Don't be afraid – I fly, I don't
5530   spin and weave. My wings are black – but you will never see
5531   them.'
5532        There's always a way out – those millions we've forgot, and
5533   everything they did ... although – behind the wall – there's
5534   rumbling, mining going on. Maybe my boss – a plan, a motor,
5535   pushing us along...
5536        'There's always that,' says Anna. 'You make your walls without
5537   a crack – no windows, then the beast arrives, opens the plaster with
5538   its horn, you see your garden's all been gobbled up, it's holms and
5539   furrows, armed men springing up.'
5540        'That's the poetry,' I say. 'There must be more, not just potato
5541   skins.'
5542        'Here's the trick,' she says. 'You know how runners fill
5543   themselves with someone else's blood – spiked up, maybe a phial
5544   of Alexander's, San Gennaro's – well: the guys who move the
5545   scroll along and let you see what they have drawn, and where you
5546   are on it – they have a special blood. Replete with that – they have
5547   short memories. Short lives – those don't appal. They don't feel
5548   pain – above all, yours... They make the story, invent it as they sing
5549   an aria so full of air, it bears you to the clouds, it lands you on an
5550   attol ... everything's unique, the centre's smoking, there's no fire ...
5551   most things are poisonous, but you can live on nuts ... there's
5552   promises of slaves that's washed ashore that you can eat or set to
5553   work...'
5554        'I see all this, dear Anna. But...' I say.
5555        'The greatness lies for some guy who can make the blood,' she
5556   says. 'Mostly it comes from holy warriors, funambulists and human
5557   cannon-balls. Since everyone aspires – what you most need is
5558   synthesis: an artificial boost, available to all. Or, better – available
5559   to just a few. You set the price...'

5560 'It doesn't work like this,' I say. 'The great men filled with
5561 Lethe blood ... it's just a fable... The scroll – it's set on automatic –
5562 it comes out with scrawls and runes already formed...'
5563 'No,' says Anna.
5564 How beautiful she is. The skin – what you see here on the tram,
5565 is limited – I bet it goes all over...
5566 'No,' she says. 'You keep the fear, it's an essential. But cut out
5567 the pain.'
5568 'Then it's what runners have,' I say.
5569 'No, no,' she says. 'When you run, you mustn't flap your arms,
5570 or pound your fists, or think of things to say. Simple arithmetic,
5571 daggers behind the tapestry ... what bosses do –all that is special,
5572 must be added on.'
5573 'I guess that long ago, people had their sage, their seer, their
5574 queen, their warrior. A shaman, too... One by one, they pass by, the
5575 tall poppies, their pictures drawn, they smirk, and scan the
5576 portraitist, easy on their elephant, the donkey trotting by ... but
5577 now...' I say.
5578 'Yes, yes,' she says. 'You need them by the thousand – nature's
5579 not equipped.'
5580 'We could concoct the stuff,' I say. 'Or denounce the use. But,
5581 since meeting you, Anna, and underneath the love, desire, that
5582 accompany this ride – I feel an overwhelming anger and despair.
5583 The vanity – oh, the vanity – it puffs your veins and shrinks your
5584 arteries...'
5585 'Exposing the trick is easy, quickly done – but earns us less than
5586 manufacturing,' she says.
5587 'Well,' I say. 'Here we both are. In a place where nothing grows.
5588 Nothing for me, nothing for you – we're sterile. We can't pick each
5589 other's flower. Or stick our prick inside its dust.'
5590 'We can't be in the place where nothing grows,' she says.
5591 'Things grow everywhere. It can't be us that isn't in the place that
5592 can't exist. We're stuck, that's true: here is the fence – but we want
5593 more, and different. You, Vince, want what you can't have – it's
5594 easy to stop wanting it. And if we make the artificial blood – you
5595 think it's not for us...? Are we so stupid that we'd sell the stuff?'
5596 'It all seems crazy, Anna – first, the flying, now the blood...' I
5597 say.
5598 'No, no,' she says. 'Think Blériot. They're all called mad until
5599 they're millionaires.'

| | |
|---|---|
| 5600 | 'They say the Russians had those first machines,' I say. |
| 5601 | 'Harassing their enemies as Moscow burned. Wings fur-covered – |
| 5602 | then buried in the permafrost. They couldn't dig them out.' |
| 5603 | 'Exactly so,' she says. 'Your business model must be fur- |
| 5604 | covered too, or else you don't get first prize.' |
| 5605 | 'This is the business, then, as they say: *le business*,' I say. 'Odds, |
| 5606 | sods, and tarts. They're the strongest, they're the motor. No |
| 5607 | compassion, no fine comprehension quite misplaced. They win |
| 5608 | because they're winners.' |
| 5609 | 'You sell so you can buy,' says Anna. 'Yourself first and last, |
| 5610 | the rest, as they occur. Remember – all heavens are disfunctional – |
| 5611 | Olympus, Valhalla. Come on, Vince, little soldier, raise your |
| 5612 | banner! That Mount Atheos – how those monks quarrel over what |
| 5613 | vegetables to plant! Listen to the songs – they'll tell you all the |
| 5614 | stories you want – "*O weile, weile wandellos!*" "stay, don't change" |
| 5615 | ... even when you're dead – wow! how you change when you're a |
| 5616 | corpse! On your horse, Vince! Remember – it's not only wolves |
| 5617 | that howl – you've the whole sky to raise your muzzle to... That |
| 5618 | song – "All I really want is to be wonderful" – that's the spirit! |
| 5619 | Your grail – it's that crucible of dragons' blood. See it foam and |
| 5620 | seethe. You'd change that for a frolic on used sheets? With me – |
| 5621 | worn thin as I am ... Insane!' |
| 5622 | 'There's no feeling in us, Anna,' I say, 'But you know how to |
| 5623 | raise me up. It doesn't matter, if it's hate...' |
| 5624 | 'Yes,' she says. 'The strongest potion you have in you – that is |
| 5625 | the thrust.' |
| 5626 | There's something here that's going to fail, to wreck. 'I don't |
| 5627 | want all of this,' I say. 'The thing we'd look for – it's like what |
| 5628 | those endless movies seek: another Ring, even the tunes. They're |
| 5629 | pits I won't fall in.' |
| 5630 | 'It's true,' she says. 'Most people involved in them, those films |
| 5631 | – they don't survive. Armour, space suits – all heavy togs. You see |
| 5632 | the trembling hands – is it the weight they bear? The guys that hold |
| 5633 | the camera – their grip is firm. Maybe it's them that brings the |
| 5634 | drugs and guns. The others, actors all, both sides of the lens – they |
| 5635 | don't survive: they fall off wooden rocks, pop the wrong stuff, are |
| 5636 | cut down on divans ... they're knifed, they have destinies bizarre |
| 5637 | with animals... You're right. Maybe it's not us, not our scenario. A |
| 5638 | past rouged up as future – the holiness has been sucked out ... the |
| 5639 | stars, the knights, the dwarves – all fascist kitsch.' |

5640 'Anna,' I say, 'let's move away from that. Forget the holiness –
5641 it doesn't suit.'
5642 'You're right,' she says. 'Inventing things. Empowering. Making
5643 a name and cash. Power to the people, all fired with the same
5644 blood... It all sounds innocent. Innocence – they won't believe you,
5645 and it isn't true. Everyone distrusts the claim.'
5646 'What then?' I ask.
5647 'We renounce our invention,' Anna says. 'All its consequences.
5648 It's buried in us. We'll forget it. The game, that one – it never
5649 started.'
5650 It's a fine idea: I look closely at her. Those aren't furrows on her
5651 face – they're lines – a net, scales – drawn with the finest pen.
5652 'It isn't age,' says Anna. 'That will come – the lines here are a
5653 plan. A city that I shouldn't want to live in.'
5654 'Just lines?' I ask. 'It's a tarmac, runways for airships deviating
5655 with the breeze. Where are the buildings?'
5656 'Oh,' she says. 'It's painful, walking in that space. You need a
5657 car – but driving's such a bore.'
5658 'That – could be a castle – a copy of those blown up or down,' I
5659 say, running a finger over.
5660 'No,' she says. 'That's a nose. Not war damage – those are
5661 nostrils.'
5662 'Expressionism in the purest state,' I say. She runs on – 'Or the
5663 plan, the face-space, might be of rooms – trapezoid. Traps – rooms
5664 full of dirty people, shooting up. Who'd want to spend a weekend
5665 there?'
5666 'If you knew exactly what your plans meant,' I say. 'The
5667 knowledge might kill. Get you thrown out. This way – you're safe.
5668 It's all – on your face, inscrutable. No transgression, and no
5669 destination. Nowhere you would want to go, but only yours, no
5670 danger, not communicable.'
5671 'You think you're clever,' Anna says. 'You've no idea – why the
5672 city was blown up, who's squatting in its spacious ruin, where
5673 those airbags are flying to.'
5674 'I don't need to know,' I say.
5675 'There,' she says. 'You've got it. If you need anything – write it
5676 on your body. It can be rubbed off. The spirit of it all, of
5677 everything, in miniature. No bass trombones – a tiny box, let into
5678 your armpit – that will do the trick. Abnegation. Know everything –
5679 keep quiet about it. Live everywhere – don't pay the rent. Life – a
5680 sip, a sniff – releases every countryside and every fruit, the sweat of

5681 every harvester. Have truck with forms, with wholes – what they
5682 call the telescope's wrong end – that shows true distances, how far
5683 you are from everything.'
5684     I kiss her – the top of her head. She turns her face, illegible
5685 beneath the *craquelure*. 'There,' she says, 'that was it. The
5686 everything. You'll remember it for all your life.'
5687     We'd long since left the tram. 'Up high – you see them come.
5688 Down low – you have more chance to run away,' she says. The
5689 building only has two floors.
5690     Her days are long – some hands of poker on the screen – 'I've
5691 friends who give me numbers,' Anna says. 'On the plastic card and
5692 on the hands. We split the winnings: losses, they don't count.'
5693 Then, it's the baseball channel, into the night – 'That diamond,'
5694 Anna says. 'It's the best I'll ever have.' I have no comment.
5695     'It may disappoint, all this,' she says, 'but every wrinkle's
5696 clear...'
5697     'Remember, Vince,' she says, 'apes are born to be sad. In the
5698 jungle – it's hetero heaven, but how glum they are. Picking
5699 themselves all day.'
5700     I don't speak, don't answer that infrequent speech. I'm not
5701 missed, it adds nothing. There was Bianca – the lady who
5702 disappeared, without a shadow, no cry. I should feel bad. No doubt
5703 they come looking, for me, the people who do that. I don't feel bad
5704 at all, but I don't want them to catch me.
5705     'The best thing,' says Anna. 'Is you don't need meet those
5706 people – the poker, there's no one real. The baseball – those little
5707 guys in uniform, you know exactly how they are. It's arithmetic –
5708 their money's not for things or services. Just swing the bat and
5709 multiply.'
5710     'We're out here on the periphery,' I say. 'More village than a
5711 *banlieue*. It's hard for me to move around.'
5712     'Poor albatross,' she says. 'Your long legs don't let you flap
5713 those little wings. Try walking. Not on the water – the sharks are
5714 waiting.'
5715     'There's nothing left to say,' I say.
5716     'Exactly – that's the goal. That's the accomplishment,' she says.
5717     'There's guys round here,' I say. 'Who want another chapter –
5718 the one about the fire. I know all about the flames – those that burn
5719 out, and there's nothing left... Their fires, though – they blaze
5720 throughout the night, the desert's black with smoke and soot ... the
5721 earth is eaten like a lump of coal.'

5722 'There's nothing new,' says Anna. 'It isn't you or me, the gangs
5723 who try to ride the world. You know how to keep clean, Vince.
5724 Remember when you walked the line, the 8s, the 18s. And now
5725 you're here, at peace, bored as you've never been before...'
5726     'It all changes, Anna,' I say. 'Another system creeps in, imposes
5727 – we don't know what to ask, what it can do. The guys that fight it
5728 – they fight us as well.'
5729     'You chatter, Vince,' she says. 'Silence was better. I have
5730 everything here set up just right.'
5731     Nothing holds me here. I could just walk away.
5732     I walk away – that was the invitation. I'm free. Except – you
5733 have to bear those coins, moist, hot in my pants. The heads of
5734 spirits that I don't believe in. That no one does now – yet, they
5735 persist, the myths that you can't live without. Maybe they unite us
5736 in our disbelief – not that I care about that stuff... I could sign up,
5737 fight for freedom, death to the occupiers ... but I'm free. Doing all
5738 that – requires I'd not be free. That's far too much ... and firing
5739 guns or digging holes. Not good jobs, for sure... All that
5740 obedience...
5741     The walking wears you down, is all.
5742
5743                   *
5744
5745     'I have experience,' I say. 'I know, everyone does. Maybe it's not
5746 always bad, admitting it. You still need a job, despite it all.'
5747     The lady laughs, as though I am ingratiating.
5748     There is no war. People are recruited, off they go, some with a
5749 band. Corpses return. There's shooting around, not where you are.
5750 It's normal, like it was, as long as I remember.
5751     I tell the boss – 'I fear I need some work.' He's thoughtful, not
5752 like the other guy, boss, who wanted to be told he should get out,
5753 forget the vanity.
5754     'It's not the money, Vince,' he says. 'That's to stop the
5755 squeaking wheel.'
5756     Oton. A Kurd, a Bosniak? Or both, or turned by cash to
5757 something else, a hybrid, in between, more shaded, more
5758 anonymous.
5759     'There's two systems, circling round,' he says. 'A global one,
5760 with guys in suits and jeans. And guys contesting. What do they
5761 wear? All kinds of stuff – disguises, uniforms... Do you believe the

5762 story, Vince? The epics? Ancient stuff, at war with ancient stuff...
5763 Does it make sense to you?'
5764 'Oh no,' I say. 'You mean – old-time religion? Clans? And
5765 dancing?'
5766 'That's it, Vince,' he says. 'Then there's the bigger scene –
5767 survival, saving the bees. Digging up everything.'
5768 'I know all that,' I say. 'That's what I think about. I know it all.
5769 But knowing ... everybody knows.'
5770 'The systems touch...' says Oton, vaguely.
5771 'Oton,' I say, 'I'll save you cash. Give me an envelope, full of
5772 notes – I'll save you time as well. The system's one. Its history
5773 means it isn't round, circular, nor like the Greeks thought, an
5774 ellipse. It's one: it's us who don't know how to deal with it. That's
5775 why you ask. You'd like to plan a paradise where you feel safe –
5776 but to get the rocks and palms, the sand to set them in, you have to
5777 sell...'
5778 'No,' Oton says. 'I could buy, instead. And build, and add
5779 security. A new system; an oval wheel. One based on guilt, not
5780 expiation. I hate socialism, knowing what's wrong and doing right
5781 – I see us wandering on the evil path – wearing my red trousers,
5782 copied on to every one of us, whistling my song, living in my black
5783 buildings, praying together to unnamed gods... My priests: my
5784 atlas: colonising my planets – playing the santur, the koiré...
5785 Abjuring me and mine, spitting on my image, pinning dead field
5786 mice to my shrines... Do you see it, Vince? The colours and the
5787 space? Only accept, Vince! Nothing to do with me – it's raking the
5788 mosaics, harrowing the pavements ... living by night... Are you
5789 there, Vince?'
5790 'Yes, Oton,' I say. It will take time.
5791 'No force, Vince,' he says. 'No power. Just people doing it. Do
5792 they want to do what they do? No! Do they gladly give their power
5793 to other guys? Of course not. It could all be open. Philosophers, up
5794 till now – they've always tried to entertain the people: now it's time
5795 to have them wander down another path.'
5796 'I see that, Oton. It's something I've doodled in my head,' I say.
5797 'For me, animals have a special place.'
5798 'Of course, we'll have them too,' says Oton. 'It's unavoidable.'
5799 'People will ask about the poor, the mines,' I say.
5800 'Well, why ask me?' asks Oton. 'I'm a rich guy – that's how I
5801 seem. What would I know about all that?'
5802

5803
5804            *
5805     'Wait here, see if he likes you,' says the lady. 'Here's the new
5806     pitcher of Manhattans.'
5807        'This is like paradise,' I say: she pours.
5808        'That means you don't know why you're there, how long for,
5809     and what you have to do,' she says.
5810        'It's early for so much alcohol,' I say. 'Watch out for your job.'
5811        'Making them – it *is* my job,' she says. 'Well – he doesn't like
5812     you. You can stay. He wants a woman, who'll replace him, do his
5813     work. You're not that.'
5814        'It's good,' I say. 'I don't understand. Nothing.'
5815        'People want to do something,' the lady says. 'They pay us. You
5816     tell them how.'
5817        'It's so easy,' I say. 'It's a joke.'
5818        'They're original things that come to us,' she says. 'You digest.
5819     They become your idea – you and your team.'
5820        She takes the pitcher in to Oton. There's shouting. I tell her, 'I
5821     don't think I want to work for anyone.'
5822        'They're ideas coming through the door, not people,' says the
5823     lady. 'I'm about to take over from Oton. Now, you've resigned?
5824     That's not a good sign.'
5825        'I liked Oton,' I say. 'But not the outfit.'
5826        'If you stayed,' she says. 'You'd always be Oton's man. That
5827     wouldn't do.'
5828        'I have loyalty, though,' I say. 'That's good. You just need other
5829     things to make a winning whole. A desk, perhaps.'
5830        'What you want a desk for, Vince?' she asks. 'No one's even
5831     told you about their plan.'
5832        'Claudine!' shouts Oton. 'I'm unhappy!'
5833        'He loved being boss,' Claudine, the lady, says. 'Now I'm boss,
5834     I think we ought to fire everyone, start over. Maybe re-hire...'
5835        'I'll go out on the road,' I say. 'Do the job.' I'm quite drunk, but
5836     it's still early. No principle's been compromised.
5837        The road forks – there's a knobbly path up to a hill – in this light
5838     it's varnished, vaguely Trecento. A wider road – Quattrocento
5839     comes to mind, with trees, some pines, some bushy-topped. A guy
5840     falls into step beside me – we strike out towards the landscape, the
5841     more recent one. 'I'm doing fieldwork,' I say to Roger, trotting
5842     along beside. 'You want opinions, then?' he asks. 'Peopling your
5843     field?'

5844  'No,' I say.
5845  'You must be from a charity, a state, a church,' he says.
5846  'We do our biz with all of those,' I say. 'They say they're for the
5847  poor, but all they teach is self-reliance.'
5848  Roger cuts some staves for us. We tramp the dusty road. 'The
5849  one place you're not poor,' he says, 'is in the army.'
5850  I'd tell him it's not true, I was enrolled – but, then, I'm a deserter
5851  too. We walk along in silence.
5852  I feel bound to tell Roger what I'm doing here. He's smiling left
5853  and right, in this painterly scene he plays the artist. What's the
5854  question I'm resolving? Nothing occurs to me – except the solitude
5855  of Oton, his tumbling mind, his military service – blows given,
5856  received, recorded, lost.
5857  'In the opera,' I say. 'King Roger was a mystic, and became a
5858  monk.'
5859  'I never heard that,' Roger says.
5860  I speed up, leave him far behind. I'm sorry for the snub, I guess,
5861  though if I apologise, it's not a snub.
5862  Redress. That's my subject. What ever redress is there?
5863  No. There's no redress, not for anything, no dirty deed, nor
5864  leaving things as they are, not your fault, or anyone's. Redress –
5865  what form? A resurrection? Something from the insurance? A tree
5866  planted, a song sung, ribbon cut...?
5867  Roger catches up.
5868  'Nothing personal,' I say. 'Just your banality, those set phrases –
5869  how they irritate!'
5870  At least, I blame myself for nothing. Nor my relatives – all
5871  honest fearing people, no victim and no perpetrator, no massacre,
5872  no genocide, no disappearances, no sentimental trips to places
5873  razed or redeveloped, memorialised. No regrets, no apologies – the
5874  family of perfect lives, no blot or smear, anonymity pursued,
5875  achieved. A tree of forbears, honey in the forks.
5876  'My brain's as full of kinks as yours,' says Roger, prodding with
5877  his stave. 'Suppose we meet the aliens – some, shaped like wild
5878  turkeys, and you say "Good morning" – if they can hear you in
5879  your rubber tent, the air in bottles on your back... They maybe have
5880  a morning every hundred years, as they go circling round, without
5881  regrets, without the massacres... Or some – medusas, feed on
5882  stomach acid – while you sleep, they fold in through your nose and
5883  live down there, as quiet as quiet... You want to swap equations
5884  with them, do they go to concerts, wave their arms...? The vanity,

5885 of wanting to make friends, like at a conference. It all comes from
5886 our cinema, our hope to be unique and kind...'
5887     There is no answer ... what might Maya, Anna say? They're both
5888 on their planets – one spinning fast, it looks like a dust devil, and
5889 Anna's, slow as if it's stuck in nothingness, a space no one would
5890 rocket to...
5891
5892                                    *
5893
5894 'I'm boss now,' says Claudine: 'Come back at once.'
5895     Roger's the hero, he must plod alone ... he'll find the garden, the
5896 teasels burning with immortal fire, the sunflowers like old gasfires,
5897 upturning, scorched... What then? You find burnt flowerbeds. I
5898 could hear him whisper, clueless, 'Ah! Hohum.'
5899     Claudine is in her room. 'If you're boss, why aren't you in there,
5900 where Oton was?' I ask.
5901     'Oh, he's in there still,' she says. 'He thought to close the
5902 chapter. You would have heard the shot. He thought he'd end the
5903 sadness so; the quarrelling, the tortures, the regrets. It's not been
5904 so.'
5905     'Perhaps he felt a new defeat,' I say. 'From you, Claudine. You
5906 closed his road.'
5907     'Oh well,' she says, 'we'll never know how things turn out. That
5908 is the beauty of the tale – there's no end yet, and when there is – no
5909 one will know...'
5910     'I'm working on redress,' I say. 'What you must pay for what
5911 you've done, what you might gain, if bad's been done to you.'
5912     'Well,' she says, 'stop it at once. "Done"?, "bad" – you all have
5913 specious claims, who knows what's wrong, what can be
5914 reimbursed, what punishments to set against rewards... Best have a
5915 ritual, a sorrowing, and not delve in.'
5916     'Oton took me on,' I say.
5917     'He didn't like you,' says Claudine. 'How are we to use you
5918 anyway? Redress – it must be put in money terms, or time. In jail,
5919 or suffering in other ways ... and Oton – surely he deserves redress?
5920 We've not been in to him. What would be the point?'
5921     'He might be waiting for his pitcher,' I say. 'Did you think of
5922 that, Claudine? What if he feels you're persecuting him, his
5923 vision...'
5924     'That's so,' she says. 'He is the only one who has a plan. Is that
5925 a merit, or a fault?'

5926
5927
5928
5929
5930
5931
5932
5933
5934
5935
5936
5937
5938
5939
5940
5941
5942
5943
5944
5945
5946
5947
5948
5949
5950
5951
5952
5953
5954
5955
5956
5957
5958
5959
5960
5961
5962
5963
5964
5965

'A vision like that,' I say. 'The grandeur – it leads to frustration, knowing you won't make it, not ever find a mate to help...'

'Well,' says Claudine, 'some mates! ... I'm really shocked – you and Roger, fighting, with those staves. They were meant to keep the dogs away.'

'Roger was frustrating too,' I say. 'He's one who wouldn't punt your vision up a hill... They weren't real weapons anyway.'

Roger was like Oton – a mind in full flower. But Oton knew the answers, and that they didn't help. Roger – didn't care. All he wanted was more road to trudge down.

'You're stood down now, my boy,' she says, grinning at me. 'Nothing boisterous! I'll cut you in – there's orders come from China now. They're running low – ideas, the soil ... all that scrabbling, now it's hit a rock, maybe it's coming to an end. So soon... It's temporary – just like you.'

There's photos that she shows – the earth is black, then in a bucket down you go, it's dark, and when you reach the end, it's black again. China – it's name suggests fragility, and bulls – who enter, smash, and run off out.

'Cut the crap,' shouts Claudine. 'Oton shot himself – he's gone, I'm boss. Now, money talks, our heads are clear and empty, waiting for our clientele. We could be lovers, Vince – it would be unethical to have you as an employee. Our problems that way would be solved...'

'I'd not get paid, Claudine,' I say. That body, blued and sweaty like a gorgonzola – alas for her, I'm not attracted.

'It's true,' she says. 'You don't attract. But – it's solutions that we seek, not things that fit.'

She's undone a button on her blouse: we clench our jaws, both of us, tight – the opposite of hungry – angry – beasts. 'You and Roger,' she says, laughing. 'Two pilgrims, turning into devils, squabbling on the mystic road.'

'No, Claudine,' I say. 'Not like that at all.'

'And walking out, across a desert and a mountain – a hostage, spy, a special soldier, Vince,' and she laughs some more.

'It wasn't me,' I say, 'another person quite exceptional, I'm sure.'

'The Chinese customs – they can smell your breath,' she says, 'and when you enter – they can tell if you will last for long enough to leave. We could send them round the world – sniff, sniff – a

5966 diagnosis everywhere, and people with short lives can do the fifty
5967 things they wanted to ... and we might take a cut, dear Vince.'
5968     'I heard it, Claudine – so has everyone. It's really not at all my
5969 thing,' I say. 'Roger was terrestrial. He's irritating. I need feel no
5970 shame.'
5971     Chinese Customs. They must have every package, every shape
5972 and smell – wonderful creatures, never on a list, messes in celadon,
5973 dragons' breath in bags... The human hearts – those whiffs of
5974 methane they send up, from when we lived on other rocks with
5975 other stars – we go there in our dreams. And will they come –
5976 maidens in uniform, at last with pigtails all erect, to suss us out...
5977     'Your visa – you'll expire before it does...' they'll say.
5978     'Do we want cash from that?' I ask Claudine.
5979     'Everything must have its point,' she says. 'Or else the whole is
5980 meaningless. Everything must travel, not see one thing, but two at
5981 least. Not to impinge – to 'ping' on some instrument, something
5982 that doesn't play a tune. Yes – the hour of death must mean a lot,
5983 dear Vince, or else there is no shape, no form or cadence, and no
5984 resolution.'
5985     To me, that's ordinary words. 'Unfinished' – that's the work to
5986 leave.
5987     'That's it, Claudine?' I ask. 'Chinese Customs.'
5988     'Will make our fortune,' Claudine says. 'Mine, at least. You'll
5989 have to wait for trickle-down.'
5990     'It's not what Oton sought,' I say.
5991     'All the founders get things wrong,' she says. 'They want peace,
5992 it comes out war. Foundation – that's the nub. You sink the piles,
5993 stand back, are shovelled in some hole – and what is built upon
5994 your foundations – it could be anything. Power-station. Amusement
5995 arcade or betting shop. Oton wanted something different: we show
5996 it all ends the same.'
5997     'I knew that, Claudine, long ago,' I say. 'Even Roger knew...
5998 And yet – it ended premature for Oton, by his will. What's built on
5999 his idea, Claudine? Where did that go? Wearing red trousers. All
6000 the other stuff I don't remember well...?'
6001     'Oton's will?' asks Claudine. 'His hand, at least,' and she
6002 giggles. 'These Chinese wizards – they'll tell the truth. Life, short
6003 or long, rich or poor – it's just a breath, a breeze, a zephyr from the
6004 south – sandalwood and mangoes. It takes so little, for the
6005 professional...'

6006
6007
6008
6009
6010
6011
6012
6013
6014
6015
6016
6017
6018
6019
6020
6021
6022
6023
6024
6025
6026
6027
6028
6029
6030
6031
6032
6033
6034
6035
6036
6037
6038
6039
6040
6041
6042
6043
6044
6045

'They couldn't have foretold Oton's end,' I say. 'Not from his lungs.'

'No, no,' Claudine shouts. 'But from his eyes!'

Chinese customs: letting things in, keeping them out, stripping the leaves off bundles, poking into spicy dusts, the ginger, the paprika – all contraband hidden within – the bones incised, the white dishes... Holding the border – *douaniers*: the peacock – Krishna – and Radha the milkmaid – setting the boundary between us and other creatures, us and the gods – the frontier where the naked man fights with the lion, both on their back legs, both valuable...

'Thirty coming in tomorrow,' says Claudine. 'Can I trust you with them? Colors and faiths – not your best shot. You only know guys like yourself...'

We put them on the métro. They're not liked – to be sniffed, and told you have an hour to live – it makes a panic. What use is it? 'It's all made up,' says Wei. 'There's big dogs, tell what is your destiny, but they can't talk.' She laughs.

It's true – the Italians call their boundary a *dogana*.

Mostly they want to start a business, those custom people.

I ask Wei, 'All frontiers, then, are in your hands – life, death, for instance. Flying and walking, fire and water, things you can't and things you want. Custom and – what? Mobility? Hard edge? Ideas? All these?'

'Oh yes,' she says.

'And what criteria?' I ask, insist. 'There must be boundaries that limit the contraries. Over ground and under, to take your customs as they're said to be. Underground, there's fire and water – that's not opposites. Is it the same for others too – that they may coexist in some dimension – maybe on a scroll, a white pagoda-jar.'

'That may be so,' she says. 'But don't exaggerate.'

'I need you for a guide,' I say. 'I'm not ready yet... I need to map the frontiers – see which are permeable. Stay over there, dear Wei,' I add. 'Don't get so near you smell my breath or look into my eyes. Like the inscription says – 'you today, my comrade – tomorrow, it's my turn.' Do you, your officers – each morning, smell each other's breath, to see if you'll get through, arrive to do some overtime, or...'

'That's what you find out if you join the service, Vince,' she says. 'I don't see you're a good recruit. You're even listed

6046 somewhere as a guy who's on the run, although long legs don't
6047 mean you can run fast.'
6048     I don't implore. It's the first day – there's time for that to come.
6049     'Listen, Vince,' she says. 'I know you've met most people who
6050 live outside the Wall. It's true – we've spilled a bit and taken in the
6051 shamans too. You can believe everything we say – but you can't
6052 trust us. We don't have a side, and so we're not on yours. I know
6053 you'd like to see what's in and what is out, what passes, what is
6054 halted, what comes in on golden wings. The problem is, dear Vince
6055 – to understand the movement – you must have a territory. If
6056 there's no bounds, there are no customs, Vince.'
6057     'No, no,' I say, 'that's pure conservatism – romantic, sentimental
6058 too. It's reaction, Wei.'
6059     'I didn't make it so,' she says. 'But look at all the other beasts
6060 around. Not there to become clay effigies. Look at earth and air –
6061 without the air, there is no earth...'
6062     'That's not what I mean at all,' I say. 'I know about apocalypses,
6063 all that stuff. I looked for something sage, dear Wei...'
6064     'I'm off now, Vince,' says Wei. 'I have to earn Claudine's cash,
6065 Down in the Underground...' And off she goes.
6066     In or out. Dead or alive. Maybe – not the most important
6067 questions. Interesting, though. The book says – we've a serpent in
6068 our belly – it fires us, we're its crucible, but when comes the hour –
6069 you smell the poison billow up. That's it!
6070     In the evening, Wei says, 'Everybody cheats, a little – friends try
6071 more than enemies. What does the cheating do? What do you have,
6072 so precious – that it's worth a risk you'll lose it? I'll take it, if it's
6073 precious – but it won't gain you a day on earth, if it's taken, or you
6074 get away. The people here – their mouths are closed, they don't like
6075 me looking at them. What's to be lost? The risk is only –
6076 knowledge, of how long they have to go...'
6077     'I don't follow, Wei,' I say. 'There's an accident. All the healthy
6078 guys are pulped – and you and they would never have believed...'
6079     'Exactly so, dear Vince,' she says. 'It's all a trick. But – maybe
6080 you have never worked a week, a month – you can't believe the
6081 satisfaction that it gives to guys like me, to have a secret, break the
6082 monotony, be seconded here...'
6083     'It's true,' I say. 'Easy money, moving about – it's granted me
6084 indifference to many things. So – tell me, what's your scheme?'
6085     'Claudine clings to everything,' says Wei. 'She knows the
6086 project – Multiple Longevity. She brought us in because we know

6087　the lines – where they are, what they're made of. What can be taken
6088　in or out. Who can stay, and who can leave. As for the rest – all
6089　have short lives. Most are full of suffering, we don't have time to
6090　meditate, exchange our suffering for wisdom, so she is convinced
6091　we are the experts.'
6092　　　'The wisdom, though,' I say, 'it's not for you.'
6093　　　'Oh no,' she says. 'We're just the guys in uniform who know the
6094　tale.'
6095
6096　　　　　　　　　　　　　　　*
6097
6098　　　'People are terrorised,' says Claudine. 'But they don't come to me
6099　and pay. They weep, instead. No one will trade intense short life,
6100　success, for tedium, decay...'
6101　　　'My career...' says Wei. 'This doesn't help. I might stay here...'
6102　　　'You're not my responsibility,' I say. 'Don't count on me. I love
6103　these capitals – but I might move on... If everything is slowing
6104　down, maybe an alp, a stream, a pitcher and a goat, enough for me.'
6105　　　'I need my hands, my arms,' Claudine says. 'More of them, and
6106　everyone ... my attributes. My pitcher and your goat. The cops will
6107　come – they say my diagnosis is a threat, the death of each is my
6108　revenge. They haven't even found poor Oton yet...'
6109　　　I say to Wei, 'You could desert. If they find you – it's no
6110　tragedy. There's always people looking for your job – the wars they
6111　have now, means killing everyone. Peace is the same.'
6112　　　'Poking into people's cases – that's no life,' says Wei,
6113　brightening.
6114　　　'I could tour,' I say, 'with my kazoo.'
6115　　　'Is that why you wear red trousers, Vince?' Claudine asks.
6116　　　'They're russet, Claudine,' I say. 'It's for Oton.'
6117　　　'That was his joke,' she says
6118　　　'That's not a bad memorial,' I say.
6119　　　'I wanted to be interesting,' Wei says, 'Even if I'm not.'
6120　　　'It always takes someone else to make you that,' Claudine says.
6121　'Me – I'm safely into history. Vince! – I guess you're still murky in
6122　the gloom?'
6123　　　'We're much nearer where we don't want to be, Claudine,' I say.
6124　　　'I haven't started with you yet, Vince,' she says. 'And, Officer
6125　Wei – I haven't begun to finish with you. Neither of you runs.
6126　You're not a pair of legs.'

6127 We'd like to live for ourselves, Wei and I – she has a common
6128 sense, adaptability, all that. It's unbearable. A mile of that – more
6129 than enough for me.
6130 'Wei,' Claudine says, 'sniffs out short lives. If you're a terminal
6131 case, the guys in white coats take you away. If you've planned
6132 some violence, you're resigned to die, or thrilled by it – then you
6133 take the other route. Terrorists, or terrorised, and sometimes both.
6134 The métro – mass diagnosis – that was scattershot. This way,
6135 there's cops, free drugs involved. We'll work out then how visible
6136 we are, the credit due, to take or bury...'
6137 'It's a horror, Claudine,' I say. 'I'm pleased I have no part in it.'
6138 'No, Vince,' she says. 'You are the expert. The wayfaring lads –
6139 those are your speciality – the sick and the committed. Both have
6140 the look – the eagle, diving like a suicide, or to feed. To kill, that is.
6141 Their eye, dear Vince. It's much like yours.'
6142 'It may not be a good idea,' says Wei. 'I see lots of trouble. I'd
6143 be much exposed...'
6144 'Nonsense,' says Claudine. 'Those who aren't wage slaves –
6145 they go mad for schemes like this. And all the good you'd do.'
6146 'Oh,' says Wei. 'The good part – I can take all that as read. It's
6147 the rest – the doing, the not doing, things not working out.'
6148 'I could have you sent back home, you know,' Claudine says.
6149 'That wouldn't suit, that wouldn't do you any good.'
6150 You can bet on that.
6151 'People believe these legends,' Claudine says. 'You can bet on
6152 that.'
6153 'You could ask my colleagues, they know rules – but only those
6154 they came with. It's all a puzzle – you go from place to place –
6155 some cities claim they're lay – then there are some where
6156 everybody has their sacred book and tries to bend its rules,' says
6157 Wei.
6158 'Come, Wei,' Claudine says. 'How you exaggerate! You're not
6159 called on to understand a thing – just go down the line: some will
6160 survive, and others too – but not for long. Then other guys will do
6161 the work of wondering how the shaky ones will end.'
6162 'It's all a matter of degree,' says Wei. 'I'd love to help – but
6163 "soon", "inevitable end", "afar" – they're terms you find in poetry,
6164 not in breath.'
6165 'You needn't fix a date,' says Claudine, turning red, frustrated.
6166 'Just think "afflatus" – poetry is borne on zephyrs' breath – or used
6167 to be. There's nothing can't be measured by the air – life and death,

6168  for sure, the space that's empty, and the space that's full of us. You
6169  need philosophy, dear Wei. A feeling for the economic side would
6170  help...'
6171       'I'll cry, Claudine,' says Wei. 'If it would help. It's not in
6172  character at all...'
6173       'You're beautiful, you two, Vince, Wei – and as you know,
6174  beauty seeks beauty, like flows to like. But,' Claudine says, 'I have
6175  this corpse to dump, a cover story too to spin. Poor Oton – ever
6176  anxious to help out...'
6177       'He never was, Claudine,' I say. 'It's true he wanted the
6178  impossible, but that was just his plan – to sunder everything that is,
6179  to spin the spheres like fruits in the machine, and have them
6180  cartwheel up the hill – and have the payout made in venerable
6181  grains from Babylon and Ur...'
6182       'That's not the point,' says Claudine. 'He's a corpse that I can't
6183  shift.'
6184       We move away. 'Of course,' she says, 'I'm not involved – it's
6185  just a bad scene. I need to see if there's some moral fence to climb,
6186  while I drag you after, Vince.'
6187       'There's no problem here, Claudine,' I say. 'The question of
6188  your guilt is yours. Do you feel guilty? No? It's settled, then. Did
6189  you do the deed? That's technology, just a fact the whitecoats
6190  probably get wrong, blame it on some travelling man. The same
6191  goes for Wei's diagnoses – the timing of our death, the how – and
6192  what it does for living... The answer is, don't stand in her line – no
6193  test! The problem disappears. Knowing it all, when you depart,
6194  especially where to – it's all unanswerable. Maybe she's wrong.
6195  Maybe you are. Forget it, like the song says.'
6196       'You're right,' Claudine says. 'We'll leave him as he is. And
6197  we'll deny.'
6198       'And I'll deny I know you too, Claudine,' I say.
6199       'I'm armour-plated,' says Claudine. 'Businesswoman of the
6200  century. I'll pay a guy to bioengineer – block out the sun, have rain
6201  and snow all year... Saving our habitat – a medal's in it, that's for
6202  sure. I take precautions – eat no food that's harvested. I take my
6203  holidays when it rains – better watch porn movies in your room
6204  than go to work in thunderstorms.'
6205       We're not impressed. Claudine shifts disaster so it falls on us.
6206       'We must make Oton disappear,' I say. 'The finger of suspicion
6207  points – at all of us.'

6208 'I'll settle this,' says Wei, 'as a favour to you all, that I'll exploit,
6209 and that's for sure.'
6210 We crate poor Oton, born in Split, and now for ever refugee.
6211 'Send him by sea,' says Wei. 'Far, far away. And we shall sing a
6212 song.'
6213 We label him. Wei instructs, 'Put "Tiger" on the box, when he
6214 arrives, he will be tiger bones. Everybody knows that's a Chinese
6215 quirk, a custom, quite above suspicion. Send him to the States, in
6216 memory of his anti-system dream.'
6217 We sing, off-key and awkward, 'If You're Going to San
6218 Francisco...' and Wei sticks a chrysanthemum in his hair. The
6219 bullet hole's invisible, amid the rot.
6220 Claudine says, 'What if there's misdirection...?' so we sing
6221 'New York, New York', just to make sure. We label him – 'To
6222 await...'
6223 'Oton didn't fit,' Claudine says.
6224 'I don't fit either,' says Wei. 'Not here.'
6225 'The question is – where does the "here" fit in,' I say.
6226 'I read old books,' says Wei. 'I know this isn't Istanbul – there's
6227 places there I'd really like to see.'
6228 'You've seen them, Wei,' I say. 'They all fit in, within the walls.
6229 Over the water, you can watch the wrestlers. Now, it's quite
6230 another scene.'
6231 'There hasn't been a single country, just the world, for many
6232 many years,' she says. 'Not since we were all in Africa. Now, you
6233 have to fit in to tiny temples, backyards, blood on the grass and in
6234 your mouth. I've done my years as border guard – oh, what a bore!'
6235 'You're fragile, Wei,' Claudine says. 'Forget the dewy dream. A
6236 word, a stamp, a visa – resolving life and death, enter, exit. Now,
6237 it's goodbye to you, precious as you are!' She leaves, making the
6238 effect.
6239 'We must pretend,' I say, 'that it all matters – the flag, the
6240 family, the character that makes us all be different and yet fit in ...
6241 shoulder to shoulder, fellowship, good cheer and bottoms up in
6242 prayer.'
6243
6244        *
6245
6246 'I never knew Oton,' says Wei, 'but I suppose he saw his slice of
6247 history and wished it had been different.'

6248    'Yes,' I say, 'he couldn't draw, but he could see, and what he
6249    saw he painted – it was what there was, and what he saw, both
6250    together. And he must have seen far off, all the named people, the
6251    big cheeses, striding and strutting. He wasn't afraid to talk to them,
6252    though it didn't seem to matter, or at least we don't know what was
6253    said. It was mostly him you'd want to know, to remember what was
6254    said.'
6255        'That's sugar,' says Wei. 'You didn't know him at all. What you
6256    say gets said of everyone.'
6257        'Listen, Wei,' I say, quite exasperated. 'You may think you're
6258    born again, starting off afresh, because you've jumped your ship.
6259    But here – you can fall, quicker than a baby. Your character doesn't
6260    matter, you can be strong or weak, left or right. You fall exactly at
6261    the same speed. It's physics.'
6262        'I don't have a character,' Wei says. 'Not yet. I wonder – should
6263    I shop Claudine, tell the police?'
6264        'Do you think she's worth all that atttention?' I ask, thinking of
6265    the trouble it would be for Wei, none at all for Oton, and even more
6266    for Claudine. And for me.
6267        'You're not courageous, Vince,' says Wei. 'I guess that leaves
6268    you time, free to do the rest. I don't blame at all – it is a point of
6269    view. No one leaves a smudge, even if they take it out on other
6270    people: in their grave there's no responsibility. It's those who've
6271    suffered, they're who ought to be remembered.'
6272        'That's sugar too,' I say. 'They aren't.'
6273        Later, she says, 'I didn't know Oton painted. I didn't see
6274    anything like that.'
6275        'It was a metaphor,' I say. 'He left bits of talk – he might have
6276    done better painting it.'
6277        'It's the rage in China, painting. They say the market's saturated.
6278    That'll be some fall!' she says.
6279        She's put a red *mèche* in her hair – she's fitting in. That snaky
6280    green and yellow dress – it fastens up the side, not what you'd
6281    expect.
6282        'I like going out at night,' she says. 'It's always been a sexy time
6283    for me. And it's certain – in the end, the light will come... It's not
6284    uniform, the black, it unrolls from the pianissimo, and makes a
6285    tower before it all spins off to lands you'd like to see, even at
6286    nightfall...'
6287        Inside her dress – her body's side – I think of pig's ribs, of the
6288    pig, slung up on hooks, its grin... 'You won't guess what I know...'

6289    he says. I remember them, the pigs, picking over fallen apples in a
6290    garden – not many pigs nowadays so lucky that they have an
6291    orchard... Another death, pig of a day for someone – like the
6292    Greeks – 'some guy told me you were dead', it goes... it ends,
6293    surprise, that this dead guy had written poetry – his nightingales –
6294    they all did that, wrote poems, whipped their slaves. But there's no
6295    poem – 'on whipping my slave' – and if I'd been the slave obeying
6296    orders, even maybe not – captured in war – better a captive
6297    *plongeur* than hanging out the flags, as back they trudge, survivors,
6298    with a slave for each to do the dirty work...
6299       'Vince!' says Wei, 'you can't be thinking what you've started
6300    off to do! Concentrate, or let me be!'
6301       'Another time, dear Wei,' I say, fastening her up. 'Suspended,
6302    not abandoned. It's our corpse I'm thinking of, and memory – in
6303    with its scythe and grin. The short sarcastic life of pigs...'
6304       'Your trouble is, Vince, you don't play the game. Don't chase
6305    the ball, even when you know it's going out of bounds,' says Wei.
6306       'You mean I'm honest, Wei?' I say.
6307       'No, you're not that at all,' she says. 'People play and chase the
6308    ball. It isn't what they want. You won't even play – that way you'll
6309    never have what it is you want.'
6310       'No one does, Wei,' I say. 'Wanting's a hydra. It means destroying
6311    time and planets.'
6312       'Then – for you, it doesn't even start. Don't look, you say, you'll
6313    never find. You won't strike gold that way,' she says. 'Anyway, my
6314    *mèche* – it works, my flame, my red light. It says "sex" in seven
6315    languages.'
6316       'It's hit and miss, Wei,' I say. 'That stuff. It's more complicated
6317    than you'd like to think. You need be a brave little soldier.'
6318       'I've been enrolled, Vince,' she says. 'You should try something
6319    courageous yourself. Deserting is brave, joining up again – even
6320    more.'
6321       'I'm a coward, Wei,' I say. 'It's an obstacle.'
6322       'Nonsense, Vince!' she says. 'That's just your lame foot – who
6323    was it had that? Oedipus? Achilles? It stops you running away.'
6324       'I could stick here,' I say. 'My hand's impregnable. I've counted
6325    out the deck. If no one talks, or gets publicity, I'm safe. Good gods,
6326    bad gods, bigoted, indifferent, an ethic quietist or progressive,
6327    mankind marching to extinction or to electronic brains – I win.'
6328       'They change the game,' says Wei. 'And people love to talk.'
6329       'Help me, Wei,' I ask.

6330     'Don't be weak,' she shouts. 'New lands! I know all about
6331 frontiers – every kind. The metaphoric ones, the geographic, and
6332 the kind you guys are squabbling about. And I'm a communist – I
6333 don't believe in them! That's why I'm here. Why are you here,
6334 Vince?'
6335     'I told you, Wei – I'm moving on.'
6336     'And I told you, Vince – I guarded the frontier – it's like the
6337 state and Lenin's cook – simple administration.'
6338     'I shan't be around, I hope,' I say. 'When you're proved wrong.'
6339     She presses on, 'You could start a militia, Vince. Everybody's
6340 doing it – you need some weapons, and there's people ready with
6341 the cash. You can run when they start bombing you. It could be –
6342 the Castilian Revenge, the Zoroastrian Resurgence... You can be
6343 prime minister, fix your own pay. Saint Augustine – there's a
6344 model! Off with the heretics! The Iron Guard, or those French
6345 torturers...' and on she goes.
6346     'It's history, Wei,' I say. 'Everyone's buried all that. Besides – I
6347 hate looking ridiculous, and saluting at parades.'
6348     'You wouldn't need to think about sex, Vince ... you'd
6349 concentrate on the price of beans,' says Wei. 'It seems here it's all
6350 soldiers, spies and sex. I'll see how good the latter is,' and she
6351 swishes away.
6352     She thinks sex is disorder, a dropping of the guard – it's not; at
6353 most a smuggling, an incursion across the border. Those provinces
6354 – they have no sovereignty. Remember the little book – that says
6355 the best frontier is a railway line, too valuable to all sides for
6356 anyone to cut, and once cut, easily repaired. A line that no one
6357 crosses, runs from my town to yours.
6358
6359                         *
6360
6361 Wei's soon back: 'You're right,' she says. 'Sex here draws much
6362 from soldiers and from spies. I hope your guys don't come to my
6363 house, to save me from myself, bring disorder, steal, partition.'
6364     'Your work,' I say, 'must have been like spying.'
6365     'Not *like* anything,' she says. 'It *was* spying. Most things are.'
6366     'You're full of conclusions, Wei,' I say, 'but nothing concludes.'
6367     'I'm young,' she says, 'I've seen it all.'
6368     'Well,' I say, 'I don't want an end banal, but somewhere
6369 between revelation and a crash.'

6370 'We mustn't talk about those things, the ends,' says Wei. 'Some
6371 are just starting off.'
6372   'It's all in mathematics, Wei,' I say. 'Locked in.'
6373   'You could say it's unlocked in ... or by,' she says. 'We knew all
6374 that. What gets in, or who ... it's all an algorithm. That stuff about
6375 the breath, the document – it was our joke. The same result – you'd
6376 get by human random. That job – the customs – is so dull... We'd
6377 do the test – then guys would feel so happy, or so sad, when we
6378 told them they would die before they could return ... or wouldn't
6379 die at all.'
6380   'It's not a funny joke, dear Wei,' I say.
6381   'Oh no,' she says, 'it's of the cosmological kind. The thing that
6382 adds an element of chance – it's bombs. Think of those people –
6383 they get called the Arabs, whether they are or not – and they get
6384 bombed, and bomb you back as best they can... Well, Arab just
6385 means "warrior" – a joke of ancient days. It leads people on... You
6386 must be, you must believe, what you were called – when you
6387 walked out of Africa. Everybody wants a piece of territories that go
6388 down – it's sharks at hungry-time. The mathematics doesn't work
6389 for them – it's scattershot and run! Shrapnel or swallow – yours the
6390 choice.'
6391   'Don't say that here,' I say. 'In other parts, it's easier – you're
6392 how you're born. And that decides it, all for ever. Here – you have
6393 to read the papers, watch the things you say. Be loyal. That is your
6394 freedom now.'
6395   'Oh, Vince,' she says, 'it always was.'
6396   'We should investigate,' I say. 'Go where they wouldn't let you
6397 out, or let me in. And – those guys... the sex? I'm curious, Wei,
6398 quite morbidly.'
6399   'Guys with their trousers off,' she says, 'look very stupid
6400 everywhere. That's my universal truth.'
6401   'That's why Oton wanted them in red, kept on,' I say.
6402   'They wanted to know what I believed. Not what I thought –
6403 believed. They had the hope – convert! Thought and belief –
6404 they're different chapters in my book,' she says. 'Belief – I've
6405 never read that one. Maybe back home we're born without. It's not
6406 like you, Vince...'
6407   'You have me wrong,' I say. 'I think, and so I don't believe.
6408 That's what the poet said. You believe to make time pass: thinking
6409 tires, and leaves you as you are, or thinner still.'

6410   'It's best to stick to flowers, primped in an ancient vase,' she
6411   says, 'or sages sleeping in the mist, their fishing rods lost in the fog,
6412   the carp, rejoicing, sing...'
6413   'The mathematics – that should let us in or out – we could go
6414   anywhere. See the Uighurs. Take along professors, people of that
6415   kind,' I say.
6416   'That's only ever about us, not other people, those people being
6417   swallowed up,' she says, and – 'You're not jealous, Vince? Of my
6418   fat pig? My, how he grunted, seeking something – not to be found,
6419   he didn't find, but all that breath! And if he'd died on top of me,
6420   he'd have been my marbled slab.'
6421   'No, no,' I say, 'amuse yourself, dear Wei, and be enjoyed.
6422   Maybe your porker was a holy man, a theologian, speleologist into
6423   the cave to find a primal purity... Those hungry guys, sitting round,
6424   can't eat because the elephant meat's tabu, belonging to the gods,
6425   who're always late...'
6426   'Listen, Vince,' she says, 'the crate with Tiger in – that's real.
6427   And us being paid by Claudine for our cover-up – essential.'
6428   'Or we could walk away,' I say. 'Like nothing ever was.'
6429
6430                                  *
6431
6432   That is what we do. Tiger's carried down the stairs. We walk away.
6433   Claudine waves the notes we'll never claim.
6434   'If we take the money, they'll think we did it,' I say.
6435   'If we don't take the money, they'll think we did it,' says Wei.
6436   'I come away with my integrity intact,' I say.
6437   'I'd like to see how Claudine ends,' says Wei. 'It's a story that
6438   can shake the world. I want to lift the curtain, see the next scene.
6439   She has her integrity as well – she could win elections that make us
6440   all bow down.'
6441   'We'll be well and far away before all that,' I say.
6442   'Suppose the people here – they decide to massacre. A group.
6443   Say – Arabs. Lock them up. Expel them. Or – Asians, say. What
6444   would you do then, Vince? Would you lend a hand?' she asks.
6445   'Of course,' I say, not knowing what's expected. 'We'd not be
6446   here, at all events. We've just to decide where.'
6447   Wei's bemused. 'I look into the faces, it's my trade – and I'm
6448   not sure. Maybe the faces are all different – that's not the point. It's
6449   the intention, the use they make of them – the eyes, the mouth, the
6450   nose. They keep the future buttoned up. Locked in, you'd say. The

6451 history calculations – they're not good. No one likes what they
6452 think are people new, inspired... I don't know where the frontiers
6453 are. What people, peoples, might do, or be induced. We could go
6454 back – the primal – but we've all been different since the dinosaurs
6455 ... there's no question here of keeping people out – they're all
6456 inside.'

6457     'Of course we think that way – it's necessary when you come
6458 into a place,' I say. 'Look around. Of course, they all look hostile.
6459 No one is carrying anything, Wei. You can't ask what they might
6460 have hidden, to declare.'

6461     'You could be a hero, Vince,' she says, 'You haven't been that
6462 yet. A saviour.'

6463     We jostle round some stalls. 'Oh, crispy, I love that,' says Wei.

6464     'The food here's not so great,' I say. 'Nor is the company.'

6465     Some guy's dog jumps up at her. 'Hey!' she shouts. 'Your
6466 fucker wolf just ate my duck.'

6467     'Come away,' I say. 'Before the insults start. That guy respects
6468 no foreign culture, you can bet.'

6469     'No, no,' she says, 'I've every right...'

6470     'Of course,' I say, and pull her after me.

6471     'The duck and I,' she shouts, 'are from Canton...'

6472     'Of course,' I say. 'The customs recognise all dialects...'

6473     'Not dialects, you idiot,' she shouts some more. 'They're
6474 languages. They're tongues,' and she sticks hers out at me – a
6475 brilliant red – the duck must be spicy too...

6476     'You've dropped, Vince,' Wei goes on. 'Once, you resisted.
6477 Now it just took that denatured dog to have you run... Dogs not
6478 allowed,' she shouts to all the crowd.

6479     'Oh, Wei,' I say. 'I used to know them all. When Rodney
6480 Hawkett was alive ... the ministers, the chiefs – I found them
6481 unimpressive, on their leads and in their kennels, robotic...'

6482     'I'm alive to that,' says Wei. 'The smuggled animals, inbred and
6483 hybrid, the wolf brought out in dogs, dogged up indeed... Robots –
6484 all the rage, that fight the wars now...'

6485     'Everyone is blameless here,' I say, but there's a crowd, and
6486 cops are sighting on us, their caps, the yellow covers, turn like
6487 sunflowers – but still she remonstrates...

6488     'If that's an attack dog, or wolf – that's what we need,' says
6489 Wei, and waves a scrap of spicy crispiness: 'Nature follows its own
6490 track.'

6491   With one bound, it is beside us: the wolf is ours. Our soldier. Its
6492   trainer stares, his lids, heavy as stones – 'We are the guard dogs,'
6493   Wei shouts out, 'This toothy mutt is one of us!'
6494       We run.
6495       Concentrate. And run.
6496       ...Cerberus, Anubis – the pointy ears, the porous nose – best
6497   have them on your side, remember space wizards, their ears – spice
6498   magicians from the starry isles, rocket dogs, empires rested on
6499   them, enduring dogged dog days, their gods coming, going, putting
6500   on their dog, my lungs sounding wolf notes ... beware the empires
6501   of the dead ... run, ventilate and pant
6502       ...we're both exhausted, though the wolf is not. 'We need some
6503   nature, something sliced fresh out, that knows the right way from
6504   the wrong,' says Wei.
6505       We don't put a collar on it. 'A lead would dissipate the energy,'
6506   says Wei. 'It will walk ahead, and if it runs away – that will be its
6507   choice.'
6508       'You'll bet on that!' I say. 'I shan't intervene. The guy, though,
6509   whose it was till now...'
6510       'He's had enough,' says Wei. 'It's clear. Over. And the animal,
6511   you see it loves its Cantonese – that was a gesture of good taste.
6512   I'm maybe its epiphany, a terminus, its end.'
6513       'It's true,' I say. 'It recognises you, your skills. The dog-wolf
6514   perches on a frontier. It's prey – it preys. The dog protects, the wolf
6515   invades. It's enemy and friend – it strolls, it slinks. It's like our
6516   world – you cross the frontier – and it's war. You trade across it,
6517   empathise – there's comradeship. But Wei – you're not at ease with
6518   our new guard, whether it is dog or wolf.'
6519       'Of course,' she says, 'It's my protection and a threat. That – I
6520   resent. It is my weakness and my strength.'
6521       'Food, Wei,' I say. 'It steals its food, and runs away – it follows
6522   who it's stolen from. A puzzle, Wei.'
6523       We exchange views on jackals, and coyotes.
6524       'We seek the moral core,' I say... 'The dog looks on, maybe
6525   measures out its time with us, evaluates how we go on, and how we
6526   navigate...'
6527       'The moral code? The dog's cuisine? You worry about things
6528   you won't be punished for,' says Wei. 'Because your prospects are
6529   so slight. The sages give examples of how you ought to act, always
6530   at crisis points – the crux, hard cases settled in a single stroke. They
6531   never touch the life, the years, creating situations where you might

6532   have doubts and fears. Ought we to do, or tell, confess, betray?
6533   Dilemmas pass away, like they were gunshots.'
6534         'We don't have tricky situations, Wei,' I say: 'So, there's no
6535   moral case to make or drop... We are becalmed, our moral gristle's
6536   gone to fat.'
6537         The dog goes out, no glance, no sign, and comes back, smelling
6538   strong. 'Nasi goreng,' says Wei. The dog sniffs at her breath, then
6539   comes and sniffs at mine.
6540         'This room,' says Wei. 'How do we pay? There's lots of others
6541   here, like we all had emergencies.'
6542         'We leave the customary sum,' I say. 'We're all in transit here –
6543   see this as a bridge.'
6544         The wolf – it leads us on. It can show the right path, it lights up
6545   the end, the hotel, hospice, anywhere for decent sleep – 'This will
6546   do,' says Wei. 'We'll doss here. The dog will be our star – but not
6547   tonight. I'm through. Our Tiger's in the hold by now, and on his
6548   way. The moral compass – it's boxed up too, high on the bridge,
6549   the captain unconcerned with us ... we're exonerated, Vince,
6550   forgiven. Whatever we should do, have done – it's on the ocean
6551   swell, a crate within a crate, no address, labelled "to await" ...
6552   Who'll claim them, Vince, those bones? Don't you have a friend in
6553   LA?'
6554         'No, Wei,' I tell her. 'Let's not bring others, in – the pardon
6555   should be ours alone.'
6556         'Vince,' she says, 'I burn, I burn – not to be extinguished, but to
6557   blaze. Will no one see the beauty of my flame, its ferocity, the
6558   colours? You were a fireman – you should know. Our Tiger's dead,
6559   he's on his way to being ash, the world is full of disappearing
6560   beasts, the people with the banners dead, retreat is everywhere,
6561   Vince, there's no stability – one step forward, two steps back. I'm
6562   burning, Vince – set me up high...'
6563         'A guide will come,' I say. 'Right now, I'm at a loss.'
6564         And so – we never mention Oton, nor his death, again.
6565
6566                                       *
6567
6568         'We've had some intimate talks, revealing everything,' says Wei.
6569   'We can roll up together in this carpet, just for warmth – but keep
6570   that dog away.'
6571         Our carpet is a fine Tabriz – faded, but the underside, its red and
6572   pink, blue and green, is like a painter's floor. The dog goes round

6573   the others, sniffs their sleeping breath, and goes outside. My head
6574   sticks out the cylinder, Wei's all inside.
6575       She kicks, as she sleeps. I wake her – 'I'm on the crest,' she
6576   says. 'Looking down is mist and leaves. I've distances to trudge –
6577   I'm not sure you have, dear Vince. It's all a picture – the Long
6578   March. Did it all happen? Shall we do it all again? You, Vince, for
6579   sure – you'll not be there.'
6580       In the morning – there's no one left but us. We struggle to be
6581   free. Wrapped up like Mongol warriors, ready for the execution,
6582   trampled so as to spill no blood. Wei asks,
6583       'I heard the people from inside the carpet, praying. Or were they
6584   soldiers?'
6585       'They're the revolutionaries, Wei,' I say. 'No one likes them, or
6586   to call them that. They're the dragon's teeth – martyrs, crooks and
6587   desperadoes, naive and saints ... corporals and brigadiers, growing
6588   scattered in thin soil.'
6589       'You can't imagine,' says Wei, 'the poverty, the masses, the
6590   abandonment, the love of death instead of nothingness...'
6591       'It's nothing we have made,' I say. 'It's not our scene'
6592       The sign over the window says – 'For your safety – don't look
6593   out.' And over there – the wheel. A priest that says, 'My child – if
6594   you don't believe, it won't go round.'
6595       'Watch out,' says Wei. 'Standing there – you are a perfect
6596   silhouette.'
6597       'The wolf,' I say, 'still at the door.'
6598       'It's no bother,' Wei says. 'It'll be with us till the end.'
6599       'I'm sure it will,' I say.
6600
6601                              *
6602
6603   'You could protest,' says Wei.
6604       'I'm an artist, Wei,' I say. 'Creating, not consuming. It's all
6605   thinking and complaining, unless you're making pots.'
6606       'I don't see what you create,' says Wei. 'You could make a
6607   scene... The warplanes here, overhead – always buzzing off.
6608   Indifference, profligacy. The helots, and the scrabble. The values
6609   hoarded by the rich.'
6610       'Creation is a smoky thing,' I say. 'What ends up on the paper or
6611   the canvas – that's just its ghost.'
6612       She's not convinced, but she's been quietened, and it all spins
6613   on.

6614     I tell her, 'The universal plan, they say – was beautiful. But lay it
6615 out in rocks and sparks, it's lost to view, the lamps keep going out,
6616 the paint's too hot and spurtles off, the surfaces dissolve, the
6617 magma underneath cracks out in steam – then, there's the
6618 infestations too. The slimy things, the fish with feathers, lizards
6619 disproportionate. Then, Wei – it's us! We can have ghosts, because
6620 we're ghosts of ghosts. The primal beauty, stuck in the sponge
6621 behind our eyes – we glimpse it – take our brush and ... there! it's
6622 gone.'
6623     'I know all that,' says Wei. 'I meant a different thing. In China,
6624 we have rich – they're good at making lots of cash. That's it – no
6625 celebrations, and no flags. But here – you let them run the theatre,
6626 say what's the good and bad... Does it irk, Vince? Once it was
6627 warriors – now it's them...'
6628     'Just ghosts of ghosts, I told you, Wei,' I say.
6629     We go down, walk around in the street. There's an army of
6630 people, mostly poor – that's how they look to me. 'You see,' says
6631 Wei. 'There's not enough rich guys here to let the poor guys have
6632 their heads.'
6633     I'm not sure it works like that.
6634     'I'd be an artisan,' I say. 'That's how art ends up. The spirit
6635 takes its form. That's it – the end. For me, no ceramics and no
6636 dance. I'd fancy maybe goldsmithing...'
6637     'It's out of reach,' says Wei. 'Vince! How do we go on? We
6638 can't hunt – and gathering, we call it confiscating – the people here
6639 don't carry stuff. They all do different things, you can't tell what,
6640 they look alike because the clothing's poor...'
6641     'Painting and books,' I say, 'those you can tout around. It's
6642 sculpture – what you've not sold takes up your space, and clogs
6643 your future ... marble blocks won't fit in the trash.'
6644     'We could sell eats – that way, what you don't sell, you eat,'
6645 says Wei.
6646     'No, Wei,' I say. 'That's too conservative. It gives no leverage.
6647 I'm sure, too, there is a flaw – it's hunger, Wei, makes you
6648 hallucinate.'
6649     'We can't beg,' she says. 'That means you've reached the end.
6650 We might ask for loans... But here, you borrow, and you know that
6651 it won't grow. It's just a weight. Here – it's all heavy stones, you
6652 have them on your back, humps – they fix your gaze down on your
6653 feet. You're tired of history, you guys. It's painful. You hope it

6654    stops, your terrifying story, and it will. You polish it and dust it –
6655    it's your furniture.'
6656        'You've seen – I'm not like that. I always choose the hardest
6657    way,' I say. 'It's my training, my challenge.'
6658        'Is that it, your quality, your point of view? Yes, I'm full of
6659    stories too, I'm made of them,' she says. 'I can convince you,
6660    because you've no idea...'
6661        'We could start a café in Russia somewhere. Or China. That's
6662    where the philosophers go, and you would have your cake – to sell
6663    or eat,' I say.
6664        We'd each prefer to carry on alone.
6665
6666                                    *
6667
6668    There's a sign, says 'Feed the hungry.' 'There!' I say, 'they are our
6669    sponsors.'
6670        'I'll pledge a million. If I have it, I always keep my word,' says
6671    Wei.
6672        We are the only hungry ones – the sponsors all are sleek. There
6673    are brioches – silent, we eat.
6674        A tall captain embraces us. 'Ah! Hungry people! How we need
6675    you!'
6676        'Too late!' says Wei. 'I'm full as eggs.'
6677        'Vince!' shouts the guy. 'One of Rodney Hawkett's men. What a
6678    benefactor Hawkett was!'
6679        'He gave his body to the fire,' I say. 'Mostly, we do that.'
6680        'A message,' says the guy. 'Around the world – you'd give them
6681    hope – information, at the least. Where you all are, the hungry, how
6682    many... You'd represent the famished, everywhere...'
6683        'Oh no,' I say. 'I'm not a humanist. We can't save all us animals
6684    – some already slip away, and some we step on heedlessly. Many
6685    get bombed, incinerated, flushed when they become a drag... The
6686    hunger's something we all live with – no more hunting and
6687    gathering ... there are laws, there's property...'
6688        'You're not religious freaks, I hope,' says the guy. 'Endure the
6689    suffering – maybe get rewards ... feeling good...'
6690        'I've not been born for anything particular,' says Wei. 'Avoid
6691    the pit, cling to your passport – that's my rule.'
6692        'Look into my eyes, Alex,' I say to the guy organising the
6693    expedition. 'You'll not have noticed. Right in the middle of each
6694    one, there's a black hole. It leads straight to our core. Nothing

6695 comes back out. It's a cave entrance. Everything enters. Nothing
6696 emerges. It's a depository, of everything, all that goes on, it leads to
6697 shelter, to nothing. A black hole, like the universe is full of...'
6698     'I understand, Vince,' says the tall captain, Alex. 'You're not
6699 willing. But you ate our cakes, so you owe us. And you'd be paid.'
6700     'We'd go everywhere?' asks Wei. 'And do anything, be
6701 anyone?'
6702     'Of course,' says Alex, 'I'd go myself. But I'm not hungry, not
6703 like Vince. And I've not renounced my frontiers, my charge, not
6704 like you, Wei. All you have to do – is be hungry. Show it to all the
6705 rest. Most will recognise it, not everyone will have the right react.
6706 Explain how it's all getting better, help will come...'
6707     'What are we looking for?' I ask.
6708     'Everyone knows that,' says Alex. 'Don't fool with me, Vince.'
6709     I don't press him. For sure, we'll find out. It might involve the
6710 slash and burn.
6711     It's a great idea. Just right for Wei.
6712     'You can't take the dog, Wei,' Alex says.
6713     'It's his,' she says. 'Vince's.'
6714     'It's best for you,' I tell her. 'Symbolically – you'll wield a hoe –
6715 a spade, a sword. An invocation. You'll call it work – it's nearly the
6716 freedom that will come when we'll do nothing, maybe we'd
6717 criticise a little, drop our line into the carp-pond, catch, toss them
6718 back in ... shoot brown shadows on the forest verge... And, Wei –
6719 you'll do the good, I'm sure. While you're alive – it's immortality.'
6720     She's happy and she's sad – that is the best. For both of us –
6721 adventures separate.
6722     'The ship is ready, Wei,' says Alex. 'Bring me back some
6723 curious things – white gourds that taste of tripe, and persimons that
6724 make you laugh...'
6725     'Oh Vince,' she says, 'come and trek the world, the poor, the
6726 powerful – we'd be both of those, magnificent in rags...'
6727     'It's right for you,' I say. 'It's just not me...'
6728     There's nothing more to say: 'Off to Cythera, dear Wei,' shouts
6729 Alex, pushing me aside. 'Press the right button, and your
6730 instructions will pop up.'
6731     'Farewell, dear Vince,' she shouts. 'This interlude will last until
6732 we both forget...' The waves are blurring her, the sails, the
6733 helmsman – the movement jiggles her about, the outlines go to grey
6734 and cloud, we both get small, so small there's no point in waving
6735 more, so strong's the swell, the wave...

6736     The wolf trots off, and I am close behind.
6737     Off she sails – away, away. Peace and freedom, far from the
6738     borders and the laws, the magistrates, police ... away the Party,
6739     away lines of longitude – there's only latitude, sweet twenties for
6740     the galleon, the super-junk – a cargo bland and tempting –
6741     bullseyes and cats' tongues, a voyage like the Chinese used to make
6742     – discovering America, away on tiptoes – spaghetti woven into
6743     belts, offloaded in Genoa...
6744     I weep. I should have gone. With her, the life, the paradise.
6745     'Feed the hungry' – there she will be, a nacreous robe, a gentle
6746     smile – distributing the taffy, blowing clouds of sherbert... The
6747     winning sign – 'No animal was harmed in the making of this
6748     dream...'
6749     Alex is staring: I say, 'We're changing the colours – yellow,
6750     grey. Sand and slush. Making a planet like the Martians did, with
6751     them all dead or underground and out of sight – the place unlivable.
6752     Maybe all the planets started so – quivering with bees and
6753     butterflies, then they were killed and filled with acid dregs by feisty
6754     suicidal aliens...'
6755     He mutters, 'New frontiers ... we must suss them out...' Then,
6756     'Vince – Wei was too fine for you.' Silence: 'We had you pencilled
6757     in as captain, Vince,' he says.
6758     'I don't navigate,' I say.
6759     'Someone else does that, I think,' says Alex. 'For you, a role
6760     imposing: there's funerals at sea, walking the plank, and mutinies.
6761     They require a lofty presence.'
6762     'I'm not sure about giving orders, Alex,' I say. 'That's been a
6763     problem.'
6764     'If there's a storm, no island near – the ship will founder, that's
6765     for sure,' says Alex. 'The water – it'll bind the cargo into floss and
6766     send it down. We send them out, those paper boats, ambassadors
6767     who love mankind – they turn to cannibals on the rafts ... those
6768     reedy sails are torn, the keel of sturdy osiers – it doesn't serve...'
6769     'They do good...' I say.
6770     'We robe them. We send them off. They do good. They don't
6771     come back. Mostly. Often,' Alex says.
6772     'You came back, Alex,' I say.
6773     'Doing good – it's a human urge,' he says. 'You get recruited.
6774     Some get eaten. Some find a hut and stay.'
6775     'Recruited?' I ask.

6776    'They live well, they get bought off. The mission's altruistic.
6777 Before there was money, there was food – so food is money,
6778 mother and son, or so you'd think. When no one's hungry – they
6779 will still need cash.'
6780    'I understand that, Alex,' I tell him. 'But – say there's a
6781 tempest... I should have gone – I know all about island monsters
6782 and their powers.'
6783    'You don't know about wind, dear Vince,' says Alex, 'Although
6784 a storm of it comes out of you.'
6785    'When you're in the sea,' I say. 'On it or under it – you're like
6786 the fish – death is all around ... Without the air, we are a poor
6787 design. A hook, a mouth, a rock that walks, eels electric,
6788 smothering – a paralysing flower... It sucks you in – past no teeth, a
6789 ribby tunnel like a man o' war's hold – you see your destiny, the
6790 anus... Your boat's gone down – you flounder, give up your soul...'
6791    'Oh, sometimes you survive,' says Alex, offhand. 'You need
6792 allies,' he says. 'They will protect you. You're like those little fish
6793 that clean the sharks – a thousand sorts of shark. How many sorts of
6794 men are there? They all need cleaning, you can bet!'
6795    'Once landed, Alex, I don't see why it's dangerous,' I say. 'You
6796 give out food. That's it.'
6797    'We give out agriculture, Vince,' he says. 'We mobilise the
6798 marginal, identify the poor, and help. That's the provocation – it's
6799 not the candy bars.'
6800    'I can imagine, Alex: I'm not just stuck on waves and fish,' I say
6801    'Women, Vince,' he says. 'They grow the food, they buy it, and
6802 prepare...'
6803    'I know all that,' I say.
6804    'Who buys the land and hires the hands, and sells the seeds,
6805 expropriates,' he says. 'Comes from afar, and sets a price... Is men.'
6806    'I'm not insensitive, Alex,' I say.
6807    'We send them off,' says Alex. 'The angels. They're judges for
6808 the end of time. If time it is that ends.'
6809    'I see them judge,' I say. 'But – the time, the time they work
6810 with: it's limited, but not the end, not yet.'
6811    'They leave,' he says. 'No one comes back. Nothing; no cargo
6812 comes to us. Maybe it ends up...'
6813    'She went down?' I ask. 'We don't know – at least, we don't
6814 know how.'
6815    'We don't know why,' says Alex. 'Was it my fault? Ours,
6816 Vince? A broken contract – at least, agreement that we wanted her

6817 to do exactly what she was sent to do, and what we wanted her to
6818 want...'
6819     'It all sounds inconclusive, Alex. Maybe you're mistaken, not
6820 responsible at all...' I say.
6821     'Oh,' Alex says, 'Unless we have some news, I'm not
6822 responsible. Rather, it would be you, the captain of the ship who
6823 didn't step on board.'
6824     'It's neat, Alex,' I say. 'You come out well.'
6825     'You're not happy with this, Vince,' says Alex. 'It's evident.
6826 Men and women. A rift in history – maybe it was normal to be
6827 hungry: – then the hungry were to make a revolution... But –
6828 suppose they'd been fed. No longer hungry... Where do they
6829 stand?'
6830     'I see your point, Alex,' I say. 'Where does that leave me?'
6831     'Oh, Vince,' he says. 'I've really no idea. Poor Wei – she went
6832 out unprepared, like all of them. If she died, she died too soon, her
6833 time not come.'
6834     'That kind of time – too soon, too late – is quite beyond me,
6835 Alex. Are you sure you went? You seem the precious type. Clothes
6836 nonchalant, the cultivated beard...' I say.
6837     'Oh yes,' he says, 'I made big friends – not great pals, you
6838 understand. The size was overwhelming, though.'
6839     'You did a deal, a dirty deal, you dirty boy?' I ask.
6840     'They have the power, the land, the seed,' he says. 'Then I
6841 played the other side – sending them off, the naive angels. That's
6842 life.'
6843     'Maybe it's not,' I say. 'If the boats sink. And – after hunger.
6844 What'll it be?'
6845     'Oh, hunger will come round again,' he laughs. 'Not just as
6846 metaphor. We'll eat the beetle stew, grass sandwiches and Coca
6847 Cola on the croquet lawn... And then? We are that way, dear Vince,
6848 and me and you ... the same. We love the edge, the void, limit, the
6849 emptiness. We climb up in the spire – then – there's the urge – to
6850 jump. Over with it all. It drives the mystic guys to make a poem, a
6851 critique – new ordering of revelation. Enough of made-up
6852 chronicles. A vision, oratorio. New chosen people, without
6853 territory, without a clan. A tool, a song and dance, to reach the
6854 truth, a diet of veracity – a text that weaves the threads of all the
6855 worms... they glow up there, dear Vince, among the mulberries. See
6856 – they excrete – the red, the blue, the green, the orange. It's
6857 beautiful, it's foul, it's homicidal, it is salvation – saving us from

6858 no one, nothing, from ourselves – a nimble fiddling with the dust
6859 we live on, that we are – but in the end, the truth is – has been –
6860 always there. At the beginning.'
6861     'But Wei!' I ask, 'why sacrifice her, Alex?'
6862     'Oh, I expect she wanted the same impossibilities as you, my
6863 friend,' he says. 'The more you flap your wings, take off – the
6864 steeper is the fall. The greater is the height that you come down
6865 from – fewer hear or see the splash.'
6866     'For sure, she wanted what we want,' I say. 'That's not my
6867 point.'
6868     'Come to my house,' he says. 'It's up a hill, it's true – but that
6869 means nothing special ... if it overpowers you, the slope, bend your
6870 head down. The road appears quite flat, and so you positively fly!'
6871     The house is full of people, coming, and, by definition, going. It
6872 reminds me of those ancient times, of Dolores, Lady Bea – their
6873 projects and recruitment; through the tall windows, we can see
6874 forays of trespassers across a handkerchief of grass: a stand of
6875 bamboos, sharpened into stakes. There's some books – a *History of*
6876 *God* – I thumb it through. Alex says, 'What an eye! The binding –
6877 quite exceptional: a sheep in sacrifice.' There's games – balances –
6878 'Those I distrust,' says Alex – swings, copied from Fragonard. A
6879 swinging trunk for two, a ride, goes round and round – 'The sun
6880 and moon,' says Alex, 'those are kissing cousins clinging on it.'
6881     It's a marvel, the house, full of brown furniture, with trompe
6882 l'oeil corridors, commodes stuffed with the testaments of kings,
6883 parleys of trumpeters at ease, things to be guessed at – a babble of
6884 ill-meaning businesses...
6885     There's two and twos, couples of strident arguers with fluty
6886 voices, making a context for a text, exchanging insults, insisting on
6887 a point...
6888     'There,' says Alex. 'That's the house. You'll have some time to
6889 see who's who, who I am, who are you, dear Vince, how do we fit
6890 the story...' and he laughs. 'You'll hear them working upstairs,
6891 adding some higher floors, beneath you – the stables and the cellars
6892 – the rumbling means a filling in, a tearing down...'
6893     'I'm surprised,' I say. 'You keep no animals.'
6894     'Oh Vince!' says Alex. 'Naughty boy! They're full of dirt, you
6895 know. You must admire my cleanliness, with all these people going
6896 in and out, the dust clings on to everything ... they all pass through,
6897 disputing – what a crew! – the sponsors, benefactors, friends and
6898 enemies from all the world. Some have the news of those sent out –

6899 the struggle and the difficulty...' His tongue frisks lightly,
6900 confidentially, in my ear – 'The others, Vince. They own the land,
6901 and we have nothing; like it ought to be – but how do we assert
6902 ourselves? How do we make our mark?'
6903     Dear Alex – how you want to love him, though you can't.
6904 'Do you want the good, the true?' I ask. 'Or just hop on the
6905 roundabout, start a big thing, your epic, all the drafts and
6906 cancellations, stories for grannies, pointed arms for youths... A state
6907 of plenty? Or obedience? Of flagellation, refectories where books
6908 are shouted out – no true food, just rabbit bones to suck?'
6909 'Yes, Vince,' he says. 'Exactly right. You have imagined all
6910 those things. You lay the keel, the fragrant lady with the wine –
6911 baptises; down the rollers goes the cruiser... Where does it go,
6912 where does it end? You're right, dear Vince – you imagine all the
6913 ports it may approach – greeted with gunfire or with tarts, all on the
6914 house... A sailor's life is that! In your heart, Vince, you've done all
6915 the trips. It's for your useless imagination that you're prized – my
6916 guslar, my minstrel singing of the all and less... That is your role,
6917 my friend.'
6918     He hugs me. I avoid his kiss.
6919 'Where are your people, Alex?' I ask, moving away. I see small
6920 animals crowding at the fence – marmosets and hares – as curious
6921 as me.
6922     He says, 'You mean, because these are so quarrelsome? They're
6923 all my people. Otherwise we'd all be dead. We'd slug it out! If you
6924 undress them, you'll find they all wear my insignia: *in hoc signo*
6925 Vince, remember. Of course, there's good and evil, but they all
6926 profess the truth. I don't ask you to join up, Vince, not with me, not
6927 just now – but, be very very careful whose team you end up on. No
6928 one gets a long life, guaranteed – the thing is, remember that your
6929 cause was just. That way, it all smooths out. That's the best life you
6930 can have. And as for Wei – she's a good shot – they train them so.
6931 She'll resist it to the last.'
6932     That's good for her, I guess. He goes on, 'This house works
6933 perfectly, just like it should. There's games. There is security –
6934 some guys come here to die in bed – they know it's peace to come.
6935 In the next room to them, high up those stairs, there's couples come
6936 to screw, to scrutinise their bodies, say what they've done that's
6937 good and not... The bourgeoisie's women, they are had in common.
6938 It was in the book. Now it's their men: in common too. You're not
6939 a bourgeois, are you, Vince? I guess your women come and go,

6940    your men as well – hardly you remember them, not as complete
6941    existences, if that is what they were – just encounters, Vince.
6942    There's many here that don't believe in what we do – gathering the
6943    people, and the cash, sending them out, accumulating more – you
6944    need a steady gaze for that. If you don't believe, you can't enjoy
6945    the house, the people setting out, new ones recruited...'
6946        'I can't live up to that, Alex,' I say. 'I'm grateful that you think I
6947    can – reach the standard. But I can't.'
6948        'It really isn't up to you,' he says. 'The standard's stronger than
6949    your weakness, Vince.'
6950        'It must be "no",' I say.
6951        'Look around,' he says. 'There's women here as well – they're
6952    open books. You've been ingenuous, dear Vince, you thought
6953    you'd run for ever, blundering and tumbling, leaving and being left.
6954    Now – look around...'
6955        He draws out someone from the mass – I guess she's an
6956    assistant. Cinzia. She says, 'I've read how our machines, like us,
6957    will all be made of helixes. That's the saliva in your cheeks. All
6958    mankind fits in a two cubic metre box, buried in Siberia – alongside
6959    the mammoth bones. And it will last for ever. Digital: that's
6960    counting on two fingers, Vince. All the info about hunger. Yours.
6961    Maybe your lust as well.'
6962        'Suppose that's metaphor?' I ask.
6963        'Oh,' she says. 'I'm sure it all goes in. When you're dead,
6964    perhaps someone will search – and there you are. Hunger and
6965    metaphor together.' We all laugh.
6966        'It sounds like paradise,' she says.
6967        'We're all reactionaries,' says Alex, laughing more. 'Here in this
6968    house.'
6969        'I'm already full of information,' Cinzia says, going off to store
6970    some more.
6971        'She's your sort, Vince,' Alex says. 'She's passionate about
6972    eternity. We wouldn't send her out – she'd sink her ship with
6973    knowing what she knows. Me – I'm not a humanist, and so – I
6974    know it all already. Just think – in Venice there's a thousand miles
6975    of shelves, a million tons of different sorts of paper: each
6976    individual, every transaction for two thousand years – all stashed in
6977    a thimble now. Down it goes – a deep hole in Siberia. A
6978    mammoth's graveyard. You dig it up, you find out everything of
6979    people that you never knew.'

6980    I wonder why he wouldn't send me out. I'm not like Cinzia – I
6981    don't know anything.
6982        'It's a complicated enterprise you have,' I say to Alex. 'All sorts
6983    get in, and do all sorts of things.'
6984        'Oh yes,' he says, 'and Cinzia has the names: recruited,
6985    infiltrated, sacrificed and willing. It comes out the same. It's to
6986    your credit, your protecting her. But – she's just a jar. A sweet
6987    person, a heart of candy. You might say – a door ajar. It goes in,
6988    comes out. Everybody's satisfied. Almost everybody. Vince – she
6989    was right for you. You didn't make your move. Too bad.'
6990        I'm at a loss. 'She was old for me, Alex,' I say.
6991        I don't want anything to do with her. My name – a deserter's,
6992    tagged in her.
6993        'There's safe houses too,' says Alex. 'Ready for an idyll.
6994    Practice an instrument there – no one will ever hear.'
6995        I could make a trip alone: to a safe place – not by sea or air.
6996        'Of course, Vince,' Alex goes on, 'you've been close to other
6997    deaths. Very close. "Responsible" – what a tough word! The
6998    sentence, as you know – it's always "Death"! That's irony! Death
6999    wipes all other things right out – it's the great pardoner, and the
7000    worst punishment,' he laughs.
7001        'I didn't do a thing...' I start to say.
7002    That's maybe worse. A waste. An indecision punishable...
7003        'I never set out, Alex...' I say, 'Not to be close to the end of
7004    others...'
7005        'And yet – they happen all around you! Known, unknown, with
7006    heavy weight or fillet-knife,' he says, and laughs.
7007        'Then send me out!' I say, daring him to set out the criterion.
7008        'Oh, you're not ready yet,' he says. 'Vince – you may never be.
7009    Always on the edge – how does that sound. The "always",
7010    naturally.'
7011        'To me, it sounds quite good,' I say. 'The moment that you test
7012    the air – and will it bear, and lift you up? The moment on the roof,
7013    on the wheel – will you resist desire, to throw your body down, see
7014    if you've a soul, and if it wings away...'
7015        'Exactly so,' he says. 'Vince – we are at one. That is my view
7016    entirely. Best wait and see, and send the others out. It's even
7017    statesmanlike. But – you can't do it here, with me. We can't have
7018    two of us the same.'
7019        'That's most unfortunate,' says Cinzia, who hears everything –
7020    her ears deep and cool, like arum lilies. 'It's a paradox. Those don't

7021 register, except as an anomaly, and over time – they're sanded
7022 down, away. They're dust, detritus.'
7023     'She means,' says Alex, listening in, 'there's no more dialectic.
7024 That's a state they once called "God". Myself – I don't believe a
7025 word – precious though Cinzia is,' and he cuddles her.
7026     Alex is a prince – he's offered Cinzia, but all she knows is other
7027 people's news. 'You're banal,' she says to me. 'Banality's my trade
7028 – but yours is instinct. You're like the animals – you think you're
7029 omnipotent because you do everything you want.'
7030     'There's something off-key,' I say to Alex, ignoring Cinzia. 'All
7031 over here. There's no bar...'
7032     'That's what you're looking for?' he asks. 'You could do that.
7033 Even take a cut. I'd send you to Siberia, you'd learn to make that
7034 hooch, the samogon. You could bury Cinzia's boxes while you're
7035 there, cover them with bones.'
7036     'No alcohol, dear,' Cinzia tells Alex. 'Remember your scenes.'
7037     'I'm just the dispatcher,' Alex says. 'Being lucid doesn't enter.'
7038     'You have a great capacity for love, Alex,' says Cinzia, holding
7039 on.
7040     'And sacrifice,' says Alex. 'I love them – off they go, in the
7041 name of doing good. Do they do it? I shan't know. But Vince – I
7042 don't think you're capable of love. And you don't sacrifice –
7043 you've nothing to do it with.'
7044     'That makes us equal, Alex,' I say. 'Except you seem quite rich
7045 and I am temporarily indigent.'
7046     'Don't forget your dog, Vince,' says Cinzia, pushing me into the
7047 garden.
7048     'It won't forget, Cinzia,' I say.
7049     'Oh come!' says Alex, 'we can't lose him before we've decided
7050 what's to happen to him.'
7051     Cinzia says, '*L'art de vivre* – the art of living – remember that?
7052 It was the rage, those old guys all gone now ... the art once
7053 mastered, living can be over shortly. Maybe that is Vince's thing.'
7054     I remember Maya wishing that her life had never started. Once
7055 wound up, though, it rolls and rolls.
7056     'You're the tough virgin here,' I say to Cinzia. 'Not Alex.'
7057     'See! I thought you'd work things out in time,' she says.
7058     'You two,' I say, 'it seems you haven't reached the core. You
7059 send them off, and that's their destiny accomplished. What have
7060 you learned? There's always more volunteers?'

7061    'Oh, the hell with it, Cinzia,' says Alex. 'Let him go. Let him
7062    take to the waves. Let's be done with it.'
7063    'No,' Cinzia shouts: we're standing on their little rockery.
7064    There's rocks the size of heads – she pelts me with them. This
7065    could end real bad. 'He's not worthy. Every dog must have its day
7066    – not him! He has no right to time, to chance, fulfilment, joy and
7067    misery. He's a butterfly. His wavering course ... can lead to no
7068    assessment, judgment – why's he here, not there? He doesn't know
7069    – no one can tell what drives him, lifts and drops him... His cycle –
7070    quite absurd: a fritillary, a metamorph – from crawler into
7071    aeroplane, worm into bird – affront to nature. Reason too. To have
7072    a mission! Choose, be chosen. How do you earn the right, Alex –
7073    tell him how...'
7074    'I'm not sure I know,' says Alex. 'I did this and that, I am the
7075    one, the only; you are my spokesperson, Cinzia. That's it – I have
7076    the key, mine is the signature, I have the automatic pen that thanks
7077    the correspondents for their wish.'
7078        I run, I leap the fence – not from fear, of course, but – this is real
7079    punishment! – I run as self-defence. This is not the answer – but it
7080    fills the moments. Cinzia bursts from her blouse, her pants, to run,
7081    to throw. In the second of the glance, the revelation of the
7082    impossible – she's desirable, she's the huntress huntable – the
7083    bloom, the wasp, the ripe peach ... she's chasing me, out of the
7084    garden, menacing ... her brown juicy pitcher's arm...
7085
7086                                        *
7087
7088    '...and so, my friend – no alcohol, so you get stoned.' This stranger
7089    steals my line. The guy – he's not my friend – we're neighbours
7090    anomalous, on bar stools, like random letters, strangers mustered on
7091    a keyboard.
7092    'No,' I say, 'we were all sober, lucid. I knew – I know – exactly
7093    what I had to do. I've always known. That's not the secret –
7094    making decisions, following a path. No – the real life – it's
7095    everything I haven't had.'
7096        The bar is dim. In one dark green alembic, there are pickled
7097    eggs, and in another – horse cocks. Either pricks the hunger and
7098    deflates...
7099    'Founding a city, curing a disease, fighting a war – those are the
7100    adventures that can justify a life of any length,' I say. 'Well –
7101    everyone's at war. Enemies, brothers, neighbours – fathers,

7102   mothers, sons and all the rest ... the sun, the moon, the rain, all
7103   threatening, the poachers and the insects, the drugs that cure, that
7104   cuddle or arouse... As for diseases – you must identify and give a
7105   name. And, you're dealing pills. The cure, the genocide – the
7106   motivation's parallel... Besides – you need a life for war or cure –
7107   existence ends before the battle's joined... That leaves the city.'
7108   I should have told it clear. I shake the guy beside me – Mirko. I
7109   say, 'You find a river, with a bend – a view of mountains...'
7110   'Sounds like old Titograd,' says Mirko. 'It's no discovery; no
7111   novelty is there.'
7112   'No, no,' I say. 'The mission. That's the point. A Faustian
7113   enterprise – the draining, damming, planting. Transforming nature,
7114   bringing reason, science to mankind...'
7115   'You need a refuge – not another heap of bricks, and guys all
7116   doing different things – like bagging bentonite,' Mirko says. 'The
7117   way is clear – we should belong beneath the water. That's the
7118   element in full expansion. There you can learn to live a new, a
7119   slower life. Your lungs? The bobbing up and down, and blowing air
7120   – that's not for creatures serious. What we must grow's not longer,
7121   fatter lungs. It's gills.'
7122   'I see,' I say. 'You take a bowie knife and slash them in?'
7123   'Don't make me regret telling you,' Mirko says. 'It's quite
7124   revolutionary. Not all the details have been pencilled in. As for you,
7125   Vince, I'm disappointed. You say the good life's everything you
7126   missed: why not say it's "justice"? I'm sure you've not had that,
7127   and nor has anyone. And yet – it's what they say they want.'
7128   'I know all that,' I say. 'My life's more street-pastoral than
7129   abstract, than an aspiration. You're right, of course – lives are all
7130   too short to do what guys had hoped, although some say when they
7131   are about to die, there's nothing left to do, they've done it all, and
7132   satisfied!'
7133   'My plan,' says Mirko, 'is on the stocks. All it needs now is
7134   someone with a blade. And cash – to pay them off.'
7135   'This is my laboratory,' he says. The lake is huge – grey and
7136   white, and down below – blue watery shapes of currents; on the
7137   shores the smoke from husks on fire, more white on white.
7138   'This is Aurora,' Mirko says. 'And this is one man and his dog.
7139   Vince.'
7140   Aurora looks quite grim. Her eyes are hungry, like an owl's.

7141       Mirko takes off all his clothes. 'Strip off, Vince,' he says. 'Down
7142   there, I have another house – you'd say a lean-to, though there's
7143   nothing there to lean against.'
7144       'I can't swim, Mirko,' I tell him.
7145       'I'll show you how,' he says. 'Remember – hold your breath.'
7146   He's gone. We watch his white shape change to blue, then
7147   disappear.
7148       'This is the village,' says Aurora. It's iron-grey. There's nobody
7149   around – 'Where are they all?' I ask.
7150       'Oh, their crap jobs,' Aurora says, offhand.
7151       Three ladies come out of a church, their heads in scarves, the
7152   Mediterranean way.
7153       'The cellars here are deep,' Aurora says. 'See how it's all
7154   designed, built on a hill. There is a backbone street – runs up, right
7155   to the citadel. There's little curvy alleyways on either side, like ribs.
7156   Then, there's the walls all round. We're mostly refugees round
7157   here. That's how they settled here – millennia, and metal ages,
7158   layered down, from bronze to plastic... We can take over too,' she
7159   says, and takes my hand and drags me round. 'This here's a good
7160   defensive point,' she says. 'You hold them here and then run up –
7161   each moment is stronger than the last. You wear them down...
7162   Think of a matrioshka – that's what the old guys had in mind...'
7163       'Does Mirko plan to live down there?' I ask. 'A new life,
7164   submarining? You, together – where do you live, what do you
7165   do...?'
7166       'Oh, he eats the loathsome things, down in the mud,' Aurora
7167   says. 'The eels. He slithers round, makes friends with them, and
7168   then – inveigles.'
7169       'This house of his, beneath the drift?' I ask.
7170       'Oh, his religion lets him have women from each element,'
7171   Aurora laughs. 'There's his mermaid. Then the fire – he's longing
7172   for that one.'
7173       'I know,' I say. 'Of course he – anyone – would long for that.'
7174       'There's the air. When he takes off – behold, a filmy one. I'm
7175   the earthy type,' she says. It's true – her face, a well-proportioned
7176   stone, clay the lips, the eyes a pale and scurfy blue you find round
7177   minerals.
7178       'You can't mean to take the village, hold by force?' I say.
7179       'It's history. That's how it's all renewed,' she says. 'You take
7180   these shabby houses, add a floor or two – then others come and
7181   chase you out. They settle in, you have their kids.'

7182    'They'll bomb you. They won't fight from street to street,' I say.

7183    'Then we'll go in the cellars too,' she says. 'Like they all did.
7184    Our cause is just. The people here – they're senile. They've forgot
7185    the story, so – their time is up.'

7186    'I see all that,' I say. 'It's not my scene, of course – but why take
7187    on a place like this, so dank and crumbling, no road in or out?'

7188    'You have a sugar heart, poor Vince,' she says. 'You need a
7189    history that toughens you.'

7190    'Money, Aurora – you need lots to make a stand,' I say.

7191    'We may have to change our names,' she says. 'That way,
7192    they'll send cash. Who can resist just causes? There's enough that
7193    can't.'

7194    'I understand there's prejudice, Aurora,' I say. 'You're a
7195    novelty. You don't fit with Mirko... Maybe you'd do better on your
7196    own... Mirko can prosper from the elements...'

7197    'It's just the same for me,' she says. 'I'm straight – I get the
7198    same deal as him. One man, from each element – or woman, if I
7199    wish. Turn and turn about – our religion can accommodate. Live
7200    the good life, that's it.'

7201    I could be the fire. The fire man. I can't imagine how we'd live.

7202    'The disenchantment was complete, a century ago,' she says.
7203    'Some whitecoats try the incantation even now – we can be saved,
7204    in peace, longlived and bland. It isn't so, Vince – we're desperate
7205    for space and water, our subsistence...'

7206    On she talks; down in the lake, I see Mirko, the seeker after
7207    wonder, renewal – a simple cut beneath the arms ... plunging and
7208    surfacing, longer the intervals before he takes a breath.

7209    'Oh no,' Aurora shouts. 'The water's spewed him up!'

7210    He's beached. We pump him out.

7211    'We're not a glam couple,' says Aurora, 'but together, we'll get
7212    somewhere, change it all. Separate directions. You could join me,
7213    Vince. You can't swim. Mirko's not for you. You don't care if
7214    there's a future, and the water's cold. You don't want a mermaid.
7215    It's to me you should belong.'

7216    'Yes,' I say, 'you're right. I'm your fire – but I've demands.
7217    There has to be first person. Action. Me. I can't find a perspective,
7218    stand back, cogitate, write it up, or down. That's sterile, teaching
7219    dead stuff to sceptics. No – it has to be adventure, and me the
7220    principal. With you, it won't work out. They'll bury you alive,
7221    Aurora. Maybe you'll be a torturer, or hang a row of people. You
7222    could change the rules – retire, and have men for all seasons: Mirko

7223 would be winter. Me, I don't have a time, a temperature. I know
7224 reality – it turns out wrong. Or dull. It's a paradox, Aurora – you, I,
7225 take the lead, you have to believe in what you're doing, or it
7226 wouldn't turn out right – and yet ... it won't. Someone will trip it
7227 up, the history you're about to make...'
7228      ...and that's the best bit.
7229      'I don't want all that,' she shouts, kicking at me. 'I need hands,
7230 sharpshooter's eyes, not a lolling head.'
7231      'Are you sure, Aurora, you want a conquest? Maybe a house
7232 would do instead,' I say.
7233      'No, no,' she says. 'First comes the battle. Then, of course, you
7234 settle in. We all forget the massacres, and if you live the good life –
7235 we can all be friends.'
7236      I see Mirko on the shore – with his nail gun he's shooting plastic
7237 cladding round a crate. 'It's an expedient,' he says. 'I'll live here
7238 under. I'll search out the treasure, and the dwarves...'
7239      'There's no window, Mirko. When someone goes to Mars, they
7240 can see the nothing all the way,' I say.
7241      'Oh, I thought of that,' he says. 'See!' There's pictures all
7242 around inside, of sharks, and treasure – bullion, mermaids, their
7243 hair in golden fillets...
7244      'This is science, Vince,' he says. 'I'm trained. If these nails
7245 don't keep the water out – I'll hold my breath. It's circular – the
7246 oboists are used to it. Breathing like that – it makes your face go
7247 baggy, but the air goes round and round...'
7248      'Aurora isn't prepared for this,' I say.
7249      'She's just another heretic. She'll change one heresy for others.
7250 That's what we are, Vince – your journeys must have shown... We
7251 are heretical monkeys. We've been cast off. Once there was truth,
7252 they say. And who told us that? Apes, Vince! In the beginning was
7253 the slime. You end in dust, my friend. Add water – and you're
7254 slime. That's the truth, Vince. Apes told the story, and we wrote it
7255 down. That's why it never is the same – each ape embroidered, got
7256 things wrong. They rhapsodised. They looked higher up the tree,
7257 they saw the shadows flickering round – the nymphs, the demons –
7258 look! up where the fruit is always ripe and tempting...'
7259      'I'm reaching that conclusion, Mirko, on my own,' I say. 'The
7260 story...'
7261      'It doesn't all conclude, dear Vince,' he says. 'Until you pull the
7262 switch. We each have one. And there's a big one, for everyone.

7263  We're not into sadomas, I'm sure, not you and I, no flirting with the
7264  end... Aurora, though – she'd do anything to get her house...'
7265  He fires the last nail from inside, shouts, 'Push me out, Vince.
7266  Have a drink on me!'
7267  I push, submerge him. His air bubbles out. The crate says
7268  'Aurora: To await'. Of course – so far, she's no address. On the
7269  side, there's a stencilled gun.
7270  The dog – it's not the swimming sort. It's loyal, I guess – it
7271  makes no rescue moves, it trots away.
7272  Here's two adventures – Mirko, Aurora – in my sights, both
7273  missed. Neither was for me; quite alien. I didn't need an ape to tell
7274  me that.
7275  Aurora stands in the village square. There's nondescript youths
7276  around. 'Help me,' she shouts.
7277  They don't know how to load a magazine. We did all that at
7278  school. I show them how. I don't approve.
7279  The eels will have revenge on Mirko – though there's no
7280  satisfaction for them there. They could expect to live a century or
7281  more – until he came and carved them up. If you believe in poetry,
7282  the importance of the things you see, the sport of words, drug-free,
7283  professional and measured – all, any of these – it's hard to fit in
7284  eels.
7285  You don't see Icarus beneath the waves – Aurora doesn't see the
7286  scene at all, of Mirko launched and disappeared. He and Icarus,
7287  those pioneers – they scarcely made their splash. To history, they're
7288  failures – and – yes, they're failures, the biggest there can be.
7289  Mirko, Icarus, eaten by the eels.
7290  Aurora's band moves slowly up the empty street. They have no
7291  flag – if they had asked, I'd have designed a beauty for them – even
7292  though I don't approve at all. If Icarus had made his flight, been a
7293  success, started the fashion – Aurora might have the aeroplanes she
7294  needs...
7295  They could divide the habitat. She on one side ... like the 18s and
7296  the 8s. Doing what she says – you'd be as safe as with the other
7297  crew.
7298  There's not much time. I'll find an attic room, it's cheap, and if
7299  you look down on the street, your head will swim. I'll write out a
7300  version of my life – short, packed like an egg – and send it out.
7301  There's tall poppies around, bosses of all kinds – they think there's
7302  a secret, or a mystery, in how they got to where they think they are

7303    – they need a follower, one with a project ambitious, transforming,
7304    in their head – but one who'll serve, crouch down before the chair.
7305        Be loyal.

# 6

## STARTING OVER

from **Blue Light**

> 'La privation de la vision béatifique
> est le degré zéro du Purgatoire.'
>
> Jacques le Goff, *Le temps du Purgatoire*

> 'And Nadab and Abihu, the sons of Aaron, took either of them his censer, and put fire therein, and put incense thereon, and offered strange fire before the Lord, which he commanded them not.
> And there went out fire from the Lord, and devoured them, and they died before the Lord.'
>
> *Leviticus 10, 1-2*

> 'Why clothe them? When they wear clothes and are under the moral law, they will assume an immense pride, a vile hypocrisy, and an excessive cruelty.'
>
> Anatole France, *Penguin Island*

THERE'S the crucifix on the wall. I'm back.

The surgeon, Dr Slavoj, says, 'We'd time to kill, so we fitted you up.'

I say, 'I thought it was simple, a thing – below the neck.'

'We found lots of things you hadn't mentioned – scars, holes.'

'The brain, the brain!' I shout.

'That always needs a tidy.'

7340     I look around the room for demons excised, discarded, wooden
7341 toys – there's nothing. He's exultant: 'We took lots out, and put lots
7342 in.'
7343     'But I'm still me?'
7344     'And who would that be? How would we know? How would
7345 you know?'
7346     I guess the head always has you saying 'me', and answering too
7347 – even if it seems a stranger. Stranger right now it seems – the feet
7348 don't flap, the fingers droop, there's gauze to stop stuff falling out –
7349 and there's a cup with things – they're beetles! Leechlike things!
7350     The Doctor says, 'Just body acting up. The brain's the thing.
7351 We're artisans, you know. Don't just fit in some bits we find, lying
7352 around. It's like making a pot.'
7353     The nurse says, 'Like making a tea service.'
7354     I ask, 'When I came in, the world was coming to an end. We
7355 even thought of waiting – seeing if it did. So – did it?'
7356     And they laugh, as if I'm a Venusian, off the ship, feeling my
7357 way, making a joke. I ask, 'And memories?'
7358     He says, 'You'll find they happen all the time. The moment
7359 passes into memory, and sometimes reappears, just like a ghost.
7360 You'll remember us, I think. The thing is to forget, forget your
7361 memories, the ones that prey on you and stop your healthy sleep.'
7362     The nurse says, 'We gave you a big collectivity horizon.'
7363     'Not communism!' I say and the two exchange a glance.
7364     'No, no,' she says, 'We're men of science, women too.'
7365     Slavoj says, 'Nothing to do with politics. All the players – us –
7366 have to think the same – somewhat the same – or else it wouldn't
7367 work. At all. Without the common land, it wouldn't be worth
7368 doing. Thinking, living. Couldn't do it.'
7369     The nurse – isn't she a nurse? – says, 'Of course we have to
7370 think and do the same, or else there'd be no reason, and no
7371 universe,' and they chuckle together.
7372
7373                              *
7374
7375     I feel it swaying. No, I'm not quite right, not yet. It sways, but not
7376 with those long, determined paces the elephants make when
7377 trotting. More like a camel, scenting something? Not a horse, that's
7378 clear, no kind of cart – if I could just reach out, I'd feel the leaves,
7379 the branches, the fat fruit, bold but friendly lizard running, flicking
7380 over the knuckles. The Sun! Seems to come and go, but always

7381 there, the worshipful, the venerable, our companion, up there it
7382 frolics through the fronds.
7383     Bearers, a palanquin, perhaps. If you can tolerate the short life,
7384 the injustice – and that's just if you're rich! And now I hear those
7385 two, I'm back again, I ask, 'How much of me could you take off,
7386 and it still be me?'
7387     The Doctor looks at me, little black eyes, 'You're the most
7388 interesting person I've met,' he says.
7389     The nurse says, 'However much we took away, what was there,
7390 or added, what was left – would still be you. There's no one else it
7391 could be, every morning you'd greet it as yourself, and every
7392 night.'
7393     'And if I die – is that still me, or are there missing bits? Or
7394 memories? In some head, lingering? Bits of that universe?'
7395     The Doctor cocks his head. He's like the dog on the disc. 'You
7396 must have asked,' he says, 'If that old guy, maybe your father, dies,
7397 would it be good? or bad? or natural? even a relief. Or just what
7398 happens, just this one time, to someone who filled spaces in your
7399 life. You can't imagine a space, without this person, always there in
7400 just the right slots ... What's you, what's memory – where do your
7401 "other people" fit?'
7402     The nurse says, 'When you see on TV, they're always
7403 brainwashing these actors and spooking the actresses – you never
7404 see a woman writer with a credit. Did you know, women have to
7405 use a pseudonym, a man's name – what do you make of that?'
7406     I say, 'But memories ...'
7407     The Doctor says, 'Ah yes, "memories are made of this". But
7408 what, exactly? Think of what you remember, then think – imagine
7409 – what you don't.'
7410     The nurse says, 'There's plenty to go round.'
7411     I insist, 'So, objectively, I consent to my death, as I do to other
7412 people's, to be part of the flux, the me that was always central, now
7413 no longer so – and for a reason that's outside, beyond ...? Like
7414 human sacrifice?'
7415     The Doctor interrupts, 'Why outside?'
7416     'You mean, that judgements are already, always, part of me, my
7417 little province?'
7418     He says, 'You make your judgements about people, situations,
7419 that don't exist, that never have, that you have never seen nor
7420 known. It's in your head. Your kind of guy – he's underneath their
7421 bombs: their kind of guy – (who's quite like you) – is under yours.

7422   What makes you judge that yours, your guys, your bombs, are more
7423   deserving? Why, you don't know the issues ... once more, is it
7424   natural, or is it bad?'
7425       The nurse nods, and checks off something on a pad. I think,
7426   '"Most interesting person" – that's what's on the protocol, they say
7427   that to all the guys, but after that, the "me" seems less alone. It even
7428   feels for others. Yet – the deaths of all! Not inconceivable, but
7429   maybe end of world is also end of reasoning. It's all quite complex,
7430   living – it seems at times there's moral calculation, others not; or
7431   else some scale, or else a protocol ...'
7432       'Then, there's history,' I say. 'All full of people, thoughts and
7433   curiosities, quite unlike me – yet as like, and different, as all the
7434   other people still alive that I don't know and can or can't imagine,
7435   who live far off, short lives for rich and poor, and getting shorter ...'
7436       They stare, encouraging, as if I'm taking my first infant's steps.
7437       I insist again, 'They said the world was going to end. Well, did
7438   it?' and the two just laugh, a horrible open genuine laugh, as if it's
7439   really funny, they're amused at the idea and not at me, so any
7440   answer would be – well, would not be funny in the least.
7441       'Well, well,' the Doctor says, laughter out of his mouth like
7442   spaghetti tails: 'This time you've really surpassed yourself. I
7443   always said, the most interesting – now the wittiest, of all the
7444   persons, that I've ...'
7445       Then, his black pupils like two black voids, he says, 'You see
7446   that guy?' and he points to another white coat, half hiding, half
7447   leaning behind a pillar. 'We're all trying to get rid of him. Life is
7448   that, even if you don't know answers.'
7449       He shows me a questionnaire and says, 'I'll tell you how to
7450   answer.'
7451       I see: 'Experience of cutting: do you find it terrifying? Erotic?
7452   Just familiar?'
7453       'We get lots of knife cases here,' he says.
7454       I disengage, but he does not: 'We see the brain,' he says, falling
7455   again into his profession, 'as a cultural landscape.'
7456       The nurse says, 'We gave you extra hunter-gatherer, it brings
7457   the ladies in.'
7458       I say, 'I'm more maso than macho,' but they go on:
7459       'The moon of enlightenment – now, that's always hard. We cut
7460   out myth and faith – when you were over there, in no man's land,
7461   did you get some spark?'
7462       'Zero.'

7463 'Here, instead,' the Doctor says, 'we have a lively time. Music,'
7464 and he shuffles a step: 'Song,' and out comes 'September Song',
7465 half bleat, half bray.
7466     'Cut the singing,' I tell him.
7467     'Don't drive your car,' he says, 'we put in lots of rule-
7468 breaking.'
7469     'So all the judgement,' I say, 'values, where has all that gone?
7470 Into that pile, with memory?' and the nurse tilts up her clipboard,
7471 and I see a sketch, a scribble, could be ethnic lunch, polyp with
7472 eyes, and then a space for Fun Time, and I see she's written '"Maso
7473 not macho" made us laugh to split.'
7474     The Doctor says, 'All you guys we get in here, you love
7475 yourselves so tight, and ask if it's all over – the world – but never if
7476 you caused it, even a bit. You weren't away too long – we just
7477 tweaked "perception".' 'So,' I say, 'I can do the things now that
7478 before I didn't dare, or thought were not for me, or even anyone?'
7479     And here's the nurse, she says, 'The choice is always yours.
7480 Evaluation – that's always the same. The rules, though – not always
7481 clear or straight.'
7482     'The rules don't come in sets of two or three,' the Doctor says,
7483 and then it comes to me, the fear.
7484     'I'm still a hetero?' I say. 'I'd got kind of used to sparring with
7485 the ladies,' and they laugh.
7486     'Why, sure,' almost in duet they cry. 'Straight down the middle,
7487 that is where we put you.'
7488     'Of course, we mean the middle of the hetero track,' the Doctor
7489 says, and I suppose I'm glad, and even thankful, though I'm not
7490 quite sure if normal tracks bring happiness or just another mystery.
7491
7492                   *
7493
7494 The Doctor's eager, and he says, 'I went biking. Trail bike, on the
7495 Andes.'
7496     'That will have been strenuous.'
7497     'I took seeds. I gave them to the locals.'
7498     'Tell me, then.'
7499     'Cannabis. I persuaded them to plant pot instead of coca.'
7500     'That must have been tough.'
7501     'The moral objective's firm. A lesser evil to replace a greater
7502 one.'
7503     I say, 'I'm not convinced you got the balance right. They were

7504    happy chewing, now they're smoking. They'll still complain about
7505    the chain of being and its consequences. Anyway, why are you
7506    telling me this?'
7507       'I thought you might like to come with me.'
7508
7509                            *
7510
7511    No one visits me – that's good. If they were old attachments,
7512    maybe this fresh brain would put them off. If they were new
7513    friends, I'd know continuity had been broken, old me departed, new
7514    me unrecognisable. All the same, it leaves a mystery – maybe I
7515    didn't tell some people I was coming in. And who were 'they'?
7516    Friends from school? Army? Monastery? The corporation? –
7517    friends are very much the same, and so are relatives – and as I
7518    muse, here comes a face unrecognised: she asks, 'Are you there?'
7519       'Absolutely.'
7520    She says, 'I was curious,' now she's two people, there's a silent
7521    man behind who pulls her back. She says, 'I'm not seeking you. I
7522    came to visit someone else, but they've departed.'
7523       'Hospitals are like that. I'm sorry.'
7524       'Why do you think this is a hospital? White coats? And
7525    clipboards?'
7526       'Feeling ill,' I say.
7527       Why has she poked herself in?
7528       'The sign,' she laughs. Everyone here is fine at laughing. If
7529    laughter were a sign of happiness or fun ... but here, it's just the
7530    side of something else. Sadness.
7531       She shows me the sign: 'No elephant rides,' it says.
7532
7533                            *
7534
7535    I hear her call the guy she's with – 'Jake' – an eager hound where
7536    moral mystery's concerned.
7537       'This place here,' he says. 'Is holistic, first they fix your body,
7538    then they talk you over. And they cut you too, but only if you pay,'
7539    and so he points to a motto, a board written in black pen: 'life is
7540    chronic, irreversible – but you can learn to live with it.'
7541       He goes on, 'They've got the right end of the stick, these
7542    laughing guys and gals.'
7543       I want to say, 'Sticks don't have right or wrong ends, or, if you
7544    prefer, they're quite indifferent.'

7545    But he's jumped ahead, and says, 'The middle of the stick now,
7546    that makes it a fine fighting tool,' and he makes some stick play,
7547    tells some history and stuff we don't want to hear – about wicker
7548    armour, diets, bronze bells and such.
7549        Here, on the floor, there's a bill. The head – 'Holistic decisions:
7550    moral and surgery'. Below, 'Easy terms'.
7551        I ask the Doctor, 'Who makes these decisions?'
7552        'Obviously,' he says, 'we all do, otherwise there'd be no
7553    contest, no game.'
7554        'When it's decided, what do we do?'
7555        'We here,' and his troupe giggles expectantly, 'do more or less
7556    what we think.'
7557        'My head,' I say. 'What did you take out?'
7558        'That again, still? Duplicate memories – lots of guys have
7559    almost identical pasts, and these cling on, they won't lie down or go
7560    away – so what's their point? School, play, growing ...'
7561        'There's no point, I guess – but then, I'm not deciding...'
7562        'Memory – in general, not a good basis for anything.
7563    Experience, now – but, there we find it's different for everyone,
7564    and then – it's here! it's gone! and back to memory, to fancy
7565    wafting free.'
7566        I see lots of holes in their holism. Is the me I've got inside still
7567    adequate for walking up and down? The street, it looks like Tokyo,
7568    the hair – the red, the blue – those whores in gingham dresses, look
7569    twelve or less, but – yes, it could just be Japan, I seem to look like
7570    other people, and I say, 'Then I'll be off. Morality can wait, I'll go
7571    down in the street and show myself.'
7572        'I'd hoped you'd come and bike with me, and spread the word,'
7573    the Doctor says. 'Of course, with pot they'd still be poor, but happy
7574    – better that than rich and lazy, don't you think? running guns,
7575    abusing kids or taking us as hostage.' He's anxious and he says,
7576    'Better the cannabis, it calms you down,' and off they go, and soon
7577    the smoke comes thick and green – wafts from underneath their
7578    door, it clogs the keyhole, the yellow-green is in our ears and in our
7579    shoes. We linger, tranquil, waiting to decide the next important
7580    thing.

7581
7582                                    *
7583
7584    That Mae – she has a playful face, but striving bears her down, a
7585    weight like marble on her head. Her Jake's a wizened thing, brown

7586    and tough, a stone without a prune.
7587         Hmmm – I could run off with Mae ...
7588         Jake asks me, 'Will you go with him, with us?
7589         'Is Mae coming?' I ask, avoiding my 'no'.
7590         'We'd bring justice. Though Mae stands for freedom, rather –
7591    but we're catching up on it, with all the books.'
7592         Jake makes raw documentaries, and Mae – 'Mae tells me where
7593    to point the eye,' says Jake. 'She knows a story, I just see what's
7594    beautiful.'
7595         Now Slavoj says, 'You'll come with me, surely?'
7596         'You're embarrassing me,' I say.
7597         Slavoj says, 'It's because you don't like me? Don't know me?'
7598         I don't answer. He goes on, 'If you knew me better, you might
7599    like me less. Even hatred. But the right thing is to do the right
7600    thing, don't you agree?'
7601         Jake takes me aside, he chews words like he's stupid, but he's
7602    maybe slow, he says, 'They always put some super in – you know,
7603    you think it's all Montaigne, the human bit subordinate to some
7604    good sense that comes from who knows where – the super sets you
7605    up, makes you a fighter. It all takes off. The axe against the door, to
7606    set the prisoners free and scrambling down the walls, they're all in
7607    white – barge-haulers, cut them free. A divine fire!' And he cocks
7608    his head for the crackle.
7609         Later, Jake says, 'If you touch Mae, I'll kill you.'
7610         We get to chatting, and he shows me his scraggy knuckles,
7611    polished like Granny's and yellow as meerschaum, well kippered.
7612         'Look at this!' he says. 'And this!' – and both arms are wearing
7613    armour. Plates. 'The hands. Lethal. With one blow,' and I think of
7614    whoever it was killed flies, just so. A terrible gift.
7615         'The arms,' he says, 'in the Galapagos.'
7616         'Those turtles are implacable. I hear,' I say.
7617         'We drop over – from the Andes,' says Jake. 'They only let just
7618    one or two a year – a decade. I got these plates there – climbing
7619    rocks, and down they came.'
7620         'He pulled the island down', I think.
7621         'It's Mae who puts the ethics in,' he goes on. 'I am pretty
7622    fearless, as you see. It's she that knows to swivel – puts the moral
7623    camber on the slopes.'
7624         And here is Mae. She says, 'He loves to boast,' but from me
7625    there isn't much for her to fear.
7626         'The world,' I ask. 'It didn't end?'

7627    She says, 'Those who are here, who're left – we need a clean: a
7628    reaming out of everything, of all the icky stuff, an irrigation of the
7629    mind, you understand.'
7630        'A document. A movie – one that doesn't move, but lifts you
7631    up,' I say.
7632        'Exactly,' she says.
7633        I ask, 'That Jake's a biker too?'
7634        She says, 'Slavoj put it in his head. He wanted a friend. It's
7635    quite incongruous. Jake's an auteur.' She's proud, but giggles.
7636
7637                                        *
7638
7639    I'm exactly the same as I was.
7640        I'm not, of course. There's the mulch of time, and maybe they
7641    switched some bits around.
7642        Slavoj says, 'Bit more right hemisphere, and you'll appreciate
7643    my verse. Bit more left, you'll see through Heidegger,' he and Janet
7644    ride the circuits in the heads, they're into literature, general
7645    conversation, and all that.
7646        I still like Jake the maniac, his flat photographer's eye. And
7647    Mae's so sweet, desirable – she's an obsessive's groupie, I fantasise
7648    her into uniform. I could risk death from Jake, and maybe get off
7649    with a beating.
7650        Janet the nurse – 'I'm not a nurse, I'm everybody's boss' – says
7651    to me, 'You're quite ready for the street, again.'
7652        But no! Going back is not the deal (the world has ended
7653    anyway, I'm sure) – and now infinity is pulling. Shall it be biking
7654    up the Andes? Or something more original?
7655
7656                                        *
7657
7658    'Up there,' says the Doctor, Slavoj, 'from peak to peak – you hear
7659    every radio station in the world. Or there is none. There is no air,
7660    then there is wind. There is sulphur, rising in plumes like the wings
7661    of monster angels, your eyes water – then you see the pyramids,
7662    down there on the plain – the sacrifice, the service. Continuity!
7663    That is being someone, that's community, the great chain. Chosen
7664    by men to meet the gods,' and his eyes are far away, two black
7665    basalt points, dreaming of surgery divine, the humans sacrificed.
7666        'Gods,' Janet says. 'Meet them or please them. Either way, it's
7667    a bridge. A highway. Us to them. Where did that world go?' she

7668    sighs. 'It's swept away, you just delve through the sweepings.'
7669         It's a thought, it brings a tear, and it's the truth. Do you have to
7670    believe the truth? Is that what belief is for? Jake is listening, pauses
7671    in silence for a little while.
7672         Then, 'That guy,' he whispers to me, admiringly, 'is set to be
7673    the biggest pusher in the New World – a veritable Cortès,
7674    Columbus, Raleigh, Drake, Pizarro – but noble too! Bringing not
7675    measles, taking not the common spud – instead, salvation! Away
7676    with the coca and its masters, no more the Indians lingering by the
7677    road, their little pokes of blueberries for sale. New Kings of
7678    Cannabis, empires of the weed. The cosmic bhang!' And     here's
7679    Slavoj, he says, 'It does you good, too, that weed. Away the
7680    smelters and the dams, on, on laughter, and the rictus grin – Mother
7681    of God, that river – so portentous – away the foul degrading work,
7682    away the mine – recline! Peace, love and garlands.'
7683         And Mae says, 'Just like before. Our fathers told us how it was,
7684    when peace and music brushed aside the nuclear dust, and all had
7685    heroes and a flag' – it's hard to stay unmoved, though it's all new
7686    to me – but then, my world is ended, that is clear, and from the
7687    ruins of the old, we build anew. New memories, new truths, and
7688    Jake has cyclist's legs, he'll make the trip, and several too, and Mae
7689    will put the ethics, moral law, into Jake's movies.
7690         'A curiosity,' I ask, 'do you ask the local guys to maybe
7691    sacrifice themselves to make a point, for you to take a shot that says
7692    it all?'
7693         'We never ask,' Jake says, 'but some will volunteer.'    Mae
7694    completes the ritual, says, 'It is a gift we offer them. To say their
7695    piece, their all. A bridge. A highway. Jake's just the crazy guy – he
7696    takes the shot, it's me who puts the ethics in,' and her face is set
7697    and firm, she's righteous, you can tell, belief and truth are one for
7698    her.
7699         I say, 'Some time I'd like to see your work.'
7700
7701                              *
7702
7703    They needed this, my interest. It fires them up.
7704         'Memory ok?' asks Jake.
7705         'Worlds end every minute,' I say. 'Memory? A broken pot.'
7706         'Don't yellow-dog me,' he snarls, 'feller, same for you is same
7707    for all.'
7708         Mae hushes him. She says, 'Memory and judgement must be

7709  the same for all, or else our movies would appear quite different to
7710  everyone, and so the moral law would lose its point. Just an
7711  opinion, leading nowhere. We're not bigots, but to build – you must
7712  start from the foundations,' and down the street we lurch, we three,
7713  Jake leaping up to grab at signs until his hands – yes, even his – are
7714  bleeding. Mae and I entwined, we are the two firm legs of our
7715  wobbly stool, Jake's the long and short leg as his fancy drives. I see
7716  a beautiful girl. She licks an ice, her tongue is long and thin and
7717  red, and in her other hand, a spliff.
7718      I think of Doctor Slavoj, say to her, 'Smoke gets in your
7719  history.'
7720      'Fuck off,' she says. Her tongue sounds numb.
7721      Mae says, 'That's good, she'll not report you, no molesting –
7722  you won't go to jail,' and I think – their camera gives immunity, for
7723  nearly everyone is keen to end on film, though cut and mute, and
7724  trusting Mae to give them resonance and words of goodness.
7725
7726                          *
7727
7728      I ask Slavoj, 'Doctor, what goes into your remedy? That girl's
7729  tongue – like a serpent's.'
7730      'My, what a genius you are!' he says. 'Synthetic pot, it doesn't
7731  coat your tongue, and not for hedonism, but to forget. That play,
7732  remember, where they put juice in everyone's eyes? Made them all
7733  forget. That was a trivial thing. My aim now ...' and he's
7734  ingratiating, 'Just think, you've nothing running through your head.
7735  You go about your day, like it's on TV. But others now, your
7736  neighbours – some are taken off by guys in uniform, they cut them
7737  up, the bits thrown to the pigs, the dogs. How can you live with this
7738  – you being normal, and beside you – atrocity! For you, for them,
7739  the magic juice. Forgetfulness. *Mann vergisst* – it is my magic gift
7740  – oblivion. To start again.'
7741      I say, 'That's why I'm interesting? Because I don't remember
7742  ...'
7743      'Maybe you don't,' he says. 'Maybe you do. At least you think
7744  the world has ended.'
7745      'It's ending all the time,' I say abstractedly.
7746      'Yes, but here you are,' he says.
7747      And so, I guess, is Mae and Jake, and they are keen to try it all
7748  again.
7749

7750

                             \*

7751

7752 Then, they're praying, down on their white knees, all clad in white,
7753 Slavoj and Janet:
7754     'Oh Earth! who permits – the synthesis of weed, when all the
7755 rest has been mined out and penetrated. Oh Sun – betrayer – shine
7756 on our resurrection, shine on our Brother here, the interesting one –
7757 ' and here they laugh, they must mean me, 'and Jake the fixer, Mae
7758 his moll, and bless the Starting Over, those who haven't grasped
7759 eternal reprise, the take-it-from-the-top, with all repeats! Bless us
7760 all, stuck in our grooves, seeking a mystery, not a truth. Passivity,
7761 not action but a drug that does no harm. Bless us all, and save us
7762 from the Great Helmsman, save us from the Great Gravedigger,
7763 save us from capital and from labour ...' and on they go.
7764     So – perhaps it's true, it's all ended, here we are, or some of us
7765 – and Janet says, 'I love that prayer,' and Slavoj says, 'So long as it
7766 evokes real things and plans,' and they giggle together.

7767

7768

                             \*

7769

7770 Here's Jake, in a huge receptacle, an intelligently designed waste
7771 bin, bullet-shaped, aluminum. It's a Wall of Death.
7772     He's on his bike, triumphant. Slowly, and round and round,
7773 with a 'heeyar-hiyar', 'hi-yi-yicky-yicky', his bandana falls, Mae
7774 grips my arm, he's faster now, the thin legs whirr like electric fans,
7775 the wheels a fuzz of zero, and he's creeping up the wall, with
7776 swoops and drops, like a swallow in a chimney – 'Why's it called a
7777 wall of death?' I ask Mae and add 'It's a bowl of accident, at most.'
7778     He's near the top, we hear the creak, the groan, the bike is at its
7779 limit, Jake is holding on – a parasite, a hard-cased flea, head is a
7780 hazelnut, seems the bike is dragging him up in teeters, down in a
7781 plunge – and wheeee, he's nearly up to touch.
7782     Mae says, 'He risks, and so he tests the moral code. He risks his
7783 life, and asks for nothing. We should all try this – though maybe
7784 not the poor and sick. It gives autonomy – which if you haven't got,
7785 this biking will not give!'
7786     'You're clear on that, at least.'
7787     'Oh yes. That's Dr Janet's rule.'
7788     I say, 'But Jake ignores the moral rule. Doctor Janet enforces it,
7789 but enforcement means you lose the choice. You cultivate your
7790 grass and take the consequences.'    'Yes, you put it in your pipe,'

7791    Mae adds.

7792       And here comes Jake, his head is circling at the rim, he's
7793    horizontal and below there's a miasma, it's sweat of Jake and farts,
7794    and trepidation, breakfast and lunch are in there too, then ...

7795
7796                        \*
7797

7798    There's a mixed conclusion, part plywood, clothes for sure, and
7799    bike all mashed – leather, oil, the tires bite in like drills – he's
7800    overtopped and some poor guy has taken Jake and bike full in the
7801    thorax, and they're broken now, all together, but Jake is fine and
7802    up, and now he's coming round to all the watchers, waving a tin
7803    cup, miniatured version of his wall, his bowl to beg with, 'Small
7804    change! Big starts!'

7805    Jake says, 'Don't mind the guy I pulped, I did the work. I took
7806    the risk. Not through surgery, and my law is not the moral law –
7807    I'm free! I'm unconstrained.'

7808    'Except by laws of gravity,' Mae whispers.

7809    Sharp as a cog, Jake's in, he says, 'Momentum, darling – that's
7810    the word.'

7811
7812                        \*
7813

7814    Now they're off. The Andes. There goes Jake, the bike. Slavoj and
7815    Janet, prostrating for a prayer, and bags of seed and copper coils for
7816    brewing stuff, and Mae is here, and she will stay.

7817    So, Jake's outside the moral law, he follows accident and risk.
7818    And Mae applauds, but longs for order, and for power. Slavoj will
7819    make you good, but he will tweak you first, so you forget. Away
7820    with memories, they blur and blot. The moral law requires an open
7821    space to work upon, synthetic pot's the cure – consensus with a
7822    grin.

7823
7824                        \*
7825

7826    I think of Mae, and fantasise.

7827       What's this? My head says 'Madame Bovary' – her skin, spotty
7828    as a fig pudding. And Mae too – refined tapioca underneath, and
7829    flecks of something sweet and pungent, and I think, 'Goddam –
7830    those doctors have me muddled up, instead of fantasies of sex, it all
7831    turns into food – and what is worse, it's food uneaten, unattainable.

7832 And here I am, I'm stuck on Mae, until some other dish is set
7833 before, a dessert in the desert, gorgonzola dreams – not that it's
7834 racism, for some crispy pork with cloves would do as well. It seems
7835 we've a taboo about blue food, so that excludes the Touaregs –
7836 though, thinking through, it isn't even plausible, for food taboos are
7837 what we most enjoy to violate.'
7838 And so I muse.
7839 The guy that Jake cut up, doing the circus act, now he's beside
7840 me, waves the Doctors off, and says, 'To sue would make me look
7841 ridiculous.'
7842 I agree, and say, 'They're going far beyond our world, our law,
7843 to make another world, another law – so stand well back or else –
7844 the wall of death could well be yours. Jake took the risk, you took
7845 the fall, and that is life, rejoice, forget!'
7846
7847                                             *
7848
7849 'I like you,' says Mae, 'because you're quite short and not very
7850 bright.'
7851 'My education,' I say to excuse myself.
7852 'No, no,' she says. 'It's quite congenital – your parents can't
7853 have been bright, to have an unbright son like you.'
7854 I think of sweetbreads with artichokes, and then of Jake, a-
7855 pedalling up and down her.
7856 'Slavoj and Janet,' I say, 'they have some big task.'
7857 'They're starting over,' Mae agrees. 'No more fantasy and
7858 brooding – they'll start a world in which you smoke, and you're
7859 relaxed, and then you do what you must do. What you are paid to
7860 do.'
7861 I say, 'The peasants will all shoot, when they see they'll lose
7862 their land to grow the natural weed – and when Slavoj starts
7863 dumping his synthetic stuff, that needs tin sheds and hydro dams ...'
7864 but all the while I think of puddings hidden in the trees, of roasts by
7865 post, and love is all around, delightful kitchen smells.
7866 'Only in wonderland,' Mae butts in, 'will you expect to find
7867 confected desserts in the forest – that's what Janet wants to stop.
7868 She sells the smoke that makes you dream – relax into the blank.
7869 Do what is correct,' and we both wonder where that leaves poor
7870 Jake, who lives his dreams.
7871 'Jake!' Mae says, 'his bum's ground down like two quail eggs!'
7872 and we both laugh complicitly, to think of him there, above the

7873   clouds, ducking the stars and meteors, his little piston legs –
7874   titanium. The effort brings your brain to zero, and to rest.
7875
7876                         *
7877
7878   'Plums,' says Mae. 'Not cannabis. That's so last century.'
7879      'Why plums? And the serenity? The blankness?'
7880      'Doctor Slavoj – he loves his tipple. The moral law, that's want
7881   they want. And booze, not cannabis. Wipe-out, not trance. No
7882   memory, and no experience, just do the good, tease out what is
7883   correct.'
7884      'Jake's bike?'
7885      'He takes it everywhere. Nothing to worry you.'
7886      I say, 'The moral law – it seems like gravity for Jake. If you
7887   don't pay it heed, it's just momentum takes you up. And if you live
7888   by day and day – then, you've no universe, not like us rich with
7889   little telephones and such. You'll love the speed, the swooping
7890   down, the roaring up – it takes you to the top, and even over. Free
7891   and damned.'
7892      'And yet,' Mae smiles, 'it's what they want, those two, a moral
7893   law that works from day to day.'
7894      'But accidents and custom do as well, or bad,' I say. 'And
7895   calculation too.'
7896      She shrugs, and says, 'It all fell down. The lot, world,
7897   everything. So now – they feel it needs some ...'
7898      She pauses, and I say, 'Reflection? Autopsy?'
7899      'No – acceleration.' she says. 'Experiment, to see if it could
7900   happen differently.'
7901      I'm silent, I accept, but Jake's bike bothers me. 'Jake?' I ask.
7902      Mae says, 'He's the monkey. He scents blood, he seeks it out,
7903   we film it, and his racing tricks make cash – for us, for Janet and
7904   her crowd. I paste on the manners, as you know.'
7905      'But he needs that cone-thing, the gravity.'
7906      'There's always mountains, canyons – he goes everywhere.
7907   There's little upkeep.'
7908      I want to ask, 'What's he like in bed?' but that is not
7909   appropriate. I ask, 'So, what's he like in bed?'
7910      'He's cheap and cheerful, like our grannies used to say. All you
7911   could want. Besides, he is a hunter, not a gatherer – runs fast, and
7912   doesn't hoard.'
7913      'Slavoj and Janet – to promulgate the moral law – must it be

7914 from mountain tops?'
7915     'It's better so – it gives perspective – in the end, it's all to calm
7916 you down, submit, accept what you are given – the real bad ...' and
7917 she pauses, and I think she stops before she says 'bad monkeys' –
7918 thinking perhaps, humour and nostalgia for those scenes of figures
7919 scurrying, the horsemen cut them down – the greatest game, the
7920 hunt, the storm, all that – 'The moral law, to be obeyed, and not just
7921 fancy, needs its punishments, its cops and judges. Otherwise –
7922 who'd care?'
7923     I say, 'Why booze, and not synthetic drugs?'
7924     Mae says, 'Janet's the smoker, Slavoj's for the booze. It's
7925 personal taste. They did a deal. There's trouble there.'
7926     I say, 'And yet they laugh, it spurts up out of them, like
7927 fountains on eternal cycles.'
7928     She says, 'Of course it has to seem like fun, and give some
7929 satisfaction. Otherwise – who'd give a spit?'
7930
7931                              *
7932
7933 Up the mountains they go, planting plum trees all the way, Slavoj
7934 and Janet, scattering the law, unburdened with those tombstones,
7935 stone tablets you can't swallow. Cycling the rings around them,
7936 their monkey humanoid, the film director, auteur Jake – his
7937 cosmological eyes that seek out corpses, dispossessions. Film it.
7938     'It's such a lonely trip,' I say to Mae.
7939     'They have each other,' she says. 'Though that's lonely too.
7940 Besides, the moral law – everyone knows what it is, it just has
7941 never stuck, attached itself. Maybe people now prefer some
7942 surgery.'
7943     There she stands. I think of rice pudding, virginal, the skin
7944 untouched, to me a bit repulsive, but exciting nonetheless. Leek
7945 soup, or lobster flesh – more palatable than Bovary.
7946     'Surgery takes the edge off,' I say. 'You switch those wires, and
7947 holy wars burst in, and purity of race or village, and off we go a-
7948 soldiering.'
7949     'Well, you must do something with your life,' she says, 'not
7950 grow a shell,' and I think of those turtles, battling on their island.
7951
7952                              *
7953
7954

7955    A cassette arrives. Here's Janet, 'Hi Mae, and that guy you're with
7956    now. How's the weather there with you, and thank the Earth and
7957    Sun we still have weather! We survivors must give thanks – and
7958    now, I've record news. Jake scaled a peak –'
7959        And here the tape leaps up, a jerky ride with lots of sky,
7960    multicoloured as it's now become, with dust and ash and atom
7961    stuff, sunsets all day, and Mae says, 'Hush! It's all imagination'
7962    and there's pause, and Jake has got to where he's going. Then – a
7963    wafting off. He's fallen, dropped – the world goes round and round,
7964    beneath, above, it's hard to say, and there's his head, the face a
7965    scream, the lips drawn thin like bacon rinds – then, swirling round
7966    and up and down – there's pyramids, and orchards now, and crops
7967    all desolate, and maize in stalks and drying on a shed. Janet's here
7968    again, and says, 'You see it all, a tragedy, no moral law could break
7969    his fall, he always lived by God and gravity and guess' – no
7970    difference made between all those, I think, and Janet says,
7971        'Slavoj thinks the fall's inevitable, it happens all the time, but
7972    specially at birth and death, and in between you may survive, just
7973    as Jake did, as you must do when pedalling, crouched like a cricket,
7974    avoiding sin and crime as you must do when bicycling – the posture
7975    that is innocent and individual, but with no choice, no holy, no
7976    profane, and no commands, just head down, eyes on the horizon,
7977    round and round those legs,' and in the video we see the world is
7978    wheeling round, and over it there's cycle wheels that's circling like
7979    cogs from clocks that's telling some short time, and then there's
7980    black and Jake is in the hole.
7981        Mae is shocked, and says, 'Jake made the wheels go round.
7982    He's quite magnificent. His best reels yet, and not a spot of blood
7983    and lymph, his last act cleansed of all that yucky stuff.'
7984        To comfort her, I say, 'That's a great act, great artist – hard to
7985    beat that one,' although you get the same effect by tossing down
7986    from buildings or a plane, a camera with a little chute to steady it ...
7987    but I don't say, and surely Mae knows how to get that same effect,
7988    and then there's Janet's head, Slavoj's, – they're laughing as they
7989    say goodbye, and 'to the next.' 'Regret, nostalgia, death – nothing
7990    to do with us, who live by law, by moral law. It's all a wall, quite
7991    blank, with no mean thing at all.'
7992        Janet says, 'Jake never disappointed, never a foot went wrong,
7993    though at the last misplaced a wheel; no victim, no real fault. And
7994    after all, a start must have its end, and every end its start.'
7995        Mae, at once recovered, says, 'Of course, it's mostly

7996  happenstance, this life. And risk – some court it, others can't avoid.
7997  But on you plough, and all the others try the same, each with the
7998  same approximations, mostly they are apostates, until the thing gets
7999  tough and then you maybe save yourself and screw the rest – but
8000  that's OK, you try again, it's like the song says, you try and try and
8001  try again ...' and I hum on, 'you're never tough enough.'
8002        Mae says, 'It's rough, not tough. You see, it's not about you,
8003  it's about your behaviour in the bad stuff.'
8004
8005                                    *
8006
8007  'Poor Jake,' says Mae. 'Of course, this moral thing's a sell-out.
8008  Slavoj and his slivovitz, Janet too, sold to the goodness biz. Jake
8009  didn't fit, he wasn't what they wanted – though he made their cash.
8010  Instinct and risk – the deadliest, most effective things.'
8011        'If they're a sell-out, Janet and Slavoj, then so are you!' I say,
8012  and she is cold, a-twisting in her dish, an invitation for the spoon,
8013  the fork.
8014        'The moral stuff just says "be good",' she goes on, 'it is its own
8015  reward, and doing so, we all agree the code is this or maybe that,
8016  and so we do the good and life is smooth. And then comes one who
8017  disagrees, philosopher or king, and there go half the guys or more,
8018  they follow him, and down the whole thing goes. It's power. You
8019  have to whip the stragglers in ...'
8020        'Mae, you look delicious,' I say, and I'm glad that Jake is
8021  absent, maybe not dead but getting there.
8022        'It's power, it's power,' Mae repeats, 'and I want some. Or
8023  lots,' and so adventure's on the table now, but power over who or
8024  what – and even why ...
8025        I guess it's true, that power-hungry's not a phase but
8026  physiological, a need that guys whose circuits in the head are all
8027  skewed out must fill, and so I say, 'It's an adventure!'
8028        She looks at me quite cold, and says, 'It's death, you fool.'
8029
8030                                    *
8031
8032  Mae says, 'We'll have to change this sex and food thing, if you're
8033  going to go to banquets. The embarrassment!'
8034        She takes a prod from a pouch, says, 'The Egyptians did it, why
8035  shouldn't I?'
8036        I say, 'Surely, I shouldn't feel it sharp?' She sticks the needle

8037    up my nose.
8038        'We haven't time to think of booze to put you out again,' she
8039    says, 'to send you to your paradise.'
8040        'It's just a garden, not a paradise,' I say, and think of dark
8041    Roumanian beer, but she is up my nose, and then I feel a twangling
8042    in the brains as she is joining this and cutting that, and those are
8043    bells! – I think 'Mascagni – operetta's quite the thing today, but
8044    vulgar,' and I say, 'I like vulgarity, small dose maybe.'
8045        But Mae is busy with her tools and says, 'It's not vulgarity if it
8046    doesn't come as second helpings,' and here come stars and
8047    birdsong, canyons, those tall blue naves with tall blue organs at the
8048    end that play like tidal waves that never come and fish so slippery
8049    that they're here and gone.
8050        'I give up,' Mae says, 'it's all a mess.' She talks of ganglia and
8051    my nose is full of broken solder, so we write to Janet – here comes
8052    a postcard, on the front, the symbol, Jake's spinning wheels, the
8053    spokes a blur, the motto 'onward, not upward', and the pair of
8054    them, Janet, Slavoj, high on some mountain, lawgivers, a book,
8055    some pointing fingers, and a sign that gives admission charges –
8056    though there's nothing to admit, no confession makes a difference,
8057    and so I guess it's just you pay to see what you should do, what is
8058    correct – as if you didn't know – and down the track again you go,
8059    the cities of the plain await, and little booths there are, you take a
8060    shot of mescal and the world is bright and tolerant ... But there they
8061    are, the pair, solid as local gods, and twice as solemn.
8062        The postcard says, 'Mae! Tweak him – we just got our sources
8063    mixed – or sauces, hahaha – a commonplace, a literary thing, this
8064    sex for food. Remote controls, that's all you need – you switch
8065    from porno to the cookery, the channels are abundant – and he is
8066    back again on track, right up the hetero middle, and with appetite,'
8067    she tries, it works, and I am back again in normal world, and Mae is
8068    beautiful, not for consumption, although she's white as mushrooms,
8069    or raw leeks – but just a simile, no more.

8070
8071                                    *
8072

8073        'Jake's trick,' says Mae, 'was being tricked. They set you up – they
8074    set him up – they say "to take this risk" and thanks will come, lives
8075    will be saved, and satisfaction general. But – you tumble down, and
8076    that's all part of it. A game, a metaphor, a paradox.'
8077        'I know about metaphors,' I say, 'that's the trouble in my brain,

8078    that embalming needle up my nose – I know you want to help, but
8079    ...'
8080         'It's that Slavoj,' she says. 'He tells you what to do, and what
8081    the consequences are. He doesn't say those consequences are not
8082    here, nor now, nor maybe ever, nor what you might recognise. It all
8083    gets muddled, people and times, taking the choice – is it the best,
8084    run to the library or the maquis, pen or gun?'
8085         And I say, 'You're beautiful, you really are, when wrestling
8086    with these things.'
8087         She's annoyed, and says, 'That's almost exactly what I don't
8088    want to hear.'
8089
8090                                     *
8091    'They want to start a colony,' she says.
8092         'An empire. Chivvying the peasants, stealing land, all that.'
8093         'To make the right choices, you must take a risk,' Mae says.
8094         'Jake took one,' I say.
8095         'Jake didn't fit,' she says. 'Those fish-eye movies, showing
8096    only what he saw – that takes you nowhere, takes you back to
8097    instinct, habit, what they taught at school. Not that you cared then,
8098    and still less now.'
8099         'I'm not engaged by plans and schemes like this,' I say. 'At
8100    least he didn't fall on anyone.'
8101         'He left the symbol of the spinning wheels,' Mae agrees. 'The
8102    ancients said that justice was a goddess, and she left the earth, and
8103    went back home, up in the stars, and no one's ever heard from her.
8104    Astraea – like my sister, last we heard, she was in Seattle, but that's
8105    further than the stars,' and she looks glum.
8106         Starting over. It doesn't seem like fun. Searching for Astraea, in
8107    the desert, on the moon or in a camp, a squat, a jail – or in the
8108    mountains, where they overlook the plain, where all feel free, and
8109    down below a white of feathers, wavelets – no, it's plum trees, their
8110    blossom whiteing everything, then the green, and purple fruit.
8111         'You'd think there were volcanoes,' Mae says, 'but it's stills for
8112    slivovitz. No human sacrifice, no drugs – except a little pot for
8113    Doctor Janet and her rites. Just healthy booze, large quantities, in
8114    those huge sheds – for socially cementing – forget the ego, socialise
8115    and drink.'
8116         'It solves a lot of problems so,' I say, but Mae is not content.
8117         'I'll tweak you more,' she says, 'and see if we can't do it
8118    better,' though I guess I'd settle for no needle up my nose, and

8119     since it ended once – the world – just let's forget the future and the
8120     perfect, leave it lie, let's not go back and trundle on, towards
8121     another future and another end, but Mae gets angry.
8122          'No, no, you coward, onward,' she says, 'that's the trip we have
8123     to take,' and maybe Astraea's hiding somewhere, coward she. But
8124     then again, there's sex and appetite and history to satisfy, and we
8125     must eat and screw and leave inscriptions too, to show that we have
8126     been and gone.

8127
8128                                         *
8129
8130          'Empires start as colonies, deposits of wanderers, marauders,' says
8131     Mae, wisely. 'My – our – colony shan't be like theirs,' she waves a
8132     hand. 'Their Empire of the Sun. Which there isn't, or hardly, any
8133     more.'
8134          'What's special about yours – ours?' I ask.
8135          'Risk. Slavoj wants an area where the drink will take you – like
8136     on a spacewalk – out beyond decisions, choices. A clock-out place,
8137     where alibis are never challenged, where the guards stand down.
8138     Peace – not perfect peace, for you awake – but paradise without the
8139     headaches and the diarrhoea. Time off, time out, no sin, and no
8140     remorse. It's your reward for doing right and being good. In my
8141     time, ours, instead – there's Risk. For ever on the edge, and always
8142     chancing. In memory of Jake.'
8143          I think: 'Fuck Jake,' but do not say. There went another
8144     wanderer, spinning his wheels, his tales, his threats, his webs, like
8145     killer discs that cut you in the back.
8146          Mae says, 'It's not just about being good. That's in all the
8147     books. Their empire, Slavoj's, Janet's, will all go
8148     sour, they'll lose the thread. The being good, the being drunk – the
8149     guys get bored, and then there's temperance, and guns, and blighted
8150     trees – and off we go!'
8151          'How about communism?' I ask. 'It all starts there, and then
8152     goes wrong.'
8153          'Yes, starts there, sort of, and ends quite somewhere else, sort
8154     of, out of control, the guys get screwed, there's history and hate,
8155     and then they've all got cars and guns – and here we are.'
8156          I think, 'Perhaps it's Janet and Slavoj I prefer – the slow and
8157     shabby ride, forgetfulness – before the paint falls off, the gods are
8158     in the spaceships waiting for the launch. Mae's got these lost guys,
8159     messiahs maybe, or just found and lost, the system's open-ended

8160  too, but struggles on – Risk! Freedom! – here too the paint falls off,
8161  the tires go flat ...'
8162      'Remember,' says Mae. 'Sex. You can have it "needle up the
8163  nose", or else – I'll show you a good time, and you can feel you're
8164  loved, protected, if you must, in the good historic way, just like you
8165  see in caves and books,' and wow! she's sure desirable, although
8166  there's power to be worked out, labour divided too – but all the
8167  same, it's better than she tweaks your brain – though what it means,
8168  this sex, I cannot tell, it's more and less than slivovitz, I guess it's
8169  risk, but while it lasts, it's better than catastrophe and falling off
8170  your bike ...
8171      And while I muse, she tells me of a fish that tastes of all fish,
8172  since the sea's too hot to breed in, and I think of the old invention,
8173  the bird with paws that's like a thousand birds, and ask, 'Did you
8174  invent it, or just contract it out?' and she says 'Silence' and I must
8175  go and spy on Janet and Slavoj, and all their enterprise.

8176
8177          *
8178
8179  Slavoj is sitting quite upright, in a blue leather armchair. There's a
8180  sign, 'Bodies we fix, brains are all the same,' but I see no
8181  instruments, no white coats.
8182      By his elbow, there's a pitcher of plum brandy, and the smell of
8183  plums and distilling them is all around, on mountain top. There is a
8184  wooden board, it says, 'The Doctor is sober', on the other side,
8185  'The Doctor is drunk'.
8186      He's sober, and he points at me, and says, 'Ah – here he is again
8187  – the most interesting. The most normal. Would sell himself for
8188  sex. Not even count the minutes. Would sell the law for cuddles.
8189  And some flattery.'

8190
8191          *
8192
8193  'How'd you get up here?' Slavoj asks, without interest.
8194      'Some guys carried me up.'
8195      'That was risky. They might have dropped you. We don't use
8196  money.'
8197      I say, 'I paid them.'
8198      He looks more interested, 'With?'
8199      'Gold and diamonds. I've got lots.'
8200      'If this is an interview, you must pay me.'

| | |
|---|---|
| 8201 | Then Janet comes in, sits in the other blue chair. There is smoke |
| 8202 | about her, and her face is lightly cooked. |
| 8203 | I ask, 'When you're both quite boiled, who takes the decisions?' |
| 8204 | Slavoj is bored, he says, 'Why, that's where states come in. |
| 8205 | They substitute – the drunken king, the addled queen – it's in the |
| 8206 | books, you know.' |
| 8207 | 'What does everyone do here?' I ask. |
| 8208 | 'They gather plums,' Janet says. 'And process them. Sometimes |
| 8209 | – under the knife they go.' |
| 8210 | I insist, 'What do you eat?' |
| 8211 | She says, 'Oh this and that. And sandwiches. A lot.' |
| 8212 | I say, 'Of course, the moral law is equal, just and universal, so |
| 8213 | you don't need lots of other stuff.' |
| 8214 | 'You know how people are,' she says, 'you give them jam, they |
| 8215 | look for jam to put on jam, and then some more.' |
| 8216 | I say, 'Soldiers? Priests?' |
| 8217 | Slavoj finishes off his jug, rouses himself, and says, 'We have |
| 8218 | all those, but under wraps. They're parasites, jam on our jam.' |
| 8219 | Janet nods and nods and says, 'We're not like Mae – she's |
| 8220 | fidgety.' |
| 8221 | 'Just interest,' I ask, 'how shall I get down?' |
| 8222 | Janet waves a hand: 'The bucket – it would not take you up, |
| 8223 | we've rules against the apostates, what Slavoj calls the "interesting |
| 8224 | ones".' |
| 8225 | I protest: 'I've always followed moral law, unless it didn't suit |
| 8226 | or didn't work, or was too intricate,' and I think, 'Well, I never |
| 8227 | dropped Jake off the edge,' and then there's whirring and a click of |
| 8228 | oily wheels, Jake's wheels are framed like clocks, they're |
| 8229 | everywhere, and though they don't tell any time, they all go off |
| 8230 | together now and then. |
| 8231 | The sun sets like a pot of goldfish leaping from a sea of orange |
| 8232 | paint. |
| 8233 | 'Stay, if you like,' the Doctors say. 'We'll have another party – |
| 8234 | victimless, of course, and no remorse. The headache's down to |
| 8235 | altitude, not booze, so don't blame us: nostalgia, if you feel it – that |
| 8236 | is up to you.' |
| 8237 | They let me down in the bucket, the apostates' bucket. The wall |
| 8238 | is sheer, it has been a climbing wall. Small ceramic heads, some |
| 8239 | bearded, some with a ring in their nose, iron tails dangling – the |
| 8240 | rock face is miles high, to climb it must have taken days. The |
| 8241 | bucket hits the side and makes a sound that booms, bell-like, over |

8242    the great expanse of – air. And far below, the orchards and the bees.
8243    All kinds of lizard – orange ones, some striped in black and
8244    green, the little crusty geckos, blobs of mustard, pesto, left on
8245    plates and dried; umber drifts on palettes – stretched out and
8246    passive, waiting for the sun that they're designed for.
8247        I think of what Slavoj had said – 'The Andes are manmade. We
8248    know, we think, so little of what they did, those former, those
8249    ancient men and women.'
8250        'They must have had material and piled it up,' I said.
8251        'Of course, not wholly manmade,' Slavoj said, a little slurred
8252    and dreamy, ready to comply. 'That would be nonsense, wouldn't
8253    it?' and laughed.
8254        Janet, laughing too, mussed his hair and hugged him to her, and
8255    she smiled at me, and turned away, pretending that the smell, the
8256    booze, was strange and quite distasteful
8257        'They have a kind of net,' she said, 'a network, that will catch
8258    them as they fall, or stop them falling wholly through, for when
8259    they're on the wall, but tied with belts, or ropes.'
8260        She went on, 'We love Mae, naturally. She'd never do us
8261    wrong, and never has. But there's so few around, the people, once
8262    abundant, – now it's hard to find them, and they're puzzled, and a
8263    little slow, demoralised, you'll see, and so if Mae starts up another
8264    colony – we need to share them round. The hands. The subjects.'
8265        'And after all,' I said, 'there's just one side, and we're all on it,'
8266    and she laughed, and shook her head, agree or disagree.
8267
8268                                    *
8269
8270    'Our friends?' asks Mae.
8271        I'm back. It takes a while. Months, years. Less. I tell her, 'A
8272    monoculture. Short of labour.'
8273        'We can import that brandy stuff and put it in our lamps.'
8274        'A dumb idea,' I say.
8275        'It's called doing a good turn. The moral law is one, you just
8276    work out the details. The light it throws – it's so romantic.'
8277        'Don't do it,' I say.
8278        'You're so hard on what I want. Besides, winching that bucket
8279    up and down! You need a tiny motor ...'
8280        I say, 'Don't play those games. Wheedle with tears, and in the
8281    end we'll all be crying.' Leave the blossoms, don't put them in your
8282    hair – with the fruit you make a pie.

8283
8284
8285     Down in the street, there's pools of guys. The ones that won't obey
8286     the law, or pick the fruit, and those who made a pass at Janet – if
8287     not good guys all, quite sympathetic, as they say. Kicked out, away,
8288     from Slavoj's colony.
8289          'We'll have to shut them up. Imprison them,' says Mae.
8290          'You can't.'
8291          'Who says? The moral law ... besides, they're just a tribe, fit for
8292     a reservation somewhere,' and I see a vulgar history is ready with
8293     its claws, its chain of being, reproduction.
8294          'If it satisfies you,' I say, 'I'll put a lock on the front door,' and
8295     so we argue on, and I am right, but often banished, and my portrait,
8296     my head, is on and off the medals that she gives for conduct, –
8297     conduct that's not good, but just in line.
8298          The problem of the guys outside remains. I say, 'They're free
8299     spirits. Risks they've maybe taken, but that's Jake's thing, risk –
8300     the great trick cyclist,' and I know I shouldn't mention Jake, who
8301     landed in a tree, perhaps, and waits to make a triumph, comeback,
8302     all bones mended, ready for another risk, another drop ...
8303          'Don't wheedle in with freedom,' Mae shouts back. 'Risk isn't
8304     freedom, it's just calculated, that is why they say a thing's a
8305     calculated risk. It's happenstance.'
8306          'Rubbish,' I say, but that doesn't help, she wants free spirits in a
8307     camp and to see what freedom does for them, and then we fall to
8308     laughing at the spirits – there they are, the Sliv from Slavoj, cases
8309     of it, and there's ads, 'you burn your candle at both ends? Slavoj's
8310     Sliv will give a lovelier light', and Mae is charmed.
8311          I say, 'You're wrong,' and she says that's misogyny, perhaps
8312     she's right, but so am I – still right! – and so we laugh and fight, my
8313     brain is back to middle tracks, you have to have it set to rights
8314     when everything has fallen down, – and nothing much to do, but
8315     put more locks on the front door.
8316
8317                                    *
8318
8319     'You'll have to sort him out, that Slavoj,' says Mae. 'Those guys he
8320     sends us, criminals – and what of Jake, poor guy, a martyr to the
8321     heights,' and I object.
8322          'Slavoj's still the king. And I'm not climbing up the wall –
8323     miles high, it's storming heaven.'

8324      'Use the bucket, then. Pay someone.'
8325      'No.'
8326      'We're the risky ones, so we go far. We owe it to the principle,
8327 to everyone.'
8328      I say, 'It's not the risk, it's the certainty. Not just falling – the
8329 wall is made for that. It's the vendetta.'
8330      I picture him, Slavoj, slightly fuddled, in his sky-blue armchair,
8331 above the clouds, the steam that swirls above the stills. The fumes.
8332 Queen Janet. It's a scene full of charm and pathos, and I say, 'He's
8333 a good enough man.'
8334      Mae's exasperated: 'He holds us back.'
8335
8336                           *
8337
8338 I pay them, to take me up.
8339      'You've got a nice deal here,' I tell Slavoj.
8340      'Just bits of everything. The more bits you have, the more you
8341 miss having some whole thing.'
8342      'There's surgery,' I say, though I don't believe.
8343      'They all die in the end. And don't do much in the extra time.
8344 My hands do dances.'
8345      'You shouldn't send us all those guys.'
8346      'You do with them as you think fit. And as for Jake – maybe he
8347 got tired of skill, and thought, 'I'll try a fall.' There's nothing
8348 wrong in failing, falling – specially if you're tired of not.'
8349      He's bored. And if he flies – off the rock, punishment for
8350 nothing, no crime, no resolution, just lives blundered and his own
8351 screwed up – so much can happen as you fall. Epiphany. The
8352 spirals bear you up, the lizards, curious – those double lids should
8353 make you pause – ceramics too: once a fine industry, exquisite
8354 imaginations, visible only as you fall, and can't record. Or in the
8355 bucket as it sounds the midday bell – winched upwards, the day's
8356 executioner, rising with his knife. The lucky guest with brandy in
8357 his paunch, descending.
8358      Slavoj says, 'I didn't want to start it up – again. Just to be fairly
8359 good – and here I go,' and he leaps up, knocks his pitcher to the
8360 floor, and shouts and spits and screams – 'And here I am, with all
8361 the killing.'
8362      To comfort him, I say, 'There's worse things. It should all
8363 balance, balance out. Anyone who's had a thought, or done a deed,
8364 will have some dead ones to their credit. That is how it goes. And

8365   that is how the judgement's made.'

8366

8367                                    *

8368

8369   'Things are getting worse, they're working out,' I say: 'There's
8370   nothing in the law that says you've got to talk things over,' and
8371   Slavoj starts to shake.
8372         I say, 'But you really ought to come, and talk to Mae,' and Janet
8373   says he ought, his hair gets mussed again, and here we are, we
8374   clamber in the bucket.
8375         Down we start to go. It's slow, it's very slow.
8376         'Did you give the guy a tip?' asks Slavoj.
8377         'No,' I say. 'I thought the honour of you being here, if not the
8378   precepts of the law itself ...'
8379         Slavoj says, 'That's good for me, but not for you or us
8380   together,' and the winch creaks, the sky is far above, the ground
8381   too's far below, and bothers us the more.
8382         He peers out, the lizards cluster, tongues suck the rope, and
8383   Slavoj screams, 'That one's a dragon!'
8384         'No, no, it wears a ruff, but there's just smoke, there is no fire,'
8385   and we go slow and slow.
8386         I shout, 'Hey, you up there,' and there comes back, 'Hey, you
8387   down there.'
8388         Slavoj says, 'We warn them against deference and hierarchy.
8389   That's why they act a bit like scum. Besides, it's time for him to
8390   come off shift.'
8391         I'm surprised and say, 'There are no clocks, so how ...?' and
8392   then those bike wheels start to whirr, and once again I think, 'Fuck
8393   Jake', for with the whirr we are supposed to pause and think of
8394   risk-free worlds, and I'm embarrassed, an apostate. Then a bottle
8395   flashes down, and Slavoj grabs at it – in vain.
8396         We hear a woman's voice, she's arguing with the winchman,
8397   and she says, 'If you cut the rope, they'll die, and there's an end on
8398   it,' and here's a slow reply:
8399         'But doing so may save other lives, for certainly there'll be
8400   others lost – we can't just have a law, we must decide, and do the
8401   likely thing,' and on they go.
8402         The lizards cluster round, and Slavoj's shaking's worse, another
8403   bottle sparkles by.
8404         We're desperate, I say, 'We need to sing! That's always been
8405   the way,' and for a while we think of what would be appropriate,

8406    and I see clear, and say, '*Moses und Aron*,' and off we go, he's
8407    Moses, naturally, and down the bucket goes, faster and faster, and it
8408    tips and shakes.

8409        Slavoj says, 'There's nothing in the law that says you must
8410    discuss, or that the hardest cases yield to chat, in any case, it's the
8411    survivor who is right, the others are just casualties of language,'
8412    and of course he's right, survival and power together make a case.
8413    He makes his sort of threat. For him to talk with Mae's no use –
8414    and down we go, there's cursing up above, it seems the rope is
8415    stronger, faster, than her arms can hold.

8416        He falls, of course he falls. The law condemns him, if he falls
8417    and kills some passer-by – especially if he saves himself, – but that
8418    is quite unlikely, we're far above the clouds, the brandy smell is
8419    sweet, and down he goes, a little spider – all his legs a-wriggling as
8420    he drops, and 'yeeeeooow' comes back like ectoplasm as he falls.
8421    He hits the clouds, they rock as he goes through, they're like plum
8422    blossom and they part, and far below I see the petals white, but I
8423    don't see him hit, or if he lands on someone sleeping underneath
8424    the tree. From far above, I hear the lady winching say, 'Oh shit',
8425    the bucket stops, I sway, some lizards come in with me, and I think
8426    how Mae will be relieved, not facing Slavoj. Then there'll be two
8427    angry queens, bereavement, all that stuff, and tantrums in the
8428    bedroom if I manage to get ...

8429        'Get me down!' I shout, and whoosh, I'm down, and there's
8430    Slavoj, the envelope that's left of him – chaplets of glass around his
8431    head. All the bottles land down here. He's been embalmed already,
8432    not a drop of blood comes out, there's just a drip of juice distilled
8433    and now distilled a second time.

8434        I find a little flask – quite Roman – fill it with his effluent, it's
8435    pure as tears, but better – you can drink it if you wish, in memory.

8436        So, off I go, as no one saw if it was suicide or accident, or even
8437    giving him the push that solves his paradox – if paradox there was,
8438    here is the law, here is forgetfulness and freedom – but after all, as
8439    Moses all he had to do was cart the stonework home. And this,
8440    Slavoj had failed to do, being instead the modern way to
8441    compromise and talk with Mae, and promise things he didn't mean,
8442    not taking things just by the book, and build a camp for all those
8443    rejects, maybe run it in a joint administration.

8444        'Slavoj has fallen,' I tell Mae, 'calling for you. And Janet,' for
8445    these lies don't seem forbidden by the moral law, they being for the
8446    best, for Mae and me.

8447 I say, 'I took some risk, but in the end, poor Slavoj – just signed
8448 off.'
8449 Mae is angry. 'Now we've to deal with Janet, the spoiled
8450 Calvinist, befogged in her mountaintop – just a tricky bucket for
8451 communication ...' On she rants.
8452 'Mae,' I say, 'you've got political skills and nothing more.
8453 Those two had an activity – nothing splendid, that is true. But we
8454 have nothing. We're just predators. If this is "starting up again" –
8455 or as I prefer, it's "starting over" – you'll have us all in uniform,
8456 and climbing walls, and you the warrior queen,' and she is even
8457 angrier, I cast her back to tapioca pudding mode. But that soft and
8458 passive skin's dissolved! Now she's more thunderbird, and flaps
8459 her wings, and flexes talons on the windowsill.
8460 'Away, away,' she shouts, 'or I'll come down and scatter you
8461 and eat your young,' and she is screaming at the rejects in the
8462 street, they're sunk in slivovitz and slink away, but they have
8463 written on our walls and door, and found us wanting – 'even the
8464 risky ones weigh in the balance', and there's not much sense,
8465 except that it's a threat, or prophecy.
8466 'We have to do things right,' I say.
8467 She's still angry and says, 'No end of fuss! Slavoj deceases
8468 when he's on your mission – I hear you're Aaron to his Moses, a
8469 role that irritates. I want no voice of god or gods a-piping round my
8470 doors, our banner's reason, firmly on the plain, leave Janet to the
8471 high and mighty mount ...'
8472 I interrupt and say, 'Butchery and bonfires, not for me, that's
8473 what the priests do, and gathering in and clothes' design – the
8474 "bells of gold between the pomegranates – of blue, of purple, and
8475 of scarlet, and twined linen" – no, Mae, let's not take that route. Let
8476 temperance be our thing ...'
8477 But she ignores good sense, and says, 'What can happen with
8478 those guys, down there on the street, no law and no abode, no faith,
8479 no offerings, just desert swarf? We'll have to make a tribe, the
8480 "tribe of a thousand tribes", pay them in booze, but rationed – that's
8481 your task!'
8482 I'm not impressed. I say, 'You can't.'
8483 'Why not?'
8484 'It's not your business, certainly not mine. My brain got fixed,
8485 and I've no mind to make some history for you,' I turn away, but
8486 she is everywhere.
8487 'You are my captain now. Courageous or not, you're all I've

8488    got. I'll call you Captain Cat, from climbing walls, and covering up
8489    your mess,' and now I see her monstrous wings unsheathed, the
8490    eagle eye – a power no captain cat, nor general cat, nor major even,
8491    could think to take home, pulsing in his jaws. I should have trusted
8492    to the bucket and the winch, to take us down together, Slavoj and I,
8493    and through the orchards stroll, our arm in arm, and talk of good
8494    lives and their ethic, questions of state. All that. And safe.
8495
8496                                    *
8497
8498    Then Mae beams and says – 'It's all beginning.'
8499        'No, no,' I say. 'It's all ending. Let it end. We're tidying up. It's
8500    all been finished,' but Mae is going on.
8501        'Janet up there, she can't have kids, the mountains are all built.'
8502    I object, and say, 'She's got field hands, and they'll soon put
8503    together some kind of clock, a calendar, gold and diamonds – I
8504    gave them plenty – and they've got Jake, Slavoj in death. Jake
8505    haunts the fields, Slavoj, the drunken one, is deity of chance and
8506    wealth – Janet too, she's in the smoke, and says some funny things,
8507    goes on for hours, repeating stuff – she's blown her sets, the left
8508    and right, synapses ...' Then I pause, for I see Mae bubbling up,
8509    then I say, 'No, Mae, not that one, not the starting up, and burial
8510    mounds and horsemen, tanks and all that. I'm not an idiot, we shall
8511    serve our time, avoid the plagues, and in good time we'll die and be
8512    forgotten. Forgotten certainly, as all the rest will go, and there's an
8513    end, another end, to all.'
8514
8515                                    *
8516
8517    'Slavoj – he was the soul of wit,' sobs Janet.
8518        I never heard him joke, but say, 'He could unleash a zinger.
8519    Yes,' and wait.
8520        I want to make my peace with Janet, though I won't go up the
8521    wall as Mae had wanted.
8522        We talk as we might have, many years ago – with two cans
8523    linked by infinite lengths of twine – she at the summit, I, down
8524    here, beneath a tree, some sounds that may be they're piped in, of
8525    fountains, peacocks white, invisible among the blossom. Blossom
8526    lasts for months or years, when there's no clocks, no urgency to
8527    pick the fruit.
8528        I say, 'Slavoj was cut, so rightly from the cutting edge he fell,'

8529 and laugh.
8530     She ignores my joke, and says, 'He was the life, the hope.'
8531     I remember him, sunk in his baggy chair, a prisoner, the moral
8532 laws severe – or else demanding arguments of such refinement,
8533 ending in such paradox, of 'hohum', or 'whoa – but then' – his
8534 brandy, his kaleidoscope, the purple fruit like murex, like jewels,
8535 like glass in appliqué ... I lose my thread.
8536
8537                               \*
8538
8539 Janet's twang comes down the string: 'You killed him. Bastard.'
8540     I say, 'He fell. Like Jake.'
8541     'Jake didn't fall,' she says. 'Was killed. Bastard,' and she must
8542 mean it was Slavoj. The doors of paradise flip open, shut. Like
8543 synapses. It comes back, the meddling with my head.
8544     'Talking of life,' I say, 'how does it go up there?'
8545     It seems to me there isn't much, but then she says, 'It's the not
8546 knowing, if we're past or future, where the present's taking us.'
8547     Poor Janet.
8548
8549                               \*
8550
8551 I'm back. Again. With Mae.
8552     She looks quite pregnant. That's a trick I hadn't mean to play –
8553 a future never calculated – but she's in triumph, Janet worsted, just
8554 some awkwardness to smooth away.
8555     She says, 'The rejects – I can't stand them.'
8556     'I am your captain,' I say. 'I shall do whatever comes into your
8557 mind.'
8558     But it's not true, and she goes on, 'You tell a lot of lies, but I'm
8559 not sure about your motives, right and wrong, maybe, just being
8560 puzzled.'
8561     Out comes the embalming needle, and she's waving it around.
8562     I shut my nose and squawk, 'No tweaks! The brain must be
8563 inviolable, otherwise the moral law is just burnt hay.'
8564     'No!' she shouts. 'You're wrong, it's all negotiable, tweaking is
8565 good until we've reached agreement on correctness.'
8566     'You made poor Jake a monkey on his bike,' I say, as best I can,
8567 'unless he's found some way, some form, of being back – you gave
8568 him death wish, and you had your way.'
8569     She's appalled. 'It's all for you, you fool, your captaincy

8570 inevitable – the best, the most refined, must win out in the end.
8571 Slavoj knew! The plan was his – Jake fell. The plan was mine –
8572 you rose! Slavoj, the executioner – natural justice. Then – over he
8573 goes!' Her voice drops, she sheathes the needle, whispers, 'The
8574 project in its polished form – is mine.'
8575     I back away, and think – from sea and mountain always comes
8576 some feisty people with their myths in place, children of heroes
8577 vanished, sea-spume in their hair, or shirts of feldspar. For a while
8578 they sort the problem out, deal with the rejects, lots of sacrifice.
8579 Maybe Mae herself will be revered, or sacrificed, or put in jail. Her
8580 child, or dodgy twins, her Remus, Cain ... her throne, her state ...
8581     'That brain of yours,' she says, 'it's on the loose, it's just a gull
8582 that floats before the storm, that trims its wings to stay above the
8583 waves.'
8584     She's right of course. I say, 'So, what's to do?'
8585     'It's the start of a dynasty,' she says, and coyly, 'Captain Cat,'
8586 and musses my hair. Words fail, but actions become clear and
8587 urgent.
8588
8589                                    *
8590
8591     I fill Mae's car with slivovitz, and it soon fastens on the taste.
8592     I search its little cupboards – a tiny pistol – here's a book of
8593 precepts. Let's see what it thinks of Mae's regime. It seems that I
8594 could run, or stay – diluting the catastrophes, it says – or try
8595 assassination.
8596     Or just wait and see, consult wise men, and women too.
8597     I drive slowly down the road, its red-packed earth is springy,
8598 and I stare around, it's like the elephant ride I'm not supposed to
8599 have. That's doctors' orders.
8600     Jake's avenged with Slavoj's tumble, accidental murder, suicide
8601 – one score for justice, though I think I hear the rolling of the
8602 cosmic dice, and say aloud, 'Poor everyone.'
8603     There's no one here. The manmade mountains, canals and
8604 canyons cut, some paths sliced through the rock, deep down. Fine
8605 heads of onions, gone to seed – it's all magnificent. No
8606 pomegranates for priests' aprons, all that to come, or else it's gone,
8607 just Janet, high above the clouds, no prophet she, and so destined
8608 for divinity.
8609     She left a pack of seeds for me, she wrote, 'plant these, for
8610 memory'. It's pot. I throw the sealed pack from the car, we gather

8611 speed, the blue and purple, scarlet, weeds flash by – and now
8612 there's white and yellow, saffron, low bushes in the sand. Faster
8613 and faster, Mae is far behind, maybe there's someone like her
8614 coming nearer, out of sight for now ...

8615     We're at the edge. I stand beside the car.

8616     Below, so far beyond, the track twists down and turns and
8617 disappears – and there it is again, it takes its course anew, twists,
8618 turns, and disappears again.

8619     There should be eagles here, maybe some rabbits, but the
8620 precept says – 'be patient'.

8621     I give the car a push. It makes no fuss – I'm quite attached to it,
8622 it's dumb and true. Then, slowly down the path it goes, and follows
8623 round the curves, but doesn't make the twist, and disappears. It
8624 doesn't make a sound, and all is as it was before, it seems.

8625     I can't stay here.

8626     I turn and walk away, and walk, and walk.

8627

# 7

# BROKEN CHORDS

*from* **Three Beauties**

REMEMBER that Kazakh boy? Dressed as a soldier. Well, he was a soldier, a Soviet soldier. Got up on the stage in the park, and did a woman's dance – with verve. Don't you remember, the scarf? The undulation? Boys, they do the women's part: sometimes they sell them, now. To do a private dance. Catamites, they've become. Don't you remember, the applause, everyone for it, the artistry, the confidence? Was it Tbilisi? Or Baku? It should have been Baku, but it seems that it was Tbilisi.' The father strains for a response, some sharing.

'No, I was a baby then,' says his son. 'You took me as your cover. You spied, all over.'

'I spied, but only for me. I was curious, not a pro. It's all done long-distance now,' the father says. 'The park... the violinist, that they said did not exist. The guy who made up verses for you, mocking your foes. Remember those red ten-rouble notes they pushed into his hands?'

'No! I wasn't there,' the son says, irritated. 'I was a baby. In the basket, in the park.'

'It was around the time your mother fucked off,' says the father, pressing on. 'We two could do another spy trip. The shopping's better now. Sell our memories. If we get back safe.'

'You have to be careful who you are. Too many lines you shouldn't cross.'

'Well,' the father says, 'you were born in Africa, so you're black. Your French is bad, that means in France you speak funny, so you're black twice over, from their Africa. In the States, that English accent – they think you're gay. So, there you are. A sort of changeling. It's always my point. My irony – "serene irony" – that's what the poet called it. Irony has no colour and no faith.'

227

8665  'They don't understand you,' says the son, 'And that's not
8666  irony – it's ridiculing the pretension, pretending that people aren't
8667  bigots, or that they're treated equal. Or that they're different only
8668  by what you can't see – what's in their heads.'
8669        'It seemed kinder, long ago. Perhaps they hid the bodies better.
8670  When I think – yes, there were mountains of bodies then, but not in
8671  colour. Anyway, my mission's passed to you. It's yours.'
8672        'What mission's that?' asks the son. 'Making yourself
8673  comfortable?'
8674        'It's not so easy either,' says the father, 'As you'll find out.
8675  You're soft.'
8676
8677                                    *
8678
8679  'I'm concentrating,' I say. 'The wax is running out my ears, into
8680  my hair.'
8681        'That's not wax, it's bad thoughts,' says the guy.
8682        'I can do the upside-down pose,' I say. 'But it does stress.'
8683        'You have to think,' he says. 'The very small, the very large.
8684  There's no big difference. Try not to get lost in either, but they
8685  should look substantially alike. There's no affect, that's the first
8686  thing. Neither the krill, nor the black hole – they're both
8687  unfathomable. Nothing to do with you, that you can change, or eat,
8688  or surf in. Or grow in pots on windowsills. That's how you should
8689  encounter everything, that's how you are yourself. Immense, and
8690  universal, tiny but basic, huge, but an infinity of end.'
8691        'I see. I understand,' I say.
8692        That's all it is, that all it takes. Seeing, grasping. From other
8693  generations, after my father's, come creations of a different size,
8694  but all the parts the same; extinct in their huge distance. They have
8695  always been – but only we identified them, with our telescope.
8696  Don't need worry about them, their impinging. Things, though, my
8697  father never knew. I am the universe. He wasn't.
8698        The teacher, the doctor, priest, philosopher – his face is round.
8699  He smiles, although it seems a smirk. 'You're my best subject,
8700  ever,' he says.
8701        'Thanks, Omar,' I say. It's what he wants, his treat. I've trained
8702  him, to come to heel.
8703        'I have this dream,' I say. 'I'm falling down this black hole,
8704  smaller and denser I become, sucked in and eaten out, like a winkle
8705  from its shell.'

'Don't worry,' Omar says. 'It won't happen. And there's no white rabbit out there in the void, when you wake up, the story ends. Watch the red dwarves don't get you, though.'

'You put things in perspective, Omar,' I say.

'Yes,' he says. 'And you want my perspective? Well, I don't give a fuck for you, your woman you don't mention, your dead mother, father – I don't care for you, and you don't care for me. I tell you people stories, and you pay me, or you make excuses, and anyway – I don't care for you. Even the law – it does not insist. Free not to care. I'd go on the streets and shout for that.'

'Yes, that's good,' I say. 'I need to hear that.'

'Work it out. Fight it out among yourselves. No moral weep, no "Do what I say, and you'll have what I've got, some day." Imagine I'm a foreigner, stuck in the country that you don't know where it is. I don't want to live up close to you,' Omar goes on.

'Don't exaggerate, Omar. Your case is made,' I say.

My agency. 'Prop. myself' – advises people what they have to do. What they can. Might. So, I have to keep myself informed. I'm interviewing Sylvia. It seems I need an accomplice.

'If I had a little sister,' I say, 'she'd be about your age.'

No, it's not seduction, nor even incest that I have in mind.

She's very cautious. 'Your agency – you liberate people? You train them? You exploit their powers?'

'Oh no,' I say. 'What you really mean is – do I ask a lot of cash? The answer's yes – as much as I can, and as much as they are able to think a thing, any thing at all, is worth. But – no freedom: just another weight – more knowledge, more uncertainties. No training – what a bore that is! It can take years, and what for? Bright ones do it naturally. Their powers? – it's clear they're not so evident. That's why they come to me. No – it's showing other paths.'

'Rich guys, without a clue?' she asks. 'That's it?'

'I could call you Sylvie,' I say. 'That's woody, pagan.'

'Have you others to interview?' she asks.

'I could have, of course. Hundreds. But I'm doing nicely with you. My father had a mission, understanding the world, preliminary to changing it, if he'd lived long enough, and had the firepower. He travelled when that was still worthwhile, with differences all around. I don't have any of this. It's like the philosopher said – "Philosophy should be the theory of what we do, not of what is." What is, is quite uncertain. Taken as it is, I'm not sure it's

8747 interesting, or digestible. Of course, if you lose me money, that
8748 path ends.'
8749     'You'd take a risk with me,' says Sylvie.
8750     'I didn't say I'd pay you,' I say. 'There's no risk.'
8751     'You're like a hundred years ago,' she says. 'Like we would go
8752 to Africa, shoot rare animals and get a fever.'
8753     'Concentrate on yourself,' I say. 'Don't consider the others –
8754 they're thinking about themselves, what it is they lack. One person
8755 can't do much, make much noise – two, even less.'
8756     'I've had battles,' Sylvie says. It doesn't show, I can't believe
8757 she won them all, and that it wasn't others had already been on her
8758 battlefields.
8759     I have no clients now, since she worked here. She has lots. She
8760 says. 'I tell them what they've done is their philosophy. They're
8761 thrilled. They're keen to do some more.'
8762     'I always wondered how guys went off each day to work, and
8763 do the same goddam thing, with no respite,' I say. 'But – careful,
8764 Sylvie! Don't take it all too literally. And don't let's make it a
8765 religion.'
8766     'Literally's the only way to take it, when it's written down,' she
8767 says: I guess it's sex, accounting for how she's so popular.
8768     'I love those Mexican trains,' I say. 'Long; real heavy metal,
8769 that's what it truly means. Yellow, and wetbacks on the top, like
8770 candied fruit on cakes. I knew a guy, worked on Canadian trains.
8771 It's military. In the caboose – you can sleep, but you can't read.
8772 That way, prophecy in your country, or anyone else's – it's not on.'
8773     'That's what it takes,' asks Sylvie, 'to be a prophet? Reading?
8774 And they can't be wetbacks, if they're on a train.'
8775     'I'm speaking loosely, Sylvie,' I say. 'And to be a prophet, you
8776 need space, and common sense. The only thing guys plan for in
8777 general, in the world – is manoeuvres. Exercises. Spying on the
8778 deadly stuff they say they'll never use. All the rest's defaults. They
8779 improvise, and call it science. Hypothesis. But what works – is
8780 army. Everything else is finite.'
8781     'I've heard all that,' says Sylvie. 'Just let my genius run its
8782 course, and then I'll think of what I've done.'
8783     'A prophet hectors, Sylvie. Prophets are bigots, and the future
8784 doesn't interest them too much. They don't foretell – the future's
8785 what everybody knows. Women can be prophets – that could make
8786 us rivals. My father thought it was in my grasp, prophesying – but
8787 the real stuff lay beyond. He used to say, "Democracy is of the

8788  Right; and don't expect benevolence. What matters is, you execute
8789  the comrades who screw up, you cut the throats of all the sons who
8790  haven't had the sense to join you. No meandering, do what you
8791  must, to the end, no musing about humanism. The rest is cups of
8792  froth, it's strut. If you're not up to this – then strum on fantasy, find
8793  your slot, your business. Crawl into it. You're just a writer on the
8794  shelves, inventing, beside the elves," and he'd laugh. Sylvie, that's
8795  what your genius is. Froth. Fantasy.'
8796      'Your father was an eloquent man,' says Sylvie, much
8797  impressed.
8798      'Well, you don't do all that being hard and realist on your
8799  own,' I say. 'It's mostly travelling, then getting old. You need a
8800  team. Then, all he had left was disappointment with his son, with
8801  me.'

8802
8803                              *
8804
8805  Even if you've seen one before, a naked body – someone else's – is
8806  a shock. You're so used to the clothes. Used to the talk about it all,
8807  the organic – and then it's there, in front of you, with demands that
8808  clothes don't make. A thing, a body, it seems unmodifiable – the
8809  things it can become – old, crippled, a cadaver the next step – seem
8810  so far away. It's not aesthetics. The cow in the field – who thinks of
8811  it, reduced to steak? Tough, the life fights back, clings in your
8812  trachea. A body, naked: it's for admiration, or for sex. The
8813  opposites. Sylvie's to be admired. Sex is mostly about you first.
8814  She's out there, beckoning. Then she's disappeared, and you're a
8815  monster, all reason gone. Scrabbling on some skin, dribbling, too.
8816  It's a puzzle – she'd see it in the same way – I guess Omar would
8817  too…. It's all philosophy.
8818      'This is a reward,' says Sylvie, as if she's always known
8819  beneath the clothes there was all this speculation, 'because you're
8820  so poor at philosophy.'
8821      'Well, that's done,' she says, when it is. 'It's something you'll
8822  remember, probably.'
8823      'It's very biological, all this,' I say. 'I remember people by their
8824  clothes. Or by their names. Omar – if he was Portuguese, that
8825  means "the sea". *O mar*. Quite inconclusive. Like having fathers.'
8826      'Two guys came yesterday,' she says.
8827      'You told them they were doing right? Were they tax, or cops,
8828  or mafia? They should leave happy that they're doing good.'

8829 'Oh, they did. Said they'd be back.'

8830 'Of course,' I say. 'It used to be empires. Now we're back to
8831 countries. I don't like them either. A country has small mountains,
8832 rivers, grass, and geese. This one has holes in the ground and firing
8833 ranges. Empires send platoons, countries send two guys.'

8834 'It's not that you go out,' says Sylvie, 'and see.'

8835 'We should leave,' I say, 'immediately.'

8836 'You're thinking wrong,' she says. 'Digging your father's
8837 archaeology.'

8838 'Before we go, we must scream,' I say. 'It's all there's left.'

8839 'That sounds a different therapy,' says Sylvie. 'I talk. Even if
8840 they don't understand. There's all these languages. It's all quite
8841 Balkan. You reach a compromise, a few words, defining you as
8842 separate.'

8843 'No, Sylvie – it's not the Balkans, not India, or China, or the
8844 Arab lands. It's right here – see – down in the canyon....' Electric
8845 buses, guys parading up and down, like they were in marching
8846 bands. New York. It could be Buffalo.

8847 We scream. There's nothing left.

8848 We don't try to be in tune – she has a good vibrato, I'm in the
8849 roots, where snakes breed and the ants reorganise.

8850 The guys below – they think we're sirens. Air raids, not death
8851 on the rocks. They run – you can run from rockets, not from rocks.
8852 They're safe. They know they aren't. America – they ran here to be
8853 safe, they armed themselves. Their fear has followed them, it waits
8854 on every block. Now from the skies, it falls, a flaming Godzilla.
8855 They pulled it with them, behind them, tugging on a leash. 'Oh,
8856 repent, repent,' shouts Sylvie, entering the spirit.

8857 'There's no need, Sylvie,' I say. 'It's no use. They'll be
8858 punished, without knowing the why or even when. It's history, it
8859 catches you. What the movies showed – all that will come and sit
8860 upon your shoulders.'

8861 We scamper down the stairs. Out in the street, Sylvie screams –
8862 'It's come! At last – it's payback day – all the good and all the bad,
8863 you'll pay for what you've done, like all the rest, and all you did it
8864 to. You're not immune – it happens to us all, to all of them....' We
8865 skitter down the street. Guys stand aside, some try a punch, a trip.
8866 They've heard it all before – the air that suffocates, the thirsts
8867 unquenchable – but never shouted out, never screamed – two
8868 beardless prophets, gorged with the words. Bonded and seduced by

8869 sex. At least, that's where Sylvie's raptus starts. With me, it's all
8870 philosophy.
8871 The cops can't decide – to shoot us, or send us with the other
8872 mad people.
8873 'We need protection,' Sylvie says: she grabs some pie from off
8874 a stand. 'Oh, I'd die / For pecan pie,' she sings. Guys assume we're
8875 a street act.
8876 'No, Sylvie,' I say, 'I don't want to attract a swarm of weird
8877 people, with their twisted hopes. We've been into therapy. That's
8878 been done too.'
8879 It's not snowing, so it must be spring or fall. You can't tell
8880 from the fruit – in the stores, it's never seasonal.
8881 I say, as we slow to a saunter, 'My father knew – social
8882 revolution would from now be made by bourgeois guys. The
8883 bourgeoisie knew all about it, revolution, and they cared. So, not
8884 the workers, not an underclass: the bourgeoisie. Behind the
8885 ignorant enthusiasts, in whose name... there always was the
8886 bourgeois guy, who knew what it was all about. The bourgeois
8887 knows the consequences, he invented them. That's what "serve the
8888 people" means. He hated them real bad, despised them. Doing the
8889 tough work – that would be the simple soldiery, the marines – and
8890 that left him to steer the ship, find the ports, ride the storms.'
8891 'Tell me something I don't know,' said Sylvie. 'Did he think
8892 that things would happen here? If we were in Warsaw, or in Rome
8893 – all round we'd see dictatorships and war, occupations, massacres,
8894 urban guerrillas, and the rest... laid down in people's heads, neat
8895 strata, the foundations. In time, there's bits of peace, the solidarity
8896 breaks down, and everyone's in therapy. Then something decisive
8897 starts over....'
8898 'Here, it's all bubbling,' I say, 'shapeless. There's forerunners,
8899 survivors – it's all a broken vase that's been repaired, all
8900 improvised – the angel on the handle pasted in the base, nymphs in
8901 the reeds all upside down and randy....'
8902 Sylvie stares at me. 'Yes, it comes to me,' she says. 'The
8903 broken vase. America. It's not the salad, not the melting pot. It's
8904 like a stew. We're farro. In the stew. That sylvan scene – where I
8905 am principal – it's all mashed up. The vase... once it was worth a
8906 lot, not now.... Now, the image is a stew, monkeys and dogs stirred
8907 in together. And elks. We're the farro, you and me, floating on the
8908 top, then sinking down. Mmmm – I love farro. Soft and malleable –
8909 it floats, sinks too.'

8910  'Well, Sylvie, sort it out, these broken images. Now, we must
8911  run,' I say.
8912      She glides along beside me, unstressed, keeping the air within:
8913  she says. 'Of course – there is a flaw. If here's a broken vase, you
8914  could smash it into shards again, make it like it should have been.
8915  But a stew... it's that or nothing.'
8916      'That's sort of what my father said,' I say, to cut her short. It's
8917  not. He wanted something different: – but not a salad, not a stew.
8918  Not something old, restored. Not liberty. He didn't believe that
8919  made much sense. Equality – he didn't think he had an equal.
8920  Fraternity? Maybe, but not with brothers, not with family. No,
8921  really, not at all. None of those.
8922      'Freedom was a negative thing,' I say, quite out of breath. 'Not
8923  having it provoked change. Not having it was a good, an
8924  accelerator.'
8925      'There's lots I don't grasp, and there's not the time or the
8926  person to ask why I don't,' Sylvie says. 'There's that sign, *La coca
8927  es vida*. Maybe it's like freedom, like your father said. And is it
8928  drugs or drink?'
8929      'Just run, Sylvie,' I say. 'Those signs are meaningless.'
8930      We stop. There's no one following. There's a waiting, a
8931  recurrence. Just two guys, going to call again on me.
8932      'What can they want?' I ask. 'My father left me nothing,
8933  nothing useful. I don't pay tax because what I get, I spend at once.'
8934      'That's not how it works,' says Sylvie. 'You're too generous.'
8935      'The mafia uses telephones. The cops – they'd want my father,
8936  but he's dead. Maybe we can't foresee a good future. The past –
8937  most of it's indifferent, and lots we'd rather that it hadn't been. Are
8938  we in some way degenerate? Is it that we aren't of use? Don't make
8939  stuff?' I ask.
8940      'Of course not, it can't be,' Sylvie says. 'That's the beauty of it
8941  here – there's millions round like us, and busy busy too. We are the
8942  grease, we help it all go round and round.'
8943      'To get elected here,' I say, 'you must believe in God. You
8944  must be pretty theological – and on the other side, it seems there's
8945  preachers, with their books. Is it my misbelief?'
8946      'Oh no,' says Sylvie, 'that doesn't matter squit. You don't want
8947  election, and you wouldn't be.' She ponders. 'You never studied,
8948  did you? Not anything.'
8949      'No, nothing,' I tell her. 'Not me, nor my father. It's all
8950  experience, all made up. And you, Sylvie?'

8951   'No! I've no qualifications, nothing like that. Quite different
8952   experiences from yours, too,' she says. 'Experience – it's all you
8953   and I know.'
8954        She sees a place where they sell – 'Oh, pies!' she says; 'Come
8955   on.'
8956        There's two guys sitting there. They're waiting for company.
8957   'Why!' Sylvie says, 'That's the guy who does my tattoos.'
8958        He might be. The other – what might he do? You pick up
8959   suspicion, it's a family thing. My father started as a Jacobin. Then
8960   it was the vanguard party. Then himself, the critical critic. Sylvie
8961   had said, 'Your father – he didn't much go for the masses.'
8962        'No,' I'd said. 'Some places, pretty large ones, he wasn't
8963   welcomed.'
8964        She's gone in, kisses the tattoo guy on the head. Imagining
8965   how it feels, the sensation, the hair, the gel – not pleasant. She
8966   thinks I've followed her, but I've hung back. The guys jump up,
8967   run after me. Sylvie stands stupid at the door.
8968        Oh shit! I think – these guys – they learn to run in all the places
8969   where the president has made his moral gestures, given history his
8970   twist. Chile and Guatemala, Grenada and Iraq – the places where
8971   he hopes for love, comes up with basketfuls of snakes. It's just
8972   about all over, everywhere, his Midas touch, turns all to dross and
8973   strass. Good cop, bad cop, flattening countries, after, giving them
8974   gifts.
8975        And all those guys – maybe they cut each others' hair, so they
8976   can recognise their pals – how they can run. They're gaining on
8977   me.
8978        A refuge? Up the steps here – seeking a small utopia, even with
8979   a secretary. My body, my system, is breaking now, sucking in the
8980   air – no longer works. The brain steps partly into a nirvana: no
8981   narcotic like the present, all the guys here are selling dope, no
8982   instructions on the packet, you make it up.... It's like Marseilles, the
8983   old quarter still resisting, nearly eighty years of it.
8984        The Indians have taken refuge here, the last massacre, in the
8985   Mato Grosso, just a few survivors, cut in half with those machetes,
8986   but still soldiering ahead, a coupla jobs to keep each half a-
8987   struggling on. There's Omar – *O mar* – you have to travel on him,
8988   on the sea, gruff and disgruntled though it is, would suck you
8989   down. Your bones are worth a dime.
8990        Oh no! The guys have caught me. The tattooer holds me down.
8991   These urban 'scapes, escapes or escapades, it's quite a situational,

8992    and the layout doesn't help you get away – the two guys kneel on
8993    me. The one without the gel says, 'Sins of the sons... are visited
8994    upon the fathers and the grandfathers, even unto....'

8995    It takes a while: they tattoo me, where I can't see. I guess the
8996    word, although I'll never read it. 'Soft'. They know all about me.

8997    Later, I say, 'Sylvie, you betrayed me. You brought me to them.
8998    We didn't run from them, we ran towards.'

8999    'I know, I know,' she says, pretending tears. 'It's the tattoo. It
9000    does no harm. I'm covered in them. It shows that you've been
9001    caught. We almost all of us are tagged – there's butterflies and
9002    swallows, that show we have escaped and now been caught.
9003    There's warrior signs to show aggression, and there's names of
9004    people you've let down, and crosses that show disbelief. They
9005    catch you, everyone gets marked, and everyone's aware of what
9006    they haven't done, or what they crave, and all of that is known,
9007    recorded somewhere.... You could falsify yours, if you wish, add
9008    words to it – "soft gold". That's for the Mato Grosso, and the
9009    mines. Or "Softer the sun, on your last morning lifts...." Wealth and
9010    art. There!'

9011    'Nonsense, Sylvie,' I say. 'People were tattooed before God
9012    told them it was a sacrilege on all the skin he wove. Now, it's a
9013    police operation, for sure. They have it written down. It's evidence
9014    against.'

9015    'Don't worry about it,' Sylvie says. 'It's nothing. It's just – a
9016    man opens me, then I close myself, and I'm alone inside again.
9017    That's all I need to know. Inside, I'm Guy Debord, though much
9018    less fun. And you?'

9019    I go along with this. Really, I'm interested in the history, not in
9020    knowing about me, or her. Things finish, then they go on again,
9021    like a big animal that eats itself, gets ever stronger, ever smaller.
9022    They're not good or bad, trundling along and eating, that's all they
9023    can do.

9024    'What do I know?' I say. 'Inside, I'm full of blood. We all are.
9025    There's no need to be a moralist, Sylvie, or unload things on to
9026    famous people. Blood – it's our food, our fuel, ours or other
9027    people's. Remember Spartacus – his profession, killing his
9028    brothers, then the revolutionary struggle, then the crosses. And,
9029    Sylvie, you snitched. That's not original.'

9030    She wriggles, rolls herself up, and giggles. '"The totality for
9031    kids" – that's my inspiration. You remember, they had Lenin
9032    saying, "I couldn't give a fuck about 'Revolutionary young

communists' either." Genius – those guys had it. Your father? He
was a passenger. I'm afraid that you are too.'

'He told me how they used to bomb the jungle, the Americans.
Our brothers. Poisoned air and fire,' I say.

'Oh, you must see how it's all different now,' she says. 'Even if
you don't, and it isn't.'

'The new guys – they're tough,' I say. 'It's true – the men no
longer sing the women's parts in Chinese opera. That's something
softening too, I guess.'

She doesn't seem convinced. Maybe she doesn't understand.
'Libs, cons, and rads – how you play on with those old games,' she
says. 'It didn't ever work like that. There's a task for you – what do
we think next? – while I'll go on, telling people what they are.'

The new guys, everywhere – they're not just tough, they're
hard. They fight for what they've got and haven't got.

Sylvie – she wears power suits – clown suits – baggy, and
ready for the wind to lift her off, a kite to snag in trees where
Jung's skeleton is perched and happy, singing to the spotted birds.
Her face is docile, though, letting the clothes do all the work,
whether they're on, or on the floor.

I wear my skates, and join with all the other suited guys,
swooping along, pretend to get to some employment before our
brothers on the trains.

Sylvie says, 'You failed your job interview. I'm proud.'

'You leering in, and your red cartwheels in the lot outside,' I
say. 'They broke the seriousness' – although I'm proud too, and
relieved.

'That was the sign of "now",' she says. 'Bear it in mind, it
cancels out regrets. Those guys – one with a tiny head, the other all
grey tufts, gummed up with snuff – if you had sought out freaks...!
Stick them together, you would make one monster. Two's a hatch.
The hairy one, the Tufty – he tried to make out with me.'

'"We need a guy who's delicate," one said. "The old regime,
this dispensation's tailing off, its sweetness draining from the hive.
The new guys, in those countries we don't know where they are,
that once were far away and now are not, they jostle you aside.
They bring harsh news. You may regret the bangs and blusters that
we brought. We're ordinary now. We are awake, the brain is clean.
We'll sell our stuff, for sure. But – from the guys that we employ,
we need an afterword. That maybe starts it all again, another
journey, just a few of us, steered by the stars...."

9074    'So, I told them, "If you want to know the future – it's civil
9075    war, city states, secessions. Invasion, occupation. Deserts, the flow
9076    of people up and down, masses like the buffaloes, the Indios, the
9077    passenger pigeons. Roaming between the mines and wells.
9078    Camping on the shale, sleeping on the broad-leafed grass, with an
9079    eye on space, where maybe they will find a home, a homestead, a
9080    square of dust to hoe." They didn't want to hear. Said I wasn't on
9081    the team. Fantasy, they said. I told them, it was just the things most
9082    people already knew, them too. They'd shut it out.'
9083    'It's what you're father said, but without the songs,' says
9084    Sylvie.
9085    'We can't believe in nature,' I say, thinking of what I might
9086    become. 'Nor sites, nor seasons, not old things, nor portable things
9087    like books and parures. Not the spirit, not the structure. So – not
9088    France, not China. Not all the terrible lessons the Americans have
9089    handed out. Where do we go, Sylvie?'
9090    She wanders off.
9091    'Omar must be right,' I think. 'Yourself. No one else, not
9092    neighbours – what a noise they make.... You must make yourself
9093    the sea, *o mar*. Swallows and regurgitates, but not a mouth, a
9094    stomach, not an anus, not a gut. That's full of everything you could
9095    imagine – all invisible, unfindable. An envelope that hums to itself,
9096    atonal: moods, colours, signifying nothing. Not silence, not beauty
9097    – just an undertow of splash and sift, a conversation about nothing,
9098    with yourself. The sea. That's what I must be, a sea that needs no
9099    place to be itself.'
9100    Sylvie's back. 'They're, you're done,' she says. 'You found
9101    your answer, like I knew you would. Not good at much, but – wow
9102    – that's what you're good at, the answer.'
9103    'That Kazakh boy – my father said – he was from the world's
9104    umbilical. Not a conclusion, but the point where all beginnings
9105    start. A fairly useless place, desert and mountain, where all the
9106    contradictions meet. That is the answer, Sylvie, to all the questions.
9107    Powerless, it's at the confluence of all the powers....' I say.
9108    'Maybe you should tell those guys, and get the job,' she laughs.
9109    'They want to know what's profitable tomorrow. I don't know,'
9110    I say.
9111    'You appreciate Omar more than you do me,' says Sylvie. 'And
9112    you steal my money.'
9113    'No, Sylvie, I've freed Omar from being just a human, but I've
9114    seen – I must be nature. The other nature, with a capital letter –

9115 that's gone. It was trial and mostly error, and it's buried. So, as they
9116 say, you must invent it yourself. Invent yourself as it. It's like your
9117 money – theft is property, and then more theft. And so on. It's only
9118 chance that Omar's name is "sea". I'm not becoming Omar – I'm
9119 becoming sea.'
9120 She's quite angry. 'Then you don't need money,' she says.
9121 'And I might go, seek love. Seek another person to do it with,
9122 definitely not you.'
9123 'Oh Sylvie,' I say, to needle her, 'don't give yourself up so
9124 easy. You'd think of me, when those armoured junks sail up the
9125 river and Kozinga takes New York.'
9126 'It won't happen,' Sylvie says.
9127 'Not real Chinese, of course,' I say. 'Just the metaphor.'
9128 'I have a new partner,' Sylvie says. 'He's for the emotions – he
9129 doesn't do philosophy.'
9130 Her new guy – sits relaxed, and twitches to her Kraftwerk
9131 discs. Sylvie moves around him nervously.
9132 I'd guess he's seventy kilos. His casual clothes cost money I
9133 could spend instead.
9134 'My father tried to save the world,' I say. 'It can't be done. I
9135 guess it was a stupid thing.'
9136 'Oh, I wouldn't say so,' he – Chip – says, quite vaguely.
9137 'I'm not trying to reassure you, Chip,' I say.
9138 'We could dance,' says Sylvie. 'Just us three – but it might
9139 seem ridiculous.' I think it would. She says, 'Chip is a Chipewa.
9140 His parents – they were Indians, but he's had the nature stripped
9141 right out.'
9142 Chip says to me, 'You should go to India. That's where they
9143 thought we came from. If you're at a loose end – there's lots of
9144 Buddhism there, just waiting.'
9145 'It was an honest mistake,' I say. 'Those airports all look the
9146 same.'
9147 'Oh, that line again!' says Chip, turning away.
9148 I say, 'Maybe what my father believed – it wouldn't work. We
9149 wouldn't want it to, if we'd survived. In the world, all that fervour
9150 died away. Left boats crammed with people looking for a beach
9151 where there weren't cops. My dad stayed true to himself, false to
9152 everyone and everything outside,' and as I say this, I wish I hadn't.
9153 It's just excuses for him. He didn't want to make us happy, just
9154 hard and tested, and then thrown aside.

9155     'We?' Chip asks sharply. 'We? None of us, here in this room,
9156 or anywhere, survives. Nor your father, nor mine. You have to start
9157 from there. Sylvie and me – is our end happiness? Some gets the
9158 club and some the needle. The rest is all ideas. We love them,' and
9159 he walks Sylvie into the other room.

9160     I say, 'My father – he spoke figuratively, of course. Those who
9161 did what he proposed, like cutting throats – you can be sure, he had
9162 a sour analysis.'

9163     There's no one left to hear.

9164
9165                        \*
9166

9167     I hear Sylvie, she's shouting, with a new voice, acid. 'Do you all
9168 need be gay, you guys? Is it the fashion?'

9169     Chip comes running out. He sits, troubled, deep in a chair:
9170 'That guy – the brain masseur, Omar – he has all the clients here
9171 that count. You're the only guy that I know, avoids the action, sits
9172 in the corner like a spider, spinning weak nets.'

9173     'It's not like a hundred years ago, everyone had conversation
9174 and a character. Now we've just the walk-on roles that's left,' I say.

9175     I'm intrigued: Chip says, 'Oh, I know most things too. The
9176 people that do them. My outfit's one of those that takes in money,
9177 churns it, out comes more, spreads like butter, makes you fat, die
9178 early....'

9179     'And Sylvie?' I ask, thinking of writing all this down. I don't
9180 know why.

9181     'She was twelve. There was the soldier – they say she had him
9182 sent away. Gunned down, of course. A victim for those ascetic
9183 guys, they say we are at war with them. They keep the score, and
9184 don't expect we heed what it is they want.'

9185     'I'm amazed,' I say. 'It's medieval. It seems that I'm the monk,
9186 deflowered. Lady Macbeth with her aria, in the next suite. Other
9187 people's lives – books with unwritten chapters.'

9188     'Well,' says Chip, 'It's not paedophilia, of course, though she
9189 was very young, our Sylvie. Those circus families, you know. At
9190 six you're eating fire, and seven – out of the muzzle. Then, it's
9191 human pyramids, and catch-me in the roof.'

9192     'Her muscle-tone, it's true ... exceptional,' I say. 'But she just
9193 does philosophy.'

9194  'She's never read a book,' Chip says. 'That's why she's good.
9195  Your trouble is,' he peers at me, 'you don't ask questions. You just
9196  juggle with the scraps you know.'

9197  'Come back in here,' shouts Sylvie, 'you renegade!' Chip grins
9198  wrily at me, and shuffles back.

9199  I hear him squeal, 'Oh no, rape, rape!' and Sylvie shouts,

9200  'I'll eat your eyes, and fill the sockets with your tiny testicles.'
9201  I guess it's all in fun, it wasn't like this between us two; muted and
9202  casual rather.

9203  It's all a mystery. 'How should we behave?' 'Do we have a
9204  nature?' 'Time shuffles the pack – what are these new cards slipped
9205  in, the old pips cancelled, not a squeak?' Are these questions right?
9206  – and see! – the answers have already changed....

9207  'Don't touch that, you creep!' shouts Sylvie, and there's Chips
9208  shouting, 'Anything but that, anything at all,' and then he's back
9209  with me, in his suit, without his shoes.

9210  'We'll never see her like again,' he says, and Sylvie joins us,
9211  looking exactly as she did before.

9212  She says, quite cold, 'Chip here – he recognises all that stuff
9213  you said, about the occupation, massacres, the entrepots, all that.
9214  He says he's had it all, it's in his genes. His people didn't make it.
9215  Well, he's still here. The only trace is, that he likes a smoke. We get
9216  it off the Kazakhs.'

9217  'I can't believe it, what you said, about tattoos,' I say.

9218  'Chip's soft as well, although he has rich deals,' she says. 'He
9219  has the mark, like you. Soft. When I'm done with him, we'll look
9220  for your tattoo.'

9221  This is not the essence.

9222  'No, it's not,' Sylvie agrees. 'What's to be done?'

9223  'Short lives,' says Chip. 'Get accustomed to them.
9224  Impermanence, not leaving stuff behind. Live as a fugitive, a
9225  warrior – everyone must be used to that, like it or not. Women –
9226  live longer, but in more pain. They make things, and these flake
9227  away. Tough kids – the ones that last the least. Plagues – think of
9228  avoiding them, not that you will. It means – walking with your
9229  nose held high, so's not to breathe them in.'

9230  'Well, Chip,' laughs Sylvie, 'you may be right – but that's the
9231  story of your folk, and where's it got you? Immunity?'

9232
9233                                    *

9234 We three – it's a domestic scene. All three, sat in a row. No poems,
9235 and no travelling. The past is bones, our bones. Now, here's the
9236 breeze before the hurricane.
9237 'My father's friends,' I say. 'One, chased out of Chile. One –
9238 walked across the desert in Ethiopia. I hear how in Moscow, there's
9239 gold leaf on everything, three kinds of caviar. It's vulgar. Not just
9240 bread and sausages, like when we were there, and there was
9241 socialism. That taste! Never surpassed. It was all a puzzle, in the
9242 end... victims and victors, tramping round. It's like the physicists
9243 say, a thing explodes when it's too big, and all the little pieces start
9244 off again, in miniature.'
9245 'No, no, there are black holes,' says Sylvie. 'Americans – they
9246 don't make good refugees. The Spanish ones do best. Male bonding
9247 and the shooting – those are a help, but almost all the other skills
9248 are useless.'
9249 'You guys,' says Chip, 'have seen so much, it hasn't left a
9250 mark. It's all just this and that, a "maybe and on the other hand".
9251 The experience has all burned off.'
9252 'Chip,' I say, air-boxing, 'I quite like you, notwithstanding –
9253 but if you want love, you'll have to pay lots more.'
9254 'I don't disburse without some service,' Chip says, haughtily.
9255 'Why – I could break you like a chocolate stick...' I say,
9256 puffing up.
9257 'Come on, you turkey cocks,' laughs Sylvie. 'That tufty guy,
9258 who interviewed – he has an island, it's used for fiscal fraud. He'd
9259 pay a trip. We'd meet the sourest of the *crème*, write a report,
9260 unmask the powerful, drink from crystal spigots....'
9261 'Oh no!' I say. 'I see it all. The bar. The maraschino – so sweet,
9262 there's grey sugar crusts around the bottleneck. Sicking in the
9263 bidet, all us three. Excess, it's not our generation's thing.... Then –
9264 these desert islands, besides the pools and bars, they're always full
9265 of sand, that grinds like glass in your best orifice.'
9266 Chip perks up. 'If you want a hobnob with some criminals, I'd
9267 truck some in. You needn't leave the room.'
9268 'You must know the President, Chip,' I say.
9269 'Of course,' he says, 'everyone knows him. If you guys had
9270 TV, you could get to know him too – send him a dollar bill and get
9271 a parchment back. He doesn't stand on ceremony, ceremony's his
9272 lymph.'

9273 'This is dangerous ground,' says Sylvie. 'We could research an
9274 occupation of the States. I'd set the terms. No armed resistance, all
9275 those bangs and stiffs. A character study, how guys would get on...'
9276 'Why wouldn't they resist?' I ask. 'All those grunts.'
9277 She shrugs, Chip says, 'Maybe they didn't feel up to it. Maybe
9278 they thought they'd lose. Maybe they were glad at last it happened.'
9279 'There's talk there is a million Trots somewhere – perhaps they
9280 had a hand,' I say, not quite convinced.
9281 'It was Ginsberg said that,' Sylvie says. 'My grandfather saw
9282 him spouting, once.'
9283 If we got cash for such a project – better not mention Ginsberg.
9284 Nor Burroughs – except for the cash registers.
9285 'If we were occupied,' says Sylvie. 'Who'd collaborate? And
9286 who'd resist, and why?'
9287 'The Feds would do the work,' says Chip. 'There would be
9288 shootings, but that's only fair, and expected.'
9289 'A different colour on school buses,' Sylvie says, fantasy
9290 taking flight. 'That would show that things were not the same.'
9291 'There'd be a civil war,' I say. 'That's always part of it. The
9292 newborns versus all the rest, perhaps. Then, there'd be militias,
9293 Swedish drill for kids.'
9294 'New clients for my loans: – maybe they would build some
9295 stuff, and make new movies too,' says Chip. 'Changing the
9296 aesthetic makes more friends than fiddling with ethics. That's what
9297 they'd change. No House. Marimbas and cembalons. Small breasts
9298 on the screen.'
9299 We pause, contemplating. 'They'd split it up, the place. Have
9300 some new capitals, and flags. Maybe take God off the coins,' says
9301 Sylvie.
9302 'I think you're crazy, both of you,' says Chip. 'That isn't how
9303 it's done. They put their new guy in, fix the elections. Don't even
9304 need to visit here.'
9305 'My father said it was like that anyway,' I say.
9306 'That's a cheap shot,' says Sylvie, laughing.
9307 'My grandfather said the same,' says Chip.
9308 'And there's another cheap one. Besides,' Sylvie says.
9309 'Without fire and water, air and hurricanes – the change would not
9310 exist.'
9311 'The best thing,' says Chip sagely, 'to be in, is autoparts. In bad
9312 times – a necessity. In good times – much the same.'

9313 'My grandfather went to readings,' Sylvie said. 'Ginsberg,
9314 those two Italians, and the Frenchie too. When things are really
9315 tough, the poetry takes off.'
9316
9317                                    *
9318
9319 I tell Omar about the project. He says, 'Asking people what they'd
9320 do when there's an invasion? They'll kill you quick as shit. You
9321 carry the plague. You add another to their fears. Just make it all up,
9322 like they do in science – that way you'll make the news, and get
9323 asked back. Now – about this mind and body problem....'
9324     'No, Omar, I don't have that,' I say.
9325     'Everybody does,' he says. 'It's like this. Of course they're
9326 different. Your body falls to rubbish. Then your mind goes, but
9327 after. Your old self is unrecognisable to your young self – but your
9328 mind connects. See, that brain up there, it's like a hank of wool: it
9329 lies supine, like spaghetti. Then, when you've knitted it – it's a
9330 sweater, a potholder. See? That's your mind.'
9331     I tell Sylvie: she says, 'I didn't have the problem. Anyway, it's
9332 not knowledge Tufty's after – it's me.'
9333     Chip says, 'All these theories, the discussions – it just lets you
9334 compete to do the cruellest things to cruel people.'
9335     'Well,' says Omar, squaring up, 'what's wrong with cruelty? If
9336 there wasn't that, there'd be no way to be kind. Besides – all what
9337 we call civilisations, they're a mix of both: – like in your head, I
9338 dare say, Chip.... There's the two impulses, side by side. You know
9339 the consequences of each – but you insist there'd be a battle, then a
9340 beautiful cohabitation You roast your enemies, we pour phosphorus
9341 down their throats. You whittle, we do *repoussé*. That's how the
9342 work is done, that's how we trudge along, better and brighter every
9343 day.'
9344     'No, not me,' says Chip. 'I want no therapy. "No God, no tsar,
9345 and no heroes", like the song says. I've had all the history I want. I
9346 sit here in my suit and shoes, and don't await the call.'
9347     Omar waves him off: he turns to me, 'Your father – he'd some
9348 trouble with those bodies too – all left lying mindless, stacked,
9349 despite the theorising,' and he laughs.
9350     'My father disavowed what he couldn't find excuses for, or at
9351 the least explain. It kept him on the hop, being on right sides all the
9352 time,' I say. 'This invasion thing – everyone's already seen the
9353 movie. If we start asking, they will want more soldiers.'

9354 'They're supposed to think they ought not do it to the others,'
9355 Sylvie says. 'Imagining it done to them. Playing the role of
9356 bleeding heart.'
9357     'You freak,' laughs Omar. 'They do it to the others so it doesn't
9358 happen here.'
9359     'You're all obsessed with bodies, that's the easy part,' says
9360 Chip. 'Just think – if you believed in spirits, you'd need investigate
9361 those too. Enough! Your project, your research – already it's done
9362 quite adequately. Sylvie makes her sacrifice, she takes the cash
9363 from Tufty – and that's the end of it.'
9364     'That's not the end of anything,' shouts Omar – 'You're all
9365 Cartesians, your naughty bodies cured by muscular minds. All of
9366 you here – you're all bipolar – depressed, you shoot, manic, you
9367 vote and feed the poor. Set yourselves right....' and on he talks, his
9368 body and his mind in two-four rhythm, words formed like pearls, a
9369 necklace dripping from his mouth.
9370     'Well,' I say, 'I need no pills and phials. Mine is the condition
9371 of the sea, thought and action one and indivisible.'
9372     'You've got things well in hand,' says Omar. 'Most of the
9373 knowledge – it's already yours. Chip, Sylvie, me – we could start
9374 up another country, run it with our skills. This guy here–' he points
9375 to me '–he is the sea. Make it an island, surrounded by this guy.
9376 The three of us could do as well as all the rest. No risk, and no
9377 attraction there; just a rock, a skimpy beach – no one would try to
9378 conquer such a place.'
9379     'Relax!' says Chip. 'Of course, you could run the world. If
9380 done well, someone would invade you. If not – you bleed out on
9381 the sand. Forget the maraschino. Your citizens back the criminals,
9382 they envy them. They have no grand design, none of them. They
9383 palaver round their secret table, within their locked walls. Why
9384 bother? Govern them? Feed them? Fill their eyes with molten gold,
9385 parade your generals with pheasant feathers on their backs? It's a
9386 delusion. Remember – "he carries the child who takes him down
9387 the lonely path". That's what keeps it going. Generating
9388 generations. Bread in the bin, that guarantees tomorrow. It is
9389 enough.'
9390     'The freaks all come to me,' says Omar. 'It's heaven and hell.
9391 The angels come to me, say it can all be saved. No heating up, no
9392 grubbing up the food and stuff it down. If only – the devils would
9393 stop stoking up and laying out the tables, killing the tasty chicks.
9394 It's civil war. All at school together, then into white coats. Now –

9395  they fight it out, with prayers and oaths. I tell them – stand on your
9396  heads, dear angels, it'll calm you down. It works.'
9397       'Well,' says Sylvie, 'I'm the happy one. No kids for me. And I
9398  can brush old Tufty off.'
9399       'For me,' Chip says. 'The money is a means. It opens up to
9400  choice – but doesn't tell you any of them.'
9401       'My father – I didn't bury him. He did it all himself, sent
9402  himself laughing up in smoke,' I say.
9403       'At least – he had the last laugh on you,' says Chip.
9404       'I knew the talk was all of breaking chains and having new
9405  ones hammered on,' says Omar. 'I prefer to live without.'
9406       'There's talk in the street about the chains, being born in them,
9407  and losing them: I believe in protest,' Sylvie says. 'I believe in all
9408  of them. It's just – standing in a crowd, waiting for some guy that
9409  I've paid his wage to come and billy me. I really can't give up the
9410  time.'
9411       'My friends,' says Chip, 'since you've no time, and battles now
9412  are all with nature – a long slog, uncertain end, nothing much you
9413  guys can do... I nudge it this way, and then that – it's mostly
9414  unproductive, I admit. But – you go in the street, it's lots of work
9415  for profit small. Big change comes trickling down, it's soup on
9416  plates, not songs and flags.... My group owns a plantation, over the
9417  hill – maybe you'd like to look it over....'
9418       And of course, we would.
9419       'Here,' says Chip, 'Here's a machete each. In the heart of every
9420  bush, there lies a fruit. Just try your skill, and gut a row or two.'
9421       'Really,' says Sylvie, 'we'd in mind a day of rest and feeling
9422  sorry for the hands, and deprecate their lot.'
9423       'Well, you're in luck,' says Chip, 'and so are they. The hands
9424  are gone – we couldn't pay enough. A favour's done to everyone.
9425  They're out, you're in, and life goes on.'
9426       'What wondrous fruit are these,' asks Omar. 'They're like
9427  pineapples, but the taste is – pastrami, or a jerky, llama strips hung
9428  in the sun....'
9429       'They're crosses, naturally,' says Chip. 'The taste's irrelevant.
9430  It's pretty much whatever you remember.'
9431       We toil all day, and Chip says the experience is one we'd not
9432  have had before or since.
9433       It's dark, 'The fruits are luminous,' says Chip. 'That way we're
9434  not stuck with nine to five,' and we slash on and stack.

9435    We roast, we peel, our sweat smells like salami or a pemmican.
9436    There's beetles too – 'Help them!' shouts Chip, and so we do.
9437    'I hope his group owns no deep mines,' pants Omar – 'Yes, we
9438    do,' says Chip, 'Hot mines, and pickaxing on your back.'
9439    'It's time to leave,' says Sylvie, deeply stressed; but none of us
9440    recalls the route we took, or how to quit the fields.
9441    'We overdid the songs and jokes,' says Sylvie. 'Coming here in
9442    Chip's old truck. We didn't see a thing... was there an aeroplane...?'
9443    There may have been.
9444    'My group owns so much stuff, it means I don't need be
9445    anywhere,' says Chip. 'Not anywhere special, at one time. No one
9446    checks. Where we come, we dig and chop, we drill and juice, we
9447    strip and trawl. So – you don't become attached to any place before
9448    you start to make it work for you. One virgin site looks like
9449    another. The stars – we haven't penetrated, but we peek, we watch
9450    them die and dwindle, we part their curtains, and with our binocle,
9451    we assess their treasures. We weigh their moons, we sniff their
9452    vapours, price their mounds and fissures. You should come with
9453    me....' and he stops, he's reached the incongruity. 'I mean, I'd let
9454    you sneak a prying glance.'
9455    'I might like that,' says Sylvie. 'That's what friends are for.'
9456    'You friends – you didn't pick as much as hired hands do,' says
9457    Chip, holding up a paper. 'That tells you all you need to know
9458    about economics – history too.'
9459    We're exhausted: Chip goes on, 'All anthropology is there –
9460    your shanks that wilt, libidos slack as empty sacks.'
9461    'And tomorrow?' Omar asks.
9462    'Is another line of work,' says Chip. 'If you're agreeable, of
9463    course.'
9464    'This has been a profound experience,' Omar says. 'Chip
9465    knows nothing like it. Since his father hung his feathers in the
9466    closet, Chip has lived in the ghostly world of not quite having, not
9467    quite being, not ever knowing... where his feet are.'
9468    'I'm sure you know,' I say. 'I'm sure money gives you a handle
9469    on some certainty.'
9470    'Oh, that's not it,' says Omar. 'Sure, he's in transit, like us all.
9471    But we've invested blood, not calculation. If we'd calculated, we'd
9472    not be here in all these vegetables. We've lived a bit of life. Look at
9473    Sylvie – she's cooked herself beyond the boiling point....'
9474    Indeed she has. She's purple, with yellow spurs, like on a
9475    gourd. We sluice her down.

9476        'That grey tongue!' says Omar. 'Try her with tequila.' That we
9477 do, and she revives, still red and purple; her dessicated breasts stick
9478 out like carrots.
9479        'I'll skip the mining, please,' she says.
9480        Omar and I – we do a dance, shuffling at first, then stamping.
9481 'That's the spirit,' Chip says, settling down to watch. Then Sylvie's
9482 off. She bounds, over the heartless shrubs, through the bamboos, a
9483 joyous hare. 'Oh no,' says Chip: 'I hope she didn't eat my fruit.'
9484        'We didn't, but she did,' I say.
9485        'That stuff's for energy. That's why the hands ran off. Not
9486 wages nor the unions. Just vital juice,' says Chip. We don't believe
9487 him – but... there goes Sylvie, up and over trees and mounds, her
9488 legs seem longer, stilts, she buzzes like cicadas do. 'Oh no,' says
9489 Chip. 'I hope she isn't going to mate.'
9490        'Chip, my old friend,' says Omar. 'You may be a tinge
9491 misogynist. Sylvie, a woman. Weak, greedy, randy too, prostrated
9492 by the sun: – maybe she's only taken on too much fuel, instead....'
9493        'It's good stuff. It burns you out, quicker than the booze,' says
9494 Chip. 'That's why they die so young, the hands. But they are
9495 strong, inventing rituals, and toiling in the sun. Those fruits – they
9496 make you glow, like working in a cobalt mine....'
9497        '...no mines,' comes from Sylvie, a glister of a sound.
9498        'Does it tell the good and evil too?' I ask.
9499        'Cheeky!' says Chip. 'The gatherers, they're like potatoes in a
9500 sack, identical, as we are told. Good and evil – they are much the
9501 same when your are hoeing rows. We don't grow potatoes any
9502 more, it's got too hot.'
9503        'The pineapple,' Omar says, shrugging off the banalities, 'Gave
9504 its name to the pineal, the eye of God that's hidden in our bone. If
9505 you believe such stuff. A blind eye – that's what we all need. Sorts
9506 out the evil problem, and the good. It isn't in my therapy.'
9507        'Well, Omar,' says Chip. 'We all do therapy, and we all are in
9508 it. It prepares us for the end. Something accomplished... maybe
9509 climbing trees, like Sylvie here.'
9510        'What else you've got to show us, Chip?' asks Omar. 'Mines,
9511 rockets, lustrous paints?'
9512        Next day, Omar and I go down the mine: there's a ladder.
9513 'Slide me in,' says Omar. The roof's a finger from the floor. Omar
9514 can't slide in. He does. 'I didn't eat the fruit,' he says. 'You have to
9515 soften up your bones. You're back to liquid cells and stuff they use
9516 to make your brains.'

9517   'Can you reach the jewels?' I ask.
9518   'Of course not,' Omar says. 'This is a shaman's trick, for
9519   spaces that aren't possible, and full of secrets too. You mustn't
9520   touch the jewels, or else you're stuck.' He lies, a huge polyp
9521   underneath the earth. I hear him slowly breathe.
9522       I say, 'Chip is hard on his friends.'
9523       Omar doesn't move, he's a jelly slice between two breads of
9524   rock: he says, 'It's right he is. He makes us show what we can do.
9525   Besides – it's too late for him, to do propaganda by the deed.
9526   What's he to do? Make a bomb? He's a money pro.... He's won, as
9527   much as you can. Others are more reflective. You knew Ojibwe –
9528   they are different up there. They plant potatoes still.'
9529       'Anyway,' I say, 'you and Sylvie – you're two remarkable
9530   individuals. You could start something off, quite new, if individuals
9531   can do that any more. Like – found a people, a past.'
9532       Omar finds this funny. He can't laugh too hard.
9533       I say, 'My father is my past. It doesn't give me much to go on.'
9534       Chip says to Omar, 'Time's up, old friend. Should we grease
9535   you out?'
9536       'A little thought will do,' says Omar, slithering. To me he says,
9537   'Too bad your father wasn't into electropop, or drugged up,
9538   winning medals for the DDR. That way would have been best,
9539   more dignified than what you are.'
9540       'I see myself carried on by some woman's dream, maybe to
9541   Africa,' I say. 'Romanticism – that'll be enough, will finish me.
9542   Then renouncing everything, her too, being miserable, and living
9543   on in disillusion. All self-made, home-made.'
9544       'Your time will come,' says Omar, not kindly.
9545       Sylvie has recovered. 'You're a rose garden, Sylvie,' Omar
9546   says. 'Patches of red and white.'
9547       'It was fantastic,' Sylvie says. 'Except – the sun, that once gave
9548   us to eat, and worship it – as it dies, and swells, it burns you up.'
9549       Chip says to me, 'I've some special work for you,' and I say,
9550   'You have no workers, Chip.'
9551       He says, 'It's all crap jobs. Technology has freed them all,
9552   those worthy hands and feet. You see how hard I have to graft,
9553   instead. The mine – no longer do we hammer to extract the jewels.
9554   We suck: and put them into sacks.'
9555       'I guess my task involves those lustrous paints,' I say. 'I bet
9556   you suck them into cans.'

9557 'Imperial green, bordeaux, and Chinese white. Alhambra,
9558 mauve, and cadmium – scorched earth and violet ecstasy...' He
9559 reels them off. 'Colour is made by light,' he says. 'The
9560 Mediterranean – that's full of light. Go – find me that fresh colour,
9561 capture it. Do what you must – the competition's there, it's stacked
9562 up into armies, and there's bombs and rockets used. They say it's
9563 for a future, but it's not. It's all for light – the colour that it hides,
9564 creates. The only worthwhile future – is light, and colour. Like it's
9565 always been. Find it for me. Then, you can share my luck.'
9566     Sylvie has overheard. 'No, Chip,' she says, 'those voyages are
9567 old chapeau. There's satellites now, that peer in your top drawer
9568 and count your socks. This sailing round and meeting tarts, and
9569 wrastling snakes, and fighting guys in bars – it's all been done. The
9570 light has been, and gone. The colour's exactly what you have in
9571 stock – "scorched earth". Don't try to fool this innocent, this patsy
9572 here. What you really want is no doubt quite nefarious....'
9573     'I want the light, the colour,' says Chip. 'Must be the Med.
9574 China, India, over here as well – it's all obscured by smog.'
9575     'He wants the paint so's to contemplate, not put on someone's
9576 house,' says Omar.
9577     'It's life,' says Chip. 'That's why you put it on your face. Death
9578 too, sometimes.'
9579     'Always back to this,' I say. 'My father said we're all too
9580 bright to have relationships. And as for families – look at the *troia*
9581 Helen, she was an early warning. Expect nothing from the dumb.
9582 Death, sometimes.'
9583     'Your father was perverse,' says Sylvie. 'Dump him. He fell in
9584 love with stuff, made excuses for its faults and his enthusiasm, then
9585 cooled off. No lesson there.'
9586     'It's true he was perverse,' I say. 'Without the perversity, there
9587 was nothing left. But I – I have to start from somewhere, before I
9588 end.'
9589     'Start looking for my colour then,' says Chip, laughing.
9590     'He can't carry it back,' says Sylvie. 'How would you? You
9591 can't paint a paint, either.'
9592     'That's for him to figure out,' says Chip, and Omar nods.
9593     'I don't mind the Mediterranean. It's good the way they let the
9594 old things just fall down. Then other things are built, they fall, and
9595 tumble in on them. Now, the churches and the mosques – falling
9596 down, blowing up. That's how it should be, making space,' I say.

9597    'And Chip, if it's trucking dodgy stuff around you want – I'll take a
9598    suitcase.'
9599        'You should bring us back a story,' Sylvie says. 'Someone must
9600    make stories that people can remember. Not fine writing. Your
9601    father....'
9602        'He was always waiting for it to start. Then he realised that it
9603    wouldn't, and he stopped talking. No story there.'
9604        'I prefer to live,' says Sylvie. 'Things shape around me. You're
9605    quite passive, you could spin.'
9606        'There's no stories now. Not that you remember. Guys aren't
9607    naive, they suspect a yarn, and if you tell a tale, they think you're
9608    conning them, or above yourself,' I say.
9609        'And they're right,' says Chip. 'You have to act, or else you
9610    contemplate in silence. Campfires, foundation epics – we've had all
9611    that. It's life and death, just when you thought you could be
9612    comfortable.'

9613
9614                                    *
9615
9616    'Of course, I shan't go,' I tell Sylvie, when Chip can't hear.
9617        'He's paid you,' she says.
9618        'Money's good anywhere,' I say. 'Go or don't go. And I don't
9619    know which colour he might want.'
9620        'It's not colour he wants. You're to set up a network, that can
9621    do anything,' Sylvie says.
9622        'No, it's not only that,' says Omar, listening in. 'You are the
9623    scapegoat. You're the one who's sent away, to bear the blame for
9624    all deeds done past and future. Chip pays you, you take on all his
9625    sins and peccadilloes, and you wander. Do you have protection
9626    over there?'
9627        'There was a Turkish woman, Aliye,' I say. 'Long ago. She did
9628    pictures in coloured inks. She had a shotgun. Maybe they ended her
9629    in jail.'
9630        'It's not enough,' says Omar. 'Chip trusts you, he doesn't like
9631    you. Sylvie and me, we do gymnastics, is all. You alone, you are to
9632    bear the sins that's in all the books, and make Chip friends all over.
9633    The colour he wants is gold, but not to spend. To eat off, and throw
9634    in the bin. He wants fuel, to carry him far and high.'
9635        'It's what we all want, more or less. It's banal,' I say.
9636        'That's why he trusts you. You're stupid, you don't know the
9637    first thing!' says Sylvie. 'You don't recognise his happiness, what

9638  he wants. That was your father's problem – he was a stone, he just
9639  rolled. He thought happiness was on a distant star. It's not, it's in
9640  the trough before you.'
9641      'You get that from a magazine, Sylvie?' I ask.
9642      I'd like to see Aliye, I think, shooting off her gun at the
9643  outside, careful not to hit anything.
9644      'Forget her,' says Omar. 'People you know are owls' pellets,
9645  full of stories. You don't want those. You want guys who represent
9646  big simple stuff: benevolence, weapons, scholarship, pills, dope,
9647  insurance, computing fantasies, guys who calculate the damage you
9648  make from landing, digging, in a sad place, and from not. No
9649  showbiz types. Chip can't do that, bring the guys, the single-
9650  minded animals together, load them on his ship.'
9651      'That way, you bury your father, again,' says Sylvie.
9652      'Why should I want to do that?' I ask. 'He's dust in the wind.'

9653
9654                              *
9655

9656  Here's Aliye, splashing inks around. 'You don't want to mess with
9657  those guys,' she says, hearing of Chip's plan. 'And all known
9658  colours – they're here, on my shelf.'
9659      Her apartment's full of stuff, 'to keep the fucking neighbours
9660  out,' she says. I pick up a bent spear. 'That's for fish, when there
9661  was so many, they sacrificed themselves,' she says. She's withered
9662  into a black grapeskin, two suspicious eyes loping round, borrowed
9663  from a self-regarding crab. 'Water refracts, you see,' she says, 'and
9664  seems to bend. This bent spear ends up straight when you plunge it
9665  in.'
9666      'I see,' I say.
9667      'As for Chip,' she says, 'remember, "Never work for anyone."
9668  That's what the good book says, that your father and I read aloud to
9669  you, in your basket. You can't start too young: learn Capital when
9670  you're six, it's yours for life.'
9671      'How'd you get your money, Aliye?' I ask.
9672      'My sister was a better artist than me. Then she died. So, I sell
9673  my stuff under her name,' she says. 'That's what family is for.'
9674      After a while, I say, 'I need a story. One that people can
9675  remember.'
9676      'Fine,' Aliye says. 'But I'll take half of what you make, when
9677  you retell.'

9678    She sits on a goatskin, and we drink some storytelling booze.
9679    'There came the day, as must it will,' she says, 'when acid were the
9680    seas, and parched the Earth. The last crumb eaten, the drops from
9681    last night's raki drunk... "Have no fear," the big chief says. "We'll
9682    activate the plan." They're all prepared, the people of the Earth.
9683    With push and scratch they all stack in – the hugest rocket you
9684    have seen, prepared to voyage up and down, until they find another
9685    earth, and there to start it all again. The last guy present is the one
9686    to start the motor, jump inside – and off they'd go. Inside it's dark,
9687    and smelly too. "Hurry, hurry up," the people shout. But there's no
9688    fuel. They've used it up.
9689        'The last guy there, he swings the handle round and round – to
9690    no avail. And there they're stuck. It's not an end with dignity, lying
9691    one atop of other, and no sacred writings there to help, and those
9692    who pray, they do just that, and likewise those that swear. And so
9693    the chapter ends. That's it, there is no more, no one survives.
9694        'You ask – "How do I know?" Well, there were three guys, too
9695    busy to pile in and maybe sceptics too – about the rocket trip.
9696    Hungry and thirsty, there they sat or stood, and talked and argued,
9697    thought of making love or doing exercise, or looking at the sky....
9698    Perhaps they spoke about the Kurds, who knows.'
9699        'Aliye, they could be Omar, Sylvie and me!' I say, entering the
9700    spirit.
9701        'Well, yes they could, but they weren't, I dare say,' she says.
9702    'You can always hope.'
9703        'Come on, Aliye, the end!' I say. 'No story without the end!'
9704        'These three guys – how lucky they were literate!' she says,
9705    eking out. 'They looked up, saw the cosmos silent, as it always is.
9706    No rocket. No new earth. They guessed the enterprise was ended.
9707    And they wrote it down. A story in its essence quite similar to
9708    mine....'
9709        She looks triumphant. I say, 'It's a con, Aliye.'
9710        'It gripped you, though,' she says. 'It roused your sense of
9711    smell. It promised you the structure. That is what matters. People
9712    will remember it.'
9713        'But Aliye,' I say, 'it's common coin. Everyone knows that
9714    tale. It's not like faith, or principles, that differ one to one. It's told
9715    a hundred times, in slightly different ways.'
9716        'Exactly so,' she says, triumphant.
9717        'It's banal,' I say. 'Capital was better, it had footnotes, and
9718    jumped about.'

'Listen,' says Aliye, 'there is no con: I've told you what you want, the story that makes your reputation. Alas, you'll be known as "anonymous". You can't have everything, fame and truth don't go together.... The point is – a network like the one Chip wants – it subverts everything. It contains all contradictions. It puts conformity into the resistance, and radicalises reaction. You think you're anticolonial? Your cash comes from the empires. You want to rule for ever? Here come your rebels, some with priests and some with jurists. They'll make you hop, and then they too will have to hop. You have to take a side – that's what you want. Which way do you jump? You find you have to jump, is all. Jump, and more jump. And so it goes. There's no state interest, nothing behind the chain of guys, no latching on to history. The network always does the opposite of what each upfront protagonist desires. It's quiet subversion. Every principle is hollowed out and voided; each dirty trick becomes a principle. There's resolution – but it's a stasis. No one wins, all think they've lost but can't see why or where. They think they should have won – instead, they're sad.'

With an effort, she tilts her neck, her eyes point upwards. The mouldings on the ceiling drip, like icing not quite set. The inky pictures seep and creep like sea-floors swept by swells.

'It sounds right, what you say. But – I don't quite understand.' I say. 'It's all quite new to me. I don't know where I stand.'

'Your father knew,' says Aliye.

She's smug. I can't say 'Fuck my father, what he knew.' It doesn't help.

'There is no stasis,' I say. 'There is a quest. New forms of power. I'm attracted. Even if Chip doesn't know what he's at.'

'You don't know what will happen,' Aliye says. 'All you think, is how you hope you won't get hurt.'

'That's the attraction, Aliye,' I say.

'It's too big for you,' she says. 'Stick to colour charts.'

All around, there is a swirl. 'This Chip,' she says. 'An American. An Indian. About as un-American as you can get. He brings us chaos as a project, not what we already know, the chaos quite fortuitous.'

'Isn't chaos good?' I ask.

'It doesn't last, my dear,' she says. 'And while it does, it isn't fun, and then when order comes – that's not fun too.'

'It's good you talk of fun,' I say. 'Chip promises a prize, to those I weave into his net. A trophy hunt – with bows. It seems in

9760 Africa, the lions are breeding fast. They're mostly in a park – and
9761 so, the little ones grow up... And then get shipped, and you can
9762 shoot them, for a price. The surplus goes to make another surplus –
9763 more and more lions, and heads to tack up on your wall.'
9764     It surprises me, it seems, not Aliye. She nods.
9765     I say, 'Chip has no workers, so there's here no metaphor. The
9766 lions – they do no work. They simply grow, they're hunted, and the
9767 chain of being gains and loses other links.'
9768     'Well, what do you expect?' asks Aliye. 'They run, that is their
9769 fun. If you refuse a bow or gun – the logic of the cull – is
9770 inescapable.'
9771     'Yes,' I say. 'You can't escape from logic.'
9772     'These networks,' says Aliye. 'They're new. Everyone has
9773 them now. Collecting, trawling. Contacting your people in the
9774 structures, and milking them, like ants with aphids.'
9775     'It's the way, it's how it's done, all over. It's like disciples.
9776 Anyone, any origin, and any faith, any colour, any tastes,' I say.
9777     'Me, I know no one,' says Aliye. 'Knowing people's
9778 dangerous. Every decade you come to me, with extravagant tales,
9779 and say how the world has moved. You seem to know the strangest
9780 guys, and yet – you're on terms with all of them. You think you
9781 know me, maybe. But do you buy a picture? Even look at them?
9782 Your father – he knew no one. He didn't like them, other people,
9783 and they didn't see him. That was how it worked. He knew he was
9784 tinier than the smallest of his thoughts. He didn't need some guys
9785 to puff him up.'
9786     There's nothing to say. She says, 'I knew about the lions.'
9787     I say, 'I didn't.' She gets angry. 'You wouldn't recognise a
9788 revolution if it dragged you in the long grass, and ate you.'
9789     She gives me a small paper, torn, blobbed with various inks. It
9790 could have been a trial. 'Take this. Maybe your boss's colour is
9791 among them,' she says.
9792     'And take these figs!' – and here's a basket, heavy with them.
9793 The branches of the figtree come in the windows. A fat log lies on
9794 the carpet, sugary with life. 'They want to cut it down,' Aliye says.
9795 'It fills the courtyard. Below is dark, real dark. The foliage blocks
9796 the gas they use to keep the young guys down. It doesn't get up
9797 here, but now it will.'
9798     The street is empty.
9799     I take a cab, the driver says, 'Those figs will do. Consider
9800 yourself as having paid.'

9801    They say they should have built the city on the other side, in
9802 Asia, where the water's fresh. Now, it's spilled over anyway.
9803    I give Aliye's inks to Chip: I say, 'Your project isn't good. I
9804 shan't be part of it.'
9805    'It's the new power,' he says. 'The network. Makes the
9806 structures work – for me, and everyone. But – if you want to be a
9807 loser, go ahead.'
9808    'Turkish politics, I bet she told you,' Sylvie says.
9809    'No, we talked about her tree. And lions. No metaphors there,'
9810 I say.
9811    'Ah,' says Chip, wistfully. 'Meeting in Istanbul, where
9812 everything meets.'
9813    'Chip,' says Sylvie, 'You're nowhere into power. You're
9814 second level. The tops is presidents and popes. Or banks. Depends
9815 on what you want to take away. You'd be behind the scenes. Those
9816 guys make the treetops move. You're just boring in the bark.'
9817    'Besides,' says Omar, 'Once it was to get a class in power.
9818 Now – the game is just to heave you up, on to some sticky throne.
9819 The best thing's for everyone to have their power...'
9820    'No, no,' says Chip. 'Everyone should have no power. That's
9821 freedom. Sow it all around – it's war of each on all.'
9822    I sit and watch them argue: I feel I'm aging. My belly loses
9823 flesh, I'm like those wooden virgins, carved from olive-wood,
9824 stomachs flat and empty, like small acorns above their legs, a smile
9825 beatified with dope, hands clasped tight to hide where there's no
9826 sex.... The meat drops off, the bones stand proud, the gristles
9827 tauten, snap and blacken. The tongue swells up, then disappears,
9828 the rictus spreads from ear to ear, the teeth are dribbled down to
9829 where the nipples, hard as garnets, brighten up from pink to purple.
9830 Inside, the tale is different, it's pap and offal, the liver with its
9831 yellow pustules, seams of blubber white....
9832    '....' Chip's been saying, then, 'As you know, I have an island,
9833 like that play where there's the storm, a bunch of guys are wrecked,
9834 they talk, and then they leave. Life in a frame – that's what I want,
9835 it's theatre—'
9836    'Plays are like that, Chip,' says Sylvie. 'There is a bunch, they
9837 talk and mime, then you go home.'
9838    'Don't patronise me,' Chip is furious. 'You creaking acrobat. I
9839 know quite well what's life, and getting on the island, and then
9840 leave. In real life, you cry a lot and eat each other. On my island –
9841 maybe you would bond, you three, and I could learn the human

9842 tricks – the ties beyond the clan, the family – ties I never had, but
9843 now are central to my plan....'
9844     Chip talks on and on. An island, with us three, to teach
9845 humanity... no bar, no games. Omar lying like a polyp on the sand,
9846 and Sylvie up a palm.
9847     'Tattoos are changing,' Omar says, changing the topic too.
9848 'Talking of islands. I saw on someone's backside – "My treasure is
9849 within." Then a monster. "Cast me not out Lest I enter into you."
9850 The cops will have to read the bards. Me – I'm clean. No one
9851 writes on me.'
9852     'Fashion's not the trouble,' says Chip. 'I want to find how
9853 humans work. I'd bring to visit you – the President of here and
9854 there, top committees too. You see, with countries, decline and rise
9855 take longer than you've patience for. It's watching tides.
9856 Conclusions – they can rarely come, and least from where you
9857 think they will. Countries and continents – they go on, much
9858 moiling, with foaming waters, flights of populations.... But when it
9859 seems resolved, you're scattered into air, gone, and missed your
9860 chance.'
9861     'I got no tattoos,' says Omar, 'because I didn't go where Sylvie
9862 went....'
9863     'This is interesting,' Chip says. 'The kind of thing I need to
9864 hear.'
9865     'OK,' says Sylvie. 'It was prison. It's the best place to catch up
9866 with literature. That's why they let me out. I passed the test. But –
9867 you come back covered in quotations.'
9868     'You must have done bad things,' says Chip, as if he can't
9869 imagine anything like that.
9870     'Oh yes,' says Sylvie, offhand, 'you start by meeting people – a
9871 guy who slept in other's automobiles. He went to India to preserve
9872 his legs. Because he drank. He sought out the ascetic life. Another,
9873 his girlfriend was a fireater. But she was young, fourteen, they say.
9874 She cheated on him, for her it ended, bad. Being with them, hearing
9875 their tales – you don't have time to earn and do dull jobs.... Prison
9876 is like war – rational and grotesque, all at once. You want to get rid
9877 of people. But – what you want is not to lock them up, the guys, or
9878 kill them. What you want is something else. That's the grotesque
9879 part, the contradict.'
9880     'Oh I'm not sure,' says Omar. 'I might want to kill guys, or to
9881 lock them up. Just that. Then prison, war – those would be
9882 reasonable.'

9883 We try to think of good answers. 'I find this subject
9884 everlasting, fascinating,' Chip says. 'To have great power on people
9885 – even if it is the kind that has no guns or handcuffs, that you feel
9886 the effect of, but not the means or the intent.... to have that power,
9887 you need to know some people, better than I do right now. It's not
9888 the arguments I want, or justifying or apologising.... It's stories.
9889 Lives. That's what I need to know about.'

9890 'It's the wrong start,' says Sylvie. 'Talking of two different
9891 things. People in the one place, they've nothing to do with those in
9892 the other.'

9893 'People need protecting from people, I guess,' says Chip.
9894 'Including me. It's pretty simple.'

9895 'I protect myself from both,' says Omar. 'Jail and armies.'

9896 'It takes you away from experience,' Sylvie says. 'Just for a
9897 clean skin.'

9898 'I lived in a place,' says Omar. 'All my neighbours were
9899 criminals. They spied on me, the scum. If you do exercises, you do
9900 it alone, no one can help you.'

9901 'I got put away for helping people I knew,' says Sylvie. 'It was
9902 a girl thing to do.'

9903 Everyone says that.

9904 Chip says, 'Well, with you on the island, I could observe you.
9905 That's an enlightened thing to do. This guy here,' he pulls me in the
9906 ring, 'he's the sea already. I lend my island.'

9907 'It's true we do a kind of therapy,' says Sylvie, 'but only on
9908 people who are well. We tell them how to live, and that is what
9909 they do. For us, the good thing's getting paid. The other stuff – we
9910 improvise.'

9911 'Exactly what I need,' says Chip. 'The human touch.'

9912 'What's in it for you, Chip?' asks Sylvie. 'Why isn't second
9913 level good enough?'

9914 Chip mostly ignores her, then, 'First level is reaching the top
9915 and then you must come down, by fall or scramble, or they unhorse
9916 you. I fancy something more permanent, not where your army's
9917 already gathered on the plain, with guys in braid and rules.
9918 "Supreme leader". That would do. Beyond argument, above the
9919 fog.'

9920 Where is this island? Halfway to Africa?

9921 'I had it towed,' says Chip. 'Here in the river.'

9922 It's red and gold and reeds. You could raise a stall, sell eels in
9923 molasses on it, blue plums battered in eggy crusts. That's an

9924 illusion. It's a flat, a stage, a platform. It's a pier's end, wrecked,
9925 deserted, amputated. I'm carried out, floated on Omar's back.
9926     Chip comes on waterski, Sylvie on his shoulders, a winged
9927 victory. I recognise her chant – and the name she's bawling out,
9928 Siddhartha. The island is more raft than rock. 'It's minimal,' I say.
9929 'It's unimpressive.'
9930     'That's how it's meant to be,' says Chip, and Sylvie and Omar
9931 nod. 'I could turf it or cement it. It'd still be flat.'
9932     'Yes,' I say, 'it's you, Chip. Unpainted boards: elsewhere, pure
9933 colours.'
9934     'They're not pure, silly boy,' laughs Chip. The three are at
9935 home. They lie on thin foam squares. 'I've brought no grand ideas,'
9936 says Chip. 'Since here, all ideas are grand.'
9937     It's so, I guess. We stretch out on our backs. We are four, are all
9938 creation.... no, we are four separated ones. We could be made of
9939 steel or jelly.
9940     It's dull, looking up at the sky, interrupted by a gull, a plane. 'It
9941 should be empty, that sky,' I say. 'It's not one thing or another.'
9942     'Then it's both,' grunts Omar. 'Fuck you, grow up!'
9943     Sylvie says, dreaming, 'Supreme Leader – it's still first level,
9944 nothing more. Everything still goes through channels.'
9945     'Second level, though,' Omar says. 'Who wants to be a Krupp?
9946 It's grovel.'
9947     'Chip, tell us how you started on the money trail,' says Sylvie.
9948     'Oh, I sold the lands,' says Chip.
9949     'Break the taboo!' shouts Omar.
9950     'I sprinkled it around, the cash,' says Chip. 'The President,
9951 other tall poppies too. They do experiments, when they find the
9952 bones. It's not all from massacres – drink and the devil too,' and he
9953 hums a line or two. 'The president comes out here – he practises
9954 his swing.'
9955     'That's the best thing I had heard,' says Sylvie, 'That he's in a
9956 band.'
9957     'Oh no,' says Chip. 'He hits his balls to where that guy is
9958 waving.' Far off, there's a black man in a coracle. A floating hole. I
9959 see there's scoops smacked in the planks here. The guy leaps up
9960 and down.
9961     I ask, 'Why'd you want a network, then? It seems you already
9962 have the best....'

9963     'Oh no,' says Chip, 'that's over here. You must think global.
9964 Remember – it is not to spend, but to accumulate. In fact, the less
9965 you spend, the better,' and we're sure he knows it's true.
9966     'See!' says Chip. 'The isle rotates. It can take off. Or be a
9967 dance floor.'
9968     It's a spinning disc. Omar and Sylvie raise their arms, their
9969 heads glow like candle-flames.
9970     'It spouts!' says Chip. The water, pink and green, shoots up and
9971 turns to spray. All four of us, we're pink and green and gold. You
9972 could pray to us. We can't respond, the platform turns too fast. It
9973 makes you nauseous.
9974     'This is living!' Chip shouts. 'I love plain things, and see how
9975 they come grandiose, and lift you up.' We're sufis standing still, the
9976 world whirls round, the water plumes. We see some secret things –
9977 there's the lady, Liberty herself, curved like a boomerang, the
9978 buildings leave their vertical, and turn to hooks and hunches.
9979     'Faster, faster!' Sylvie shouts, and she is airborne, her little
9980 slippered feet do *fouettés* in air. Omar spreads out, sticks to the
9981 boards, a treacle-smear with eyes.
9982     'See, you idiots!' Chip shouts, 'this is what you get if you have
9983 lots of cash! Experience quite unparalleled....' And we would stay
9984 for ever, us and the rest transformed. It slows. 'Enough!' says Chip.
9985 'Sometimes it makes you speak with tongues—'
9986     'Oh, I am sure I was,' says Omar, quite entranced, 'You
9987 couldn't hear me for the spume, and the machinery.'
9988     'Hey! Hey, you guys with seawrack in your hair!' It's the guy
9989 from the floating hole. 'The President is on his way!'
9990     'He's always calm,' says Chip, 'so we don't spin him up.'
9991     Are those the dragon boats? The galleys from republics of the
9992 sea? No.
9993     'He loves that paddle-steamer,' Chip shouts out, and now he
9994 hugs the guy.... His office makes the President tall enough, gives
9995 him a jaw. He smacks the balls away. The guy in the coracle waves
9996 his arms – 'A hole in one, each shot,' he lies. It's over. 'He's so
9997 keen on ritual,' says Chip. 'He doesn't say a word. I'm sure he saw
9998 you lurking there.'
9999     'Chip!' says Sylvie. 'No one can party like you can. It's all
10000 been most extravagant – the company baroque, the twirling killed
10001 the thirst and hunger dead. Now we could sleep, our questions quite
10002 unanswered.... The guy was clearly level one. Nothing to say, he
10003 made no observation sharp or dull. What a pain, to end like that!'

10004     'My father said Stalin was always very cordial,' I tell them.
10005     'But he can't ever have met him. His daughter liked to dance.'
10006         We go back to the shore. The guy in the coracle lies there,
10007     coiled sleeping like an asp. Does he live without resentments?
10008         Sylvie says, 'Chip – the President, he doesn't know a thing.
10009     Nor all those guys who visit ... they're emptied out as walnut
10010     shells.'
10011         Chip makes some mild complaint. Then Sylvie screams at him,
10012     'We don't know what's going to happen next. Don't you grasp?
10013     We're terrified.'
10014         'It's been like that since they fitted us with brains, and made
10015     them so's they pointed backwards,' Chip says, trying to calm her.
10016         'This time, it's different,' Sylvie says. 'That's why we cling so
10017     to our bodies – how they torment us! – write on them ... so's to do
10018     what? To recognise ourselves when we are lost? To show more
10019     difference? We see the others driven to the edge, and then beyond,
10020     we see them lying there, as flat and calm as Omar. Into the pit they
10021     go. Some have numbers, so you can tell them. We have writing and
10022     designs. It's our insurance. What will happen? We don't know – we
10023     have the fear, as if we knew.'

10024
10025                        \*
10026
10027     'You can have clients,' Sylvie says to me, when I am settled in, 'but
10028     not when I have mine. I'll give them some Jung today – he's dry.
10029     Take their minds off their minds.'
10030         'I'll only stay a day or so,' I say. 'Your clients seem so
10031     complicated – their problems!'
10032         'Oh, they burrow into those,' she says. 'If only they'd admit
10033     how scared they are – all the rest would scud away. Imagine if they
10034     had a pantheon – those spirits to placate... they'd have no time for
10035     therapy.'
10036         All this – it's not the work I want to do.
10037         Sylvie says, 'Another week, and I'll be cured. There's nothing
10038     wrong with me, of course, but in a week, I'll give it up. It was good
10039     I had the chance from you. First, it was college boys, then rich
10040     deadheads, thinking of something else – then you, looking for a
10041     sugarplum. After – there was Chip – so much more interesting.'
10042         'It's useful to know all this,' I say, put out.
10043         'There is no mystery,' she says. 'Those guys who started off by
10044     studying the ants, the bees – that was genius pure!' She's quite

10045 delighted. 'It's about stability, the durability of the realm, the death
10046 of the leader, or their idea, and their regeneration. There's a
10047 condiment of divinities. Beautiful people, mostly, but capricious.
10048 There's a judge, at the end.... And temples. Stone or paper.'
10049     'Don't tell me there's a trial,' I say.
10050     'Oh, there's trials, but they don't matter much,' says Sylvie.
10051 'It's the judge with a garrotte who counts.'
10052     'Did watching the golf put this in you, Sylvie? Or did you just
10053 read it somewhere and forget, and now it pops up back?' I ask.
10054     'No, not the golfer. The guy in the coracle. He's always there,'
10055 she says. 'Ready to catch and lie.' She laughs. 'The balls they shoot
10056 at him....'
10057     'Once you know this, Sylvie,' I tell her. 'There's only to stand
10058 aside.'
10059     'That's what you do,' she says. 'Spying's in your blood, your
10060 father's blood. That's it – you stand aside. You don't join any of it –
10061 the dance before the hive, guarding the queen, transporting the
10062 larvae. You pry, you tell, you know, but you don't do. Neither
10063 support, nor yet subvert.'
10064     'Neither way seems to have much point,' I say.
10065     'That's because you are an ant,' she says, 'who'd like to be a
10066 bee.'
10067     'You're hitching up with Chip, I guess,' I say. 'You can do that
10068 because you're a beauty. The details... the stories, the parades, the
10069 rhetoric that comes in many shades – they just adorn the plan. It's
10070 not your plan, you're not the architect, but a builder – yes. The
10071 great design's to make the state that won't endure, seem
10072 everlasting. The detail doesn't matter. You're all chrism, Sylvie.
10073 You're an enchantment. There you sit, upon the empty throne
10074 beside the emperor. Rising with him, instructing what to do.'
10075     'It's not the upward curve,' she says. 'It's that the fall should be
10076 magnificent, part of the trip. You should believe in tumbling down
10077 with all the passion, the delight, you feel in soaring up.'
10078     There's nothing great in being beautiful. There is anxiety you'll
10079 get more spots. Yet – after all, it must be great, that 'being
10080 beautiful', just like the poet says.
10081     'It's not I'm beautiful,' says Sylvie, 'Just the proportion's right.
10082 I'm not the beauty – it's my skeleton. To butterflies, we're quite a
10083 sight – the little heads, the stumbling feet, the colour uniform and
10084 bland. No flight, no metamorphosis. Tiny eyes.'
10085     'You're with Chip full time?' I ask.

10086 She evades. 'There's trouble in the palace,' she says. 'It takes
10087 two to pull the President from his bed. It's absurd, his depression –
10088 when he took the job, he knew he had to kill people that he didn't
10089 know. There's his two helps, one wants the succession, the other
10090 sees he has the power to put an end to everything, and can't decide:
10091 to spare or to exterminate. They get him dressed. I'm not surprised
10092 Chip keeps his distance.'
10093 I say, 'Omar says they feed the President jokes, like – "This
10094 guy – they came in to arrest him, though he thought he was clean.
10095 They took guys off for being in the wrong tribe, having wrong
10096 passports, thoughts or friends... so, the guy thought he was covered.
10097 But no – they caught him for being left-handed... it seems that
10098 someone with a knife...."'
10099 'The ones who laugh at that – it shows they're friends. That is
10100 the test,' says Sylvie.
10101 'Chip must be clean,' I say.
10102 'He's depilated thoroughly,' Sylvie says. 'I wear black so you
10103 can't see what's written on me.'
10104 'That's not work, Sylvie,' I say. 'What you're trying to do now,
10105 with Chip. His schemes – they come across to you as fantasies, like
10106 you've been sniffing smoke....'
10107 'Work?' she shouts. 'You call it work? I fed them
10108 Schopenhauer. It comforted. But I could tear their flesh – it'd be
10109 consistent. Everyone should bear their burden, like I do, and Omar
10110 too.'
10111 'But – Chip?' I ask.
10112 'He has the marvels – you have seen them. They're made to be
10113 ephemeral. It takes so little to transform – a pistol shot, it brings the
10114 forest down. Remember Yugoslavia – the shot led straight to Hitler.
10115 Then – to everything thereafter. So it is with Chip – a small report...
10116 a supernatural push or prod. The voyage starts, the launch....'

10117
10118 *
10119
10120 Sylvie calls. I'm invited. 'Yes, it's a launch. Maybe of my face.
10121 We're having a reception, not a party – so, that means you don't do
10122 sex upstairs.'
10123 There are no mariners there, so it's not a proper launch: it's
10124 mostly guys in suits, exchanging tips.
10125 'My,' says a woman, 'You look out of place. You come in off
10126 the street to look for eats?'

10127 Her name's Roxanne, on her badge: she's maybe got tattoos
10128 that show the guys she's been with, and I peer...
10129 'No, no,' she says, 'It's just a chest, there are no trophies there
10130 – you needn't stare.'
10131 'I do her music,' says Roxanne. 'It's up this loud so guys can't
10132 overhear. But for a fee, I'll rent you a device that let's you listen
10133 in....' And she does, though it's not worth the sum.
10134 'There he is,' Roxanne says, 'Chip. The man without the
10135 qualities, that means he must have all of them. Who knows what
10136 plan they have, those two? To conquer heights – that is for sure, but
10137 who's to push, and who's to pull, Sylvie or him?'
10138 'Well,' I say, 'I'm really curious. Were I to find the cash,
10139 maybe you'd find what Sylvie does, or wants to do?'
10140 'Oh yes,' she says. 'I love to spy.'
10141 I insist – don't work for someone else. It makes living in any
10142 kind of way quite difficult. 'You mustn't think you work for me....'
10143 I say to Roxanne, and she says, 'Oh no, of course not. I love prying
10144 into other people. That's how you live, and feel alive.'
10145 The guys stand round, in little clumps of two and three. The
10146 music covers them. My father would have felt superior, to all their
10147 secrets. Objectively, I guess he was on their side. He wasn't one for
10148 purity, for an idea that chases people to the fields and starves them
10149 as they dig and plant. He didn't want to start things off again,
10150 taking the better, arid path. 'Behind the drive for altruism, there's
10151 always some self-indulgent boss,' he said. He liked guys small,
10152 impure, he felt at home with them, looking down.
10153 'You know,' says Roxanne, 'Chip doesn't plan a thing. His
10154 cash sweeps him along. Myself, I think those terrible experiments –
10155 if you don't share something of them, you've really lost all hope.'
10156 'What can you mean, Roxanne?' I ask. 'It's quite incongruous
10157 here, I'm sure. What experiments?'
10158 'Oh well,' she says, 'some of the Chinese things. Pol Pot.
10159 Where you're happy that it didn't happen to you, but—'
10160 'Is Sylvie into that?' I ask. 'She's quite farouche. She didn't get
10161 it from me.'
10162 'Oh,' says Roxanne, 'with you she got to study the philosophy.
10163 Peasants, cities – all that stuff – it doesn't bother her. It's the
10164 parabola, the gesture, the ambition – that's what matters. And your
10165 father. Like me, she's keen on spying – that cop who said he didn't
10166 know what side he's on, but on the whole.... and ended as director
10167 of the Cheka, for the Bolshies.... He fascinates.'

0168     'It's all new to me,' I say.

0169     'That's what it's supposed to be,' says Roxanne.

0170     The straight guys have all left, there's only us two, and Chip

0171 and Sylvie, left. Roxanne goes on, 'The music scene's all over.

0172 Movies are miniature. Good looks and tits – we've seen them all.

0173 The politics is guys in suits. Now, it's our turn: it's what you said.

0174 Farouche. It's voodoo in our heads, without the fooling with those

0175 animals. It's climbing up to fall straight down. It's digging up the

0176 dead and burying them again. Apocalypse as farce.'

0177     Sylvie joins us: she says, 'It's worshipping the deities... you

0178 know they don't exist, and watching as they bring the lightning

0179 strikes and plagues.'

10180     'I thought Chip was involved with cash?' I say.

10181     'Of course, that's needed,' Sylvie says. 'But it flows in and out,

10182 just like the sea. Just like you say you are. You gave me some ideas

10183 – ideas you hadn't got, you as the sea, digesting everything, always

10184 renewed, more acid, saltier, lifeless too.... Just depth and motion.

10185 Me, skimming, never making land...'

10186     Chip stands and nods, his polished head waves slightly to and

10187 fro, like an old-time radio valve.

10188     'It sounds all symbols,' I say. 'Beautiful satanists, all that.'

10189     'You soft guys – to you it's enough things come up as art and

10190 heritage,' says Sylvie. 'Never the real thing. All this intent – reason,

10191 belief, calculation – the results, you understand, are quite arbitrary.

10192 Justice finishes as revenge, guys in iron boxes savaged by pitbulls.'

10193     'Begin from the other end,' says Roxanne, trying to help out,

10194 'You might reach the grand things you started with.' She doesn't

10195 sound sure. I think she doesn't care too much.

10196     'What deities have you and Sylvie had enshrined?' I ask.

10197     'We get them from a book, and try them out on vacant lots,'

10198 says Roxanne. 'Picking out the beauties – then quick sex in animal

10199 disguise. Lightning displays, of course. Sometimes we have to

10200 goad them on.'

10201     Maybe Roxanne's spoofing me. She's soft and sugary, Turkish

10202 delight, your eyes run over her like hands. 'It's true,' she says. 'I'm

10203 not proportional. But the material is there, stacked up by clumsy

10204 fingers.'

10205     It's true, she's like the blobs of dough a baker leaves and bakes

10206 when he's laid out a tray of perfect biscuits, each one as beautiful

10207 as Sylvie – yet, it's so, the material is the same.

10208   'Good looks is coming back. It's been unmentionable for years,
10209   though fortunes were still made on it,' Roxanne says, and wriggles
10210   noncommittally.
10211       I say, 'I recommend an expert – he will change your shape,
10212   brain patterns too, – an oriental cast as well, if you will buy the
10213   book,' and so by puffing him I've been a friend to Omar, and his
10214   trade.
10215       'We'll see how far Chip goes,' says Sylvie. 'Will he run, or
10216   will he fall? It's an experiment, but one he wants, perhaps. Another
10217   fall: there's been so many ends, another one will scarcely rock the
10218   room.'
10219       'Besides,' says Roxanne, 'some of us – we never had ancestral
10220   lands. He has an enviable past, that only he has access to.'

10221
10222                                   *
10223

10224   Omar tells Chip, 'Beware your women. There's a game in play.
10225   They waft you up, to see if you will fly, and if you fall – it's just
10226   more fun.'
10227       'Who told you that?' asks Chip. 'Of course – there's always
10228   been quite other Indians. Even the wrong sort – building those
10229   pyramids and torturing their equals on the top. Say "Indian" –
10230   we're the fall guy. I thought all that was past. You people – you all
10231   came from caves, not washing, eating grubs – but that's been put
10232   behind you – I dare say you never think of it. Besides – where'd
10233   you hear all that?'
10234       'Oh, well,' says Omar, 'that's what politics is.' He gestures at
10235   me, as I'm listening at the door. 'The secrets are the ones that you
10236   don't tell, or even think.'
10237       He limbers up. 'I'll show you guys! Wrestling. The deal is –
10238   keep your weight low, full of gravity. That's what politics is –
10239   *gravitas*. Say, do, what you like. If you don't have *gravitas*, it's all
10240   smoke and crackle.'
10241       He crouches, flat and dry as a cowpat on the mat. The other
10242   guy – looks stretched, as if he's down from his cross, starting his
10243   second sporty life. He's long. He doesn't need to bend. He flips
10244   Omar over, as if he were a leaf. They try again. He spins Omar like
10245   a frisbie.
10246       'Yes!' says Omar, feigning triumph. 'That's the lesson! Even
10247   when you do things right, there is some freak who makes a fool of
10248   you.'

10249 He strongarms the victorious crucified wrestler out the door.
10250 'Great demo, Fritz,' he shouts, when the guy has left. 'You see,
10251 Chip – it isn't just you Indian guys. Maybe you should avoid to be
10252 a group. The groups – they end up bad. Neanderthals, Armenians,
10253 those Carthaginians, Hereros, Jews and communists – the dark
10254 wing settles over you. There is no count, no trials, no fancy
10255 explanation. Apocalypse that follows on the one that's gone
10256 before.'
10257    'Omar,' says Chip, 'we know all that. Now – it's not the
10258 groups. It's everyone.'
10259    'We all go on, living as if we're immortal – but only the richest
10260 ones are going to make it,' Omar says. 'Chip, you're one of them.
10261 Don't you feel like taking some of us with you, ever upward, like
10262 they say?'
10263    'No,' says Chip. 'I don't even know if I'm going anywhere.
10264 Some have castles, some have islands. I have an island. You guys –
10265 there's not much work for you. You've all the time you need to
10266 have your brain pick out some scheme – just think, if you were
10267 hoeing maize, you wouldn't even know the questions.'

10268
10269                 *
10270

10271    'It's true, Roxanne,' says Sylvie. 'I screw men so's I can criticise
10272 them. More intimately. Am I sick, Roxanne?'
10273    'It's your forte, Sylvie,' says Roxanne. 'Don't give up on it. It's
10274 a victory.'
10275    'If you say,' says Sylvie, 'but now, there's Chip. It's time to
10276 launch him too. We are the horse, we know the way. He just sits
10277 atop and whoops. People get tired of everything, even of
10278 pretending. He's the new. There was paternalism, then markets,
10279 then the intimate. It's waves, Roxanne. Sit higher up the beach,
10280 they won't reach you, not today. The worst thing you can imagine –
10281 it's already happened. Or it's still happening. Chip: stripped and
10282 hairless. Expect no good of him – but differences. Extremes. Those
10283 you've not considered. They won't do you good. But – he's the
10284 great change....'
10285    'Yes, yes,' says Roxanne, 'the change while we wait.' She sees
10286 me lingering round the door. 'Hey,' she shouts at me, 'write to your
10287 boss that we're all gay. Or indifferent. That way, they'll get no
10288 blackmail money from us.'
10289    'I don't have a boss. Everything I do, I do for love.'

10290 'Sure, you have a boss,' says Roxanne, 'A boss is your fetish.
10291 You pinch it, try to pull its head right off.'
10292 'I'm sure that's what Jung said,' says Sylvie, trying to calm a
10293 storm. 'This guy's quite innocent. He spies and lurks because he
10294 doesn't know a thing.'
10295 'I'm stifling in here,' Roxanne says, taking off her top. 'This
10296 city! Chip – doesn't he have a space somewhere? We could do
10297 sport. Here – it's the words, written on the walls, guys in the
10298 automobiles – they shout them, don't mean a thing....'
10299 'Don't be precious, Roxanne,' Sylvie says. 'They're insults.
10300 That's not so hard to grasp. What pisses me right off – it's all the
10301 art they do – they say it's valueless, ephemeral, or else it's up to
10302 you to make it mean, look harder, the gesture, yes but no! – the
10303 artist is the work? oh no it's you! And on it goes.... The fucking
10304 venue's just the same, and so are you, and so's the guy beside who
10305 tries to press your thigh. Roxanne!' she screams. 'It's all the same!
10306 But dull! Repetitive and obvious....'
10307 On she goes, till Roxanne says, 'I know, dear Sylvie. That's
10308 why we both want something new.'
10309 'And that won't be the same, the same parabola, those goddam
10310 words?' shouts Sylvie. 'And put your top back on, Roxanne –
10311 we're not equipped for fondling here.'
10312 Roxanne is blushing, but I don't think it's shame. Sylvie calms,
10313 she says, 'Once, Aphrodite intervened in this. Now, all is up to us.
10314 Why were we left to fix this shabby scene without a help, a
10315 prompt?'
10316 We have no answer, and I think she doesn't wait for one.
10317 'I'm hot, Sylvie,' Roxanne says. 'I wish I was like Omar, living
10318 in his body all the time. Where does Chip live? In the grasslands?
10319 Hot, Sylvie – it's not about the universe, or brotherhood. It's too
10320 much power, we use it up, it goes nowhere but in our skin, it makes
10321 us sick....' She weeps.
10322 'Come, Roxanne,' says Sylvie, cuddling her. 'It all will pass.
10323 There is a law that says, that everything runs down, there's less and
10324 less. It is the only law we have, no good it does to us.' She
10325 brightens. 'Maybe Chip could rent an iceberg – it is all the rage.
10326 We're towed to see the animals. We're cool, so cool. They take us
10327 off when it is time.'
10328 I say, 'Chip exploits his environment; once he was a wolf, now
10329 it is offices. Until the fox comes – with better technology. Humans

10330 fear the fox, who kills more than he can eat. He's a rival, so they
10331 hunt him down with dogs.'
10332     'You don't mean "technology",' Sylvie says.
10333     'Yes, why not?' I ask.
10334     Later, Roxanne says to me, 'There's nothing to spy on, in
10335 Sylvie.'
10336     'I don't pay you in trust, Roxanne,' I say. 'It's only cash. Just
10337 tell me anything at all.'
10338     'Innocence,' she says. 'Lots of people seek it. It's not
10339 recognising evil.'
10340     'You're thinking of the fox?' I ask.
10341     'We're good guys, as we are,' she says, 'but if you say our
10342 lives are at risk, there's someone out to get us – each one will resist
10343 in their own way. Without appetite, or with it.'
10344     'We're good guys,' I repeat. 'You can hardly tell each one of us
10345 apart.'
10346     'You spies,' says Roxanne, 'you have more rules than most of
10347 us. I see you – making the rules that ship the people off. Omar –
10348 won't risk his body – but I can see him sign a warrant. And as for
10349 Chip.... Sylvie too.... No limit.'
10350     'There, Roxanne,' I say, 'that's some secret you've just told.
10351 You're worth your pay.'
10352
10353               *
10354
10355 'I don't believe in renting,' Chip says. 'There's always someone
10356 waiting, somewhere. So I bought.'
10357     We're sitting on this iceberg.
10358     'Are you bored, Chip?' Omar asks.
10359     'Never,' says Chip. 'I just look this way. They'll snap us. Then
10360 we're done.'
10361     'No, Chip,' says Roxanne. 'We've to see the animals, before
10362 they all die out. But I don't see them – there's just birds, and dark
10363 things in the sea.'
10364     'You have to wait, Roxanne,' says Sylvie. 'They come in ones,
10365 they're not like us, a pack.'
10366     'Our pics – they'll be on all the little screens,' says Omar.
10367 'We're a story without words, in just one line. But – I've lain here,
10368 made a shape. That, I'll leave – and join them on the boat that's
10369 towing us,' and so he does. His outline disappears, quite fast, and
10370 Roxanne says, 'We're not melting – all else is.'

10371       'That's not the point,' says Chip. 'You don't need believe in
10372   what we do. How we are solid, and the ice – it's all ephemeral. But
10373   – it's a step, obligatory, like in beauty and the beast. A look, a
10374   glance, of love, that must intrude, reveal.'
10375       'It's right,' Sylvie says. 'The ice isn't just to chill Roxanne. It's
10376   being a family, loving the beasts. You have to show it, lots of
10377   loving, so you can be good at something else.'
10378       It comes into my mind – the Moscow store, the GUM. My
10379   father said to me, small boy trotting after, smelling strangenesses
10380   and pickles, until I was just a nose with legs – 'This here is set out
10381   like the *grands magasins*. You might see Proust, coming up the
10382   stairs. Making his purchases of biscuits.' Perhaps you might.
10383       I saw a lump of ice, bigger than this iceberg – since I was
10384   smaller then – 'It's to cool the caviar', he says. Then came the
10385   thaw, the melt, right down.
10386       'It's all for our campaign,' says Chip, 'whatever that's about.
10387   Don't take it serious. There's no bears to punish you, however hard
10388   you look.'
10389       The ice is disappearing, and we jump on the boat, leaving the
10390   sets of eskimo boots behind. They were included in the price. They
10391   bob away – 'I had a wastebasket one time,' Roxanne says, 'made of
10392   an elephant's foot. Those boots – they bring it back.'
10393       'Well,' says Omar, 'there's our extreme. The cold. Then the
10394   warming.'
10395       There's nothing much to add. How are those animals, the ones
10396   we didn't see – how are they doing? Maybe they were there, we
10397   didn't know enough to recognise them. Probably, it was reciprocal,
10398   the ignorance, and they stayed well away from us.
10399       I feel Roxanne slide her hand into mine. 'It wasn't real,' she
10400   says, quietly. 'The foot.'
10401       'I didn't think it was,' I say. The hand seems boneless, quite
10402   indeterminate. A toad. It squeezes – oneTWO, oneTWO....
10403       Then Omar rises up. 'Not now, Roxanne,' he says. 'I've
10404   pondered this one, over time. You two can hear it first.' Of course,
10405   she's fascinated, so am I. Roxanne lets me go.
10406       'The thing is drugs,' says Omar, in a voice that's rich with
10407   minerals. 'The history of the world. The sports is all about it – guys
10408   who play and guys who watch. Football! There's guys who
10409   couldn't read a paragraph, they watch for hours. And what? Is this
10410   drama, like you're overseeing ants knit shawls? Of course, there's
10411   lots of criminals involved – you see the hammer? That's a convict's

0412 ball and chain, it's canting talk, for thieves. Throw it away, your
0413 manacle, far as you can. And see them, crazy in the park, with their
0414 jumps and spears and sticks. That game they call pelote? It's a
0415 giveaway: you spell it p-e-y-oh-t-e. That's the sense....

0416     'And all the stuff the feds have seized – they don't flush it, you
0417 can bet. It's for the army, so's they can do the things they do.
0418 Politicos – the calm! Unnatural. They're sending out those flying
0419 bombs, and yet they're on TV, with jokes and what their kids have
0420 learned at school, and sorry for the blood and stuff, and doing little
0421 dances....'

0422     'That's all well known,' I say. 'What's new, Omar?'

0423     'The pyramids,' he says. 'They never found a spoon or pan.
0424 Those guys – they didn't eat. Each hefted up a six-ton block and
0425 made a shape – for what?.... a tomb? A boat? A plane? It's like
0426 religion: – those lists of names, not heard before or since. Hazor?
0427 Ziking? Names for your kids? I'll bet! The walking dead, speaking
0428 with tongues, the flying here and there, bilocation and the word of
0429 God – "just wait, I'll take it down, I've got some gold plates
0430 somewhere here...."'

0431     'We've heard it all before, Omar. So what?' I say, and Roxanne
0432 says she's clean – 'I wouldn't do the dirty stuff,' she says, and
0433 here's her hand come creeping back....

0434     'Indians – they drink,' says Omar. 'But don't do dope. Chip's
0435 maybe the first who wants to do his thing without a fantasy, as
0436 realistic as they come. Just think – those cow boys they were up
0437 against. Forget their feminine side! Transmogrified, they were. Not
0438 lady into fox – boy into cow...!

0439     'I don't see what's your point,' I say. 'Old Marx – he said it all.
0440 It's opium. Or something else you've stashed there in your shoe. It
0441 is the human race, it's how it's fuelled; that is its history, Omar. Get
0442 reconciled!'

0443     He's quite deflated. Roxanne says, 'No, Omar's right. It is a
0444 thing to be explored. I'll spy it out. I'm clean, and so's you two. I'll
0445 spy out Sylvie too. Maybe all the things she does, and Chip as well,
0446 is all because they're clean? Is that the plan – to see things as they
0447 really are? No mirror, and no telescope?'

0448     I feel it's kids' talk, this, but I've got free of Roxanne's hand at
0449 last.

0450     'Dammit,' says Omar, quite disconsolate. 'I thought I'd got it –
0451 the mystery of everything.'

| 10452 | 'Maybe you have,' says Roxanne, sliding a podgy hand in his. |
| 10453 | 'It's just it's all irrelevant to everything.' |
| 10454 | 'I'll try the vertical,' says Omar, rising up. He takes a pair of |
| 10455 | shining stilts, with springs, and bounces up and down. |
| 10456 | 'Do you always bring those, on a boat?' Sylvie asks Omar. |
| 10457 | She's standing beside Chip – the two of them, tall, frantic, on the |
| 10458 | bridge... like Rimbaud's king and would-be queen. |
| 10459 | 'Well,' Omar says, 'it strikes at any time, the hand of destiny. |
| 10460 | There's some in charge that want to end it all and quick, and others |
| 10461 | castled in their offices, settled for the long haul. Sometimes a |
| 10462 | circumstance will bring them both together. It's called a window of |
| 10463 | opportunity. The pistol shot – and then, the army that's only to |
| 10464 | parade, not fight, is dashing to the front. The dream you're |
| 10465 | emperor, everywhere – it gets a nudge: there go your warriors, |
| 10466 | whittling their darts, fulfilling every wish of yours....' |
| 10467 | 'There's the ideas,' says Chip. 'The saving people, doing noble |
| 10468 | things...' |
| 10469 | 'I thought I'd covered that,' says Omar huffily. |
| 10470 | 'Intentions ought to get some points,' says Sylvie, making |
| 10471 | peace. 'Hey guys – how's my getup look? We won't ask votes for |
| 10472 | our campaign, or set down op-ed stuff. Just be important, meaning |
| 10473 | grandiose things – by being here, upfront and mostly silent.' |
| 10474 | She wears a plastic apron, not much more. It looks like fur. |
| 10475 | '"Lounge leopard" is its name,' she says. 'We'll put them on the |
| 10476 | grasslands. Real ones, leopards, pecaries. No lectures on the |
| 10477 | authenticity, please – we've heard it all before. You give a hand to |
| 10478 | evolution – no one thanks, nor should they blame.' |
| 10479 | 'Ah yes, the grasslands,' Chip romances, as if they weren't |
| 10480 | there always, just behind his eyes. 'We'll stock them. Stockyards – |
| 10481 | maybe that's the word?' |
| 10482 | 'No, Chip, no!' screams Sylvie. 'Fuck it, fuck you! This won't |
| 10483 | change the world, nor any thing! I could be Sissi – this time, it's me |
| 10484 | that pulls the trigger. I live on, become the empress, building |
| 10485 | plywood cities. No Franz Ferdinand – just my interminable old age, |
| 10486 | fucked by black horses. As the whiteys' star goes down – the |
| 10487 | Spaniards will invade, of course. Some life into the dance... |
| 10488 | Flamenco on the Pink House lawn. Open the silver mines – oh no! |
| 10489 | the Indians have a low-grade guerrilla going on, where there's no |
| 10490 | maps.... What's to come next? – junks up the Hudson, your |
| 10491 | Ambassador limo won't run on this new toxic oil.... And none of |
| 10492 | it,' she screams still louder, 'none of this is mine. It will all happen, |

10493 even if I'm lying on a sheet and having Borodino red-tattooed upon
10494 my bum!'
10495     We're all on guard. Chip hears he's to be victim of his suicide,
10496 Sissi will spin some tale, convince the cops, take the top spot.
10497 America won't need to change its name, but all the rest will
10498 change. No more fried egg sandwiches – Madrileno eggs in rancid
10499 olive oil, paella full of grit, you pay in silver oblongs, look like
10500 they been sucked and stamped with cleats.... We see it all, the
10501 future. There is nothing new. It's all different, but you've imagined
10502 it this way and that. That's why you spy. That is the point. The
10503 future is a country known, that you have helped to make... it
10504 doesn't frighten any more....
10505     'What did your father want to find?' asks Roxanne. 'Or did he
10506 just pass on?'
10507     'Not finding things,' I say. 'Just watching. No one to pass on
10508 to....'
10509
10510                                    *
10511
10512     'Hey, guys,' shouts Chip, white and frayed. 'Guess what – I've lost
10513 all my money... I had it banked, and now it's gone, without a word!'
10514     It was our money too. It was our upholstery. He may not have
10515 realised.
10516     Desperate, he says, 'They say the iceberg broke the bank. You
10517 pay by weight, it seems. It's on the futures – wow! Each kilo is like
10518 gold. The guys must know it's getting hot, and ice is on the outs...'
10519     'No, Chip,' says Sylvie. 'It's all your companies. They
10520 circulated stuff, they didn't do a lot. And if the leopards eat the
10521 cows – the price of cows goes up, and you can't pay to compensate.
10522 You see, my dear, nature is all a to and fro.'
10523     'They should have said,' says Chip.
10524     'You looked so beautiful, the two of you,' says Roxanne.
10525 'Declaiming French upon the ice.'
10526     'At least it wasn't Mallarmé; sequins and trollops,' Omar says.
10527 'Sex below zero – you can't even notch it up.'
10528     I remember the book that ends, with satisfaction,
10529 disappointment. Your lover going out the door to join her friends,
10530 routines: how she didn't care for anything "but the mouth-organ
10531 and the pistol". Pretty sexy too, that end.... Chip's lost his cash...
10532 what's there to say?

10533   'Imagine,' Sylvie says. 'It's been blown up by inflation, and
10534   then there's Hitler. Or Sarajevo, and they gave you a shoebox full
10535   of dinars when you changed ten bucks.... Then came the massacres.
10536   Your cash has just been stolen, Chip. Goes on someone else's pile.
10537   Making the country strong....' She laughs.

10538   'At least,' says Chip, 'they're thieves that know how valuable
10539   the cash can be. It's not some sleazy guy who sells your stolen
10540   medals in the pub.'

10541   'I never knew!' Roxanne says. 'Chip – what you get your
10542   medals for?' To me, she whispers, 'Sylvie took her share. I hope
10543   she didn't bank it all....'

10544   'Disaster for you guys, not for me,' says Omar, limbering up.
10545   'School should tell you what to do when you are poor – not when
10546   you've made it. My clients see me as a relative. When things are
10547   bad, I'll go and stay with them. That's what they're for, the
10548   families.'

10549   'Omar,' Roxanne shouts, 'things are worse than looking for
10550   free loads. They say there's fighting everywhere. The Guatemalan
10551   army's moving west to join up with the gangs. The Mexicans have
10552   made a bridgehead north of Juarez. There's rebels everywhere. It's
10553   not the million Trots – it's everybody else, with guns and
10554   principles....'

10555   'Roxanne!' says Sylvie. 'You listen in to all those spoofing
10556   radio stations – it isn't happening....' but Roxanne says, 'I'll send
10557   my little girl away – maybe to Italy, someplace like that, and she
10558   can work and send me cash.'

10559   'You have a child, Roxanne?' asks Omar, quite amazed. 'How
10560   old?'

10561   'Oh, three or four. She doesn't live with me. I can't stand kids.
10562   But once abroad, she'll work – they set them to it, over there,' she
10563   says.

10564   'I'm not fighting anyone,' says Chip, 'I want my money back,
10565   is all. Horseriding, painting faces – it's no answer, when you search
10566   for cash. Besides, the President will sort it out. He seems a docile
10567   guy. He's trained for football coaching, I believe.'

10568   'No, no,' says Roxanne. 'He believes those hostile guys are
10569   terrorists and foreigners. He's ordered up atomic shells....'

10570   'They'll never bomb the property,' says Chip. 'They're there to
10571   see it stands.'

10572 'When there was that Easter thing in Ireland, Chip,' I say.
10573 'They said the Brits would never use artillery against the buildings
10574 – but they did. Learn the lesson! – that's what my father said.'
10575     'You two are shadows,' Roxanne says to me. 'You and your
10576 lurking parent. Unless you take a side, how can we like you both?'
10577     'That doesn't prove a thing,' says Sylvie. 'It doesn't seem there
10578 was a pistol shot, nor anything, not like the European wars. It must
10579 be spoof, and we won't need to pick a side.'
10580     Chip says, 'If I had cash again, I'd hire a landau – you could
10581 recreate the scene. Turn on the bridge – and then this guy....'
10582     'No, Chip,' says Roxanne, anchored into spoof. 'We're not that
10583 interested in your histories. At least we ought to check it out: these
10584 civil wars – they're pretty serious things.'
10585     'Maybe you guys should form a pact,' says Omar. 'Look for
10586 the truth. The guys round here – they say they all can carry guns.
10587 So, unless they simply like the weight, they'll use them too. Seek
10588 out the reality – and then decide. In or out of it.'
10589     'We could retreat to my island, for a spin. I doubt the President
10590 is using it to shoot into the coracle,' says Chip.
10591     'No, no,' says Sylvie. 'That's just the skill you need in war.'
10592     We reflect, briefly.
10593     Then Chip says, 'You guys – this is from the funnies. All I
10594 want – is my cash back.'
10595     'Oh,' says Sylvie. 'I saw them at the bank. It's all quite regular,
10596 no longer having it.'
10597     'I love this!' Roxanne says. 'After the fantasy – there's the
10598 fantasy.'
10599     'And are you sure you ever had the cash?' Omar asks Chip.
10600 'You always seemed so calm. No work was evident.'
10601     'If there's trouble,' Sylvie says, 'the Chinese will sort it out for
10602 us.'
10603     'Maybe we should check it out, see if there's a civil war,' says
10604 Chip. 'Though good info's hard to come by now.'
10605     'We've Chip, we must take care of him,' says Sylvie. 'Chip!
10606 You're a burden now, you and your powerful friends....'
10607     Chip's island: we wanted to see the Chinese junks go sailing up
10608 the Hudson, bringing a respite, and some order that we didn't want.
10609 I hoped to see the coracle guy cheering them on, and being
10610 cheered; those guys in white baker's caps, saluting, ranged along
10611 the ship's side like beading on tea trolleys.

| | |
|---|---|
| 10612 | 'The mechanism's broke,' says Chip. 'My island doesn't spin |
| 10613 | no more.' |
| 10614 | 'Send Omar down,' says Sylvie, full in charge. |
| 10615 | There's no one in the coracle: it's a nest of tiny balls, like turtle |
| 10616 | eggs. |
| 10617 | Omar dives to check the motor, and we see his bald head going |
| 10618 | down, the water colours it, first tanned, then dark jade, then |
| 10619 | disappeared, 'Like a medusa,' Roxanne says, in wonder – and I |
| 10620 | realise, it's Omar is the sea, not I. |
| 10621 | So what am I? |
| 10622 | Omar doesn't reappear. We hadn't asked if he could swim – it's |
| 10623 | not a thing you ask. He just changed elements. |
| 10624 | The island doesn't turn. |
| 10625 | Those water colours – maybe one was the colour Chip sent me |
| 10626 | to seek out |
| 10627 | 'Should we tell someone?' Roxanne asks. |
| 10628 | 'Who? What?' Sylvie says. 'If there's a war, they'll need some |
| 10629 | unknown guys for the memorials. That's Omar's noble destiny. The |
| 10630 | good thing is,' and she pulls the four of us together, close. 'There is |
| 10631 | no general conflict. Big beasts die, their parts are carried off, then |
| 10632 | some fresh things hold the centre stage. We see an end, but it is not |
| 10633 | the end. Just repositioning.' |
| 10634 | 'That's the philosophy, then?' asks Chip. |
| 10635 | 'Oh no,' says Sylvie. 'Philosophy is what we do. We don't do |
| 10636 | much. Your cash had crimped our minds. Now, from your ashes, |
| 10637 | we shall rise....' And she flaps long wings. |
| 10638 | 'Omar was the immortal type,' says Roxanne, wiping a salty |
| 10639 | tear. 'It's all salt water now – the brokers in Manhattan go about on |
| 10640 | stilts; for now, it's just for practice. Omar's safe, a pickled fish in |
| 10641 | an enormous barrel.' |
| 10642 | Ah yes – those barrels, full of fish. Moscow – when it was the |
| 10643 | new land, we from outside, riding and singing, into the storm of |
| 10644 | dust.... My father – must be chuckling somewhere, embracing |
| 10645 | Omar. Their last grasp. |
| 10646 | 'Come on you!' says Sylvie, pinching me. 'Remember the |
| 10647 | judgement: "soft". No pickled dreams. Toughen up.' |
| 10648 | 'I'd hoped for more,' I say. 'Where shall we go, Sylvie? A |
| 10649 | militia in the woods, Trots armed at last?' |
| 10650 | 'Oh no,' she says, majestic. 'I might set up a band, but not a |
| 10651 | *bande*, not *dessinée*: nothing comic. And you? You want love? The |

0652  hurricane?' And she's all over me. 'Pouf!' she says, a seadrift of
0653  spit comes over. 'I'll blow you far away!'
0654      'No, Sylvie,' I say, 'not love. It's being loved I want. Not the
0655  warmth, the certainty, my father sought – but something that makes
0656  up for him, the vacuum.'
0657      'All my friends – all the people here – are spies,' she says. 'It's
0658  nothing. It is all the same, and has been always. It's civil war, but
0659  all the pieces, most of them, stay on the board. One day, a lot will
0660  disappear.'
10661      She's still on top of me, I see Chip, his face grimacing, as if
10662  he's peeking through an *oblò*.
10663      'Poor Chip,' says Sylvie. 'All his bloom's rubbed off. Not
10664  much when he'd cash. And now – a wooden Indian with a smirk.'
10665  Chip gestures, without words.
10666      'We're off!' says Roxanne. 'Sylvie and me. My daughter isn't
10667  safe here. They can't pay the soldiers. It's the end. We'll take her
10668  off – Greece, China. Leave her there.'
10669      'Where there are nomads,' Sylvie says. 'The richest experience
10670  I can think of. Packing up the yurts. The lucky girl. Yes, here it's hit
10671  the wall. Now, it's the crumble.'
10672      'Ours is a girls' trip,' Roxanne says to me. 'You can't come.
10673  And I resent that you don't like me.'
10674      'I don't want to come,' I say. 'I'm seeing Larissa. We were
10675  babies together.'
10676      'Talk to Chip,' Sylvie says to me. 'He may be missing Omar.'
10677      'I doubt it,' I say. 'He just needs a happy pill.'
10678      Sylvie and Roxanne choose a song, and leave; the child is
10679  packed away on someone's back.
10680
10681                                    *
10682
10683  Larissa's here.
10684      She's dark and anxious, Larissa is, head down, jerking like a
10685  bird, pecking at where she puts her feet.
10686      She says, 'Your father parked us close, thought we would
10687  bond. It wasn't so. Two bundles in a Georgian park.'
10688      'My father wanted the true faith. When he saw it wasn't there,
10689  he sought the truth. Disappointed once again, he ended up, longing
10690  to be wise,' I say.
10691      'That is exactly it,' Larissa says. 'Your father came to Moscow
10692  at the very end. He wasn't wise at all.'

10693
10694
10695
10696
10697
10698
10699
10700
10701
10702
10703
10704
10705
10706
10707
10708
10709
10710
10711
10712
10713
10714
10715
10716
10717
10718
10719
10720
10721
10722
10723
10724
10725
10726
10727
10728
10729
10730
10731
10732

'It seems beyond our understanding now,' I say. 'Things started falling down. They didn't stop, they haven't stopped. He'd nothing he could sell, and they'd no cash to buy. And then things fell down everywhere.'

Larissa's always expectant, waiting to be found. Parked in a park, and now, 'You live well here,' she says, 'doing nothing but some commenting.... I could stay here, all quiet and good with you—'

'No,' I say. 'It's not a good idea. You're earlier than my memory – and so, I'm bound to love you, but that's it. The end. Goodbye, Larissa,' and she goes. She's not contented.

She comes back at once, carrying a weight. 'No Larissa,' I say. 'If that's your baby in a basket – I've nothing in exchange. The one baby that I know's evacuated, gone to China. Here, it's all smashed up, there's strife....'

'You should reproduce,' she says. 'Better than socialism. Shows faith in future things.'

'That one's gone to China,' I say. 'It'll get toughened up there. But it's safe. In China they've got everything – socialism, capitalism, armies, dissent. I guess it sounds like here, a bit, but more confident.'

'My, you're banal!' Larissa says. 'Is that your best? I hope they put it with the nomads – that way it has a little chance....'

'There's no food or water, and it's hot,' I say.

'It's the way of life, you useless idiot!' Larissa says. 'Remember what they say – 'man never sets himself a problem he can't solve', or something like. Besides – they've television, so the kid will sit and watch, like all the rest.'

'I don't know who sets the problems now,' I say, 'But if the saying has it wrong....and you might say it often is....'

Then – here's Roxanne and Sylvie, back again and joyful, 'Yes!' they say. 'The Chinese have a thing about too many kids – the nomads took our little one without a word.'

'You trafficked her!' Larissa says.

'Oh pooh!' says Roxanne. 'She was glad to go. And here's another one, I see....' She whispers, close to Sylvie. Then she says, 'Chip should take one. Take his mind off cash, and give him company.'

'Of course!' Larissa says. 'that's the ideal. He'd teach her how to ride and paint her face and buy and sell the real estate.'

10733 It's all girls' talk, but it's decided; I'm relieved. A good deed's
10734 being done, a problem solved. I think of Aliye, her tale: I say,
10735 'Before you go, Larissa, you should tell a tale that makes us
10736 think, and possibly rejoice.'
10737 'No, no!' says Chip, 'First we must sort our families out.
10738 You're gross, you two, you're pigs! Those stereotypes!'
10739 'Chip,' Sylvie says, 'You haven't understood. We're
10740 naturalists. We're working out the new – what you must want, what
10741 you must do, all that. The structure and the urge. Experience, but
10742 no metaphysics. The principles for all cohabitation.'
10743 Larissa says, 'It seems to me that here – it's going strong.
10744 There's life that's going on...'
10745 'No, no,' says Sylvie, 'You see the bars and clubs are full – it's
10746 just because the rest is falling – if it hasn't fallen – down.'
10747 'You're moralists as well as pigs,' shouts Chip. 'You want
10748 another set of rules to suit yourselves. I don't want this woman! Or
10749 her child!'
10750 'Well,' Larissa says, 'I won't go back, so there. Sylvie, you're
10751 right! We need new structures, and new rules, and who should go
10752 with who, and tell them what to do – and whether you should steal
10753 or booze or take some pills.... We never loved the state, and now all
10754 round it's falling down, and we must make things up ourselves. It
10755 all was cash. When the state can't pay its guys – that is the end. No
10756 regrets – into the whirlwind we shall go, determined, proud....'
10757 'And with eyes closed,' says Chip. 'Someone still has my cash
10758 they stole. That's nothing new.'
10759 'Tell us a tale, Larissa, then we'll sort you out,' I say, 'Chip
10760 too. There's nothing we can do, when all is crumbling, and there's
10761 no Aphrodite, taking sides and nudging spears, turning aside the
10762 blades. The heroes – they have all gone down. And no one cares to
10763 carry their cadavers off....'
10764 'Not all things fall apart,' Larissa says. She tells her tale.
10765 'Beside me, when I had just been born, there was another basket,
10766 with a little boy. Time passed. He had a dog, then lovers, order and
10767 ambition, a degree in architecture.... I remember – those dogs with
10768 bushy tails, the village lads who walked them down the track – it's
10769 asphalt now, and lined with bricks and lo-rise buildings.... What
10770 were we to do, when he was ready to be conscripted in the army?
10771 How could we get him out? – for he was marked "soft" at birth,
10772 and he was mine, my destiny, my beginning and my end.'

10773    'Oh no,' I say, 'that wasn't me. And your child's not mine,
10774  Larissa. I wasn't there for long, besides, they can't conscript a
10775  foreigner.'
10776    She's blank. 'It's just a tale,' she says. 'It isn't you. It hasn't
10777  been for years.'
10778    'If that's your tale,' says Chip, 'Larissa, you'd better stay well
10779  clear of all creative trades.'
10780    She doesn't care. 'Your father,' she says to me, 'knew
10781  everything. He was the best of spies. He couldn't do a thing with it.
10782  All the knowledge – some of it the truth... he couldn't warn the
10783  bosses. Couldn't praise them. Couldn't say, "History's against you,
10784  your end is more than nigh." Instead, he left a Moses basket, right
10785  beside me. That was to be my history—'
10786    'I know all this,' I interrupt. 'I too know everything. It is a
10787  curse. You can't accomplish anything. No one listens, no one hires
10788  or fires you. You're undercover, quite invisible, sat in the park. My
10789  father left me there, abandoned. He'd got bored. Like Roxanne.
10790  Except – my story isn't yours, Larissa. Your tale's invented. I am
10791  not your destiny. My father – he returned. Carried me off. I wasn't
10792  born beside you. The child's not ours.'
10793    'This stuff is dense and deep,' says Roxanne. 'I just dumped
10794  my child – now, here's another to sort out. Then, there's the moral
10795  base of everything we've to decide. All this while Armageddon's
10796  moiling up the road....'
10797    'It's always so, Roxanne,' says Sylvie. 'The future's all
10798  planned out and written down, you find the project long long after,
10799  in the ruins, as a scroll or book, when you've tacked together
10800  something else...
10801    'America: it's the metaphor for everywhere, the point of union
10802  where the world's played out. The molecules – they dance, and
10803  then they clash. Turn into bombs. It mustn't trouble us, the ultimate
10804  war is not the end. It's dialectics, friends. We must anticipate the
10805  finish, and thereafter....'
10806    'But Sylvie,' Chip complains, 'We've lost our scientist, our
10807  engineer. Omar: the sea, engulfed, sunk into the pickling. Now – to
10808  protect ourselves: – do we dig, or do we climb? The pit? The tree?'
10809    'The people here,' says Sylvie, 'Live in the metaphor. They
10810  think that where they are, is all the world. It's like Chip's people
10811  thought, when they had only bows and arrows to kill each other
10812  with...'

10813   'Oh come!' says Chip. 'That's simplified! Larissa – just leave
10814   your child and basket here. We are survivors – on our tippy-toes
10815   we'll leave.... The ancients said the child would speak in Hebrew
10816   if you let it be. The linguists think that's so today. It speaks no
10817   Russian yet, so we shall see....'
10818       'That way it will avoid the Schul,' says Roxanne.
10819       All is resolved – posterity, all that. I'm free to be the sea again,
10820   absorbing everything. Anger and calm, following each other like
10821   big and little waves.
10822       'The whole thing, the future, is to be decided here, and now,'
10823   says Chip. 'Sylvie! The moral order you're concocting – it's more
10824   than bleak. There's punishments for sure, but no rewards. "All men
10825   are brothers" – but there is no family. "Respect for all" – but
10826   you've none for yourself, still less for me....'
10827       'No, Chip,' says Sylvie, angrily. 'It's good you're firming up.
10828   But what you want is going backwards, to those fictions – exactly
10829   what has got us here. Exhortations no one will obey.'
10830       'Sylvie,' I say, 'both you and Chip are stuck. People do what
10831   they can get away with – useless giving them more rules. See –
10832   they got away with all Chip's money....'
10833       'Money's not a skin,' Roxanne says. 'You can't wear it like the
10834   suit you came in.'
10835       'Yes you can,' says Chip. 'That's why I got depilated. Cash on
10836   me is like a carapace, a shell. Or a tattoo.'
10837       'We need more stories, that's for sure,' says Roxanne. 'I could
10838   put a coda on Larissa's effort – you two, brother, sister – seek each
10839   other; and there's a quest for Chip – his treasure, his sparkling
10840   roots, the colour he aspired to....'
10841       'You guys!' says Sylvie. 'Stop inventing. Look what's
10842   coming!'
10843       Larissa's overwhelmed: she says to me, 'There was a war when
10844   first we met. We were young, to be its casualties.'
10845       'There's nothing terrible in that,' I say. 'War is our condition,
10846   like wolves have to eat carrion, poor noble things. Here, they found
10847   some mechanisms, so's they didn't need to fight at home, but it was
10848   always there, and coming; in the past as well.... Now – the
10849   question is, what's to be done?'

\*

10853   Chip has more pasts to cancel than the rest of us.

*Unsteady States, Volume 1*

10854 'Hey, guys,' he shouts, in military mode. 'Energy fruits – now,
10855 that'd be the thing! New colours that would stretch your eyes?
10856 Occupation? Civil war? I can't wait for all those things!'
10857 'He means – to simulate,' Sylvie says. 'It's good we settled
10858 with those kids. The family's an awful place to start. He'll
10859 construct some futures. Like Potemkin, the prince of plywood. He
10860 has the tools—'
10861 'No corny stuff,' says Chip, 'No fantasy. No Martians, Thai
10862 tanks in the Bronx, coming to my aid.'
10863 'So long as it's simulation, science, not fantasy, I can't object,'
10864 Roxanne says. 'Go ahead, Chip. But remember – there's the
10865 National Guard. Every state has its army. When things are
10866 crumbling, each one goes its own way—'
10867 'Oh no!' says Chip. 'I hadn't thought of that. For sure, I'll find
10868 one that'll help me get my money back. One of them will do a deal.
10869 Wyoming, do you think?'
10870 Chip's scenarios are fairly stark. 'Sylvie,' he says, 'you can
10871 have a little band, and get protection from some guys. Roxanne –
10872 I'd hate to think of you as victim, but those religious types would
10873 spit you out – you don't go near to them. Larissa and this uptight
10874 guy' – and he points at me – 'you've both got pasts as fellow
10875 travellers. You'd better hope you're not found out—'
10876 'Oh Chip!' says Roxanne. 'How you make us suffer. Penned in
10877 those tanks, the submarines, the rockets – even when we're not
10878 incinerated – the atmosphere is dense and stuffy. I do believe – you
10879 get off on our hurt.'
10880 Chip doesn't care: he sketches in a beautiful old Dodge, that's
10881 full of nail bombs. 'Better keep your heads down for that one,' he
10882 warns us, 'if it hits a bump.'
10883 It's almost beyond imagination, as if Aphrodite's there, making
10884 the well-laid guns miss their targets, or she knocks your arm, just
10885 as you try to bayonet your awful officer – some guy who worked in
10886 advertising....
10887 Sylvie's fulfilled – a warlord, a warlady – working with her
10888 militia, working with everyone, punishing those she doesn't like or
10889 who can't pay.
10890 'It all ends well, because it ends, and order is restored,' says
10891 Chip. 'Although maybe my money's not.'
10892 'Come on, Chip,' Roxanne says. 'Almost everybody says that
10893 war is hell, and that's where bad guys ought to go....'

0894     'That's as maybe, Roxanne,' says Chip, swiftly inputting data
0895 to his valve-like skull. 'That monotheists' alliance was a dud. Now,
0896 what complicates things more, each army issues its own currency.'
0897     'Omar would have brought the calm,' I say, hoping by this to
0898 bring it on.
0899     'Omar deserted long ago,' says Sylvie. 'He was a refugee
0900 before the battle started.'
0901     'Maybe you'd all better be,' says Chip, still frantic. 'Refugees.
0902 These guys will fight it out, then someone will give us cash, and we
0903 can buy more arms.'
0904     'This science,' Roxanne says, 'it's more uncomfortable than
0905 being shelled, cooped up in Chip's parameters.'
0906     'Where's your spirit of community?' Chip asks. 'At least, of
0907 sacrifice, or patience? This is a drill, an exercise – take it in that
0908 spirit, as it comes.'
0909     'Where's Aphrodite?' asks Larissa. 'I've heard of her, but she's
0910 not up to much. Goddess of providence – she is what we need.'
0911     'She's used to only one big battlefield,' says Chip. 'Now
0912 there's too many, and she can't divide. Besides, there's talk of
0913 revolutions, and the gods get scared at mention of the word. They
0914 jumble it all up.'
0915     'There's no hope here,' I say. 'Chip: find us a mountain – one
0916 where they won't dig or drill. A forest, desert – anywhere so's we
0917 won't have to flee to Canada.'
0918     'They wouldn't take us,' Sylvie says, 'Our breath would hasten
0919 up their melt.'
0920     'The stars!' Larissa says. 'Maybe they'd take sides?'
0921     'The cosmos doesn't give a toss,' says Roxanne, her morale is
0922 wilting, her words come from the street...
0923     'No, no,' says Chip. 'She means the actors. Those that aren't
0924 just painted on. Italians all take Jewish names – they don't know
0925 which side is theirs. No, we can't look to them. With luck, someone
0926 will occupy us, or drop us arms.'
0927     Each against all – or was it all against each? My father doesn't
0928 give a lead, although it doesn't mean all are the same, or that
0929 there's no good choice.
0930     'A safe place, Chip!' I say again. 'I know it's all in fun, nothing
0931 means quite what it says, but all the same—'
0932     'No, no,' shouts Sylvie. 'I am in the game, and I will stay there.
0933 Chip! Keep them coming, cards and options. Some decent spies I

10934 need – not this one here—' and she punches the muscle in my arm,
10935 '—as soft as jello.'
10936     'How fortunate my kid is safe and trekking with the yaks,' says
10937 Roxanne.
10938     'That's crap,' Larissa says. 'The nomads disappeared before
10939 the Jews, and no one cares... and where's the kid I dumped?'
10940     They shout at Sylvie, who shouts back. From someone comes
10941 the cry, 'Let's get her!' – maybe from all three.
10942     'Listen!' shouts Sylvie. 'I'll stay here – the Durruti column is
10943 my inspiration, though I may change my name. Louise Michel –
10944 that comes to mind. I'll find some clean and feisty guys – or gals,
10945 for preference – no flab, no therapies....'
10946     'They'll think you're all religious freaks,' says Chip. 'Besides
10947 – I love you Sylvie. And remember, this is not a game, it's science,
10948 but it isn't happening.'
10949     'But it will,' says Sylvie, 'and thanks, Chip, for the warning of
10950 your inner swell. That is your problem. Deal with it.' And to me she
10951 says, 'Don't talk to me of politics, coherence – your father'd no
10952 adrenal gland, and nor have you. "Soft", both of you. You didn't
10953 enter in the storm. You sneaks.'
10954     'They'll inflate you, Sylvie, then they'll cut you down like
10955 rhubarb,' Roxanne says. 'That's how it works. They take you at
10956 your ambitious word, and then they do for you. It puffs them up.'
10957     'It's all romance,' Larissa says. 'Roxanne is right. They cut you
10958 down – your ideas don't die, they go back in Pandora's vase, and
10959 they are sealed inside.'
10960     'It doesn't bother me,' says Sylvie. 'All that you say – it
10961 doesn't change a thing.'
10962     To that, there is no argument which holds.
10963     'Sylvie's mission... it reconciles her to what comes. And what
10964 she does.' Larissa says. 'I don't believe in it myself.'
10965     'Just think,' says Sylvie. 'All those people, wanting to go home
10966 to where they've only memories. I can't do anything about all that
10967 – I just do what's right. It's true – I'm beautiful – my bones are
10968 beautiful, at least. But – what can you do with them? Make soup?'
10969
10970                         \*
10971
10972 Sylvie leaves.

10973     'She's not a humanist,' says Roxanne. 'That's quite *démodé*
10974 now. She wants recruits, not converts. Maybe I shall stay with her.
10975 Beauty attracts, you know – so does her lean mind.'
10976     'I know what happens,' says Larissa. 'Sylvie turns malevolent,
10977 her gang loses a stand-off, Roxanne gets killed trying to protect her,
10978 when she's up and over that wall, already on the run.'
10979     'She's always been malevolent,' says Chip. 'None of us was
10980 worth her effort.'
10981     'Look, Chip,' I say. 'Are you quite sure that everything has
10982 fallen down? It's all disorder? Suppose it's just got larger? A pact
10983 between the guys? Sweep away what doesn't serve, that holds them
10984 up – and it's a scheme between the strong, with all their spies, and
10985 all the other likewise, from the world entire.... Suppose that, Chip?
10986 Then Sylvie's in the maelstrom.... There was so much I had to
10987 ask....'
10988     'The only thing you soft guys ever want to ask,' says Chip, 'is
10989 "does she love me?" Well, I can answer that. The beautiful are
10990 quite incapable of feeling love for any person but themselves.
10991 That's what the ancients taught, and they were right. You
10992 contemplate the beautiful. That is what it's for. It doesn't fit inside
10993 your truckle bed, my dear.'
10994     'Well, yes,' I say, 'that would have been one of those things I'd
10995 ask... but I had trusted you, dear Chip, to map it out for us, the
10996 future....'
10997     'And you did right,' says Chip. 'Besides, there's no one else to
10998 trust. But – my science was a plan, a plot: the simulation... well, in
10999 science and in politics, there's bulls, there's bears. The aim is all
11000 the same. You knew my aim was one and only one – to get my
11001 money back. What was the link with somehow pumping Sylvie up,
11002 and living on a mountain with you guys, while all the places where
11003 my cash could hide came toppling down?'
11004     'Yes, Chip,' Roxanne says, 'put it like that, we were imprudent.
11005 We wanted to believe.'
11006     'Suckers,' Larissa says.
11007     'I may have maybe... misled Sylvie,' Chip says. 'There's gangs
11008 and civil war all right – but those guys, all over in America –
11009 they're quite rebarbative. You cross them – and they'll drive you
11010 mad, and then they'll blow you up. No, not a metaphor alone – but
11011 chemically too. Bang bang!'
11012     I say, 'It's all because of Sylvie's beauty – you wouldn't
11013 contemplate, but tried to screw... and then you were humiliated....'

11014    There's the truth, I think, and although I've told it, that's a thing
11015    you never do....
11016        'Well,' says Chip, cool as cool, 'she'll go down fighting. Sylvie
11017    rides a horse so thin it can't be targeted. Maybe she wears lucky
11018    beads, who knows. It's an intense experience, this struggle for
11019    existence. She'll show that Schopenhauer was wrong – she's never
11020    bored, and so she must believe in God.'
11021        'So what?' Larissa asks. Chip has no reply. I think he's often
11022    bored.
11023        'I ought to follow Sylvie, tell her these truths,' says Roxanne,
11024    much disturbed. 'In my own way – not beautiful – I loved her. For
11025    sure, the truth will save her.'
11026        'From what?' asks Chip. 'And why? She can't help being
11027    beautiful, and when that ends – she ends as well.'
11028        Who knows of Chip's perfidy? To promote is to expose.
11029    Encouraging Sylvie to ride her papery horse is to sacrifice her.
11030    Who knows of Sylvie's perfidy? Not even Sylvie.

11031
11032                                    *
11033
11034    She writes to us:
11035        *'I need a touch from Aphrodite – I'm maybe her only true*
11036    *believer here. The wars – civil and less so – are so loud! I'm made*
11037    *for being seen, not heard. The people here are used to noise, it's*
11038    *their asbestos blanket.'*
11039        'Oh no!' Roxanne says. 'She's so confused. It's the racket, all
11040    around. She comes from here, but, returning, it's quite another
11041    scene. They eat and drink – dormice and larks' tongues isn't the
11042    half of it. All painting their little shapes and opening strange
11043    restaurants.... the pyramid, the cube, the wavy line, something to
11044    do with Gauss. They build them all, especially the pyramids...
11045    stones and cement, so high they block the light....'
11046        'We know all that, Roxanne,' Chip says. 'It's because the price
11047    of land is high, the buildings must be high as well. We've lived
11048    there, in the canyons; makes you want the stars.'
11049        'Oh yes,' Larissa says, 'you want the stars, and they will have
11050    them, bottled.'
11051        'Larissa, what have they told you?' Roxanne asks.
11052        'Well,' Larissa says, stretching out, 'they take a little drift of
11053    star, and when one dies, they make a new one, to the size they
11054    want.'

'What nonsense,' Chip says.

Sylvie writes, '*I'm the only one here without hope. The others – busy, trying not to be destitute, or even poor – they don't see how desperate it is, how it's all going down.... They wander through the ruins, eating rich foods. Don't they see the sky? Feel the cold, the heat?*'

'Poor Sylvie,' Roxanne says. 'It can't be just her autobiography. She's lost her hope, because there is no hope.'

Should I feel responsible? I didn't merely contemplate. I was intimate – she, much less. She – not at all. I don't bring this up with Chip.

'*They'll surely find me and my comrades,*' Sylvie writes.

She's so much time to write – a will, an epitaph. She doesn't have a cause, so they can pick her off the street, or leave her there, broken, abandoned.

She says, '*The state – it seemed to be disintegrating, but it's what all these people need, to make them whole. They're bubbles, released into it, the state, like bubbles in champagne. Smaller and smaller it gets, but – there are scores of them, a hatch of mini-states, all tributary to the massive one that we can't see. We hear it, though. My band.... It's different – we are a nest of bees or ants, and I'm the queen, the only one with wings....*'

'I must find her, help her,' Roxanne says. 'At least I'll spy on her.'

'No, no,' says Chip, 'She's gone. Gone in the head. She says all this to have you come to her, Roxanne.'

What Sylvie says – they're things you say when you're about to disappear, and start again as something else. I don't say so, but I've seen it all before.

Roxanne goes to look for Sylvie: Larissa says, 'That's great, Roxy.'

Roxanne says, 'No one was closer to me, ever.'

She doesn't come back.

Chip says, 'Sylvie will have gone under. Underground. But they'll know where she is. Besides, a group like hers, there's always someone who will spy. And come to that, they'll know where we are too – not that it does them good.'

I ask Larissa, 'Whatever happened to your kid?'

'Oh,' she says, 'Roxanne placed it. I didn't think Chip was quite suitable – I didn't like his views on money. I hope it goes with the nomads. I had no special plans for it.'

11096      'Those agencies,' says Chip. 'They don't like taking prisoners.
11097      They're not interested anyway in what you've done – it's networks
11098      they are after.'
11099          'My father said where we were, some people used to hide,'
11100      Larissa says. 'But mostly they were working where they oughtn't.'
11101          'My father knew some people who did hide,' I say. 'If you're
11102      well hidden, you don't count for anything.'
11103          Chip seems discomforted. 'I don't expect Sylvie did anything
11104      except some metaphoric statement. No real damage, nothing they
11105      might track back to me – not that it's all about my cash...'
11106          Larissa says, 'You're not involved in all that jacquerie, I hope?
11107      That so-called spontaneity? Common sense, know-nothings?'
11108          'I didn't think you cared, Larissa,' Chip says, embarrassed,
11109      'about the detail, the quality, all the theory stuff...'
11110          She turns away from Chip, 'His superficiality...' she says.
11111          I think – if Omar was the sea, and everything that's in it – to
11112      reproduce his medusa shape, he makes a journey of ten thousand
11113      kilometres, up to the New Siberian islands. Seeming to drift, but
11114      pulsing with determination, there to divide, a hundred stinging
11115      mushroom canopies, and on and on, to the world's end. An
11116      enterprise so far beyond me....
11117          'Omar's drowned,' says Chip, intervening. 'On his first ever
11118      helpful gesture. That shows you! That should make you think!'
11119          'You shouldn't just drift,' Larissa says. 'You need to have a
11120      plan, like I do.'
11121          'Everybody plans now,' Chip says, 'I planned.'
11122          'No,' Larissa says. 'Plans with an aim. Not forecasts. Forecasts
11123      know there's storms. Everyone already knows it.'
11124          'That sounds like communism,' Chip says, 'then, Larissa,
11125      you're another carbuncle on our collective toe. Imagine who was in
11126      Sylvie's gang – not counting spies! People making gestures, people
11127      who read; relativists and dogmatists. All of them,' and he glows red
11128      with frustration. 'Exactly the kind who cancel each other out, and
11129      are explosions waltzing down the street.'
11130          'Chip,' I say, 'no one has joined those ends together. Being a
11131      suspect's nothing. It's the last thing that would make you stand
11132      out.'
11133          'Fuck it all,' says Chip, 'we'll all be guillotined for being
11134      terrorists. Let's go to my mountain before it's all shipped off.'
11135          'That's a Seventies thing to do,' I say. 'But none of us can play
11136      an instrument, so I guess it's all right now.'

1137     'None of us can express themself,' says Chip. 'Instrument or
1138 nothing. Not even Sylvie.'
1139     'I can,' says Larissa loudly, 'and you'll all of you hear me
1140 pretty soon.'
1141     'All I know is, I was robbed,' says Chip. 'That puts me on the
1142 side of justice. But not equality.'
1143
1144                             *
1145
1146 Chip's mountain glows. 'I like big stuff,' says Chip. 'It's tailings.
1147 It's other mountains stripped and dumped – but, see! This greenish
1148 yellow here is cobalt. Don't touch the red – it's slag, or maybe
1149 artificial rubies, anyway, it's hot. You see, I don't do little things
1150 like nose jewels, writing songs and such. This blue and purple –
1151 looks like feldspar, but it chars your feet. Don't breathe too deep –
1152 you may be stuck with crystals growing in your lungs....'
1153     'It's magical, your mountain, Chip,' I say. 'It's quite unique,
1154 and not a metaphor for anything.'
1155     'Usually it's pyrites, those lumps, but sometimes they dump
1156 gold, to steady up the price and keep it high,' says Chip, dribbling a
1157 ball of lapis lazuli. 'It's a dirty job, picking through, making a
1158 fortune from the dirt. I prefer to cool myself, and watch it burn and
1159 glitter. It's not everyone has a pile like this.'
1160     We sit around. Sylvie writes: '*Sex, drugs, and what comes after*
1161 *rock. You'd think they were calm – I've done those three myself,*
1162 *and added gambling and drink. In its own way, each is a blessing.*
1163 *All together – you can find them in the same spot. You can go*
1164 *through them all in an afternoon, and in the evening read your*
1165 *Schopenhauer. But here – they're distributed with violence.*
1166 *Beatings and flagellations. Biting off a rooster's head – it's nothing*
1167 *to what guys put guys through here. My theory? – I guess it's all for*
1168 *cash and influence. What interests me is the real tough stuff – the*
1169 *power, the metaphysics. What my gang is for. But – a little debt can*
1170 *have you lose a leg: a kicking's just routine. The soldiers and the*
1171 *agencies – what happens between comrades! Imagine when they're*
1172 *let loose on all the rest....*'
1173     'She's really soft,' Larissa says. 'The barrack's where it starts,
1174 of course. They have some officers – they set it off.'
1175     'Sylvie's tasty to look at,' Chip admits. 'She wants to move
1176 things on. It signifies for her, I guess. The most she'll get's a good
1177 death – a quick one. You can't read much into that.'

11178    'Striving's the thing,' Larissa says. 'The end will disappoint,
11179    but that's the way it is.'
11180        Chip seems to find Larissa cute. He says, 'This mountain
11181    here's a pile of junk – but people covet it – that gives it sparkle.'
11182        'Oh Chip,' Larissa hugs him. 'It's so full of energy, your hill.
11183    Poor Roxanne – she'll have gone trotting down the street, there's
11184    doorways, people, all is normal, then – she's snatched! Small
11185    rooms, without a mirror. "Come clean – you're one-dimensional.
11186    We'll suck your lymph, from now, your life is just a paper sack."
11187    That's what they say, the good guys and the not. We shan't see her
11188    again,' and Larissa snaps her knees into the vertical, and leaps like
11189    Sylvie did – over the jasper blocks where we are sat –
11190    somersaulting up and down, sounding that kletzmer doodling as
11191    she goes.
11192        'No, no,' shouts Chip, as she showers us with chalcedony
11193    drops, 'Not kletzmer – sing us a song like in the olden times...'
11194    Larissa stands majestic, sings,
11195        *'Everywhere is corners*
11196        *Every stair leads down –*
11197        *Down among the jazzmen, singing like a frog,*
11198        *Singing like a princess, waiting for the kiss,*
11199        *Kissing in the mirror, changing all the shapes,*
11200        *Being something different, every time you sing....'*
11201        'Ah,' says Chip, almost tearful, 'Those Soviet ballads! They
11202    may have been butchers there, but they knew all about writing
11203    songs.' He turns to me, 'Brings it back, no doubt? Not like my
11204    cash! Nothing brings that back.'
11205        I'm not much moved. 'Spying's quite against new things,
11206    going back and moving forward,' I say, coolly.
11207        'Anyway,' he says, 'Roxanne won't reappear, but her sort's
11208    immortal. She'll reproduce, like Omar. You won't tell her kids
11209    apart. Sylvie – she won't waste gestures; not for her a slogan and
11210    crazy shooting. She's in the war, she'll slog it through. No second
11211    lives for her. First time's the last time – that's her.'
11212        'Does Sylvie have it?' Larissa asks. 'The Idea? If you don't
11213    have It, there's the maximum – of "frightfulness and terror". That's
11214    what the philosopher says. Of course, you may have It, and It may
11215    be crap.'
11216        'Oh, Sylvie knows philosophy,' says Chip. 'That's why she's
11217    gone to war.'

11218  'The trouble with God,' says Larissa, 'is that the appearances
11219  are quite arbitrary. But you can't be arbitrary too – you must be
11220  humble. Follow, and submit. Philosophy's quite arbitrary, but
11221  there's lots of them. War is arbitrary, when it happens to you. I
11222  shouldn't say that God is quite like war, like what Sylvie's got
11223  mixed up in. But – it is so.'
11224      'Well, Larissa, I think that nonetheless you've left things out,'
11225  says Chip. 'It doesn't bother me. I believe in lots of gods, including
11226  gods of war – but they don't say what I should do, because they're
11227  arbitrary, just as you say, Larissa. It's true they want some
11228  visibility, but there's so many of them – and they reproduce – they
11229  settle for respect, not love. And not obedience. They don't tell you
11230  what they want until it's all been settled, done.'
11231      'You may be right,' Larissa says. 'But mine was a hypothesis.
11232  I'm a sceptic, but once you think you've sighted the divinity and
11233  made your pact, you're off the map, to put it philosophically.'
11234      I feel quite lost. Those two can argue in the void, while I – my
11235  father too – just hung around, and gave bent guys some cash to
11236  snoop for us. Now, like Omar, my father floats in the sea. They are
11237  the sea. Expanses remembered, like yourself, your life, over,
11238  sucked to the pips. Maybe in memory there's a dance – no song.
11239  Just empty mouths. And nothing about the rest, nothing at all. My
11240  father said the bad things – all those, were over by that time... and
11241  then, besides, everything had changed, changed utterly. Now, I'm
11242  here: bad things all over.
11243      'You never plugged into anything,' says Chip to me. 'Just
11244  turned stuff down – and turned your nose up.'
11245      'No, it's the fear,' I say. 'We used to fool ourselves it all would
11246  turn out good. Now, it's the fear....'

11247
11248                                    *
11249

11250  'These little movies,' Chip says, 'you can't see a thing. This one
11251  sent to us – there's dust.... That swirl could be my secret colour?
11252  It's apricots and gooseberries, mixed together....'
11253      'Of course you can't make it out,' I say. 'It's what happened to
11254  Sylvie and Roxanne. It's over like a spit. It's war photography –
11255  things travel fast. Too fast to see and count.'
11256      'It says there's an "unnamed",' Larissa says.

11257
11258
11259
'Oh, that'll be Roxanne,' says Chip. 'You mustn't think I sent her out for reasons selfish or banal. It was her false hope that did for her.'

11260
11261
11262
'Hopefulness is just an attitude,' Larissa says. 'My granny had it. It's not really hope. It's more a call for luck to perch on you.'

11262
11263
'You killed them both, Chip. You had them killed. You knew they could be killed....' I say.

11264
11265
'We need to be precise,' says Chip. 'So far – it's just a storm of dust. At any time, and anywhere.'

11266
11267
'I've seen these images before,' I say. 'There is no hope. Not for Sylvie, not Roxanne.'

11268
11269
11270
11271
11272
11273
11274
11275
11276
11277
11278
11279
11280
'Well, now,' says Chip. 'Responsibility's an idea that's quite more complicated. But – death – that is simpler... in a complicated sort of way. We have religions – they see death quite differently from you.... Resurrection, then an Armageddon. Sacrifice, then paradise. Rebirth, all that. Recycling. Believe or not, it's up to you. Then – there's the ghosts. And concepts – they're immortal. Having a thousand jellyfish, that look and act identically to you... they breed. Has the medusa died? No, no – it's species being. There's no head jellyfish, no living one, and so there's no cadaver. The values – lots of talk of them. They're immortal too, of course. And Sylvie – when we didn't see her, she could write. We saw, we read her words. There she was. And Roxanne: didn't write, and didn't speak. She was invisible. But, there's no corpse....'

11281
'Chip!' I say. 'You set them up. They're dead. No argument.'

11282
11283
11284
11285
11286
11287
'Relax!' he says. 'Beauty fades. It settles. What it was, goes into the soil. I'm like that – a deep one. Like Proust – remember him coming in your store, looking for Magdalenes, sweet ones? Maybe he'd have found Larissa!' Larissa shrugs and pulls away. 'Remember, there's another French guy who's appropriate, who talks of "*l'étoile stalinienne du bonheur*". There's a thought!'

11288
Larissa says, 'You're bleak, Mister Chip.'

11289
11290
He laughs, and says, 'I see you're always hungry for my marvels. I've the one left – a stand of trees, quite central.'

11291
11292
11293
There it is: it says 'Reserved'. 'I hate those guys,' says Chip, 'who occupy the nature, crowd round, sell their caribu sandwiches and their tangled artwork....'

11294
11295
11296
11297
There's straight black trees: branches like scimitars. 'The branches chime,' he says. 'It's all tuned steel. When there is wind – there's always wind, of course, because we're voyaging – they make a carillon.' And so they do. They jangle to and fro.

11298  'If only history had paused at 1913,' Chip says, ears cocked
11299  and hand wagging roughly in time to the sound. 'Berg's three
11300  orchestral pieces – they would have shown another way.'
11301      Larissa and I consider this, quite lost in ignorance.
11302      Some guys in sporty clothes climb in the garden. At once, Chip
11303  breaks off a branch, and, whirling round, uses it as a scythe to
11304  menace them. They tell him to fuck off, but it is they who run. 'It's
11305  just the way I am,' says Chip. 'It's really all quite arbitrary, but
11306  sometimes it's well-aimed as well.'
11307      The intruders shout insults. 'See?' says Chip to us. 'You want a
11308  new society for scum like that? You know all about new societies,
11309  Larissa, back there in Moscow... So do I – they paid us back all
11310  right! We flying chips got a new society, and then another, and
11311  another! Sylvie will discover – you too,' he swings his scythe at
11312  me, without rancour or intent, 'You go to fight – the old you'll not
11313  get back, the new – your bones will go to pickle if it comes.'
11314      'Chip, I didn't realise you identified,' I say. 'It's not just about
11315  Indians, it's everyone.'
11316      'No, no,' Larissa says. 'There's change, improvement, even
11317  through the fighting. That's why we send our kids to nomad bands.
11318  To wait it out.'
11319      'They said that after the emperors would come the *intelligenty*.
11320  But it was all bandits and soldiers,' I say.
11321      'And never my turn,' says Larissa.
11322      'You mean what was new, along with those musicians?' asks
11323  Chip, disdainfully. 'They didn't ride horses – they put the horse
11324  inside themselves.'
11325      'Oh,' says Larissa, 'Not that sort – I mean, when educated guys
11326  drank coffee *mit Schlag* and ate tiny cakes – where they make the
11327  chocolate, like Linz. And places that changed their name, like
11328  Agram.'
11329      'Rich kids,' says Chip. 'Like I was.'
11330      'My father said the toiling masses—' I begin.
11331      'They toil. By definition,' Chip says. 'Like your father didn't.'
11332      'That's cheap,' says Larissa. 'When you two were on the
11333  mountain, on your judges' thrones – I thought *How fine their
11334  minds, how small the meshes of their nets*. Nothing can escape
11335  those well-tempered minds.'
11336      'Ah yes,' I say. 'We were tranquil back there – judges, with no
11337  crime laid out before us like a mess of entrails. But now it's

11338    brought it back. Omar. How Chip manoeuvred him – *o mar* –
11339    becoming sea, and drowning in it.'
11340        'Nonsense,' says Chip. 'Omar had studied an expansion,
11341    assimilation, of all things thrown overboard, whipped into storm
11342    and sea-drift. Including him. He knew his destiny! ... It was his
11343    element, you fool! He went where he had striven to end up – the
11344    sea!'
11345        'And yet,' Larissa says, 'he took that mucoid form. A jelly.
11346    Strange.'
11347        'Yes, well,' says Chip. 'He had to move around, of course. In
11348    the deep, you can't use legs.'
11349        We see our accusation hanging over Chip – the axe that longs
11350    to fall, but doesn't manage it, to cut through the doubt, the neck,
11351    the bridge that links the head to all the rest, clarifying all. Guilt
11352    without recourse.
11353        Just then – a wind arises. Every branch seeks out its note. 'I
11354    didn't plan all this,' says Chip, 'The architect arranged that we
11355    should hear those pieces every time a breeze tuned up. I'm not a
11356    fan of Berg myself – and now a note won't sound, the branch I
11357    broke.... Reminds me of my iceberg, melting right away. Still, I
11358    have my mountain, glowing, precious.... But – if only we had
11359    followed Berg, there'd be no pistol shot, no Sarajevo tumbling it all
11360    down.'
11361        The sound is massive, hot and cool, it stirs my memory. It
11362    bears me and Larissa back to our baskets in the park. *Calme, luxe...*
11363    before us – our whole untouched lives, a path. A fantasy. I say
11364    aloud, 'If only we had taken it, that path – upward and onward....'
11365        For a moment, Larissa leans against me. But I am not the
11366    father of our child. I watch, I don't walk along the path, its flowers
11367    and stones, its steep inclines.
11368        Chip struggles, trying to reattach his scythe.
11369        He's anxious to be away. 'I'll check on what is left of mine,' he
11370    says, 'Then I'll come back for you.'
11371        We are alone. Larissa, not much loved, or sought....
11372        'Hey!' Larissa says. 'All the guys here are actors! This city's
11373    all a theme park, with some dressed up as animals, and some as
11374    chorus....'
11375        'You go fight in places no one's heard of, it's clear it'll all
11376    come back on you,' I say. 'The guys here – should have thought of
11377    that. Maybe they hadn't read of what they'd done. There will be

1378  *casseurs* – they come first. And then the civil war that guys here
1379  haven't heard about.'
1380        Chip is a threat for us, for both of us. Perhaps Sylvie left a
1381  word?
1382        How can you escape, fleeing before the warriors who fuel
1383  themselves with their own horses' blood? Those Romans....
1384        'Lots went to Armenia,' Larissa says. 'And some elsewhere, to
1385  wait until the Prophet came along.'
1386        'Well,' I say, 'We should leave quick. I know how these things
1387  work. Sylvie would have discovered that.'
1388        'If you're quite sure...' Larissa says. 'But I'd be sorry to leave
1389  Chip, a man who has a garden with steel trees that chime with 1913
1390  music, from Vienna too.'
11391        'It's clever, I admit,' I say, 'but very limited.'
11392        'But,' Larissa says, 'you're soft. It's written into you. I think of
11393  all these strident people here – whatever they now fear and suffer –
11394  you know, they'll suffer ten times worse. They think they're safe.
11395  They've escaped from somewhere, and now they're bunkered up.
11396  They think, "It will not happen here, we'll never have to choose –
11397  resistance, collaboration, lose your stuff and cash, no food or drink,
11398  no sleep... we've passed all that to other guys, in places we have
11399  never heard of."'
11400        'Chip won't get his money back,' I say. 'It's no good choosing
11401  him, Larissa.'
11402        'Oh, it's not about the money,' she says. 'It was that insult:
11403  Magdalenes. I'm not his biscuit, sweet or bitter. Nor his cup of tea.'
11404        'We'll leave,' I say. 'Find a safer place, and then I'll say
11405  farewell to you.'
11406        'I feel quite safe enough right here,' Larissa says. 'Although
11407  you said this here was the world, and not a proper country.'
11408        I assure her, 'Larissa, we won't leave the world. Don't stickle
11409  over definitions.'
11410        There's a message from Sylvie. 'That means she's alive,'
11411  Larissa says.
11412        Of course, it doesn't.
11413        It says, 'There must be a better place. And if there's not? My
11414  companions here are Korean, most of them. *Juche*. That's what you
11415  need, iron self-reliance. People in this city – each one has a ghost
11416  upon their shoulder, some stranger. Some unacknowledged guilt. A
11417  corpse in their name. A responsibility not taken.

11418     'This expanse – for so long, it's been an easy place to rule.
11419  Lots of odd guys take the wheel.... So, it starts small, the war of
11420  each, the war of all, the one you should avoid. It can go on for
11421  lifetimes.'
11422     We pause. I say to Larissa, 'Chip says you are a communist.'
11423     She says, 'We all would like a better place,' and then, 'Poor
11424  Roxy.'
11425     I say, not much convinced, 'She was obedient to beauty. They
11426  used to say you can't do better than serving beauty.'
11427     'Sylvie will fight, resist,' says Larissa. 'But, why did Chip pick
11428  on her? What must she think she's doing there?'
11429     'She saw Chip as he was,' I say, 'that's always hard for guys to
11430  take. He made her take a side. Then, he wanted to toughen me, so's
11431  it was worthwhile his being dominant. You, Larissa – he wanted
11432  clean and pure. You could not imagine that. We weren't malleable,
11433  and so – he dropped us both. I'll be pushing you along from now.
11434  There's no future in my being soft. Besides, there's only you left.
11435  The rest have spun away.'
11436     We think about our prospects: I say, 'Spying – for me, it's
11437  completely done with.'
11438     'Chip never spoke to me,' Larissa says.
11439     'It's not important, if you're him. Cash, history – that
11440  communicates as well,' I say.
11441     'There's no war, no fighting here,' Larissa says, 'I guess it's
11442  still in the periphery.'
11443     'We could try Wyoming,' I tell her. 'Look for your child. Our
11444  child, if that's how you see things.'
11445     'It surely wouldn't end up in a place like that,' she says.
11446  'Though people drift away.'
11447     'Yes,' I say. 'Like Omar. Just float away. Even Aphrodite's
11448  quite indifferent, or absent as she always seems to be.'

About the author

John Fraser lives near Rome. Previously, he worked in England and Canada.